WHEN WE CHASED THE LIGHT

ALSO BY EMILY BLEEKER

WHEN WE CHASED THE LIGHT

A NOVEL

EMILY BLEEKER

LAKE UNION
PUBLISHING

Published by Lake Union Publishing, Seattle

www.apub.com

Amazon, the Amazon logo, and Lake Union Publishing are trademarks of Amazon.com, Inc., or its affiliates.

ISBN-13: 9781662517075 (paperback)
ISBN-13: 9781662517068 (digital)

Cover design by Shasti O'Leary Soudant
Cover image: ©Leonardo Baldini / ArcAngel

Printed in the United States of America

In memory of Dan Sackett, who inspired so many of us to find and follow our light

PRESS RELEASE

Vivian Snow's Personal Belongings To Be Auctioned

More than 95 items once associated with Hollywood icon Vivian Snow will headline a live auction at Christie's on October 27 at 10 a.m. PDT, in Beverly Hills, California. Bidders may attend in person or online.

One of the most notable items in the collection is a series of handwritten postcards from Father Antonio Trombello, close friend and suspected lover of the subject of the 2023 award-winning documentary *Bombshell*. The former Italian POW was at one time thought to be the secret father to Vivian's daughter, two-time Oscar winner Gracelyn Branson.

"This series of communiqués are the only known material artifacts that establish any connection or communication between Fr. Trombello and the famous leading lady," reads a release from her estate.

"I discovered the postcards by chance while preparing her daughter, Gracelyn Branson's, personal archives for auction," Peter Lawrence, historian/collector, explained.

The postcards—which Christie's estimates may be sold for $2,000 to $3,000 apiece—feature art by Fr. Trombello and messages in his handwriting.

Those wishing to own a piece of Snow's history can bid on letters from her years as a USO performer; promotional photos from her early days with MGM and Twentieth Century-Fox; her sunglasses, medical bills from Silver Hills, perfume bottles, and cosmetic jars; and an address book containing the phone numbers of fellow celebrities as well as doctor to the stars, Dr. Spencer Youngrin.

"Christie's is honored to represent the legacy and lore of Hollywood's glamorous and iconic star Vivian Snow," the group's executive director Montgomery Sly said. "This auction brings us closer to understanding the real person she was. These artifacts offer a glimpse into her deeply private world and provide a window into the true love story she may have lived off camera."

VIVIAN SNOW

Auction

Lot #1

Hand-drawn postcard labeled: The Chapel in the Meadow
    Pencil on cardstock. Small rectangular church with religious details
on the inside walls.

    CAMP ATTERBURY, IND. AUG 07 1943 5:30 PM

    Dear Mrs. Highward,
        The chapel is almost completed. The archbishop
will be back before the snow comes. See you then?
        God be with you always—Father Antonio
Trombello
    (Translation from Italian)
    Passed by censor 4

CHAPTER 1

August 13, 1943
Camp Perry
Port Clinton, Ohio

"You're on in five." Betty, our stage manager, pops her head into the dressing room and waves a handful of fingers at me.

"I'm ready. Just a quick touch-up." I slather on another layer of red lipstick.

"Rouge too. You're looking a little pale." Her comment isn't said out of concern. All business, that's Betty on a show day. And she's right. Though I usually try to cover up my naturally olive complexion, the past few weeks, I've been feeling the wear and tear of the road. I haven't been home to Indiana since immediately after Archie Lombardo said yes at my audition six weeks ago. I had one day to pack up my belongings, resign from my position as interpreter for the Italian POWs at Camp Atterbury, and say goodbye to everyone I've known and loved my entire life.

Papà was furious, which I guess is his default emotion. He ordered me to stay home, but by then he'd found out that I'd eloped with Tom, so there wasn't much he could say or do to force a married woman to comply with his wishes. My sister, Aria, on the other hand, was heartbroken. Her tears and pleading nearly convinced me to cancel my train ticket and pack away my suitcase forever.

"You promised you'd never leave me," she said, a piece of grass from her garden stuck in her hair. It was a hot day, officially summer, just two weeks since I'd said "I do" to Corporal Tom Highward, the same day I'd assured Aria I'd always be there for her.

At fifteen, with Papà still recovering from his accident at the plastics plant and with Mamma in the sanitarium permanently, I know she must feel abandoned. But truly, I left to save her.

I make a good wage on the road with the USO Camp Show, and I send most of it home. Plus, signing with Archie Lombardo from Music Corporation of America is an incredible opportunity. After the war, whenever that may be, Archie can open doors I'd likely never even know existed. And while I'm on the road, I can rub elbows with the established Hollywood elite.

I've already sung backup for the Andrews Sisters and danced behind Danny Kaye. My voice isn't as strong as it used to be, not since the horrific night in the gymnasium when my life changed forever, but it's improving every day. One day—when it's back to normal—Archie says I have a solo waiting for me somewhere on the road. I'm hoping to be promoted to the Foxhole Circuit, which could take me into the war zones of Europe or the South Pacific.

I rub some reddish-pink cream onto my cheekbones and blot my lips to even the coloring. I look like a typical chorus girl: long lashes, dark hair pinned back, figure-hugging leotard. Unlike at home in Indiana, on tour we have nylons: thick, flesh-colored tights that give the appearance of long, bare legs without breaking the morality clauses plastered all over our guidebook.

The bruises on my neck are long gone. At first I hid them with scarves and then with greasy foundation and now, no one would ever guess someone had grasped my pale throat so hard I felt like it might snap. As I run my fingertips down my seemingly unmarred neck, the pink scar on the side of my throat covered by foundation, I can't help but feel the invisible clutch of Tom's fingers even now, two months later. It's a choking sensation I'll never forget, just as memorable as our first dance or the first time we made love in the back seat of his borrowed car. Each moment was life-changing for different reasons, and I'm growing to regret every one of them.

I toss my makeup into my vanity kit and blink away the tears that always seem to surface when I let my mind time travel. Father Theodore says it's better to focus on what's to come than what's in the past. I try to remember his counsel while I'm away from home and away from the confessional of Holy Trinity, my hometown church. Holy Trinity is the only place I feel safe anymore. There and with Trombello.

Antonio Trombello is so many things—an Italian soldier, a prisoner of war, a colleague, a confidant, a savior, and a priest. While I'm traveling across the country, he's still behind gates of metal and barbed wire.

His postcards come sporadically, with a hand-drawn image on one side of the cardstock and a brief message in Italian on the other. I'm not sure how his cards find me on the road or how they make it through rigorous censorship on the base, but I'm guessing my former boss, Lieutenant Colonel Gammell, has something to do with it.

Trombello's most recent card has a pencil sketch on the front of a nearly completed chapel at Camp Atterbury, a boxlike structure with tiny portraits inside the open front wall and a simple altar along the back. It's beautiful, what he and the other POWs built. A place of worship inside a place of confinement. "God is the only true freedom," I remember Trombello saying as the committee met to plan the chapel.

If Aria was filled with sorrow and Papà filled with anger when I told them I was leaving to tour with the USO Camp Show, Trombello seemed filled with joy. Not that I'd be leaving, no. But Trombello knew better than anyone why I needed to run away.

Tonight, I'm onstage with Danny Kaye, playing a part in his comedy number. It's a small role, I'm mostly a human prop, but Mr. Kaye chose me out of the whole crew of twenty girls. He saw something in me he hadn't seen in anyone else. And that makes the cheesy material and minuscule stage time priceless.

I stand and straighten my glittering uniform and tilt the matching top hat pinned into my hair, but just as I get to my feet, my stomach rolls like I'm going to be sick.

I've never had nerves like this, not back at home at the USO on Main Cross Street. There I'd take off my Vivian Santini persona, the quiet, dowdy daughter of Italian immigrants, and put on my Vivian Snow persona, vibrant, full of life and confidence, to fill the role of every young soldier's dream girl. But now that I'm Vivian Snow onstage and off—the frailties of Vivian Santini find ways to make themselves known.

I take a swig of coffee, quickly pop a peppermint in my mouth, and swallow down my nerves. I try on a smile. A family portrait tucked into the frame of the mirror smiles back at me. And the latest postcard from Trombello. Just as I get my nerves under control, a knock comes at the dressing-room door.

In the mirror, I watch as two men in uniform push open the door and walk in without waiting for an invitation. Both wear MP bands on their left arms and stand in a ready position. Military police. My heart nearly stops. I know exactly why they're here.

"Excuse me, miss."

A trumpet trills in the background. I spin around, away from the mirror, and smile at the officials.

"Sorry, fellas—that's my cue," I say, checking the buckles on my shoes and making eye contact so I don't look guilty.

"Are you Vivian Highward?" the taller of the two men asks, his hand resting casually on his gun. I shiver at the sound of my married name. I haven't heard it since leaving Edinburgh, Indiana. Archie and the performers here just call me Snow.

"I . . . I am."

"You were married to Tom Highward June seventeenth in Edinburgh, Indiana. Is that correct?"

"Yes," I answer, my smile dragging at the corners. An explosion of applause and a rush of heavily breathing girls flood into the room, their makeup dripping from perspiration. The first performer to cross the threshold, Margie, gasps.

"Oh no. No," she whispers, reaching back for Carol's hand, creating a bottleneck. The chatter quiets, and a reverent silence spreads through the crew. I know what they think—they think the military police are here to tell me the worst thing any of us can imagine: my husband is dead.

"Snow. Snow. Where are you? The band's been vamping for over a minute now. Get your ass onsta—" Betty cuts off her snarky comment as soon as she sees the uniformed men in the middle of the dressing room.

"Oh. Well. I see," she says, curling her lips over her cracked tooth, the closest thing to empathy I've ever seen from her. "I'm sorry, doll. Need me to send out Barb?" Barb's second on the list for the part; she's rehearsed once or twice but always with a cardboard smile on her face and a scared look in her wide eyes. I can hear her shuffling around in the background, ready to take my spot.

"No, I can do it," I say, keeping my gaze steady on the officers. "If it's all right with you, that is," I say calmly, placing the wrapper from my peppermint onto my dressing table and putting the half-dissolved candy on top of it, licking the slightly sticky residue off my fingertips.

The tall officer nods and steps back to let me through.

The girls in the room watch in hushed awe as I calmly walk past. The show must go on, as they say. And I must find a way to perform knowing some of these young soldiers in the audience have wives who, sometime soon, will face uniformed men giving them news that'll change the course of their lives.

"You know you don't have to do this," Betty says, escorting me to the stage, where I can hear the music playing and Danny talking to the men in the audience. Betty's husband is overseas already. They have a little boy who's at home with her mother while she's on the road. She writes to her soldier every night, long letters, multiple pages. Betty's usually jealous of the women in the group, the long, slender dancers, the rich-voiced soloists, and the charismatic comedians. But for once Betty isn't jealous. No one wants to be me right now.

"I know." I rub my lips together and focus on the stage lights. "But I need to."

And I step out into the intense heat of the spotlight. Danny Kaye welcomes me warmly.

"You good?" he asks, giving me an extra spin and holding me a moment longer, searching my face for a clue. I'm sure he can see it, the worry, the stress, the fear in my eyes.

Onstage, I forget the outside world. Under the lights, energized by the applause of the watching servicemen, I can't think about Tom, the MPs, or even angry Papà and tearful Aria. It's just me and Danny and a world we're fashioning out of thin air.

"Of course," I say. He nods and spins me out into the middle of the stage. From the corner of my eye, I can see the rest of the USO showgirls lined up in the wings with concerned looks and crossed arms, hugging each other more for their fears than my pain.

As he introduces me, the crowd laughs. A whistle comes from the mass of male faces as I wink at the audience. A few soldiers call out phrases I'm glad I can't entirely hear.

I say my next line without flinching, making sure to avoid any further glances at the wings. The next ten minutes go by in a blur. It's not my best performance, but it's good enough to get not just one round of applause but two.

We usually give a brief encore, and tonight is no exception. The music starts up again in a short reprise of the little comedic ditty. As it closes, we take a bow and I escape to stage left before any impromptu numbers can be added. Danny doesn't know about the military police waiting for me in the dressing room. He will soon, though. I can already see the assistant stage manager talking to him offstage. I turn away, refusing to see his response, his pity. I don't deserve it. Not a whit.

The girls touch my shoulder as I pass through on my way backstage. They've all changed into their closing-number costumes, which I'm supposed to rush and do as well, but not today. The MPs let me dodge them once, but I shouldn't push for twice.

The girls march out to center stage, and I take each of their gentle well-wishes with me as I return to the dressing room. They think they're giving me privacy to receive my bad news in solitude, but they're all wrong. I already know what message I'm about to receive.

These men, these military police, are not here to tell me my husband, Corporal Tom Highward of the Eighty-Third Infantry, is hurt or injured. They are here to tell me he's missing. And not missing in action in some respectable way. No. Tom is gone. Tom has been absent without authorization for more than thirty days.

That means—Tom is a deserter.

I unpin my hat as I step through the dressing-room door. The officers are talking quietly by my mirror, holding Trombello's postcard between them as though they're trying to decipher his message written in Italian.

I'm not surprised. I knew the military police would show up eventually.

This isn't the first time I've been interrogated. The first round of questions came when Tom didn't report to duty at Camp Atterbury. The MPs came to my house, asked me questions and asked Papà questions. It was from those military men that Papà found out I'd eloped with the young GI he'd met only once. When the men left, I lied to my father like I've become far too accustomed to doing. I told him that Tom was off at training and the MPs were mistaken. Because Papà speaks very little English, he didn't fully understand the MPs' questions, making it easier for me to spin a story. After that, I heard nothing more from the military police. Lieutenant Colonel Gammell waved away any suspicion of me, his secretary, thinking me incapable of misdeeds and having nothing but bad things to say about my missing husband. But Gammell is all-powerful only at Camp Atterbury. He can't protect me anymore. Tom is supposed to be at Ranger training in Tennessee, and because he didn't show up, I'm guessing that's why the MPs tracked me down.

"Mrs. Highward. We're sorry for the intrusion but we have a few questions for you. Would you mind if we found somewhere more . . ."

"Private?" I finish his sentence, slipping into a long robe. They watch me, this time greedily rather than suspiciously, like they want to know what my body looks like beneath the silky material.

Betty clears her throat and grabs the MPs' attention.

"There's an office just around the corner if you'd like to wait there while Miss Snow gets changed into something more . . . appropriate." She holds out her hand like she's going to escort the officers herself if they don't stop gawking.

"Oh, of course," the shorter of the two men stutters, looking at his shoes like he's been scolded by his first-grade teacher. They follow Betty out of the room, still holding Trombello's postcard.

As soon as the door shuts, I unzip my unitard and wrangle off my tights, then slip a casual skirt and blouse on over my highly structured strapless bra and silken panties. I want to get my interrogation with the MPs over with before the inquisition starts with my castmates.

I'll tell my friends Tom is missing—no further details are needed. They'll make assumptions, and I won't correct them.

I wipe off as much of my stage makeup as possible before sliding on the low heels stored in my cubby. I look at myself in the mirror one last time. There's still enough rouge on my cheeks to make a priest blush, but I can't do anything about it at this point. I step away from the mirror, ready to face the moment I've been dreading.

I'll answer as many of the officers' questions as I can, and I'll tell the truth—I don't know where my husband is. After they question me I'm sure they'll talk to Tom's family, and they'll say the same thing. Eventually, everyone will find out what I already know.

Tom Highward is a ghost.

And I should know—I'm the one who made him that way.

VIVIAN SNOW

Auction

Lot #2

Hand-drawn postcard labeled: Altar Cross
  Pencil on cardstock. Metal crucifix.

CAMP ATTERBURY, IND. SEPT 20 1943 11:30 AM

> *Dear Mrs. Highward,*
>   *The word has come that my country is no lon-
> ger at war with yours, God be praised. Great joy in
> our camp. Perhaps we will leave this chapel behind
> soon—proof of God in war. Time will tell. God be
> with you always.*
>   *Your friend—Father Antonio Trombello*
> (Translation from Italian)
> Passed by censor 3

CHAPTER 2

September 30, 1943
Waukegan, Illinois

The wind off the lake is cutting as we rush down the metal staircase, out of the Naval Station Great Lakes auditorium. We just finished our last show of the night. It's time for dinner, and then we'll mingle with the sailors before getting back on the road to the next town. I can't seem to recall what base we're headed to next. I go where Betty tells me and I do what Danny assigns, and I keep my head down so no one asks too many questions. I'm worn out, more exhausted than I've ever been, that's for sure. The other girls complain about the food, rotten sleep schedules, and the breakneck pace of travel. But for me it's the stress of the secrets I carry.

A slight dusting of frozen rain has come in off the lake. It's early for the icy temperatures of the lake-effect storms that plague areas along the shore. I cringe away from the stinging ice pelting my cheeks when I hear my name.

I look out at the crowd of men, waving and calling out compliments, and see one fellow at the back in plain clothes, dark trench coat, and tilted hat. I clutch my stomach, and vomit stings my throat. Margie takes my arm and whispers, "You okay?"

"I'm fine. Just a little hungry."

She nods. We're all hungry. I've paid more attention to my waist size in the past few months than in my whole life. We're reminded every day that our bodies are now on loan to the US government, and Betty keeps a close eye on all of us.

But that's not really the reason I feel ill.

They found me, I think, panic putting my senses on high alert. I look for a place to run but see nothing except a sea of white uniforms and sheets of frozen rain.

I think they've found me at least once a day. Whether it's a man in the audience who isn't laughing or a deep voice in the hallway outside my hotel room. One day my act as the wife of a missing soldier will falter, and my mask will slip. They'll find Tom's body, wherever Trombello hid it. Or one of the other prisoners who helped him will crack. Or maybe Tom's wealthy family will hire enough PIs to figure it all out. Or a reporter—a nosy reporter.

"Vivian!" I hear my name again, this time closer. The man in the trench coat is only a few feet away. I glance over my shoulder and nearly laugh. It's not a detective or MP or private eye or investigative journalist. It's my agent, Archie Lombardo, huffing toward me.

"Archie! You're here!"

"Yeah, doll. Said I'd come. Got you a few hours off. Come on, I'll buy you dinner."

I check with Betty, who waves me away like she's fine with me going but also slightly annoyed. She's softened a bit since hearing my husband is missing in action. No one checked my story, thankfully. Now half the Camp Show stares at me with a distant pity, and the other half dotes on me like I'm a wounded creature. I'll add it to my list of things to feel guilty about.

"Go. Go!" Margie says, pushing me toward Archie. I stumble across the path and follow him to his waiting car. He looks at my threadbare coat and fussy hat and urges me into the running Cadillac.

"Come on, dear. You're gonna freeze your keister off." I'm shivering, but the heater in the car thaws my fingers and nose. We make small talk as he drives, and the car fills with a thick cloud of smoke.

I've never seen Archie Lombardo without a cigarette in his hand, including during my audition in Indianapolis three months ago. Archie tracked me down after sneaking into one of my Edinburgh USO shows and gave me his card, some words of encouragement, and more than anything—hope.

At his office after the audition, with a half-smoked cigarette turning to ash in his left hand and a blunted pencil in his right, he waved me across the room to the chair placed in front of his desk and slid a contract across the wooden surface. I signed with very few questions, and he's kept up with me ever since. I try to remind myself he probably treats all the girls he signs the same, but I can't help but notice the way he watches me with paternal-like pride when I perform, and in those moments, I let myself believe he sees something special in me.

I like making Archie proud, that's why I'm dreading our meeting today.

I went to confession during a stop in Virginia, but my story seemed to overwhelm the elderly priest, so I snuck out of the confessional before telling him of my worst sins and receiving absolution.

Tonight, I'll make another sort of confession, and this time I won't be able to sneak away without consequences. But I owe this to Archie before he finds out some other way.

~

At Louie's on North Avenue, Archie sits across the table filling his glass with chardonnay. I haven't been able to stomach the aroma of alcohol since smelling it on Tom's breath the last time I saw him. Even across the table, I can pick up the sweet, fermented scent.

Archie holds out the open bottle as an offering, but I wave it away.

"No thank you," I say with a smile, trying to mollify him before I break the news.

"I'd think a good Italian girl like you would appreciate fine wine," he says, placing the bottle on the table before taking a sip.

"Oh, I do. I think I drank wine before I drank a Coke. Watered down, of course."

Archie nods and says, "My parents were the same, but if I give my little Bobby even a sip, my wife says I'm raising an alcoholic." He takes a puff from his cigarette and another drink from his glass, and I wonder how he can taste anything other than wine and smoke anymore.

"At least take bread so I'm not eating alone. Mario is bringing out some of my favorites. You'll love the risotto. Just like my nonna used to make."

Though Archie agrees I should keep my maiden name under wraps for show-biz reasons, we're both first-generation Italian Americans, and we've bonded privately over our shared heritage. Perhaps that's why he feels justified in pointing out all the "foreign-looking" traits he'd like to see wiped away as completely as I've removed my father's name.

My eyebrows must be plucked thin—daily. And he's already told me I need electrolysis on my hairline to bring it up at least half an inch. I don't have the money for it—yet. I'm sending home every paycheck to Papà and Aria, but Archie has made it clear that before we head to Hollywood, in a fairy-tale future after the war, my hairline will need to be addressed.

As four dishes of pasta with sauces of various colors are presented to the table, my stomach growls, and I regret not eating lunch.

Archie fills a plate with hefty servings of each dish and slides it my way.

"I can't complain about a girl watching her figure, but one night won't hurt. I insist."

Steam tickles my senses, and immediately I'm transported back into that little kitchen where I made chicken parmigiana every Sunday night while Papà listened to the radio. Aria bounced between helping with dinner and reading one of her old books. I wouldn't let her knead the dough without first checking her nails for dirt. This is the real problem with a familiar feast—the memories. Or even more malignant—the regrets.

But I haven't eaten all day and I'm missing dinner with the cast, so I can't feel too guilty indulging. I drive my fork into the pile of sauces and pasta and take a bite quickly, avoiding the most delicate flavors and the richest of regrets.

"There we go," Archie says, as if encouraging his daughter to eat her greens. He slurps up a long strand of mozzarella from his first bite of lasagna. Then, with his mouth half-full, he continues our discussion, somber this time.

"I heard the news about your fella." He gives me a look of pity as I silently curse his secretary for being a gossip. "Danny told the whole story to Sylvia. She wants to meet you. They're quite the team. And that damn Lew Wasserman's been sniffing around about this new girl Danny's been dancing with. I'm telling you, doll, he'll be knocking down your dressing-room door by the time you get to New York in a few months. So watch out. I've got your back, don't you forget that."

Lew Wasserman. I hide a gulp. Lew is the biggest agent at MCA. He represents Bette Davis and James Stewart and every megastar on their roster. And Lew Wasserman knows my name. *My* name. He's a star maker. He's a dream granter. He's a . . .

My stomach drops. It doesn't matter. None of this matters.

"You don't have to worry about New York," I say solemnly.

"I know. I know. I don't mean to insult you, but you've got big things coming, doll. Big things. I'm telling ya—Christmastime in New York, that's when Lew will make his move. Keep your guard up, 'cause I'm an understanding guy, but I also believe in loyalty, you know what I mean?"

"I'm not going to New York," I say, staring at my plate. He continues as if he hasn't heard me.

"And he'll bring furs and jewelry. I've seen it. That's how I lost Rita back in '39. She was two-timing with Lew and finally gave me the Dear John before signing with Columbia."

"Archie," I say, knocking on the table to get his attention.

"I know. I know. Don't worry," he says again, pretending to listen to me. "But New York . . ."

"I'm not going to New York in December," I say, with force this time, raising my voice. His face scrunches up into a twisted landscape of wrinkles.

"You're not going to New York?"

"No." I swallow down my nerves and nausea, speaking slowly. "I think it's best if I don't."

His eyes narrow to a thin line and he leans across the table, his tie precariously close to the vodka sauce on his fettuccini.

"Best? Who's telling you that's the 'best' idea for your career, huh? Who got to you?" He's waving his hands like Papà does when he gets angry. It's been months since I've had to calm someone's anger, but the instinct bubbles up. I snatch the wine bottle by the neck and refill his glass to the top.

"No. Nothing like that. I promise."

"Hollywood? Is Lew sending you to Hollywood?" His silverware clatters against the fragile porcelain plate, and the bartender takes notice. I wave him off with a covert gesture. The last thing I need is an audience for my confession.

Archie doesn't notice. That's the thing about people consumed by anger—it distracts them from any perspective but their own. I make myself small, quiet, and apologetic.

"I'm not going to Hollywood, Archie. Around Thanksgiving I'm moving back home—to Edinburgh."

His tantrum halts immediately as he finally seems to hear me.

"Wait. You're quitting?" He picks up the nub of cigarette from the ashtray where it's been smoldering, takes a puff, and then follows it with a long drink from his newly filled glass.

"Yeah. Well, for now at least," I say meekly.

"I know you're worried about your soldier, but if you go home 'for now' there might not be a 'later.'"

"I'm not quitting because of Tom. Not exactly . . ." I stutter and twist my fingers into the edge of the white linen tablecloth. There are so many secrets I've been keeping, but there's only one I've told no one—no one but a country doctor far enough away to keep my visit a secret.

"I'm expecting a baby."

I'd had my suspicions—the nausea, the fatigue, the swelling of my bust and waist. I was hoping for a simpler explanation, pneumonia or anemia, but it turned out to be the simplest and oldest explanation of all time: a baby.

"In a few months, I won't be able to keep it under wraps any longer."

He extinguishes his cigarette and stares at me for a moment, his gaze drifting to my midsection as if he's trying to diagnose how far along I am.

He finally speaks in an understanding, gentle voice.

"There's a doctor in Brooklyn I've worked with before. I'll get you an appointment. You can't be too far along, so it shouldn't be a problem." He takes out a small notebook from his coat pocket and starts scribbling. "We'll tell that Betty lady you've got the flu. Believe me, doll, you're not the first small-town gal to get her head turned on the road and get knocked up."

What he's suggesting sinks in, and my easygoing, placating approach swings into indignation.

It's true that I wasn't married to Tom when I first let him inside me. I had to confess to Father Theodore the next day, and Tom and I were married soon after, but that doesn't mean I'm the kind of girl Archie's making me out to be.

"It wasn't like that," I say, lowering my voice.

"Oh, I'm sure it was true love." Archie's sarcasm rings in my ears like the farce my love turned out to be. He slides the folded notebook page across the table and scoops up another mouthful of linguini. "It doesn't matter who or why. It only matters what you do next. And next is Dr. Montgomery."

Why won't anyone listen to what I want? They all tell me what to eat, what to wear, what my eyebrows should look like, what my name is, and apparently whether I will have a child or not. Why can't I decide what's best for me?

"I'm not going to see that doctor, Archie," I say, pushing my plate away and grabbing my purse. "I'm having Tom's child."

I shove my chair back, and it screeches against the varnished wood floor. Tom wasn't perfect. I wasn't perfect. Our marriage, short as it was, also not perfect. But this child growing inside of me is the one perfect, innocent thing in my life, and there is no way I'm going to let it go—not for Archie, not for Hollywood or the US military, not even for my dreams.

I toss my hair back over my shoulders in my grandest Scarlett O'Hara fashion and stomp out of the restaurant, leaving a dining room full of staring onlookers. My heels hit the sidewalk, and the chill in the air registers on my bare arms and legs, but I'm too heated with outrage to care.

This might be the end of my time with Archie and the Camp Shows. Instead of getting on that bus in the morning, I might need to find my way to Indiana instead. I wanted to go on one more leg of the tour, to finish big and then go home when I had no other choice. I wanted to pause my dreams, not demolish them.

"Miss Snow! Miss Snow!" The street is empty, so I can hear the huffing and puffing of my now-former agent rushing up from behind. I pretend I don't notice and pick up the pace.

"Miss Snow! Stop. Please."

I don't know how the heavyset middle-aged man caught up with me so quickly. I stop in my tracks and spin around on one heel. Archie nearly slams into me but stops short, napkin still tucked into his collar, not even wearing his hat.

"Don't do that. Don't run away." He gulps for air and then coughs. His lungs sound heavy and thick with fluid. I turn toward him, tearful but still resolved.

"I'm sorry, Archie. I can't do what you're asking me. I just can't . . ."

"No, doll. No. I'm the one who should be apologizing." He rubs his hands up and down the front of his shirt like he doesn't know what to do with them. "Tom's your soldier? Your husband."

I nod. Tears push into my eyes. There they are, the expected tears of a war wife waiting for news of her missing husband. They finally appeared—real, sincere, heartfelt tears, just when I needed them most.

"Oh my. Yes. I see now. I see," he coos kindly, the emotion making him nervous.

He holds out a fresh-looking handkerchief. I take it and dab at my wet cheeks.

"What's a few months off, right? You're flat as a board still. Stay that way for a few more weeks, and then we'll get you home. Soon enough you'll be back, and we can pick up where we left off. Okay?"

"You sure?" I ask, hoping he's not just appeasing me.

"Absolutely. I've known from the first time I saw you on that stage that you're special. Really special." Even if his words are tainted by sympathy and pity, it's a comfort to know I'm worth chasing after.

"We'll keep things hush-hush till you can't hide that little belly of yours. You'll keep dancing your ass off with Danny and making every soldier from here to the Eastern Seaboard fall in love with you. Sound good?"

"Sounds good," I agree. He's telling me everything I've wanted to hear since the first time I suspected I was pregnant. My baby, Tom's baby, isn't the end of something. It's the start of something brand new.

He guides me back toward the restaurant, and I lean against his arm as cars rush past one after another, their thick exhaust choking me. The cold wind gusts off the lake, and I can't help but shiver as he continues making promises.

He'll keep my secret, he says. He'll help me return home in a few weeks, he says. He'll send me back out on the road after the baby. We're still Hollywood-bound—he'll make sure of it. And I try to believe him because I have no other choice.

VIVIAN SNOW

Auction

Lot #3

Hand-drawn postcard labeled: Chapel View
   Pencil on cardstock. Wildlife on a small pond.

CAMP ATTERBURY, IND. OCT 08 1943 11:30 AM

> *Mrs. Highwood,*
>   *Sunday, 17 October, the chapel will be dedicated by the archbishop. Lt. Col. Gammell said you'd be in attendance. I hope to see you then.*
>   *Yours in God—Father Antonio Trombello*
> (Translation from Italian)
> Passed by censor 1

CHAPTER 3

October 17, 1943
Edinburgh, Indiana

"When will you be leaving?" I ask Trombello in Italian after the final "amen" of the dedicatory services. It's a cold day, and my question leaves a cloud of condensed air behind.

"I won't know for a few weeks, perhaps months. Rumor has it our unit will be stationed in New York or Boston." He squints at the cross atop the chapel, his chapel.

The completed Chapel in the Meadow stands in front of us, just outside the fence lining the Camp Atterbury POW camp. The gates will be extended now that the work is complete, and the chapel will be an official part of the internment camp. I saw this project go from proposal to foundation to finished structure when I worked at Camp Atterbury, and though the chapel is no larger than Papà's front room, it's stunning to me. Lieutenant Colonel Gammell knows what it means to me. He pulled some strings to get me here today, and I'm filled with gratitude.

But the men who built the chapel will use it for only a short time. Italy has surrendered and this past week proclaimed its allegiance to the Allied forces. Trombello, and all the rest of the Italian prisoners inside this camp, are no longer our enemies.

In the weeks and months to come they'll have a choice to make—sign their loyalty over to the Italian Service Unit of the US Army or be transferred to a high-security POW camp until the war is over. Trombello says he will choose peace. I shouldn't be surprised. Though he defended me on the most violent night of my life, I've never seen my priestly friend want anything more than good for his fellow men.

"I'll miss this place," Trombello says with a wistfulness I don't understand.

"The camp?" I ask with a shocked chuckle. "Not many men love their prison."

He shrugs and turns to face me. His cheeks are brushed red by the sharp wind, his hair, once neatly combed to one side, now a restless landscape of dark strands curling up at the ends.

"Paul spent much time in prison. Timothy. Peter saw an angel in his captivity."

"And Daniel was tossed into the lions' den, but he didn't wish he could stay with the lions when they opened the gate in the morning."

"Ha. Yes. True. True." He pushes his hands into his wool trouser pockets. "It's not the walls I will miss."

"It's the lions?" I quip.

"Some of the lions."

Trombello looks down at me, his rich, dark eyes holding on to his true meaning, leaving me to guess. The wind whips across the lake behind the chapel, and I shiver.

"You should get out of the cold," he says protectively. "You must think of the baby now."

The baby. I told him when I first arrived at the dedication about the passenger I'm carrying. Which means I've trusted him with every single one of my secrets.

I sniff, the breeze having numbed the tip of my nose. I don't want to go, but he's right, the jeep is idling at the fence line, and if I don't get in my seat by thirteen hundred hours, it will take off without me, and I'm on a tight timeline. Camp Atterbury is only three miles from my childhood home where my father and sister still live. It's time to let them in on the news I've been keeping close to my heart, the same news I told Trombello today. But when I leave, I have no guarantee of ever seeing my friend again.

"Will you write?" I ask, already knowing the answer, thinking of the stack of his postcards I keep in an old cigar box in my suitcase.

"When have I not?"

"True."

Emotion swells in my chest, and tears start to gather in my eyes. He's been a sincere friend. When he heard Tom screaming at me after the POW dance in the middle school locker room, he left his gentle, priestly behavior behind and confronted Tom, knowing that as a prisoner he could face countless consequences. He fought until he lost consciousness and would've died if Tom had had his way.

After waking up to see the tile floor covered in blood and a knife in my hand, Trombello took Tom's lifeless body away. He assured me I was safe. He promised God understood what I had to do. And today, when I told him I'm carrying Tom's baby, he suggested I let the innocent child believe its father was a hero. There's a peace that accompanies Trombello's advice, as though God's mercy is accessible if I shelter this child from the truth. We both know that the story I'll tell my child about Tom is a lie, but it's a beautiful lie, the kind I wish I'd been told as a child to shield me from the darkest corners of my mother's soul.

"God be with you, *figlia mia*." He takes my gloved hand and squeezes gently.

"As with you, Padre." I kiss the chilled skin on the back of his hand and dip my head in respect, trying to memorize this moment in case it's our last.

He releases me and I rush off to the waiting vehicle, my legs frozen through and my cheeks damp with the tears I held in until Trombello could no longer see my face. As we drive away, I don't look back. I'm not sure I'll ever return to this place, this chapel. The only hopes I take with me are for the child growing inside me and a future where I can see Trombello again without a fence surrounding us.

~

The gravel on the driveway leading to my modest childhood home crunches under my low heels; my heart leaps in my chest. If I didn't know better, I'd think the butterflies in my belly are the first signs of the baby growing inside of me, but it's too early for that sort of thing. I smooth the front of my dress down flat, hoping to keep my little passenger a secret until the exact right moment.

I approach the ranch-style house with my head held high. I'm a married woman now. Papà doesn't have control over me anymore. In his mind, my husband does, but what happens when my keeper is dead? Perhaps that means I'm in charge of my destiny for once.

"Vivi!" Aria bursts out the front door and rushes down the front steps dressed in Mamma's old gardening coveralls, tackling me before I get halfway up the drive. Papà stands in the doorway, smiling, leaning on a carved wood cane, his leg wrapped in gauze to his knee. He looks gaunt, his skin an unhealthy gray and his dark pants held up by a belt with additional holes punched in the leather. When Aria slams into me at full speed, she can't knock the breath out of me, because it's already gone. Papà is unwell.

"You look so fancy," she says, melting into my arms. "And you smell fancy too." She buries her nose into my neck, and I wobble on my heels, still struggling to breathe normally. "You smell like Mamma."

"It's just drugstore perfume," I muster as she steps back enough that I can see her. She's grown an inch or two, her hair is wild and looks like it hasn't been combed through in at least a week, but the color in her cheeks hasn't changed, nor the playful glimmer in her eyes that the normally shy sixteen-year-old only shares with her family.

"How long do we have you?" she asks, grabbing my hand and leading me to the porch, where Papà looks like he's gritting his teeth through unbearable pain to stay upright.

"My bus leaves at five." Aria's smile falters, and the sparkle dims like electricity flickering in and out during a thunderstorm. "But I can make dinner before I go," I offer, interlocking arms with my baby sister.

"We . . . we'd have to go to the store," she says, staring at her boots as they peek out from the rolled cuffs of her pants at each step.

"I'll ask Papà for the car," I say self-assuredly, though I'm not positive my marital status will give me that much leeway.

"Okay." Aria's smile returns, and I wonder how slender she is under the oversized coveralls she's wearing. I leave my bags at the bottom of the stairs. I'll have to retrieve them later because it's clear I'm the one who'll be carrying things in our family from here on out.

"Ragazza mia. Sei a casa." *My girl. You're home.* His voice is gravelly but pleasant, and his moist eyes frighten me almost as much as his angry ones do. I'm not used to this version of my papà. I lean in to hug him and kiss his cheek. I can feel his shoulder blades beneath his thin button-up shirt. The arm grasping his cane trembles, and the faint smell of something foul wrinkles my nose when we embrace.

"Siediti, Papà. Non dovresti stare al freddo per me." *Sit, Papà. You shouldn't stand in the cold for me.* I know not to mention his leg and the weakness I read in his frame. It would be too much shame for my proud father. But he'll let me dote on him, especially now that I'm a married woman. That's the culture he was raised in and the way he raised me. It's now my time to look after my father. He's done his work, he has fed me, clothed me, housed me, and protected me. Now, he can allow me to care for him in return.

"Sto bene. Sto bene." *I'm fine. I'm fine.*

It's no use arguing. Papà will insist he's fine until he's blue in the face, but I can tell he'll let me help him inside the house without any resistance. The smell follows us, and I have a terrible suspicion I know what it's from and what it means—his leg is infected. I get Papà settled onto the couch. The box of cigars Tom gave him before our first date sits on the side table like a trophy, and a glass with traces of amber liquid at the bottom is beside it.

"Papà, I'm going to make you dinner."

"That's beautiful, *passerotta*. Aria's a good girl but knows too little about the spice of life to bring flavor to the food. Maybe you can teach . . ."

"Yes. I'll teach her, Papà. We're going to Danner's. And I'll leave some good meals for you to have in the icebox until I come back."

"When you come back? What does that mean? Next year? Two years?" Any time I spend away from home he defines as endless.

"No, Papà. No. Soon. Very soon," I say softly, on my knees tucking a blanket around his now-slender midsection.

"Soon?" He squints at me and seems to decide I'm serious. "The Hollywood man is sending you home? Or are your feet all worn out from dancing?"

"No. Neither. And it's not forever. I'll go back after . . ."

"After they find Tom?" Aria asks from behind me. I thought she was in the kitchen, and when I look back at her, I see far more worry in her features than a girl her age should bear. I have plenty of good news to tell my family, my success on the tour, the baby, and the money from the ring, even if I can't tell them where it came from. But when I take note of that hope in my sister's eyes, I see the sad parts of her world. Here she is—raising herself and taking care of a sick papà while her sick mamma is locked away in an asylum.

I skirt her question about Tom, knowing far too well that if we waited for my husband's homecoming, we'd be waiting forever.

"Christmas."

"Christmas? How long will you stay?" Aria asks.

"A few months." I don't mention the baby. It's not time yet. Before I leave tonight, I'll tell them. I'll share it one nibble of happiness at a time. "Archie made the plans already. I'll go back next spring if I'm still needed."

"Or unless your husband comes home to take care of you," Papà says with a grumble.

I swallow my guilt and nerves at each mention of my husband and put on a smile to cover up my emotions.

"He already is taking care of me, Papà."

"I knew it. I knew they found him!" Aria trills, clapping her soil-caked hands.

"No, Aria. No." I shake my head and hate seeing Aria's hope evaporate. I take her hand and Papà's, creating a chain. Aria is already crying, and Papà's lips are set in a line of stone. "It's unlikely Tom will be coming home."

Aria lets out a small "Oh" and sinks into the chair kitty-corner to the sofa. I can't look at her. She didn't know Tom, neither did Papà. They met him, sure. They understood the *idea* of my husband but not who he was when his breath was thick with whiskey and his hands became weapons. Goodness, I didn't know him either, did I? But we all know it's a tragedy to lose a husband. They can't find out it's my fault that I'm a widow, so I must let them cry for me.

I whimper and cover my lips to keep my regret from spilling out. Papà must think I'm crying for Tom. He caresses my cheek and whispers, "I'm so sorry, *passerotta*. Forget this war. Forget this dream. No more head in clouds. You are safe at home with your papà."

"I'll come home for a while, Papà. Tom left enough to take care of us for the time being. I already paid Mamma's bills. And we can pay for the house. And when I get the rest, you can put it in savings. And we can take you to a real doctor to get your leg fixed once and for all." I pass him the slip of paper I got from the jewelry store where I sold the diamond out of my wedding ring. Three karats. Thousands of dollars. Plenty to keep us afloat until I figure out what's next. "Look."

Papà takes in the number on the page, and his eyes widen. Aria, who is still fighting off a full-blown crying fit, peeks at the total on the slip.

"Oh heavens," she says, stumbling back into the chair.

"This is yours?" Papà asks, his unkempt eyebrows raised so high they disappear behind his hair.

"Yes, Papà. It's ours." I touch his shoulder, squeeze Aria's knee, and then rest my hand on my belly, counting my unborn child. "All of ours."

Aria doesn't pick up on the gesture, but Papà's eyes narrow when he notices the subtle tell. He glances at my face and then at my hand placement and then back at my face. I hold my breath and wait for his reaction. His daughter coming home pregnant—without a husband.

But he doesn't explode or toss accusations.

Instead, he says, "You're my brave girl, Viviana." Papà's tone is gentle, like how he used to coo at baby Tony or the way he talks to Mamma as she stares at the walls when we visit her at Mount Mercy. I always wondered why I never got that version of Papà. Now it's my turn, and I can hardly hold in the guilt that comes with it.

I don't feel brave, but I'm home now—or I will be soon enough. And even though I'm adding another mouth to feed, I also have a confidence that's growing. Because I won't let my family starve. I won't let them fade away like a strip of film melting in a movie projector. I'll do whatever I have to do to take care of them and to keep that light in Aria's eyes from being snuffed out entirely.

VIVIAN SNOW

Auction

Lot #4

Hand-drawn postcard labeled: Peddocks Island
    Pencil on cardstock. Shoreline and seabirds in flight.

FORT ANDREWS, MASS. MAR 1 1944 11:00 AM

> *Dear Mrs. Highward,*
>   *It is cold here, but I find joy in seeing my country-*
> *men in one place. I pray for you, always. May peace be*
> *with you now more than ever.*
>   *Yours in God—Antonio Trombello*
> (Translation from Italian)
> Passed by censor 5

CHAPTER 4

March 17, 1944
Edinburgh, Indiana

"Look at you, carrying everything on your own." Mrs. Danner tsks and waves to her waifish son, Barry, as I grab the paper bags with our weekly load of groceries. He's one year older than Aria and dropped out of school to help in the store after his father enlisted in a moment of patriotic fervor. "Hurry up, boy. Help Mrs. Highward with her things," she orders Barry, even though he's moving as quickly as his lanky body will allow.

I blush. The whole town treats me like a little china doll since the news of Tom's death spread through the gossip network.

Vivian Highward—the town's newest widow, daughter of immigrants, soon to be mother of a poor fatherless baby. The gossip worked in my favor too. Papà needed his leg amputated after another infection, so the women's group of Holy Trinity brought us meals for a month. Last week a box of baby clothes and lovely hand-quilted baby blankets was left on our front porch by a mysterious patron. Papà says it's charity and we don't take charity, but my pride won't stop me from feeding my family or keeping my baby warm. Anyway, God tells us to be charitable, but how can anyone be charitable if we're all too good to receive charity?

Barry has his arms around the groceries before I can protest.

"Are you walking, dear? I can have Barry drive you home," Mrs. Danner says, her judgment worn like a fancy piece of jewelry she's proud to display.

"No. I have the car today."

"Well, thank the Lord, if you excuse the expression. You should be home with your feet up, if you ask me."

"They could use it, for sure." I point to my swollen feet, the tops spilling over the edges of my only pair of shoes like bread rising in a pan.

Thankfully, Papà lets me use the car more often now for groceries and to drive Aria to and from school. Only six weeks out from his life-saving surgery, he's battling pain both physical and emotional. No one told us that we'd mourn the loss of Papà's limb, independence, and way of life. He didn't only lose his leg, he lost his job and ability to care for his wife and children. The only bit of joy for Papà lately is the dream of his grandchild—which I did not expect.

"Well, don't hesitate to call if you need anything. Barry can deliver. Right, Barry?" Mrs. Danner doesn't give him a moment to respond before whispering loudly like she's keeping a secret, even though the only other person in the store is a woman in an expensive suit staring at gardening supplies on the back wall: "We'll waive the delivery charge because of your . . . circumstances."

She glances at my giant belly at the exact moment the baby stretches, pushing its bottom up under my ribs with a swift kick. I wince and rub the area gently.

I still don't feel comfortable with strangers, even ones like the fancy woman in the gardening section. Trombello says raising my child well is all God asks of me. But what if he's wrong and my act of self-defense leads me to a life behind bars? What would happen to my Trombello? To my family? To my baby?

I shake the nerves away. I'm safe here. For now, at least.

"You're very generous. Thank you." I give her a forced smile.

"Don't mention it," she says with feigned humility. I pull on my gloves and fasten the top button on my overcoat, letting it drape over my midsection modestly. No one talks about pregnancy in public, no one even says "pregnant" unless in hushed tones, as though just hearing the word could force an otherwise innocent girl to get impregnated instantly.

I hurry and try to hold the door for Barry, but my belly blocks his exit, and we do a little polite dance, far different from the moves I was doing onstage with Danny Kaye just a few months ago.

When I told Danny my cover story about Tom and my tiny reason for leaving, his shoulders slumped.

"Sylvia warned me. She warned me." His wife, who is also a composer and creative collaborator, had just written a song for Danny and me to perform on tour together. "She said we'd lose you to Hollywood or the Foxhole Circuit but this—damn it, Snow. Damn it."

Seeing Danny be serious was painful. During rehearsal and performances, he was loose and funny but also nimble on his feet. I soaked up every minute of his sunshine and talent. To leave his light and venture into the unknown was terrifying.

"I'm sorry, Danny. I'll be back . . . after . . . if you'll have me."

"Don't you get it? There are hundreds of you out there. Hundreds of gals have dreams and can charm an audience. You're special but not so special that no one can replace you." He downed the rest of his drink and then poured another.

"You're not special" should be the motto of show business. And though his words were harsh, I know he didn't mean to be cruel. He wasn't telling me anything I hadn't heard before.

"I get it. But"—I touched his shoulder, and he watched me in the mirror—"what choice do I have? I didn't plan on what happened with Tom. And now I'm alone and I'm going to have a baby . . . and . . ."

"Shhh." Danny sighed and patted my hand affectionately. "I'm being a selfish fool," he said, as though the angel on his right shoulder had finally caught up with the devil on his left. He beckoned me to sit in the chair beside him. And just like Archie, Danny made promises and predictions of success and triumph, working hard to undo the damage of his initial outburst.

"Vivi!" Aria's voice brings me back to the present. She skips up to the car in her oversized peacoat and the rain boots she wears year-round, or at least when she can sneak them past me in the morning. I'd forgotten we'd planned to meet at Danner's, and I jumped in fright at her greeting. I'm always jumpy now. I wonder if that reflex will ever go away.

"What are you? A superspy?" I ask, my heart beating so hard it must've scared the baby enough to make it stop wiggling for a minute or two.

"It's not my fault you're as jittery as a jackrabbit lately. Oh!" She looks over my shoulder at Barry. He's waiting at the closed trunk to load the groceries. He doesn't look impatient, though. I'm sure he's not exactly anxious to get back inside, where his mother will likely yell more orders and he'll wish he could go back to high school and be a kid again. Aria blushes and clams up, her cheeks flushing.

"Barry!" I call out to the long-suffering bag boy. "I'm so sorry. Here. Aria, you move faster than I do. Help him, will you?" I pass her the keys and a quarter to give as a tip. She shoots me a look of annoyance I seldom see from my helpful little sister.

Aria is shy, and though she's bold and playful at home, she hardly speaks in front of others. Especially not boys. I used to be shy too. Papà'd made me so scared of the world and men that I didn't know how to recognize the warning signs in Tom. As I danced at the USO and worked at Camp Atterbury, and my friendship with Trombello and the other men on the chapel construction committee grew, I learned. But it was too late. I want better for Aria, even if she finds me annoying in the process.

I climb into the front seat, my belly barely fitting behind the wheel. The car bounces when Barry closes the trunk, and moments later Aria is on the passenger side, her face still pink from the chill in the air and . . . maybe something else.

"Here. He didn't want it." She drops the quarter into the unused ashtray with a clink.

"He didn't want a tip?" I ask, confused. Maybe it's because his mother said the thing about not charging for deliveries, or maybe he just felt bad for us. Or maybe . . .

"I think he fancies you," I say, even though I have no evidence to back up my claim.

"Ew. Stop." Aria crinkles her nose, which just makes her more adorable.

"It's okay to like boys, Aria. Especially nice ones like Barry." We pull away from the curb, and she crosses her arms.

"I don't want to like boys. Not yet. They're too . . . complicated."

"Yeah. I can see that. They sure do complicate things," I say, my belly tightening like it does lately. My doctor says it's normal, that's how your body gets ready for childbirth. I still haven't gotten used to the uncomfortable sensation.

We make it home so quickly it seems silly that I drove. The sensation releases, and I blow out a heavy breath of relief. Aria hasn't noticed and continues with her thoughts.

"I'm never getting married. It looks terrible. I'll be an old maid or a spinster. I like that term—spinster. Can I just be a spinster now?"

"You're sixteen," I say, chuckling, remembering a time when I considered becoming a nun rather than submitting to a man. "You don't know what the future holds. One day you'll meet a man and fall in love, and then I'll tell him you wanted to be a spinster and we'll all laugh."

"Never. I swear."

Aria shakes her head as I pull into our gravel driveway and put the car into park. Little pieces of hair have come loose on the sides of her ponytail. I want to take her to the salon and get her a bob, but she says she's fine with her long hair and that she doesn't want to spend the money. I think she's afraid of looking pretty.

"Time will tell," I say, wiggling my way out of the car. Aria retrieves both bags of groceries and is halfway up the front porch before I can make it to the trunk. I close it and take a step to follow Aria inside, when another tightening spreads through my midsection like a rubber band pulled taut. I touch my firm belly and let out a slow breath, surprised at the intensity of the sensation. If this is practice for labor, what will the real thing be like?

"You all right?" A young woman with a dignified East Coast accent, dressed in a white mink ribbed jacket over a green lace skirt and a matching emerald-colored art deco hat with a wisp of a veil on the brim, appears out of nowhere.

I recognize her. This is the woman I saw at Danner's store browsing the gardening section. I saw her slip out of the store when Aria surprised me by the car. And now that I see her up close, I think I've seen her one other time, as I was leaving my doctor's appointment in Columbus earlier this week. I couldn't help but notice her on the street and the flowy cream-colored pants suit she wore regally like Katharine Hepburn, without a single wrinkle in the silk fabric.

"I'm fine. Thank you." The grip on my middle releases slowly, and I can breathe normally again. I pull my purse back up onto my shoulder and straighten my spine.

"Oh. I see," she says as I glance beyond her. There's a dark car parked at the end of the street right in front of Mrs. Lee's house. It looks like a government car. I squint at it, my heart racing. Wait. It's not a government car. It's something more . . . shiny . . . expensive.

"I better get inside," I say, backing away toward the house. The finely dressed young woman doesn't return to her car or move. She watches me with her purse clasped in front of her.

"Please, don't go. Can I have one moment of your time?" Her plea sounds eager. If she didn't look so well put together I'd think she was a traveling salesperson or a religious zealot going door to door, saving souls.

"I'm so sorry. My father is ill, and my sister needs my help with dinner . . ."

"It'll only take a moment." She follows me a step or two, and I feel like a field mouse pursued by a pampered house cat.

"Maybe another time," I say, knowing I'm being rude. I'm at the front steps now. But I'm slow, my new weight making climbing stairs awkward. The woman catches up, her cheeks glowing now and expensive perfume filling the space between us.

"I picked out your ring," she says, out of breath. "At Tiffany's. I would've been at your wedding, but it happened so quickly, and I couldn't sneak away."

I stop on the second step, my heart racing. She *is* here to see me. I'm not being paranoid. My ring clinks against the metal railing when I lean against it for support. The Tiffany box that came to my doorstep after my wedding, only days after Tom died from the knife in my hand. A week before the bruises on my neck had faded away and I joined up with the USO Camp Shows. A month before the cut on my throat could be hidden with makeup instead of a bandage. Three months before I realized I was carrying Tom's child.

"Moira," I say, seeing it now. Moira Highward, Tom's younger sister and biggest supporter. The color of her sandy blonde hair is a perfect copy of Tom's, her eyes too.

"You know my name?"

"I do." Tom called her spoiled but sweet. He told me they grew close when they both had measles. Their older brother, Richard, died in the bed next to them during that same illness, and their younger sister had been born with limitations and lives in a special home much like my mother. I don't know a lot about his family except for the rumors of their great wealth and prestige, but the one thing I do know for sure is Tom loved his sister dearly.

Her eyes glisten, and her mouth turns up at the corners, just like Tom's smile.

"Do you know where he is?" she asks. Neither of us has said his name yet, but we both know who we're referring to. As I answer, another spasm begins, hardening my belly and making me short of breath.

"No. I haven't seen him for months. The MPs have been out here more times than I can count," I say, panting. I put my free hand on my midsection, leaning nearly all of my weight into the railing. "You?"

"The MPs, yes. Reporters too. But Daddy paid them to go away. They don't know about you, though. Daddy doesn't want anyone to know about you or . . ." She looks at my tented dress and half-buttoned coat. "But it's not like you're some girl he ran off with. You were married in a church. You're his wife. That's his baby."

She lists these facts as though she's had this argument before with her father. I don't stop her, hoping I can wait out my pain before needing to speak again. She continues her speech, close enough for us to touch now.

"I'm so sorry, Vivian. I didn't think my brother could be such a cad. He loved you like mad, or at least I thought so. Daddy hired a whole troop of private detectives, but no one's found him yet, not in Canada or Brazil or anywhere else.

"I know many men are scared off by war or fatherhood or both. But I didn't believe my brother was capable of cowardice, so I thought maybe marriage wasn't what it was cracked up to be or something. But then I saw you. You're lovely."

She says the last phrase like she's finally found the right word after sorting through a thousand wrong ones. The pain has passed, and I can stand on my own.

"I'm sure there's a good reason he's not here, or at least that's what I tell myself," I say, without an ounce of bitterness in my tone. Tom was not a hero, not for me at least. But I've made the decision to shield my child and my family from the truth of who my husband was. I'll do the same for Tom's family, the best I can. Out of repentance, yes, but also selfishly so they'll leave me and my baby alone.

Moira raises her eyebrows, and she rubs her lined and painted lips together.

"That's what I mean. You're lovely. My brother doesn't deserve you." She shakes her head.

"I don't know about that . . ." I shift my weight, my back and feet aching. I want to go inside and check on Papà and make dinner and pretend I'm just another war wife having a baby with her husband overseas. That's one thing I have in common with Moira's father, Mr. Highward. I don't want my story to be told, not the real one, at least.

"Look at you standing here in the cold," Moira says, taking in my discomfort and assuming it's purely physical. "You've got to be worn nearly dull." She shakes her head and rummages through her purse. "Daddy would slaughter me for being here, but I want to help until Tom comes to his senses. Here. This is my maid's address and phone number. You can reach me there without Daddy finding out. I can help you, financially."

She holds out a card with her name printed on it and a series of numbers and addresses on the back like she'd been planning on this moment all along.

"Oh, I couldn't," I say, pushing it back, already drowning in shame from selling the diamond from my wedding ring that *she* bought. I couldn't take another penny.

"Take it, Vivian. Your baby deserves it. Until Tom shows his lousy face again, that baby is the only heir after me. Daddy thinks I'll get married and have lots of children, but do you think these little hips can handle that?" She jokes, but the meaning behind it is real. My baby is a Highward, the only other Highward for now. Who knows what'll happen when they realize Tom isn't coming back? They could take my child and there'd be little I could do to stop them.

"I'm sorry. I'm just not used to asking for help. Papà's a proud man . . ." Moira cuts in.

"Let's leave the prideful silliness to the men, shall we? Besides, you're family now."

"Family. Yes," I echo and take her card to placate her. I won't call, not for money. And I hope she has a dozen children and forgets all about my baby.

After a few more pleasantries and questions about due dates and plans for the future, Moira leaves and I enter the house feeling as though I've walked a thousand miles rather than the few steps from the car. Another sensation takes me, this time spreading its tension to my lower back and making me drop my purse and Moira's card.

"Vivi?" Aria asks, concern in her voice as she enters the front room. "Are you all right?" I'm not all right, not anywhere close. But I'm not used to admitting that to myself, much less to anyone else.

"I think I just need to sit down for a bit," I say, stumbling into the armchair. Aria runs into the kitchen for a glass of water, and I can hear Papà calling from his room, still bedbound from his surgery.

"What's going on?" he shouts. "Someone tell me what's happening."

I don't know what's happening any more than he does, but I do know that he will never know what's truly happening in my life. No one will—other than me and perhaps my dear friend and confidant Father Trombello. And God—if he's even listening (to a sinner like me).

VIVIAN SNOW

Auction

Lot #5

Hand-drawn postcard labeled: Sanctuary of Cathedral of the Holy
Cross
    Black ink on cardstock. Church interior, marble columns, and lines
of wooden pews.

BOSTON, MASS. JUN 3 1944 1:30 PM

> *Dear Mrs. Highward,*
>   *Thank you for the photograph of young Grace. She
> looks much like her mother. Good health to you both.*
>   *Yours in God—Antonio Trombello*
> (Translation from Italian)
> Passed by censor 1

CHAPTER 5

June 23, 1944
Norways Sanitarium
Indianapolis, Indiana

The baby whines in the back seat. Papà is asleep in the passenger seat, his head against the doorframe, and Aria rocks the basket back and forth trying to stop the impending eruption.

"Shhh, little one. Shhh." Aria places a rubber nipple in the baby's mouth. "We'll need to feed her soon."

"I know," I whisper back and glance at my watch. I thought we'd be at Norways Sanitarium by noon or I'd have fed her at our last stop. We've been driving since early this morning. "Think she'll make it a few more minutes?"

"Maybe. But you know how she gets when she's hungry," Aria says with a giggle, and I hold back a laugh. I could let her give Gracie a bottle, but selfishly I like to be the one to feed her.

Little Miss Grace has been a screamer since half past midnight on March 18. Only six hours after Moira Highward drove away in her fancy car, I met my daughter, Grace Maria Highward. A red-faced, light-haired, blue-eyed treasure whom I love more than life itself. She loves her mamma's arms, her auntie's kisses, and her nonno's grumbly voice. We've all been healed by Grace—Papà's leg is nearly recovered,

Aria's smiling more, even in front of strangers, and my Grace has made me feel as though I may one day be forgiven if I can give her a good life.

"We're almost there," I say, glancing at the map of the city of Indianapolis. We left nearly everything behind in the house, rented out to a group of nurses from the hospital at Camp Atterbury. Our car looks like an ant carrying a ridiculously oversized crumb home to its queen.

Today, Papà starts his job as groundskeeper at Norways Sanitarium. We moved my mother here after I transferred all the ring money into my new bank account that I was able to get as a married woman with my husband "away at war." When I saw the advertisement for a sanitarium closer to home, with private rooms and state-of-the-art treatments within our budget, I couldn't refuse. As the staff came to know Papà from his frequent visits, they took pity on his plight, "supporting" his two daughters, one married to a soldier who was missing in action, and a potentially fatherless infant granddaughter.

I'm still unsure if Papà's leg is healed enough to endure hours on his uncomfortable and ill-fitted prosthetic, but Aria insisted she'd find no greater happiness than helping him tend the grounds so they can live closer to my mother. I, on the other hand, am conflicted about the change.

Leaving Edinburgh is a relief. It's the only home I've ever known, but with the MPs showing up every few weeks, it's getting harder and harder to keep Tom's AWOL status under wraps. The more miles we put between us and my hometown, the more I know it's right. And even if my time at Norways is temporary, it will be the closest thing to having our family all together since the day Tony died in Mamma's arms.

But Mamma doesn't feel like a mother to me anymore. Mamma now is either so heavily medicated that she can't form words or so frantic that she pulls out patches of her hair and begs in Italian to go home. Mamma now is still scary sometimes. Mamma now, I'm terrified of turning into one day.

I've taken one life. And so has she.

I turn the '38 Oldsmobile up the long tree-lined drive, angling to fit between the stacked stone gateway off the brick street. In front of the large Victorian mansion are tracks embedded in the street that lead to downtown Indianapolis. And though I know what waits for us inside the grand old house, for a moment I let myself imagine that I'm a movie star and I bought the place for my parents as a gift.

But the trees that line the path bring me back to reality. The sanitarium is named after the Norway maple trees that populate the grounds, green now but brilliant yellow, orange, and red by fall.

"Papà! Wake up!" Aria says in English. We've been speaking more English at home to help Papà prepare for his new position. Aria and I cannot always be around to translate.

Papà sits up, groaning as he adjusts in his seat.

"Siamo già qui?" he asks, rubbing the sleep from his eyes.

"In inglese, Papà," I prompt. He grumbles and speaks slowly.

"Us here for now? Quick."

"Yes, Papà. We got here quickly. It helped that you slept the whole way," I say slowly, hoping he understands. I give up when I see his confusion and translate for him, an old habit from my interpreter days at Atterbury, I guess.

I park in the bend of the drive outside the grand front porch and pointed turret. The house is imposing and looks like the setting of a Gothic horror movie where secrets are buried in the basement or somewhere on the grounds. I can't imagine how this dramatic backdrop wouldn't agitate the more paranoid patients at Norways.

I help Papà out of the front seat, where he stretches and adjusts his prosthetic under his pant leg. His limp is noticeable and he's still using a cane, but overall he's more active than he's been since the injury a year and a half ago.

I turn to see Dr. Wells, the head of the facility, saunter down the sturdy front steps. Two women in tailored nurses' uniforms follow, and a large man with muscled arms in a white uniform accompanies them like a bodyguard.

"Mr. Santini! Welcome!" He's a friendly doctor, on the younger side, and not nearly as serious or stern as the director of Mount Mercy, where our mother used to live. There, they used harsh punishments, and often I'd see marks on Mamma's arms and legs where they tied her down.

Here, they're cheerful, though still firm. Dr. Wells gives his word that they'll try innovative new therapies. Papà believes Mamma will be healed here, but I'm not as optimistic. Any hope for my mother's cure only brings compounded pain in the future when nothing changes. But I do like her improved living situation, and even slight improvements over her catatonia or mania are meaningful.

"The whole family is here, at long last," Dr. Wells continues. Papà tries to respond in broken English as Aria crawls out of the back of the car with Grace in her arms. Normally, I'd feel the urge to translate, but the baby's whimpers have stolen my attention.

Her infant-sized patience will run out soon. I prepared two bottles this morning. She's nearly weaned from nursing. I know it's necessary to get her used to a bottle since I'll be leaving for the road in a few weeks, but sometimes it's painful to feed her the concoction of evaporated milk, water, and Karo syrup as instructed by our family doctor instead of the milk that aches inside my breasts. I still sneak her into my bed at night for a feeding and again in the morning, but soon she won't need me, at least not for food.

"We can find you a private room inside, Mrs. Highward, if you like," Dr. Wells offers, beckoning one of the nurses forward. I have to be respectful. Dr. Wells and this facility have given us all so much hope and stability, and I don't want to lose that. But I would rather keep my child out of the madhouse for as long as possible.

"Thank you, but I think some fresh air will do her good," I say with a polite smile. He assesses me with a barely perceptible hum and cocked head like I'm one of his patients.

"I'm sure it will do both of you some good," Dr. Wells finally agrees. "Mrs. Harris, please take Mr. Santini and Miss Aria for their tour. And,

Lucas, please show Mrs. Highward to the back garden. I'll bring you to your family once the little one is satisfied."

He speaks with kindness and an authority that's comforting but also unnerving, like he's in charge of not only the asylum but my family as well.

As Aria and Papà follow the stern Mrs. Harris into the house, I head toward one of the trees in the side yard with a glass bottle clutched at my side. My heels sink into the soft grass, and I end up walking on my toes. Baby Grace's whimpers have grown into wails. Little tears leak out the corners of her squinted eyes.

"Oh, little baby. Oh hush," I say, settling onto a shaded bench, kissing each of her hot cheeks and nuzzling her soft baby face. She smells sweet and a little sweaty, so I unwrap her blankets and find a comfortable position as her cries ring in the open air of the massive front yard. I pop the rubber nipple into her mouth and rock back and forth and hum a lullaby as she gulps hungrily. Her blue eyes rest on my face, and she calms in my arms, relaxing into a puddle of limbs and squishy bits.

We sit in the cool peace of the yard, and I close my eyes, pretending her satisfied sounds work as a harmony to the song tickling my vocal cords. A light touch on my shoulder interrupts our solitude.

"Is your baby?" an accented voice asks. I glance at the woman behind me, expecting to see the white of a nurse's uniform. Instead, I see a middle-aged woman in a neat blue dress, cinched at the waist with a simple belt. Her hair is dark and held back in a low braid with only a few strands of silver hinting at her age. Her face is lined but not deeply wrinkled, and there is a glossy sadness in her rich brown eyes. No matter how long it's been since I saw her last or how long since I've heard her speak a sentence, I know immediately who this visitor is.

"Mamma," I say, the word catching in my throat. I called her that ten years ago when I came home from school to find Aria abandoned in the empty house. I searched the rooms for her and my tiny baby brother, Tony. His bassinet was empty, as was her bed, the kitchen, the basement.

Back then Mamma could be as wild as a dragonfly, flitting in and out of our home, or she could be a sad shell Papà tried to manage with pills and wine. But once she found out she was pregnant with baby Tony, she found peace, and to him, she was the mamma I'd always wished for. That day when I saw the back door standing open, I called for her outside, listening for any clues to where she might be. The car still in the driveway. Her coat still on the hook. Tony's baby blanket on the ground.

I should've stopped my search. Every nerve in my body told me to. But I didn't listen. Perhaps it was God trying to spare me. Or was God trying to keep me from saving her when I couldn't save him? Tony.

I found them both in the creek behind our house—Tony, blue in my mother's arms, Mamma alive but near to death. Mamma lived. Tony was buried in a tiny casket in Rest Haven Cemetery. Since then I haven't been able to look at the color blue without thinking of that day, and I haven't known how to forgive Maria Santini for being so sick that she sacrificed both my childhood and my brother for her illness.

She's lived in an institution since she awoke from her deep sleep to find she'd killed her own child.

Trombello says I should pray to soften my heart, that she didn't choose her illness any more than one chooses measles or tuberculosis. And what he's kind enough to leave unsaid is, my mother and I both have blood on our hands.

"Your baby?" she asks again. I've rarely heard her voice during my previous visits. Usually, she's lost in heavy medication or madness. Now, she stands in front of me tidy and speaking in broken English. Perhaps Dr. Wells's miracle treatments are working. A nurse stands in the distance watching the interaction.

"Sì. Tua nipote," I say in Italian. *Yes. Your grandchild.*

She cocks her head and squints at my face and then at Gracie.

"My?" she asks in English again, transfixed by the nearly satisfied baby in my arms. The bottle's nipple squeaks as Grace drinks the last remnants of milk.

"Your granddaughter." I put Grace on my shoulder and pat her back, urging out any bubbles that settled in her stomach. Most women have mothers to advise on motherhood and childcare, but my mother doesn't even recognize me.

She walks around the bench, her feet dragging slightly like they've been weighted down. She was always beautiful, my mother, especially before she was institutionalized. Men would stare despite the solid band of gold on her left hand. Even now, I see the curve of her jaw, the bow of her lips. I'll always wonder how life brought her to this point—and I'll never stop worrying that I might face the same fate.

"Mio piccolo tesoro," she says, leaning down to Gracie's level, calling her a little darling. No. Calling her "my little darling." My heart swells with a touch of hope. Does she know who I am? Who Gracie is? Has my mother caught up to the rest of us in reality?

"Her name is Grace Maria. After you," I explain, in Italian this time.

"Grazie a Dio per questo miracolo," she says, and I echo the sentiment in my mind. *Yes. Thank God for this miracle.*

Gracie whimpers and squirms, my attempts at burping her not yet successful. I bounce her slightly and pat faster, shushing to keep her from exploding.

"Qui. Dammela," she says, telling me to pass her the baby like she's a real grandmother and hasn't been in an asylum since my childhood. I recoil. The last time I saw her holding a baby, it was my deceased brother.

"I've got her," I say in Italian, switching the now crying baby over to my other shoulder.

"Give. Me," she says in English, putting her arms out. "Give me. Give me. *My* baby."

"*My* baby. Your grandchild, Gracie." I try to explain, not knowing what language I should speak anymore. "You are her nonna."

Gracie is wailing now, and I'm doing a poor job of comforting her, distracted by my increasingly agitated mother. I glance back at the nurse, who is speaking quietly to the attendant Dr. Wells ordered to escort us after Grace's feeding. Neither seems to notice the tone change in our interaction over the sound of the infant's cries.

"You took my baby. You took him. Give," she screams and lunges at me, her eyes clouding over with a desperate fury. I wrap my arms around Grace and lean back, my mother's nails catching the skin at my wrist. I don't loosen my grip.

"Help!" I cry out, and the fear from the night Tom nearly killed me floods back in. Trombello is not here to save me, and I'm not holding a knife. This time the only thing in my hands is a baby. "Help me!" I scream as my mother tears at my fingers, working to rip my hands off Gracie, who is as frantic in her panic as her grandmother. We fall to the ground just as I see Dr. Wells leap off the front porch, yelling instructions, and Lucas, the attendant, only a few steps away.

The big burly attendant and the nurse pull my mother off me. They pin her to the ground, and Dr. Wells takes a syringe from his coat pocket and measures a clear liquid, which he injects into her arm. I scramble to my feet, my face wet, shushing my baby and myself in the same moment.

I can't watch as Lucas and the nurse take the madwoman who looked and sounded like my mamma a few minutes ago into the big house. I stumble across the lawn, hoping I'll see Papà or Aria but also hoping I can spare them this crushing disappointment. I rock Gracie back and forth over and over, hoping if she stops crying, I can stop this stifling panic that makes me want to escape my body.

"Mrs. Highward, are you all right?" Dr. Wells is by my side, inspecting the bloody scratches on my arm. I keep rocking, half-aware, half not. "Mrs. Highward? Mrs. Highward." Dr. Wells takes my face in his hands and flashes a light in my eyes, calling my name.

Aria is here. She takes Gracie, who's finally stopped crying. Papà talks to me like I've heard him talk to Mamma, calm but with an undercurrent of fear. Dr. Wells says something about taking me into the big house and giving me something for my nerves.

And immediately, I'm back in my body. My arm stings where Mamma scratched me, and the back of my head aches from where it hit the ground.

"I'm fine," I say, my voice breathy but sure. "I'm fine."

"Mrs. Highward," Dr. Wells says again, this time like he's welcoming me home. "You've had a little shock. You should rest."

I clear my throat and straighten my hair and skirt, ignoring the grass stains down my right side and the tear in my only pair of nylons.

"That's not necessary, Dr. Wells. Thank you kindly, though," I say as though I'm speaking from a script. He gauges me with a raised eyebrow and then nods like he approves of my resilience.

"Then we'll move forward with our tour of the grounds if you'd like to join us in the back garden."

"It would be my pleasure," I say, playing my part well. Aria whispers that I can go inside and rest, but I decline, taking Gracie in my arms and following Dr. Wells with my head held high. I won't allow them to think I've lost my mind, even for a moment. Because there's one thing I know for sure: I will not be a patient in a place like this. Not today. And if I can help it, not ever.

VIVIAN SNOW

Auction

Lot #6

Hand-drawn postcard labeled: Boston Shipyard
   Blue ink on cardstock. Empty docks and shipyard from a distance.

BOSTON, MASS. AUG 3 1944 1:00 PM

> *Dear Miss Snow,*
>   *I'm sorry to have missed you. I heard you sang like an angel. May God keep you safe in your travels.*
>   *Blessings to you—Trombello*
>   (Translation from Italian)
>   Passed by censor 3

CHAPTER 6

December 29, 1944
Undisclosed Location
French Countryside

It's frigid here in France. Where it's not frozen, there's mud. And where there's not mud, there's snow. And where there's no snow, we sleep. The Foxhole Circuit is a cast of funny men and beautiful women who entertain the soldiers and help them forget about the war for a while. And when our company manager, Willy, says "Go," we perform. Around camp, I wear the same uniform as the enlisted men most of the time. Onstage, I'm usually in stockings and a unitard or a short-sleeved dress with my legs showing, but I don't feel the cold, because as soon as I get in front of a crowd, I'm warmed by the cheers of the soldiers.

We're so close to the fighting we can hear the shells exploding at the front and have spent more than one night hiding in a dirt shelter to stay safe. I conceal the details of my proximity to danger from Aria and Papà. I haven't seen them since I left home at the end of July. Gracie can sit up and feed herself peas and is starting to crawl. I've seen none of it, and the ache of missing her keeps me up at night almost as much as the sound of the explosives.

I was told I could return home for the holidays, but then the Ardennes Offensive started on December 16 and all leave was canceled.

We keep moving east, which means something good must be happening, but no one knows when we'll go home. I guess that's pretty normal when it comes to war.

"Ready for your solo?"

Larry Rockford, the handsome embedded journalist who travels with our Foxhole Circuit Camp Show, peeks into the tent wearing head-to-toe camouflage. He has wavy brown hair held in place with the help of some scented pomade and a sly smile that keeps me warm out here in the frozen wasteland of war.

"Don't you ever knock?" I challenge, feeling the urge to flirt. Our evolving friendship makes me excited to wake up in the morning but also scares me nearly as much as the air raids and Nazis. Besides, I'm married. Or at least that's what Larry thinks.

"Knock, knock," he says sarcastically. My playfully annoyed grumble emits a burst of condensed moisture into the air that matches his.

He slides in beside me and stares at our reflection in the small, portable mirror I use to apply my makeup. He smiles, as though he likes what he sees. Then his eyes rest on a snapshot sticking out from the frame around the reflective glass—me and Tom outside Holy Trinity on our wedding day. I was wearing a borrowed wedding dress a few sizes too big, and Tom was in his uniform. Grace was there too, though I hadn't realized it yet. I'd known him only six weeks, and I'd let him inside my heart, my body, and my life forever. I should've been more careful with my eternity.

"What did you say your husband's name is? Tom?" He snags the picture for a closer look. I like Larry and he likes me and that's literally bad news, at least for me. Everyone else wants to get on Larry's good side. He decides who gets mentioned in his articles and newsreels. He's in charge of the camera, too, and who ends up America's darling or just an unknown backup singer. Larry can bring the spotlight in your direction, which is good news as long as that light doesn't expose things better left obscured.

"Yes. Tom. But I'd rather not . . ." I take the photo and replace it on the mirror as Larry continues his friendly interrogation.

"What was your married name again? Wasn't it Highward?" he says as though he already knows the answer.

I shudder at the Highward name. Everyone here believes my husband is MIA, and I've never mentioned my legal name to anyone in the circuit. Behind my back some say he's likely dead, others hold out hope for his return. And when they think I'm too far away to hear, they talk about how I had his baby a few months ago. But if Larry digs into Tom's family or the truth behind his disappearance, it's not only bad publicity I have to fear but possibly prison. So I keep him at arm's length, as difficult as that's turning out to be.

"Larry. Knock it off," I snip and put on another coat of lipstick, buying myself time to come up with a distraction. He continues.

"It has a ring to it. Highward. Did you know there's a big rich family named Highward? Have a lot to do with steel and have some big government contracts."

"They sound delightful. Can't imagine why I spend all my time here with the likes of you," I say, trying to sound uninterested.

"Well, it's hard to resist the scenery and fresh air, not to mention my charms . . ."

"Ha," I laugh, feigning a flirtatious ambivalence that's fitting for my onstage persona, Vivian Snow. Here I'm more Snow than Santini, and there's no trace of Highward. Until today.

"I think there's a Tom Highward in that family too." He reaches across my body, blocking my view in the mirror, to retrieve the small portrait of Grace and holds it up to the light. "The wealthy Tom Highward has gone missing too. What a wild coincidence."

I rub my lips together and replace my supplies in the metal container that keeps them sheltered from the elements. Makeup is as much a part of my costume as the sequins. These fellas haven't been near their girls for months, if not longer. I've had more than one soldier tell me that it meant the world to see an all-American girl. I take it seriously, the comfort we bring. That's why I can't let myself get distracted by worries from home, secrets, or feelings for a certain nosy writer.

"I'm not sure what you're insinuating," I say, yanking the picture out of his hands and placing it back in the mirror, which I close with a snap. My heart thumps like it used to when I'd audition or when Papà lost his temper.

"You're frightened," he says, studying me. I stare at the floor, though it likely won't help. My quickened breath will give me away as much as the fear in my eyes.

"No," I lie.

"Yes. You're scared shitless. You're shaking like the new recruits during their first air raid."

He touches my chin and forces me to look at him. He towers above me, taller than Tom by six inches at least. But it's not his height that frightens me, and there's not a touch of anger in his eyes. It's the way he looks at me, like he can see into me, like he wants to know every bit of me. It's one thing to let Trombello see the truest version of myself; he stood by my side during my lowest moments, and he still brings me comfort. But Larry has a pen he can dip in poison at any twist or turn. After all, he's a journalist, and his entire reason for joining our tour is to spin stories that'll keep the American public spellbound. It's clear he suspects I'm hiding something about Tom, and he's itching to get it published on newsprint.

"I'm just nervous about the show." I shake my head again, knowing it's some of my worst acting.

Larry leans in.

"That's a bunch of bullshit. I've never seen a single nervous twitch out of the great Vivian Snow."

He watches my lips, and I know it would take so little to change his focus. We've been stuck in the same group since August, when we sailed out of Boston. At first I thought him a cad, a philanderer, but I'm almost sure he's not any of those things. He's a reporter, yes, but with a poet's heart. I've seen him write letters home for men wrapped in bandages who can't hold a pen. I've seen him pass his rations to a pair of French orphans begging on the side of the road. He's a good man. But is he good enough to keep me safe?

Good or bad, our physical attraction is undeniable at this point. One brush of his skin against mine does more to heat me from the inside out than a steaming cup of coffee. As he angles closer, I know so many temptations would be satisfied if I pulled him into me. I've only kissed one man in my life. I wonder if they're all the same, if kissing Larry would produce the same symphony of sensations I had when I let Tom kiss me in the back of his borrowed Cadillac. Or the explosions of emotion that came with our passionate wedding night. Would I live the entirety of my life never experiencing that feeling again?

I close my eyes, my lips parting. The growing tension between us is at a breaking point. His hands are on my shoulders as I anticipate his lips on mine. He leans in. I lean in.

His breath warms my face as he whispers, "I heard Tom Highward has a secret wife and child he abandoned and that his family pays handsomely for the press to turn a blind eye to the scandal."

My eyes fly open. Larry's gaze is soft, but also analytical, and it terrifies me. I stumble backward on my heeled shoes, the dirt floor uneven. My folding canvas chair clatters to the ground, spilling my cosmetic kit. I want to slap him or curse at him, instead I stare as I try to regain my composure. He looks like he's about to speak, when the tent flap opens a crack.

"Hey. Call was five minutes ago. Let's go," Willy shouts without entering. Grateful to have a reason to escape, I grab my helmet and run out into the cold after Willy. I'm slowed by the mud and heels, but it's better than walking with Larry. My throat is dry, and I can barely make small talk once I catch up.

"Get some water, would you? You sound terrible," Willy orders once we reach the rest of the cast: Kitty Barrett; her husband, Don Rice; and a new girl—Nancy Walker. We're all made up and polished. Beneath our large overcoats, we ladies have on nylons and pretty dresses.

On the outside, we wear smiles that don't belong to us, though we're all cold, tired, and scared for different reasons. All of us make up an odd little family. Danny wrote our show along with Sylvia. He's supposed to join us for a few performances as soon as he can get here safely. And Larry will be with us the whole way, reporting on the war, our victories and triumphs, and any interesting stories about us that will keep morale high and papers selling fast back home.

"Break legs," Nancy says with a smile. She's new. This'll be her first time in front of a group of heartbroken, battle-weary men. The first time with mud in her shoes and shouting into a crackling sound system.

"Yes, break a leg," I echo with very little emotion. I sound burned out, embittered. How? This is what I've always wanted to do, what I used to dream of when I performed on the small stage at the Edinburgh USO each weekend. I thought when my dreams came true, they'd also make me happy.

As Don and Kitty head onstage to warm the crowd, I take off my overcoat. The freezing air brings a flood of goose bumps on my arms and legs. I notice Larry coming up behind us and make myself look busy with my zipper.

I haven't recovered from our moment in the tent, embarrassed that I thought he wanted me when all he wanted was a headline. Now that I suspect his true intentions, I need some time to think through my side of the story before he corners me again. So I'm relieved when I hear Don start in on my intro. I squeeze Nancy's hand for good luck.

"And now for a little of what we know you've been waiting for—our very own Miss Vivian Snow and Miss Nancy Walker to share a song and dance. Give these gals a warm-as-possible welcome!"

Cheers break out. Nancy raises her eyebrows and lets me onstage first, and I meet Don at the microphone. I shout out a gracious hello, which leads to more applause, catcalls, and dog whistles. Nancy blushes and waves, and I make scripted small talk with Don before leading into our first song in a three-part harmony.

It's then that the stage shakes, knocking me to my knees, an ear-piercing explosion reverberating inside my skull. Behind me, Nancy screams at the top of her lungs, though I can barely hear it. The audience changes from boys taking a break from their wearisome job back into soldiers.

On my hands and knees, I cover my head as another explosion hits, presumably closer this time. The canopy above the platform starts to collapse, and the heavy beam cracks. Nancy is frozen in place, still screaming, though I can't hear her. I find my way to my feet and dive across the stage, wrapping my arms around her waist.

"Go! Go!" I shout, shoving her down the stairs toward three men in uniform holding our helmets, gesturing at a foxhole a few feet away from the now collapsed stage. One of my shoes is gone, and my dress is covered in debris. Nancy's dress is ripped down one side, her slip showing. We'll freeze once the panic leaves us, but that will hardly matter if we die on our way to the foxhole.

"Get down!" one of the soldiers shouts. We duck behind a wall of sandbags as another explosion rocks the camp. Mud coats my arms and the side of my face, but I don't let go of Nancy. She's not screaming any longer. Now she's trembling and stunned like a frightened animal in front of a predator. I'll have to drag her the rest of the way.

With the help of another soldier, we carry her through the mud to the foxhole. I scramble down the makeshift ladder and strain to get her over the ledge. As another explosion shakes the ground, I cover Nancy's body with my own, my eardrums rattled and ringing with a low whine.

A soldier rushes us a few feet down a tunnel to a shallow alcove where several figures are huddled.

The first face I see is Larry's.

"Thank God," he mutters and looks like he wants to embrace me but is too wary of Willy and a cluster of young soldiers watching our exchange. Instead of offering words or an embrace for comfort, he brings me and Nancy a stack of blankets, one of them his, I'm sure. Our fingers touch, and his caress warms me.

He retreats, lights a cigarette, and tucks a hand into his pocket, leaning against the earthen wall—watching. It's the only thing he's allowed to do during this conflict other than write.

As I sit on the damp, muddy floor of the foxhole, Nancy curls into me, covering herself entirely with a blanket. "I've got you," I say, encircling her with my arms as I pretend that she's my little Aria, frightened during a nightmare, needing comfort, needing my embrace, our body heat the only thing keeping us from hypothermia.

We sit like that for what seems like hours. As the world gradually grows quiet outside the foxhole, Nancy's shoulders shake, and tears finally find their way to her face.

"Shhh, darling," I whisper. "Shhh."

With my eyes closed, I begin to sing "Amazing Grace," to myself at first and then to Nancy. A shifting weight nearby catches my attention. My eyes open, and I notice that Nancy and I aren't the only ones finding comfort in the old hymn. As each line comes from my lips, more soldiers turn toward me, the whites of their eyes the only way to tell what's human in the darkness and what's a wall of mud.

We stay in that hole till the sun has set and the air is still, and I sing the comforting hymns of my youth. It's not a true performance, my voice ragged from the debris and tight from the cold, but it's one I know I'll never forget.

"It's safe now," a soldier says when I pause, my mind growing blank as if the cold stole my memory of anything outside of this cavity. Nancy and I don't move at first, finding the words hard to believe. Nothing here is safe, not really.

Willy urges us to our feet and helps Nancy climb the ladder at the dead end of the foxhole. As we exit, a great rush of applause follows us. I stop and glance behind at the gathering of soldiers, a larger crowd than I could've imagined when I first started singing to young Nancy Walker.

"Wave or something," Willy directs. It feels forced and a touch inappropriate looking down on a dirty cavity full of young men who dive for cover or reach for a rifle every day. But Willy is the boss, so I put on a big smile, give a giant wave, and blow a kiss off my mud-caked fingers. The response is nearly as deafening as the explosives were. I blush and hold back my tears. If they can't cry, neither can I.

Willy rushes us up the ladder, giving orders, and I stagger through the mud, shivering in the dark, damp night. Larry walks by with a wink. I don't return it, instead listening to Willy's plans for getting us back onstage within the hour.

I can hardly understand his instructions, my ears still ringing from the explosions and my head buzzing with the implications of Larry's whispered accusation. With the line between life and death so thin, it's easy to forget there's more to be afraid of than an unexpected explosion or a piece of hot metal hurtling through the air. Some truths are nearly as threatening as the faceless enemy we just escaped. In this instance, the man holding the weapon destined to ruin my family isn't anonymous, and until a few hours ago I thought he was my friend. I'm starting to wonder if I was horribly, horribly mistaken.

VIVIAN SNOW

Auction

Lot #7

Hand-drawn postcard labeled: Cathedral of the Holy Cross
    Pencil on cardstock. A large, round stained glass window above a set of cathedral doors.

BOSTON, MASS. DEC 13 1944 1:00 PM

Dear Miss Snow,
    The work here is hard but steady. I have more fear for you than for any other. I pray for your protection all the days. May God keep you safe in your travels.
    Christmas wishes—Trombello
    (Translation from Italian)
    Passed by censor 2

CHAPTER 7

December 29, 1944
Undisclosed Location
French Countryside

"Get warmed up and cleaned up best you can. Nothing fancy. Just fatigues. You go on in an hour," Willy orders when we're almost back to my tent. I think it's the third or fourth time he's explained the schedule, but I'm finding it difficult to pay attention. Rattled from the shelling and hours in the foxhole but also from the bomb Larry dropped before any explosions started.

"An hour? But . . ." *I'm tired. I'm hungry. I'm scared,* I think, but I don't say.

"I'll take Nancy to get checked out by a doctor, but be prepared to fill in both spots." He doesn't wait for a response, and I accept his assignment as though he's a general and I'm a private.

I wash up quickly with limited provisions and change into the camouflage pants and jacket assigned to me back in Boston. A man in uniform waits outside and escorts me to the makeshift chow hall with my newly applied coat of makeup covering the mud I was unable to clean off. I wonder briefly if I should offer to help Nancy get changed, but when the smell of coffee hits my nostrils, my good intentions falter.

Maybe she'll crack. Some do, I've heard. Some fall apart and get sent home without ever putting one foot onstage. I don't get it, that lack of tenacity. Keep getting up, that's what I say. Get up more times than you fall down, or else you'll end up like my mother in some sanitarium, thinking your granddaughter is your dead baby. I shake off the memory of that moment. In many ways, I'd prefer battlefields and foxholes to facing my mother again.

I slide into an empty seat and take a bite of the baked beans on my plate. They're bland and cold, but I've learned to never take a meal for granted out here.

"Whoever first said 'The show must go on' had no idea how far Vivian Snow would take it," Larry says as he sits down next to me and offers a cup of hot coffee. I flinch but force a smile and gesture to the full mug in front of me.

"I think you'll need more than one," he says, brushing a bit of dried mud off a spot I missed on my ear and then dusting the remnants off my shoulder.

"Scandal. You're gonna get my rations cut," I say playfully, keeping the tone of our conversation light. I'm too worn down to face any further discussion about the Highward family.

"No one will report you after that performance you just gave. I think half the camp is in love with the beautiful and bold Vivian Snow."

I shake my head and sip my coffee.

"I hope tonight's show is what they remember."

"Tonight? As in, they're putting you onstage now?"

"You know how it goes." My trembling hands make the coffee slosh in my mug. It's warm and the smell comforting enough that I don't mind the bitter taste it leaves at the back of my throat.

"I know. I know. But the Walker girl is crumpled on a cot in the field hospital. And Don twisted his ankle climbing that damn ladder. It's the size of a grapefruit. You and Kitty gonna do it all?"

"Maybe. It's fine, Larry. It's what we do." I finish my first cup of coffee. He nudges the one he brought closer, and I don't resist this time. I drink again, pretending to be cool despite the nervous tremor shivering through my whole body.

He sighs and studies me, and then he shakes his head.

"Why do you do it, Viv?"

"You know why." I put my mug down and rest my chin on my fist, cocking my head. He doesn't know everything about my family, but he knows enough to answer this question for himself.

"Your little girl?" he asks, and I nod.

"And my papà and Aria and . . ."

"Tom?" he completes the sentence. I shake my head. He chose the wrong person to fill in the blank.

"No. My mother. She's sick. She's been sick for a long time. They all depend on me."

"Then why not go to the Highwards and ask for help?" he asks. I stiffen at his renewed line of inquiry about the Highward family. His question seems sincere, though. Like he's asking as my friend and not a reporter. His smoky breath touches my cheek, reminding me of when I waited for a kiss from him that never came. I shift away.

"Stop, Larry," I say quietly, wishing I could scream it. He continues as though he didn't hear me.

"They're rich. Like, *rich* rich. Your girl is the only grandchild in old Mr. Highward's family line. If they knew about her, they'd surely want to help."

I bow my head, remembering Moira's visit that brought on Grace's entrance into this world. I want nothing to do with the Highwards. Even if life would be easy with their money and prestige—I'm not stupid enough to think it wouldn't come with a price. When they finally realize Tom is never coming home, they could take my daughter away from me.

"They know," I say firmly.

It's almost call time. I get up without warning and drop my dishes in the return. He follows me like a sniper stalking his target. He doesn't care about me. I'm just a story to him. It's a story about a small-town girl and a big-town boy who ran off together until the boy ran off altogether.

"And they don't want to help? Why? Unless—" He stops in his tracks, falling behind as I keep walking toward the stage. Then he rushes to my side. "You weren't married?"

"Go to hell," I spit, horrified, stomping away, fury clouding my vision.

How dare he? In this day and age, it's only slightly better to be thought of as a whore than a murderer. And Archie already explained the morality clauses I'll be up against if anyone decides to claim Grace is illegitimate or that my husband is a potential traitor. Besides, I promised Trombello I'd tell Gracie that her father was good, even if it isn't the full truth.

Larry catches up to me again as I arrive at the stage. We're both out of breath, but Larry can barely put together two words. I'm early for call, which means we're alone in the tattered pavilion near the platform. The canopy above the stage is gone, and it looks as though the lighting system endured damage as well. Three large jeeps are parked near the stage with their lights pointed upward.

"Hey. Stop running away. I didn't mean to offend . . ."

"Don't talk to me ever again," I growl, the burned coffee churning in my stomach making me want to vomit.

"Whoa. What the hell?" he says, sounding hurt. I don't give a flip if I hurt him. He'll get over it. But if he messes this up for me, I may never recover. My family may never recover.

"Tom and I were married June seventeenth last year in Holy Trinity by Father Theodore," I say defensively. "That's in Edinburgh, Indiana, if you need to know. Get out your precious notebook and write it down. You can look it up. We have one child, my little Gracie. And she's her father's spitting image."

"My God, Vivian. Don't you think I know that?"

"But you just said . . ."

"I meant that they must think something scandalous happened. The Highwards. Or else why would they let you be out here in this hellscape when they could take care of you for less than they spend on bubble gum? Goodness knows they spend enough paying off reporters who know more than they should about where your knight in shining armor is now."

"Where Tom is?" I ask tentatively. "Where is he?" I ask as though I don't know. He can't have guessed the truth, that's impossible. Or at least I think it is. He stares at me, and I blink up at him, waiting.

"The family says he's on a secret mission. You say missing in action. But we all know, us reporters. We know where Tom Highward really is."

The Chapel in the Meadow flashes through my mind. Likely that's his final resting place, where Trombello buried him. Though he's never confirmed it, I can't imagine any other place he'd have put Tom after giving him his last rites. Would they tear it down, the chapel? Would they dig up the foundation to investigate what happened to Tom? Would I go to jail? Would Trombello?

"Canada," he says matter-of-factly, and I blink again, not expecting that response. "It's where all the rich boys go AWOL. I guess it's easy to get cold feet and run off. Especially when you have a wife your parents don't approve of and a kid on the way. Everyone is dying to break this story. It's a dynamite tale of love, wealth, and betrayal."

The alternate reality Larry illustrates is painted with harsh colors and stark contrasts. I can easily see the salacious headline now. HIGHWARD HEIR: TRAITOR. It's the least harmful explanation of my husband's absence, but it's no good, not if I want to keep working with Camp Shows, Inc. Not if I want to get a studio contract one day. Vivian Snow, wife of a deserter. No way will I pass the morality check with that infamy in my past.

"Please don't write that," I say, my voice small and swelled with emotion. "Please." I'm nearly begging now. "I don't have much money, but I can get some." I clutch his arm, my anger turned to desperation.

His eyes narrow and then soften, and before I know it he has his arms around me and my head pressed against his chest.

"Hush your mouth right now," he orders, but not angrily like Tom or Papà. There's shame in his voice, shame and something else I can't identify. "I don't want your money, you silly girl. Tom Highward's family already offered me money. I want to help you. That's what I've been trying to tell you, but you keep running away . . ."

"Help me?" I shove against him, playfully. He pulls me in tighter. "You could've just told me. You scared me half to death."

"I'm sorry. I needed to make sure you weren't hiding him."

"Well, I'm not."

He nods. "I know." He's holding me like he thinks I might blow away in the cold night breeze. "And I needed to make sure you weren't still in love with him."

"I'm not."

He nods again. "I know."

He kisses the top of my head and whispers something about life being unfair, and I melt into his embrace. I haven't been held by a man off the stage or off the dance floor since Tom. I've thought about Larry's arms and the thrill they might give, but this peaceful feeling, the protection I experience with his body sheltering mine, is unexpectedly delicious. It's like I can let out a breath I've been holding for a long, long time. I can't get enough of this feeling. I work my hands around his waist, pressing his warm torso against my slender frame, taking in his sweaty, tobacco-tinged scent. He pulls away and holds me in front of him like a rag doll.

"Hold up, sweetheart. I'm gonna lose my mind if you touch me like that, and as much as it kills me to say it—I need to have a few brain cells working if we're gonna figure this thing out."

"I'm sorry. I didn't mean to. I just . . ." I retrieve my hands and shove them into the pockets of my fatigues.

"I know, doll. I know." He caresses my cheek and chin before putting his hands in his own pockets, matching my stance. "Listen. Time is short. I'm not the only one on this story. I just talked to my source a few days ago, and if we're not careful, we're gonna lose control of this thing. I'll be damned if Tom Highward and his family think they can toss you on the pyre as some sacrificial lamb. I've got a better idea."

My head is spinning. I think I understand. Larry wants to protect me from the Highward family, who will not blink an eye if my reputation is ruined. With my reputation intact, I still have a chance for a future where I can take care of my family on my own. He was telling the truth when he said he wanted to help me. What if Larry isn't my potential enemy but my potential ally?

"I'd love to hear it," I whisper. The crowd is filing in, and Nancy is walking toward us, all cleaned up and talking to Kitty. It's almost showtime—again. But Larry doesn't let the activity distract him, and he regains my attention and holds it as he returns my whisper.

"Let's kill Tom Highward."

VIVIAN SNOW

Auction

Lot #8

Hand-drawn postcard labeled: George Robert White Memorial, *The Spirit of Giving*
    Black pen on cardstock. Bronzed angel fountain with wings extended.

BOSTON, MASS. MAY 14 1945 3:00 PM

    Dear Miss Snow,
       To know you are safe is a great blessing. I will meet you in one month, as you request. Find The Spirit of Giving in the Boston Garden. I will be there at five.
       See you soon—A. Trombello
    (Translation from Italian)
    Passed by censor 3

CHAPTER 8

June 14, 1945
Boston, Massachusetts

I hold up the postcard and match it to the fountain in front of me—a bronze statue of an angel towering over the quiet park corner.

As I make my way toward it, I see two girls whispering to each other behind gloved hands. One points, and the other giggles. I have some idea what's going to happen next. When Larry implemented his plan, I had no idea how effective it would be, but over the past five months, my husband has been declared a slain hero and I have risen in notoriety and acclaim.

At first, I rolled my eyes when Larry recounted the responses to his articles about me. And when Aria's and Papà's letters started to include retellings of their interactions with friends and acquaintances, even the nurses at Norways, I assumed it was familial pride that made them believe I was becoming a star. But when the news crew showed up in France to film a special segment that was then shown before films in movie theaters across America, I started to wonder what life would look like when we got home.

And now I'm here. It's been two weeks and a total whirlwind. I've barely slept or eaten between parties and official appearances. There's hardly a corner of town where I haven't been asked for an autograph or set off a knowing tip of a hat.

"Excuse me, miss. I'm sorry to ask but—are you Vivian Snow?" The smaller but braver of the two girls is at my elbow, a piece of paper trembling in her hand.

"Yes, I am," I say, smiling softly.

"We saw your show last night. And the newsreel. Did you really sing in a foxhole?" she asks, and I nod, telling the story for the thousandth time.

In return, she tells me her name, and her friend rushes over and shares hers as well. I listen to their stories as I sign my stage name to the page they provided me. One girl is from Nebraska but is here for the Women's Airforce Service Pilots, and the other girl is a childhood friend visiting her husband in the Chelsea Naval Hospital. They're both young, so young.

I'm a keeper of stories now. Men, women, and children alike eagerly tell them to me. I wonder if I'll ever tire of hearing these stories, of signing my name on scraps of paper and giving smiles that mean so much more to the recipient than they do to me.

"Could you write to him? My husband, Charlie, I mean. I know he'd lose his mind getting a letter from you." She presses an address into my hand, and I take it with a nod.

"I will."

"Thank you," she says with tears in her eyes. She and her friend rush away, giggling like the children they were only a few summers ago.

"Will you truly write?" a voice says from behind me.

"Trombello!" I recognize his accented cadence immediately and spin around to find him standing in front of the fountain.

Trombello looks nearly as angelic as the life-size bronze angel looming over his shoulder, even though he's dressed in a neatly pressed khaki uniform with a green patch on his sleeve that reads *ITALY*. Something comes over me at the sight of my dear friend and pen pal. Even though we've never embraced before, I run up the stone steps and throw my arms around his neck. He chuckles and stands awkwardly at first, then returns my hug with a tentative pat on the small of my back. His shoulders are firm and fit. I can tell he's doing physical labor for the Italian Service Unit.

My wits return and I step back, out of breath from the excitement.

"Look at you," I say, taking him in. "I'd hardly recognize you if I walked past you on the street." He has filled out and looks more like a man than the skinny, youthful idealist I met more than two years ago. His black curly hair is short but visible under his cap, and his naturally olive complexion is dark from what must be hours in the sun.

"I could say the same of you, signora," he says, blushing under his tan, shoving his hands in his pockets. His shy smile is charming and touches my heart.

"Oh, no. Not signora," I correct, looking behind me as though someone might overhear, my paranoia not completely resolved just yet. "I'm Miss Snow, remember? But you should just call me Vivian. Did you see Larry's articles? The ones I told you about?"

He nods and transfers his weight.

"I did. I read them all. They are true? The stories?"

"Yes. Well, mostly true, at least," I say, remembering when Larry finished the story about Tom's death and my moment in the foxhole, the way the thin typewriter paper crinkled in between my fingers as I tried to read it lying beside him in bed.

"Ah, yes. Mostly." Trombello nods knowingly but doesn't seem ashamed of the truth. If God is as forgiving as Trombello, there may be hope of redemption for me yet. And yet I still feel the need to explain myself, unable to imagine losing his trust.

"Tom's family doesn't want his name in the papers, so Larry made the story work without using their names. They can go on thinking Tom ran off, and I can go on as a war widow. No harm, no foul."

"And your daughter? Will she know who her father is?"

"She's too young to know anything," I say, brushing away the question.

My little Grace. I haven't seen her since I shipped out in July last year. Even then she was starting to prefer her zia or her nonno.

If she doesn't even know who her mother is, why does it matter if she knows who her father is? I wonder, bitterly, my heart no longer warm and connected to Trombello but aching with regret. He must read the truth in my response.

"You did what your family needed. You'll go home now. You'll be her mother and she won't remember otherwise," he reassures me, but it doesn't help. I stare at the stone under my feet and tell him something I haven't been allowed to write about in my postcards.

"I leave again in two weeks for the Pacific. Another tour. I'll be gone for . . . who knows how long?" In Europe, the war is over, but it rages on in the South Pacific. I'll go home, see my family, and then ship out again. Larry will be going too.

"Another tour? Back to where there is war? Why, signora?"

"Vivian. You must call me Vivian."

"Yes. Scusa. Viviana." He uses the name Papà has used for me since I was a little girl, and I don't correct him, too focused on defending my decision to go on another overseas tour.

"Someone must care for my family. You know that. Larry talked to Archie. They both think if we continue his column from the Pacific, I'll have enough leverage to sign with a big studio. I can move my mother to a better hospital by the ocean and buy a big house where Papà can retire and Aria can plant a garden and Gracie can call me Mamma."

"Ah, Larry. Vedo. Vedo." *I see. I see.*

"You see what?"

"Niente," he says. *Nothing.* He huffs and takes off his hat, walking in a circle, and I watch him, confused and frustrated at the turn our conversation has taken.

"There must be other ways," he says, in English this time. "Safer ways. These men should stop putting you in harm's way to make money."

"Safer? That's not fair." I stomp my foot but then lower my voice, realizing I'm nearly shouting. "It's not Archie's fault or Larry's. Everyone's in danger, Padre. It's war. Everyone is making sacrifices—because of war. Your family must miss you, but you are here. Because of war."

"Questo lo so bene," Trombello says solemnly. *This I know well.*

He stares off into the park. Trombello hasn't seen his home or family since he left Italy in 1941. His country has been ravaged by war, and his family has not been left untouched. He's no longer an enemy, but he's also not a free man. And I've no doubt he's a different man than he was when he left his home and church to care for his brothers who'd been conscripted in the army.

"I'm sorry, Padre. I didn't mean . . ."

"Lo so." *I know,* he says, patting my shoulder and then turning his eyes up toward the winged statue witnessing our reunion.

There's a scripture carved into the stone beneath the angel's bare feet: *Cast your bread upon the waters; for you shall find it after many days.* I've been short-sighted. No one has made more sacrifices for my safety than Antonio Trombello. If it weren't for him, I'd be dead or as good as dead in a prison cell. I slip my arm into his and put my head on his sturdy shoulder.

"I'll be careful. I promise I'll come home."

"I pray for this, but . . . ," he says, his gaze focused solely on the statue. As I wait for the rest of his sentence, his rigid muscles begin to relax against my touch. "I'll be gone when you return."

"Oh," I respond softly, understanding the sadness in his reply. With the war in Europe over, Trombello will be sent home. It might not be right away, but eventually we'll have an ocean between us—again. Unless . . .

"You could stay," I offer, meekly, knowing very little about the logistics of the postwar repatriation process. All my thoughts are half fantasy. I clutch at his arm and angle my body toward him. "Come to California. Start a new life. You look more American than you realize, and your English is good. Really good. There has to be a way. I'm sure Larry could help. He seems to know people. Archie too . . ."

He appears to consider the idea for a moment, but at the mention of Larry and Archie, he shakes his head.

"No, no, piccola. Questo non è il piano di Dio." *This is not God's plan.*

I'm unsurprised. I'd have been far more shocked if he'd agreed to my suggestion.

"I know. I just hate the idea of you leaving."

"You can come to Italy. Bring your father. See your history," he offers, though I don't think he expects me to accept his fantasy either.

"Perhaps. One day." I trace an invisible circle with my toe, disappointed. Our dreams are getting us nowhere. Then, I get an idea. If we're going to play pretend, we might as well enjoy ourselves. I tug at his arm. "Come to dinner with me. And dancing. I'm meeting some friends, and Larry's coming in from Europe tonight. Finally." At the mention of an entourage, he starts to reject my offer, but I don't let him. "I won't take no for an answer. Larry knows who you are, and I'll tell everyone else you're my long-lost cousin or something. It's our last night together—let's enjoy the now for once in our lives."

He shakes his head, pensive. My glossy red nails press into his sleeve, and I plead, putting on a little of my Vivian Snow charm.

"Dobbiamo battere il ferro finché è caldo," I entreat. My father said this when anxiety or hesitation kept Aria from trying new things—*We must strike while the iron is hot.* "Please, Padre."

"Non Padre," he corrects after a gap of silence. *Not Father.*

"No?" I've pushed too hard—offended him, taken him for granted. I'm not his responsibility, not his family or congregant. And now that he's leaving, I may never hear from him again.

"No," he echoes, taking his hat from his back pocket and angling it on his head, ready to leave. "Cugino." *Cousin.*

"Really?" I laugh with relief.

"Assolutamente," he declares, offering me his arm. People are watching, but I'm growing accustomed to that.

VIVIAN SNOW

Auction

Lot #9

Hand-painted postcard labeled: Edinburgh, Indiana
    Watercolor and black pen on cardstock. Cornfield at sunset.

BOSTON, MASS. AUG 14 1945 3:00 PM

> *Dear Miss Snow,*
>   *I believe you may wish to see a bit of home when you are so far away. Soon, I will return to Salerno and see my own home again. I wonder if it will feel the same.*
>   *May God protect you always—A. Trombello*
> (Translation from Italian)
> Passed by censor 3

CHAPTER 9

June 14, 1945
Blinstrub's Village
Boston, Massachusetts

There is a line outside of Blinstrub's Village. The overhead lights flicker in the twilight of the summer evening, and I adjust the strap on my emerald-green cocktail dress and mink shawl. Trombello waited in the lobby of my hotel while I changed.

The transformation from my day dress into elegant dinner wear took less than fifteen minutes, and that included powdering my nose, freshening my lipstick, and teasing a little bounce into my hair. I sprayed a puff of Rochas Femme in the air as I walked out of my hotel room, tossing the three or four messages I'd found shoved under the door onto my bed as a reminder to read through them tonight.

Though, with Larry back in town, I'm not sure whose room we'll end up in. That's a secret I *won't* share with Trombello, not yet at least. Larry is my fiancé. We'll be married once we've found a way to make the rumors of Tom's death more than gossip. It'll mean a death certificate or an official burial, and that'll take time. Till then, we play a very complicated game of pretend, and hiding in hotel rooms under false names is only one layer of the façade.

At Blinstrub's a short man with a heavy Boston accent stands behind an elevated podium with a large book in front of him. "Reservation?" he asks.

"Fairbanks. They're already inside," I say, pointing to the velvet curtains between us and the bustling crowd and big band music. He looks at me with a raised eyebrow and then at Trombello and the patch on his shoulder.

"Marco. Table three." A young man with a wispy mustache, wearing a tuxedo and white gloves, nods at the host and then at us.

"This way," he says, holding open the curtain with an outstretched arm.

We duck under the green velvet, and the golden tassels tickle my cheek. The room is enormous. Thirty or so banquet-length tables, jampacked with well-dressed men and women, surround a large, elevated stage and dance floor. A second-floor balcony drips with diners as well. The dance floor is covered from corner to corner with couples, young, old, and in between, swinging their hips to the big band music played live. It's the first time in my life I've walked into a hall like this as a participant and not a paid performer or a volunteer dancer.

I glance at Trombello, who must be more stunned than I am at the grandeur of the space and the overall frivolity and laughter filling the smoky room, but it's not shock I see on his face—it's a smile. As he takes in the Scandinavian-inspired details on the balcony and the buzzy conversations from the tables we pass, he seems entranced.

"Have you performed here?" he asks, dipping down to make sure I can hear him.

"Not here." I shake my head.

"But, like this?" he asks with enough genuine curiosity that I don't feel judged.

"Yes, a lot like this." A memory flashes across my mind of muddy fields, air-raid sirens, and men wrapped with bandages, wincing with every smile. "But also not like this."

"I see," he says with a chuckle, as though I've told a joke, not catching my meaning.

"Here we are," Marco says, sweeping his arm toward one of the tables that skirts the dance floor. There are several open chairs that must have been recently abandoned for the dance floor or powder room. Patrick Fairbanks leans back in his seat with a cigarette in one hand and a tumbler of whiskey in the other. He's watching Caroline Evans, a young chorus girl we picked up six weeks ago in Paris, in a gauzy yellow gown, swaying through the crowd with a man in a fancy suit whom I haven't seen before. Kitty and Don are half-drunk and all over each other, clearly in immediate need of a hotel room. Sharon Nasser sees me first, though. Her knee-length cobalt dress, a shade that complements her bright eyes and light complexion, looks like blue lightning across the cornfields on a warm summer night. Why she's sitting out a dance with so many lonely soldiers on leave in attendance, I'll never know.

"Vivi! There you are!" She pops out of her chair and throws her arms around my neck. She smells of Chantilly and bourbon. "You missed dinner, silly."

Patrick's jealous stare leaves Caroline and her dance partner at Sharon's exclamation.

"Damn, you're a sight for sore eyes," Patrick says, standing and running his gaze over my dress and figure, leaning across the table to kiss me on my cheek. Trombello stiffens beside me as though he doesn't like the hungry way Patrick looks at women.

"Hey, Patty!" I say, smiling at the comedian.

"No Larry yet?" Patrick asks, eyeing Trombello with some of the jealousy he'd been sending in Caroline's direction. He's the tour's resident comedian, and he hates any of the men who take our attention from him, other than Larry. It wasn't exactly easy for Larry to break through Patrick's surly exterior, though mentioning him in his dispatches seemed to help.

"I think he's gonna meet us here after he gets in. I left him a note. Hopefully he has a suit . . ." My thought drifts off. I didn't consider that detail. Who knows what made it over in his luggage? All I know is his approximate return time—other than that, his journey home is a mystery to me. One thing I've gotten used to in this war is *not* knowing things.

"Eh, there's barely a dress code anywhere anymore. He better come, that lucky bastard of yours." He's back in his seat, taking in a mouthful of smoke before I can introduce Trombello.

"So, who's this?" Sharon asks, noting the patch on his sleeve with raised eyebrows, as Kitty and Don kiss passionately in the background. My cheeks are hot, and I'm embarrassed. Trombello must think my friends are degenerates, though I guess in the eyes of the church we are all unworthy in the sight of God. But Trombello doesn't seem to judge, not me at least. I'd be heartbroken if something changed that.

"This"—I clear my throat and link my arm with his and squeeze— "is my long-lost cousin, Antonio Trombello."

"Ah, from the home country, eh?" Patrick says, friendly now that he realizes Trombello isn't a rival. "Glad you all came to your senses and made your way over to the right side."

"Antonio. What a lovely name. Are you the one who's been sending Vivi all those pretty cards?" Sharon asks, batting her eyelashes and swaying her hips ever so slightly to the music like a reed blowing in the breeze.

"Perhaps," is all Trombello says, blushing.

"He draws them himself. I keep telling him he's an impressive artist."

"Gosh darn, sweetheart, you sure are. What are you waiting for? You two should sit. Here, by me." Sharon is interested, and Patrick starts to grow cold again, watching Caroline as the song slows. Trombello and I take the empty seats. I order us both a drink as Sharon asks basic questions and Trombello gives basic answers.

"Heard you Italian boys really know how to have a fun time. You get out much?"

Trombello shifts in his seat and takes a sip of water as our drinks are delivered.

"Not really," he replies, his accent warm and lovely for me to listen to in contrast to Sharon's sharp New York clip.

"So you're a shy one, huh? I like shy ones. Right, Vivi?"

"She does." I laugh, thinking of all the times she's found the wall-flower in the room and coaxed him into a conversation that ended in his declaration of love.

"She'll flirt you into a state of passionate love if you're not careful, Tony," Patrick says, shortening Antonio's name without permission. He tosses the last of his drink back and waves for the waitress. Trombello flushes.

"Antonio has someone waiting for him at home, so he's not exactly shy. He's . . ."

"Devoted?" Patrick finishes my sentence, not knowing how right he is.

"Yes, devoted. Completely," I agree, and Trombello nods. Sharon seems to deflate but then perks up, scooching to the edge of her seat, glancing at the band and full dance floor.

"Doesn't mean you can't have a little fun. Don't you like dancing?" Trombello looks confused, but before I can explain, Kitty and Don excuse themselves for the evening and drift away on a cloud of love and desire. Sharon huffs, annoyed.

"I don't know why they came here, anyway," she says as we watch the couple get swallowed up by the crowd. "I know if I had a man I loved and we only had one day together before he was shipping out, I'd spend the whole time in bed."

She giggles and raises her eyebrows at Trombello, who understands this implication. A slow song starts, one I've sung a hundred times at least: "We'll Meet Again."

"Oh my Lord, woman," Patrick shouts. "That's all you think about. Get your ass up. I'll dance with you." Patrick's moved to our side of the table with his hand out. Sharon pushes it away.

"Shut up, Pat. I think Antonio was about to ask me something . . ."

These two have onstage chemistry that's spilled into their offstage life, and it's a constant tension we all have to deal with, especially now with Patrick's current obsession with the young, nubile Caroline Evans. But whenever I get annoyed at their childish ponytail-tugging flirting, I remember that I'm in love with someone I shouldn't be, and I try to laugh it off. But I can't let Sharon use Trombello in her little jealousy games.

"Antonio owes his cousin a dance first, I think," I say, standing and taking Trombello's hand, "Right, Tony?"

He looks as though he gets my joke, but he doesn't let go of his wineglass and remains speechless.

"See, I told you. He wanted to ask *me*. Didn't you? Who wants to dance with their cousin, anyway?"

"She's not *my* cousin," Patrick says, readdressing his hand to me. "How about it, Viv? One quick dance before Larry gets here and spoils our fun?"

I hesitate. I've danced with Patrick more than a few times. He has wandering hands and a dirty mouth, but I've dealt with worse. Larry might grumble a bit if he walks in and sees us, but he'll forgive me after a kiss or two. But I hate the idea of leaving Trombello behind to fend for himself with Sharon.

"I'm sorry. She's occupied," Trombello says, standing. It might not be a common American colloquialism, but I'm happy with the meaning.

"Yeah, Pat. I'm occupied," I say as Trombello wraps his fingers around mine.

"Shall we?" Trombello asks.

"Absolutely." I enjoy the pained looks on both Patrick's and Sharon's faces as Trombello leads me to the steps near our table. He spins me out on the dance floor and then back into his arms as though we've been partners for years. The fluidity of his movements surprises me so much that I crash into his chest rather than following gracefully.

"Oh gosh. I'm sorry."

"Per così poco," he says into my ear, telling me not to worry. The song is slow, and we settle into a comfortable sway.

It takes me a moment to think of what to say. This is my friend Trombello, who knows more about me than any person other than God. But I never thought I'd be in my friend's arms in a smoky club with sultry voices backed by a full orchestra guiding our feet. So I try to think of what I'd say to someone who knew less about me, a stranger or a man who just wanted to dance with a pretty girl.

"You're an artist *and* a dancer. So many hidden talents," I say in our shared tongue.

"Eh, there are things that are not hidden but left behind, I think. Many passions I've abandoned for more important ones."

"Ah, yes. Devoted. That's a perfect word to describe my . . . cousin."

"Yes," he chuckles with a touch of darkness to his tone. "Cousin."

I'm not sure what to say next. Small talk doesn't remain small with Trombello, and I don't want to argue again about going overseas for another tour or his plans for the future, so I stop trying to force a conversation and instead submit to the languid pace of the music.

Each sway and turn seem to make us more aligned until I close my eyes and let him take us across the crowded floor, dodging pairs of lovers, strangers, and friends. This is what I've always felt with Trombello—synchronicity. When we are close, we are one. I trust him more than I trust myself.

The last chorus of the song changes key, and emotion elevates inside of me in a similar way. Nothing will be the same after tonight. I'll move on with Larry, with Gracie and my family, and Trombello will return to Italy to his collar, robes, and a life of service. He's always been holy in my mind, but at Atterbury, he was our guide, my guide. Soon, I'll have no claim to him, and he'll belong to everyone else.

"You can't forget me, Antonio. You have to swear to me," I plead, staring up at him as the song comes to an end.

"Forget you?"

"When you go home. Don't forget."

Antonio Trombello looks down in my eyes as though he's looking into the eyes of God or perhaps facing the gates of hell.

"I should forget you, Viviana."

An ache fills my chest, and my eyes well up.

"I understand," I say, putting space between us, attempting to break the invisible cable that's held us entwined. I dab my tears with my fingertips and match my step with the crowd as we exit the dance floor. Trombello walks beside me. He doesn't touch me, but I still feel it—the connection. I can't look at him or I'll get tearful again.

We return to our place at the table. Trombello's wine waits for him, and my mai tai, full of half-melted ice, seems less appealing now. Trombello excuses himself to use the restroom.

"I could just gobble that man up, my Lord," Sharon mutters as she watches him walk away. The singer's clear preference for Trombello irritates me, and I'm worried I have the same look on my face that Patrick gets when he's watching us girls with another man.

"I wouldn't know. He's my cousin."

"Ha! Your cousin, my ass. No one looks at their cousin the way that man looks at you."

"Sharon. That's terrible. He's family," I deflect.

"Who is he, really? Are you sleeping with him?" She tries to whisper but can't control her volume while under the influence.

"Shhh. No. Of course not. I'm with Larry. Anyway, Antonio is my—"

"Cousin. Sure. Well, if he ever gets over you, maybe send him my way, okay?"

I'm completely tongue-tied. I'm about to bite back with another denial when a deep voice calls my name.

"Vivian. What are you doing here?" For half a second I think it's Larry, here at last, ready to tell us about his many adventures, to meet Trombello, to start our life together. But it's not Larry. It's Willy. He's a stickler for the rules and is rarely if ever invited out with the performers.

"Me? What are *you* doing here? I thought you were with Larry."

His forehead wrinkles as though he doesn't understand me.

"Vivian, honey. I need to talk to you in the lobby. Come with me, would you?" He sounds like a grandfather talking to his favorite grandchild. I've never heard such softness from this military man, even when bombs were falling. He threw a holy fit when he found out Larry and I were getting close, preaching about morals. But once he heard Larry's story about Tom's heroic death, and my baby girl back home, he softened up. Not this soft, though. This is new and unnerving. I follow him reluctantly, used to taking orders.

"Sit down," he says, pointing to a velvet-covered couch in a quiet corner of the lobby.

"I don't want to sit down. What's the matter?" I demand, the anxiety crushing my chest. Over Willy's shoulder, I can see Trombello. He's just exited the washroom and is watching me. From the look on his face, I think he assumes Willy is Larry and can tell I'm upset.

"Oh God. I didn't want to be the one," the stodgy director mutters, lighting a cigarette and taking a long drag before speaking again. "I told Marty to tell you. It'll be in the paper in the morning, so you've gotta know . . ."

"What, Willy? What's gonna be in the papers? What did Larry write? What?" I think of all the ways I may have exposed my secret. Was Larry pretending to love me to get money and fame? How do I defend myself and my family? Will I be disowned? Do I let Papà adopt Gracie? Or maybe Moira with all her money. Or do I run? I eye the door. I could make it if I leave Trombello behind. I have money now. Gracie and I could disappear. Or I could stay and tell the truth. Trombello saw it all—he could testify.

"Larry didn't write anything. The article will be about Larry. Listen, doll, his plane went down in the Alps."

He spits the news out quickly, and my ankles collapse. I grasp Willy's thick forearm to keep from falling. Trombello is next to me immediately, holding me up and looking at Willy as though he's to blame. Sharon, who followed us out, is on my other side. Neither knows the news I've just learned.

"So, they're looking for him?"

Willy helps me into a chair. Trombello stands behind me. His hands on my shoulders are the only thing keeping me from falling over.

"They'll find him. Larry's stubborn. They'll find him."

Willy shakes his head.

"They did find him, honey. I'm sorry, Vivian, but—Larry's dead."

VIVIAN SNOW

Auction

Lot #10

Hand-painted postcard labeled: Soldanella Calabrese, Calabria
    Watercolor on cardstock. Plant with small purple flowers with long,
slender petals.

SALERNO. ITALIA. 01 APR 1949

> *Dear Vivian,*
>   *I received your letter today. Many congratula-*
> *tions on your new contract. Your family must be so*
> *very proud.*
>   *—A. Trombello*
> (Translation from Italian)

CHAPTER 10

April 23, 1949
Twentieth Century-Fox Studios, Stage Two
Hollywood, California

"Cut!" The director's voice echoes through the soundstage, and everyone on set lets out their breath at once. But this isn't a sigh of relief. Tension is mounting, and I know if we don't get the take right, we could be here all night. At the helm is Glenn Carver, the award-winning, innovative director with notoriously high standards.

"What the hell's his problem this time?" George Sanders, my handsome and accomplished costar, grumbles. He's earned the right to grumble. George has more experience onstage and in front of a camera than anyone in this room, and his smooth, upper-class British accent adds to his air of authority. I, on the other hand, am a new face at Twentieth Century-Fox. After filming a few too many gangster and horror pictures, silly romances, and solemn morality tales, I had my first big-time movie at MGM, but then my small-claims contract ended, and I switched sides after some heated negotiations. Now, I'm the leading lady on a high-budget film. Archie says this movie is my "big break," even bigger than *Summer in Salerno*, which premiered a few months ago, or at least it has the potential to be. If I can get this kiss right.

I can tell by Mr. Carver's harsh tone that he's irritated. We've tried this moment nearly thirty times. Too much passion. Too little passion. Not the right angle. Too loose. Too tight. Too much and too little all at once. It's maddening.

There's little lust to an on-camera smooch, especially with all the rules and regulations that keep us within the Hays Code.

"Keep your tongue to yourself, George. For God's sake," Mr. Carver shouts from his director's chair.

"For God's sake yourself. I wasn't even close . . ." George bellows, taking off his suit coat and tossing it on the floor, reminding me of Gracie in the middle of a temper tantrum the last time I was home for Christmas.

As the men hurl insults at one another, my hairdresser and makeup girl take turns fixing all the smudges and out-of-place hairs. My ability to remain small, which I learned from my father's explosions, has served me well in this tempestuous town. After losing Larry, I almost gave it all up. I went home to Indiana and cried into a pillow as my little girl slept by my side. The first man, whom I had loved blindly, was dead, and the second man, whom I had loved wholeheartedly, was also gone. I didn't know how to go on.

The night I got the terrible news, the world swirled around me. I felt like a figurine in a shaken-up snow globe. Trombello, with Sharon's and Patrick's help, found a way to get me back to the hotel. As Sharon peeled off my dress and loosened my shoes, Trombello and Patrick collected the pile of notes and telegrams that'd been pushed under my door. I'd have known sooner if I'd only looked at them when I went back to my room to change.

With a few drinks in me and a pill that Sharon slipped in my mouth when no one was looking, the room grew gray, then black, like storm clouds changing a bright spring day into a foreboding twilight.

The only brightness in that night was Trombello. He was by my side as I drifted to sleep and also when I awoke several times in the night. The next morning, though, he was gone, and Sharon had taken his place. I didn't even get to say goodbye or thank you. Sharon, in a newly pressed dress and fresh coat of makeup, stroked my hair and encouraged me to take sips of black coffee. She told me how my "cousin" had refused to leave. Trombello—always my guardian angel.

For being a city named for angels, there are very few heavenly creatures in Los Angeles. Trombello is back in Italy and I'm here—with a grown man in the throes of a hissy fit. George eventually stops shouting and stomps out, with Mr. Carver cursing at him across the soundstage. We all know what this means. The women stop fussing with my face and hair.

"Let's break for lunch. We'll try again at three," Mr. Carver barks, and his assistant director calls out more detailed instructions. The crew step away from their positions and head off to the commissary, and I follow. Archie tells me I should spend more time at the commissary to "see and be seen," so I force myself to go out at least once a week.

"Miss Snow! Miss Snow! Hold on. I'll walk you." Mick Mitcham, the screenwriter who penned our current project, *Moonshine on the River*, runs up behind me. He's a little older but not out of his twenties, though if he keeps smoking and drinking the way he does, I'm sure he'll look ancient in no time.

Mick has a very obvious crush on me. Not on me, actually, on starlet Vivian Snow. He's generous with the number of lines he writes for me, but I find his attention off-putting for many reasons, especially because of the wife and two kids he has at home.

In this business, married men tend to forget their vows anytime their wife is out of the room. Many actresses take advantage of the male sex drive. Sharon says her sex appeal is the only way to level the playing field in a business run by libidinous men. But I'm not willing to sleep my way to the front of the camera. I've heard that Sharon calls me a hypocrite behind my back because of my relationship with Larry and all the articles he wrote about me, but that was different—or at least I have to believe it was.

"Good afternoon," I say, smiling while keeping an arm's length between us. Mick drifts in my direction, and I stray farther to the left every time. He's a handsome man with a strong jaw sporting an outcropping of stubble no matter the time of day. It's the writers' look, I've noticed—dark circles, scratchy shadows on their chins, the smell of stale smoke following them like a puppy follows its master.

"I have some pages for you. Rewrites. I gave you a great moment at the end of the first act. Thought you'd do something good with it." He hands me the sheets of paper as we walk.

"Oh, you're a dear. You didn't have to come down here just for this," I say in my best Vivian Snow voice. I show more gratitude than I feel. A production assistant could've passed along the script, but Mick is filling up an invisible ledger with my debts to him for favors I've never asked for. One day he'll come to collect, and he expects I'll pay up. But Mick is mistaken.

"It's always a treat to make you smile, Miss Snow." He holds open the door to the commissary, and I thank him with a nod, not a smile.

"I know how busy you boys are. I truly appreciate your work." If I let the conversation go on much longer, I'll have no choice but to eat lunch with him. I scan the room, hoping for a familiar face.

In the corner booth, Bette Davis and Spencer Tracy are in an intimate tête-à-tête I wouldn't dare interrupt. A lovely girl I met in my training courses sits alone in the middle of the room with a simpering pout on her face, waiting to be approached. Betty Grable sits alone, but there's a reason for that—she's a raving bitch, and we all know it. She has a particular hatred for the fresh-faced ingénues Twentieth Century-Fox cycles through every few months. I would rather walk into a tiger's cage with a sirloin strapped to my rump than sit down at her table uninvited.

There's a group of chorus girls chittering in the corner and a few cowboy extras chomping down their meal as though they're still in character. Either I slide in with a table of unlikely bedfellows or suffer the company of Mick and his philandering.

"Vivi! Oh my Lord almighty, you're a sight for sore eyes." Johnny Scott, my costar from my last low-budget film, appears as though he'd been summoned by a genie fulfilling my unspoken wishes. His debonair Southern drawl, which he hides well on-screen, leaks out in his greeting.

"Johnny! Look at you, all dapper. What brings you to this side of town?"

Mick glances between the two of us, trying to evaluate our level of connection. Johnny hasn't even acknowledged his presence.

"I'm here for a . . . meeting," he says carefully, not exposing too much of his business in the social hub of the studio. "But I saw you from across the street, looking a vision, and couldn't help myself. I had to say hi and congratulations."

He embraces me and places a timid kiss on my cheek. He's a good-looking young man with dark hair, a cleft chin, and mischievous blue eyes, definitely a face made for the silver screen. He was easy to work with too. No temper tantrums like George.

"I was about to have a quick bite. Would you have time to join me?" I ask, and a huge grin blooms across his face.

"I wouldn't miss it for the world," he says.

We both seem to remember Mick at the same moment.

"I'm so rude. I'm sorry. I should introduce you both. Johnny, this is Mick Mitcham, one of the brilliant writers on *Moonshine on the River*. Mick, this is Johnny Scott. We worked on a western at MGM last year. He's set to be a giant movie star, so I'd get used to his name if I were you."

Johnny beams at my compliment, and Mick glowers. The men shake hands and share some benign words.

When they come to a place of awkward silence, I turn to Mick.

"See you tomorrow?" I say sweetly.

He looks Johnny up and down again, sighs, agrees, and walks away, his shoulders stooped.

"Blech. Writers give me the creeps," Johnny says as we're shown to our table. I laugh at his unflatteringly honest response.

"We wouldn't be here without them, love."

"I don't know. I think I could do their job pretty easily. They just make stuff up. We make it come to life. Sometimes I add my own lines."

"During the Camp Shows, they encouraged us to ad-lib, but I've yet to meet a director who agrees."

"That's right. You did those USO things. I saw a few of them in Guam. You ever go there?"

Did I ever go there? I was supposed to go with my Larry. It was supposed to be another arm of our publicized tour. We were supposed to be living this postwar life together. But he died and I had to make a choice—stay home and fade into obscurity or ignore my grief and move forward. Papà wanted me home. Aria wanted me to fly free. Archie threatened a million deaths if I didn't get on that ship to Hawaii. I didn't need to ask Trombello for his opinion. He wanted me as far away from bombs and war as possible. I didn't listen, and I'm still not sure if he's forgiven me yet.

"I did. Twelve weeks. It was . . . different than I expected." Beautiful women placed strings of flowers around our necks when we arrived in Honolulu, as though we were starting a vacation, but the flowers were a lie, it was all a lie.

"Me too. Thought it'd be all coconuts and pretty girls, but I ended up in New Guinea with the army's 594th Amphibious ESBR with five hundred men. We were lucky to see one dame a month, and the jungle rot was out of control. Lost a toe, you know."

"Oh, I do know. Don't tell a soul, but I have a false nail on the littlest toe of my right foot because of the dang jungle rot. And Jerry Colonna got it so bad that he spent a week in the Honolulu hospital, thinking he'd lose his leg."

"The comedian? Really? Damn. I had no idea." A waitress brings us coffee, and we both order something simple off the menu. "You know—I used to judge those Hollywood boys doing the USO shows for not enlisting, but it helps to know some of them left their fancy houses and cars and pretty wives and sacrificed *something*."

I think of the closed coffin at Larry's funeral and his mother sobbing into the dark fabric of his father's suit coat. I remember the long, glowing eulogy in the *New York Herald Tribune* that spoke of Larry's short life, mentioning his academic and professional accomplishments but leaving out the way he snorted at puns even though he pretended to be above them, or how he kissed my temples after each show when my head pounded from lack of food, water, and sleep. He not only knew the names of every member of the cast and crew but also the names of their family and friends from home. No, that was the obituary I wrote in my heart and couldn't share. I shook his parents' damp hands, knowing they were ghosts of a future family that died with Larry. He may not have died in battle, but he did die in service to his country.

"And now look at you. All prettied up with a big contract at Twentieth Century-Fox." He shakes his head, smirking softly like he's thinking about something he can't tell me. "You caught a leprechaun, didn't you? How many wishes do you have left, huh?"

"Wishes?" I balk at the idea that magical wishes granted me the current state of my life. I'm a working actress. I have my name in the credits of more than fifteen films. My family is cared for, and I've signed a contract with a studio that guarantees me work for four years. He doesn't know the path to get here included a sick mother, a debilitated father, an abusive husband, a sad sister, a lonely daughter, a dead lover, and disappointed friends. My life is not composed of wishes. It's more like a tapestry of mostly blackened strands that give a vivid contrast to the bleached, brilliant ones.

"Yeah. Does your leprechaun have a name? How small is his house?" Johnny jokes, and I keep my gloomy thoughts to myself.

"If my contract came from a mythical creature, it wouldn't be filled with so many caveats."

"Caveats?"

"Yes. My hair. My weight. My clothes. My love life."

"That's a lot."

"It's best you know before you sign. They're not joking over here at Fox. They mean it. They want proof."

"Proof? Of what?" Johnny asks between bites of his pastrami on rye. I nibble at my tuna salad sandwich, still more worried about my makeup than the knot in my stomach.

"For me? Well, proof of my marriage. And then Gracie's birth certificate, which I'm sure they checked against the date on my marriage certificate," I say with a lowered voice and raised eyebrows.

"Your husband? The one who died in France?"

"Yes."

"And you gave it?"

"I did." It was the last thing Trombello did for me before returning to Salerno. The only person who knew Tom's true story took a train to my hometown of Edinburgh, Indiana, and bought a grave for my husband and a headstone. Larry gave Tom a hero's story, and Trombello gave him a resting place. It was enough for the studio, and so far it's been enough for the press.

Larry left the Highward family out of the story entirely. Tom Highward's full name was mentioned only once, with no reference to his steel-magnate family. Moira wrote me a letter after the article came out, said she'd kept up with me through the newsreels. She told me she was getting married soon and asked if Tom really was dead. She said their family held out hope he'd come home one day, but her father and uncle were grateful for the article because it put an end to reporters threatening to write about Tom being a possible deserter. She offered me money and asked for a picture of Gracie. I never responded. A few weeks ago I saw a picture in the newspaper announcing the birth of her first child—a boy. I won't lie, I breathed a sigh of relief. The Highward family can go on believing Tom is alive as long as they leave my family alone.

"Not one leprechaun was involved. I swear."

"I'll stop chasing rainbows, then, I guess." He chuckles sardonically, and I worry I've jaded him.

"Chase your rainbows, Johnny. Just know that any magic you find at the end is magic you've made yourself."

"You're not just a pretty face, are you?" Johnny pushes his plate forward and rests his elbows on the table. With his chin on his clasped hands, he watches me, one eyebrow raised. I blush, and the sleeping butterflies in my stomach twitch as though they're awakening. I'm about to brush off the compliment and calm the fluttering in my midsection when Mick appears at my elbow.

"Miss Snow. I'm sorry to bother you, but . . ." I jump at the interruption, and Johnny muffles a low growl of what I'm assuming is frustration. I take a deep breath and put on a kind look.

"Everything all right, Mr. Mitcham?"

"Yes. I mean, no. I mean. You have a call."

"A call? Who?" I scarcely ever get a call on set. Archie, occasionally. A publicist setting up a photo opportunity or sham date for his client. The only other person who has my number is . . .

"Your sister," he says, panting like he ran the whole way from our soundstage.

When I gave Aria this number, I said very clearly, "Emergencies only."

She laughed me off. "You worry too much."

"I know. I know. But just in case."

"All right," she said, clearly humoring me, "just in case."

Emergencies only. I glance between Mick and Johnny. Johnny's clearly trying to decide whether he should be worried about me or deck the interrupting writer in the nose. Mick looks self-satisfied that he's found a reason to derail my one-on-one with the handsome actor.

"She's on hold so we should probably go," Mick urges.

Emergencies only. There's no time to waste. I toss my napkin on the table and thank Johnny profusely. He sputters some well-wishes, offers to pay the bill, and says he'll call me soon. I have to stop myself from running back to set as I dodge scenery, prop pieces taller than my house, and a string of chorus girls on a smoke break.

With sweat streaming down the sides of my neck, I burst into the side entrance of Stage Two, and Mick guides me to a metal staircase that shakes with each step and leads to the second-floor office. I reach the top with my lungs burning, ribs pressing against my corset. The door is painted a faded blue, thinning in spots where I can see the original wood underneath. I reach for the knob but stop short.

I can't face a world without Gracie in it. Everything I've done and sacrificed is so that one day I can be a real mother to her. If I lose her now, I'll die, I know I will.

Mick catches up quickly, and in the fog of fear, I forget how to be the panderingly manipulative Miss Snow. I grasp him tightly by the shoulders and give a slight shake, my voice raised.

"Did you hear a little girl in the background? Did you hear a child?" I ask. Grace already feels like a gift from God I wasn't supposed to receive. I'm constantly afraid he'll realize his error and take her back. I cover my mouth, suddenly ill. I can't hold my tears.

Mick holds his sweaty handkerchief to my cheek. What disgusts me more than the smell of the perspiration-soaked cloth is the gratification he seems to get from seeing me in a weakened position. He's the kind of man who only gives so he can take, and I'm tired of it.

"Don't touch me," I say, slapping his hand away so hard the handkerchief flies over the rail, fluttering two stories to the cement floor below.

"What the hell?" He recoils from my assault. "What's your problem? I'm just trying to help."

"I don't need your help," I say, squaring my shoulders. My eyes dry without the assistance of Mick or his nasty, soiled handkerchief. He looks like he's going to lash back at me, when the blue office door opens inward with a whoosh. On the other side is the trim figure of director Glenn Carver.

"Miss Snow. There you are." He escorts me inside with a light hand on my lower back. "Your sister's on the line. You may use my office for privacy."

He points me through a dark sitting room and another set of doors, blocking Mick from following. I can hear their conversation faintly in the background as I approach the phone lying on the large oak desk. Nausea turns my stomach again till I almost wish I could vomit just to relieve the pressure. Placing the handset against my ear becomes an act of pure courage.

"Aria? Hello?"

I hear swishing on the other end of the line and then my little sister's voice.

"Vivian. There you are. I'm so sorry to call you at work, but it's an—"

"Emergency. I know. It's okay, hon. Just . . . just tell me. What's wrong?"

She's crying. Reflexively, my throat tightens, and I know I'm not far off from my own breakdown, but I try to remain calm, for her sake.

"Do you need a doctor? Not those quacks at Norways. I'll have Archie find someone good who'll do a house call."

"It's too late for doctors," she says tearfully.

"What? What do you mean?" I know my voice is too loud, more like a shriek than a shout. Carver stands in the doorway now. It should bother me that he's watching my turmoil as though he's recording a scene, but truly, I barely notice him there.

"It's too late," she says, frantic.

Too late. The words fall from the sky to crush me like a firebomb. Aria is sobbing now. I want to go home and hold my baby one more time. I want to beg Trombello to come across the sea, to carry me again.

It sounds like Aria sets the phone down on the counter.

"Aria! Ari! Pick the phone up, sweetie. Please. Please, Aria," I beg. I wait for the phone to go dead, but instead a small voice on the other end changes everything.

"Ma? Is that you?"

"Gracie? Gracie, baby. Are you all right?" Relief outweighs confusion, and I'm crying a different sort of tears.

"Yeah, I'm okay. I had school. We drew flowers. I'm the best flower drawer in my class. Mrs. Chapman says so."

"You know I've always thought so. Prettiest flowers I've ever seen drawn by the prettiest girl I know," I say, sniffling.

"Are you crying?" her little voice asks. I don't know how to explain the mix-up and why I sound so sad. So I respond honestly.

"Yeah, honey. A little."

"I cried too. Mrs. Chapman said it was okay. Auntie Ari cries a lot, though."

"Why are you crying, honey?" I ask, concerned not only by Gracie's tears but also by Ari's surprising behavior. Gracie doesn't answer, because my sister yanks the phone away despite Gracie's five-year-old protests.

"Hey! I was talking. Stop . . ."

Aria's voice is thick and tearful but also unusually bitter, like lemonade without any sugar added. Lately, she's had unpredictable switches in her mood that confuse and concern me. Maybe this outburst is one of her swings. Or maybe she's grown tired of raising my child and taking care of our parents. I don't blame her—it's been too much for too long. I vow I'll fix things once I know for certain what's gone wrong.

"Papà's dying. Come home."

She hangs up.

Stunned, I place the receiver on the phone's base and then lunge for the wastebasket, barely reaching it before I lose control and vomit. Carver slaps a box of tissues onto the desk in front of me, a trail of spittle dripping off my chin.

"You have two weeks," he says gently, without asking any questions.

From the moment I met Glenn Carver across a room during my audition, he's reminded me of a polished version of my father. He's younger than Papà by twenty years or so, but he has the same stern, headstrong attitude. The way he runs his production with an iron fist, leaving no room for contradiction, reminds me of how Papà ran our home. And now this unexpected compassion—also like Papà.

"Thank you, sir," I say, with a quiver to my voice. He nods and walks out of the room, his heavy footsteps rattling the metal stairway outside. I call Archie and fill him in on the news. He promises to make arrangements for my trip home and sweetly gives his condolences. Archie is nothing like Papà, but he's like the father I always wished I'd had. So I let him take care of me occasionally, especially in moments like this. As we finish the call, I take a handful of tissues, shove them into the belt of my costume, and return to set. I have to hold it all together because that's my job in this family. I hold it together—no matter what.

VIVIAN SNOW

Auction

Lot #11

Hand-painted postcard labeled: Giardino della Minerva
    Black ink and watercolor on cardstock. Courtyard and window box of flowers overlooking the sea.

SALERNO. ITALIA. 15 APR 1949

Dear Vivian,
    Only now I saw a poster of your new film. I knew you'd end up a star.
    Blessings to you—A. Trombello
(Translation from Italian)

CHAPTER 11

April 27, 1949
Norways Sanitarium
Indianapolis, Indiana

The house on Tenth Street located at the rear entry of the sanitarium doesn't feel like home, it never has. I've lived here off and on since we put Mamma in Norways, but it's been my daughter's home since she can remember. The one-story cottage has white pine siding, neatly painted blue trim, and hedges of blooming lilacs that fill the two-bedroom home with a welcoming fragrance. My father and sister have made a Garden of Eden of this place. The grand Norway maples out front are the only original greenery that I can identify. Usually, I visit in the fall or winter months for holiday celebrations, but to see their creations in full bloom, I'm moved. Aria is the artist here, and Papà is her hands.

Two cars sit outside the pretty house. One is the green Oldsmobile sedan we drove up here five years ago. It looks no different. Aria never got her driver's license, and Papà can't drive with his prosthetic. The other is a shiny new two-door Ford I've never seen before.

My driver, Tito, maneuvers around them and finds an open spot on the grass.

"Thank you," I say, passing a five-dollar bill over the seat between us.

"Oh no, ma'am. I'm supposed to wait," the middle-aged man says, refusing my payment. He'd been standing in the station with my name handwritten on a sign. I'd planned to take the bus or a cab, but I couldn't exactly tell Tito to leave. He said very little, just that he'd been hired as my driver. I made a mental note to thank and scold Archie when I got back to California.

"What is Mr. Lombardo paying you? I'll match it. You can tell him you waited." I wink at him in the rearview mirror.

"Mr. Lombardo? I'm sorry, miss. I was hired by Mr. Carver. And he told me to stay with you until next week. Day or night. Anything you need."

"Mr. Carver?"

My director? Archie or even the studio I might believe, but sour-faced Mr. Carver?

"Yes, miss."

I shift, not wanting to be shadowed by a driver or butler or babysitter or whatever Tito is meant to be. But I can't insult my director. I remember the box of tissues he gently offered me after I received the news about Papà. There must be more to Glenn Carver than the hardened shell we see on set.

"Thank you. And I'm sorry."

"Don't be sorry, miss. It's my job."

"All right, well then. Just thank you, I guess." I grab my purse, and Tito pops out of the car, retrieving my suitcase. It's small and looks like a plaything in his hefty hands. "I've got it, Tito. Thank you."

"Yes, miss," he says again, waiting outside the car as I walk up the front steps. I sure hope he doesn't stand there the whole time.

I go to ring the bell and think better of it. Papà is inside, ill, dying, gosh, maybe dead for all I know. He had a heart attack while working in the back fields. Aria found him, and he was rushed to the hospital.

The prognosis was given—Papà would die. There's no other outcome possible. So he asked to go home and die in his own bed.

I check the doorknob. It's unlocked, so I enter the house unannounced. A solemnity hangs heavy in the room. There's a smell to it, like the stench of Bactine that fills every corner of the sanitarium. I remember this stink from after my baby brother died, when Mamma was locked away, and I remember it from Larry's funeral. It's the perfume of tragedy, I guess.

"Vivian, is that you?" Aria comes into the room carrying a tray, and she looks like she's aged a few years at least. She's thinner than ever and has puffy splotches under her eyes. I can see Mamma in her—not the lovely, young version of Mamma but rather Mamma when she was trying to not lose herself to her sadness. I shouldn't be shocked—the way Aria spoke to me on the phone about Papà was so unlike her. But she's had to carry so much. It's unfair. If I've had to hold things together, she's had to hold things up.

I drop my bag.

"Let me carry that, darling." I take the tray, though she doesn't seem to want to give it over.

"No, you've been traveling. You should rest . . ."

"Shhh, now. I think one of us needs rest, and it's not me. Uh, where should I put this?"

"In the kitchen," she says, wiping her hands on her coveralls and reaching for my suitcase.

"Don't you dare. I can carry that."

Aria holds up her hands as I place the tray on the kitchen table. When I return to the living room, she's peering out the window.

"There's a man in that car."

"Yes, dear. It's a silly thing. My director sent him. I'm sure the studio made him—to keep an eye on me."

"That *is* silly. As if *you* could ever do anything scandalous."

You'd be surprised, I think, removing my gloves and stashing them in my purse. I quickly change the subject, sitting beside Aria on the couch.

"How is he?" We haven't even said a proper hello to one another. I haven't had a chance to ask where Gracie is or when she'll be home. We just picked up in the middle of a conversation as though greetings were useless.

Aria sighs and settles in right next to me, curling up into the crook of my arm like when she was little. I cradle her and kiss the top of her head. She doesn't make a sound, but I'm sure she's crying.

"Oh, sweetie. Shhh." I pet her hair and let her mourn, holding back the litany of questions that've been running through my head since her call. Heavy footsteps from the hall startle me. A man in a tweed jacket and dark-rimmed glasses emerges from the shadows. I don't recognize him. I jolt upright, startling Aria.

"Dr. Youngrin," Aria says with a gasp, as though she'd forgotten he was here.

"You never returned, so I thought I'd make sure you were all right."

"I meant to come back but—"

"I interrupted her tray delivery." I complete the excuse for Aria, and some tension leaves her waifish body.

"You must be the oldest daughter," he says, studying me closely.

"I am. I'm Vivian Santini." I use my maiden name. That's who I am here—Santini not Snow or Highward. I won't sit by my father's side as he dies with any other name than the one he gave me at birth.

"Pleased to meet you," he says. "I'm sorry it's not under better circumstances."

"As am I," I say, looking up at the man.

"Your father is a fighter. I believe he's been holding out to see you."

"Yes, he's been asking for you," Aria says, sitting up beside me.

"Me?" I know Papà loves me, but to call to me at his darkest moment? That surprises me and touches me deeply.

"The only other person he asks for is Mamma. She came over one time, but it was a disaster. He didn't recognize her, and she didn't recognize him."

"It's possible he won't remember me either," I say, not sure if that'd make it all easier or harder. "What do you think, Dr. Youngrin? Do you see this often at the asylum? I know Mamma hasn't recognized me in years."

"The asylum?" he asks, shoving his hand in his side pocket and retrieving a pipe and tobacco tin, lending an air of higher knowledge to his appearance.

"Yes. I guess I assumed that's where you work. I'm sorry. Are you making a house call from the hospital?"

"No, Vivi. This is *your* doctor," Aria explains.

"*My* doctor?" I scoff, examining Dr. Youngrin with more care. He's in his early thirties, I'm sure, and has a bit of a Cary Grant look to him, with the dark hair and friendly brown eyes. "I haven't needed a doctor since I had scarlet fever two years ago."

"Not for you. For Daddy. He said you sent him from Hollywood or wherever."

Youngrin clears his throat. "I should clarify. I'm here because of Miss Snow, but Mr. Carver sent me."

"Mr. Carver?" I repeat, stunned.

"Your director? Again? Goodness, Vivi. He must be the kindest man."

"Kind" is not a word I'd use to describe Glenn Carver. Tenacious, yes. Aggressive, at times. Gentle, once or twice. The driver, the doctor—is it control Carver's after? Making sure I return to set on schedule? Or does he have a God complex, like any good director?

Aria, for one, seems grateful.

"Very kind," I echo, wondering how well Dr. Youngrin knows Glenn Carver. I change the subject. "Can I see him? Papà, I mean."

"In a few moments. We are finishing a . . . procedure." He's vague in his explanation, and I'm surprised that I don't mind. Carver is presumptuous to insert himself in my life, but it's nice to not be solely responsible for taking care of my family.

"I'll freshen up a bit. Let me know when you're ready for me."

Dr. Youngrin agrees and returns to his work. Aria gives me a real squeeze and a proper hello, explaining that Dr. Youngrin and his nurse flew into Weir Cook Municipal and have been here for nearly twenty-four hours straight. I've been on the train for twice as long.

"You look exhausted," Aria says, walking me to the bedroom she shares with Gracie. "You should rest until you can see Papà. Gracie will be home in an hour, and goodness knows you'll need to regain your strength before she gets here." I can't deny it—I'm tired, overtired.

Aria leaves to do some chores, and when I sit on Gracie's small bed, her scent poofs up from the blanket and mattress. After slipping off my shoes and removing my suit coat and the pillbox hat pinned to the top of my head, I dive under Gracie's covers.

Soon I'll say goodbye to my father. I've spent countless years managing Papà—his rules and his temper. It's been a lonely road. At times, I've felt so small and helpless, at the whim of everyone else's needs and wants before my own.

I shiver and pull up Gracie's crocheted afghan, taking in another breath of her smell, my eyelids growing heavy. As tragic as Papà's loss is, I know Aria and I are standing on the threshold of a freedom we've never experienced. Without Papà's controlling will, we must figure out what we want as individuals, what we need. Over my lifetime I've learned to ignore the part of me that has desires. I don't know if it's there anymore. And if it is, how do I know if I can trust it?

~

"Let's make your hair pretty." I brush my mother's thinning black-and-silver locks back into a low bun at the nape of her neck as she cradles her little doll in her lap, softly singing a lullaby. It's the first time I've visited her bedroom inside Norways Sanitarium. Gracie will be here in a few minutes to play dolls with her grandmother. The little girl processes grief like a butterfly flitting from flower to flower, taking sips of the sadness but mostly remaining in flight away from the loss. I worry what will happen when her wings are tired and she has to sit in the heartache she's running from. But for now, if it helps, I'll bring her to see her grandmother to show off the new doll we bought at Block's department store this morning.

Mamma has been in love with Gracie from the moment she first saw her. Over time, and under the watchful eye of staff, Gracie has found an unusual but true friendship with her grandmother. Especially since Mamma had the new procedure done on her brain. It was supposed to help level out her astronomical highs and rock-bottom lows, but from what I've seen it's left her blank. She remembers none of us other than Gracie, who she thinks of as her little friend. With the groundskeeper's cottage only a few steps from the sanitarium, they play dolls together nearly every day. I could barely tell the difference between their giggles when I found them playing last night after Papà had passed.

Maria Santini is a different woman than she was during my first visit to Norways. Since her surgery, she's become still, quiet, and completely demure. There's no fire or passion anymore, no outbursts either. Now she's just a pretty older lady who looks a little like my mother but acts a bit like a child. She has no idea her husband died last night, and we've decided not to tell her. Aria's eyes are red from crying, and I have to keep a handkerchief close by to wipe my running mascara, but Mamma doesn't notice.

"Does she understand me?" I ask Aria as I pin Mamma's bun in place. She's standing in the doorway, watching.

Margot, the nurse supervising our visit, answers before Aria can.

"She hears you. Right, Mrs. Santini?" She speaks to Mamma tenderly like she's a child. Mamma nods and goes back to caressing her baby doll.

"Gracie is on the porch, hoping to see her. Do you think she'd like that?" I ask Margot.

Mamma's head lifts.

"Gracie?" she whispers eagerly.

"You can ask her yourself," Margot says, gesturing to my mother. I swallow and put on a stiff smile.

"Would you like to see Gracie? She has a surprise for you." I speak to her like I would speak to Grace, touching her shoulder lightly. Mother smiles back.

"Yes, please," she says as though she's been asked by a teacher if she'd like a treat.

"All right. Let's go! It's cold today so what do we need?" Margot asks, clapping her hands.

"A jacket?" Mother says, confused at first and then proud of her declaration.

"That's right. Show me where it is, Mrs. Santini."

Margot helps her dress, patiently waiting through each step. Usually spending time around Mamma makes me feel scared or angry at all she's taken from us. At this moment, though, I feel compassion for my parent who cannot remember how to button her coat or buckle her shoes and whose dolls are more like children to her than her daughters.

Aria moves beside me, watching the nurse at work.

"Margot is helping Mamma learn how to take care of herself. She reads all the latest medical books and practically knows more than the doctors." Margot, a young woman not much older than Aria, blushes and waves at her like she's shooing a fly away.

"Oh, hush. I'm fresh out of school, that's all. I've read a lot, but the doctors have seen more than books can teach me."

"She's too humble," Aria whispers. "The doctors here get mad when she pushes back, so we gotta keep it kind of quiet."

"You're too kind. I only want to help where I can," Margot adds, and her rigid exterior seems to ease. I glance between the two young women and can see the mutual respect they share. I've never understood why Aria is slow to make friends—she's witty and loyal and passionate and has the greenest thumb I've ever seen.

I can see that Aria blossoms in the sunlight of her friendship with Margot, even during this dark time. The wilting I saw yesterday and heard on the phone earlier this week diminishes as they interact. Aria's been forced to stay dormant—frozen in her life's progression while she makes evolution possible for everyone else. It can't be good for any one of God's creations to be in the shadows for so long.

Once Mother is fully dressed and her doll wrapped in a soft blue blanket as though he were real, we make our way down the wide front stairs with polished banisters and a fine wool runner that reaches into the foyer. Tall wooden pillars frame the foot of the staircase, and flowers stand on podiums to either side. If it weren't for the men and women in white uniforms and patients shuffling through the halls like walking dead, Norways would look like a lovely holiday retreat or the home of an elderly businessman living out the remainder of his years in luxury.

But it's not. It's no more than a prison for most of the people here. For some, like my mother, it's a necessary penitentiary. Mother is treated well, or the best she can be, considering the circumstances. But I've always found this place chilling, and until this visit I've refused to step inside, as though it were a trap that might clamp down and never let me leave.

"This way," I say, taking her elbow and leading her toward the door. Margot and Aria walk a few paces behind and seem pleased with my willingness to help my mother. I may not have been a present mother with Gracie, not yet at least, but I know how to take care of people. I know how challenging Aria's life must be, because I once lived a similar life.

We can hear Gracie chittering on the front porch, conversing with her dolls or maybe a nurse. My mother's features perk up and she glances back at Margo, excited.

"Gracie?" she asks.

"Yes, Mrs. Santini. Gracie," Margot replies patiently. I find myself smiling and am surprised to see the same expression on Aria's face.

As we step outside, the spring air hits us, still cold but welcoming and fresh with the smell of pine mixed into the earthy scents of April. Gracie sits on the swinging bench where Aria left her before we went inside to get her nonna. She's curled up under a blanket with a doll cradled in her arms, the new one with real hair and porcelain skin.

"Gracie!" Mamma calls out, grabbing the young girl's attention.

"Nonna!" Gracie chirps. "I have a new doll!"

"She's pretty," Mamma says, pulling her arm from my grasp as though I'm a nurse keeping her from her fun. She climbs onto the seat beside Gracie.

Gracie throws her arms around Mamma's neck, and I jump forward reflexively, sure my mother will scream or claw at the little girl, as though her nerves are raw and exposed. Margot puts out a hand to stop me from intervening. I look at Aria with concern etched into my face, but she nods. I hold my breath as the old woman who looks a little like me takes my daughter into her lap and hugs her like she's a living doll. For a moment I pretend my father can see it, his wife caring for their granddaughter like he'd always dreamed, his grown daughters looking on with pride.

But I'm here to take care of them now, my sister, my baby girl, even Mamma. No more running away. No more excuses. No more acquiescing to the rules of a man in my life. With my contract signed, I have enough money for a home and enough power to get help for anything we need. As we bury my father, I will say goodbye to more than the man I've loved and feared for most of my life. I'll also say goodbye to my past, to Indiana, and the memories here.

Then, I'll take my girls to Los Angeles with me, and we will start a new life, together.

We aren't perfect, us Santini women, but there's good here, and now that Papà's gone, it's up to me to protect them—no matter the cost.

VIVIAN SNOW

Auction

Lot #12

Hand-drawn postcard labeled: Port of Salerno
　　Pencil on cardstock. Virgin Mary statue on a stone ship.

SALERNO. ITALIA. 10 MAY 1949

　　Dear Vivian,
　　　　My heart is with you in your time of need. Much comfort to you and your family.
　　　　In prayer—A. Trombello
　　(Translation from Italian)

CHAPTER 12

May 2, 1949
Rest Haven Cemetery
Edinburgh, Indiana

It was a beautiful funeral—well attended by those who have known my family since they first settled in Edinburgh before I was born. Back then, my parents shared the house with Mamma's cousin, her only living family. Papà's family remained in Italy with no interest in coming to America, though Papà made the offer time and again. I think Papà was lonely without anyone else but us around to talk to in the language of his youth. And once Mamma went to the asylum, he had no one who remembered his home and longed for it like he did. Cousin Frido ran off with a married lady from town and moved to Kentucky or some such place, leaving Papà with the house payments and no secondary income. But Edinburgh felt like home enough, so we stayed.

Plus, Mamma had always refused to return to her life in Italy.

"It's all dirt there. Dirt in the houses. Dirt in their minds. Dirt in their hearts." And Mamma wanted more. She wanted to live a truly American life. Sometimes I think that's why she'd go through her wild seasons, leaving home for a few weeks, feeling like she was really living.

Papà would pace the house, an anxious, angry mess while she was away. She'd come home. They'd fight. Mamma would cry and lock herself away. Aria and I would observe like audience members watching a play they could get pulled into at any moment without warning.

Even though it's never acknowledged, the town knew of my mother's health struggles, and when we lost Tony, the church was almost as full as it is today for Papà. But unlike Tony or Larry or Tom, Papà had grown old, or at least old enough to have experienced much of life's roller coaster. They say his heart gave out—it was just his time. I wonder if his heart had been limping along, half-broken all these years.

The only one not in attendance today is Mamma. Her break from reality is a secret our family has kept for more than a decade. We've had many stories, but Papà always had a promise at the end of every one—his wife would be home soon. He told his friends from the factory that Mamma was joining us in Indianapolis after Gracie was born. And since I know Papà would've wished it, I'll make sure that these people never find out my mother is no longer the dark-haired beauty with coal black eyes and a mischievous smile who loved her children but also loved dancing, singing, and laughing.

I know her absence will give the town's gossip mill plenty to whisper about, but it'd be worse if she were here, dull eyed and childlike. And now they have me and my career to whisper about instead. So I let the ladies gossip, holding my head high while wearing a Dior suit and letting my wedding ring glitter in the sun at Papà's services.

If there is gossip about Papà's missing wife, there'll also be chatter about the striking young doctor following me around. Dr. Youngrin hasn't left us other than when sleep or decorum makes parting necessary.

He was there when I held Papà's hand for the last time and told him I loved him. Papà could barely speak, and when he did it was in the language of my home and childhood.

"You look thin. Do you eat?" he asked. Instead of being offended that his last words were critical, I took it to mean that he cared about me. Everyone in Hollywood wants me to watch my weight and waist size, but my father wants me to be well nourished. There was something I liked about that.

"Yes, Papà," I said, crying and kissing his thin and ashen hand.

"Eat more," he said, and I laughed with tears in my eyes.

"Of course, Papà."

"What am I saying? You care for us. You feed us. You'll be good. My good, good girl."

He touched my cheek and caressed it as he spoke of my goodness. My father's approval has always been so hard to earn, so far away, so desperately far, but I could never stop reaching for it. Finally hearing it spoken, I soaked it in, let it light up every dark corner where I used to hide when he frightened me or when I couldn't tell the truth about myself or my life.

"Take care of all my little birds, will you?" he asked, chillingly aware he was in the last stages of dying.

"Of course, Papà," I said as well as I could through my emotions.

Dr. Youngrin watched on.

He also watched a few hours later after Papà had slipped into a coma and as Aria and I held each other, seeking the steady comfort of a mother in our sisterly affection.

"I'll never leave you again," I pledge, holding her tight against my chest.

"I'll stay with you and Gracie forever," she replied, her arms wrapped around my rib cage.

Youngrin was there when Gracie gave me a tentative hug after not seeing me for so many months. She doesn't really know me when our time together is mere punctuation in the story of her life.

"I have no father or grandfather now, do I?" Gracie asked after she kissed Papà goodbye. He'd doted on her, in love with the free spiritedness of his fatherless granddaughter. He'd been a father to her in all the ways he could manage, more than he'd been to me or Aria.

"Nonno will always love you, darling. Even from heaven. God just needs him more now, that's all," I said to comfort her.

Gracie crossed her arms and stomped her foot so hard the lace trim on her socks continued to shake after her foot landed.

"I hate God!" she shouted, which on a good day would send a chill through my heart, but today of all days, with the veil between heaven and earth so thin, it sent up the hairs on the back of my neck.

I choked. "Gracie! Take it back!" But she refused.

"No way. He took my daddy *and* he wants my nonno. He's mean. And selfish."

The priest was waiting in the front room to give the last rites. I was sure he would hear her and storm in with a lecture on sacrilege and my failures as a parent. But he didn't.

I rushed to correct her blasphemy. "God isn't mean, sweetheart. He's all that is good. He will make you feel warm and safe. All you have to do is pray . . ."

At the mention of prayer, Gracie dodged my embrace and ran out of the room in a grand exit worthy of Bette Davis. I could see Dr. Youngrin trying to hold back a smile, which lessened some of the horror of hearing Gracie denounce God as my father lay dying in front of us. My whole life I've barely dared to question authority figures like Papà or Mr. Carver or Archie—much less God. I have more to learn from my courageous little daughter, I'm sure.

Dr. Youngrin was also there for Papà's last breath when his spirit left his mortal coil, and we knew we'd just shared the same air as him for the last time in this life.

He was there at Norways talking to Mamma's doctors when I visited her before leaving for the funeral.

And he's here now, at Papà's grave, watching the coffin as it's lowered into the ground. I eye him from behind my handkerchief as I dab at the corners of my eyes. Just like the driver Tito, there's no use in trying to get him to leave. I'm sure if I forced him out, he'd go. But to what end? I ignore him through the rest of the service until he fades into the crowd after the final amen.

"I miss my dolly," Gracie says, holding Aria's hand as we leave Papà's grave with the mourners who accompanied us to his burial.

"I know, sweetie, but you gave it to Nonno," Aria explains softly. Gracie had placed the doll in her grandfather's coffin earlier that day. At the time it'd seemed a tender, selfless moment of grief. But children don't always understand when things are gone, especially when they're gone forever.

"We can get you a new doll, love," I say, taking my daughter's other hand so we're joined in a chain. She yanks it away.

"I don't want a new one. I want Harriet. I want my Harriet."

I kneel, feeling everyone's judgmental eyes on us.

"She's with Nonno now. We can't get her back," I try to explain, but Gracie clamps onto Aria's legs, sobbing.

"But why not? Go ask the man. I want her. She's mine. Please, Zia. Please." This sorrow is not only for her doll, I think. It's for her grandfather, her only father figure. She's just a child lamenting the loss of something I wish I could give her back but that will never return.

Aria looks to me as though I'll magically know how to comfort my child just because she came from my body. But as much as I adore Gracie, she doesn't look at me as a mother. That's on *my* list of things I mourn.

"Hey, I know what we can do, Gracie." Aria's voice is filled with exaggerated excitement, which teary-eyed Gracie picks up on immediately with genuine enthusiasm. I wait just as eagerly for Aria's solution. "Let's visit your daddy. He's right over here, remember?"

The thought fills me with dread. We've visited once since Trombello purchased the headstone. Gracie was shy at that time, confused. But today her eyes light up, and she follows Aria to Tom's stone, marked with a date of death that Trombello and I agreed on together.

"Daddy!" Gracie cries, speaking to the headstone with more ease than she speaks to me. I dry my eyes and hold back a sob.

"I'm five now. I play piano and I sing like a pretty angel, or that's what Nonno says. I help Zia Ari lots and lots and have a pretty room with lace curtains. Ari said we can make taffy today, and I can play with Mary Lou from school tomorrow . . ."

A group of women from the town watch with hands over their mouths or hearts as my daughter embraces the headstone as though it's her living father. They leave, likely whispering about Tom's heroic, tragic story, a story that's a safeguard for me and my family but a shameful fabrication. What would people say if they knew the truth? I can imagine their justified disgust, and it haunts me: "How dare that young woman use the war and our brave boys to hide her sins? How dare she make money off the sentimentality of our scarred nation? How *dare* she?"

"Nonno died," Gracie says, with a little pout. It's pointless to stop my tears now. Aria puts her arm around my waist, and I put mine around hers.

"It's just us girls now," Aria says, resting her head on my shoulder. I kiss her hair. She let me tame it this morning, and it smells of rose oil and the cool spring air.

"We'll make him proud. I'll make sure of it," I say. We are my father's legacy. We have to keep moving forward, for ourselves and also for Papà.

"He was already proud of us," Aria says, sniffling as we watch Gracie. She makes the statement with a confidence I don't often see in her. "We need to make ourselves proud now, I think."

The comment takes my words away. Make myself proud? Is that even possible? I can't guarantee I'll ever reach that seemingly unattainable goal. I don't have to respond, though, because Gracie interrupts, leads me to the headstone, and puts my gloved hand on the curved top.

"Say hi to Daddy," she says, smiling up at me expectantly with her twinkling blue eyes. Her tiny fingers press mine into the stone before she lets go and watches me closely. Tom isn't here, but I'd be a fool to think that mattered. I swallow my anxiety and reluctance and clear my throat.

"Hello, Tom," I say. I haven't spoken to him since the day he tried to kill me and I plunged a knife into his thigh, severing an artery. I'm uncomfortable saying his name out loud.

"Go on. Go on," Gracie urges. I don't know what she wants me to say, but I continue, aware Gracie is watching, and off in the distance, Dr. Youngrin looks on.

"I see you've met Gracie." I smile, and Grace giggles. "You have a good little girl here, Tom. She's smart and funny, and you'd love her as much as I do, I know."

"Say 'I love you,'" Gracie directs from behind me, where she's huddled against Aria to stay warm. The wind picks up, stinging my damp cheeks.

I don't feel it anymore, but I need Gracie to feel like she came from love, so I say it with as much emotion as I would if Glenn Carver were directing me with the cameras rolling.

"I love you, Tom." I caress the stone as though it's his cheek turned to granite and then return to my spot beside Gracie and Aria. I look out over the cemetery where my father and my husband are memorialized, where all of us might rest in a family plot one day. Life is so damned fragile.

Grace takes my hand.

"Can we go home now, Mamma?" she asks, looking up at me. Me—not Aria. I smile softly at my little girl, who looks so much like her father. I might not be in love with Tom anymore, but I do love what he's given me.

"Of course, darling."

We return to the Chrysler, where Tito is waiting. He has a lollipop sitting on the back seat for Gracie. She gushes her gratitude to the stocky, dark-haired man.

"Aren't you a softy?" I whisper to him through the front window before climbing into the car beside Gracie. I'm full of appreciation.

"Oh, it's not from me," he clarifies. "I don't like sticky candy in my vehicle, but I told him I'd make one exception."

"Him?" I question.

"Yeah," Tito says, using his thumb to point at the car parked behind us. "It's from the doctor. This too." He passes me a prescription bottle with small white pills inside. It has my name on it and instructions for use written on a folded piece of paper wrapped around the brown glass.

Dr. Youngrin's engine starts and then idles. I can only assume he's waiting for us to leave. He tips his hat, and I nod my head in his direction as a thank-you before I scooch into the back seat next to Gracie, who is already devouring the multicolored confection. As we make the long drive back to Indianapolis, where we'll pack up the only home Gracie has ever known, I unwrap the note from around the container.

At the top of the page: *To help your nerves. Dr. Youngrin.* A short list of dos and don'ts as well as a few contraindications follow.

"What's that?" Aria asks, returning to reality after daydreaming while looking out the car window. I palm the bottle and slip it into my pocket along with the note, my heart pounding.

"Nothing. A little mix-up," I say, hoping she won't press for more information. She's seen our mother take far too many medicines "for her nerves"—the last thing she needs is to worry about me taking them as well. I don't need pills, at least I don't think I do . . .

She shrugs and returns to watching the landscape flash by, and I do the same, uncomfortably aware of the cool bottle inside my skirt pocket, lying against my thigh and giving me a dose of reality stronger than any medicine it could contain.

Could it be Dr. Youngrin was sent here by Glenn Carver to take care of *me*—to be *my* doctor? I blush and touch the bottle in my pocket, relishing the feeling of being important enough to be cared for, protected.

Glenn Carver, what an unexpected man. Perhaps inside that tough, take-no-prisoners exterior there's a tender heart that's motivated by more than money and fame. Perhaps he's like the men I've loved the most.

Perhaps he really is kind.

VIVIAN SNOW

Auction

Lot #13

Hand-drawn postcard labeled: Cathedral of Nola
    Pencil on cardstock. Cathedral with five arches atop Roman columns and a tower with a cross on top.

NOLA. ITALIA. 09 JUL 1950

> *Dear Vivian,*
>   *I have been moved to Nola. The air is fresh here, and the people are full of faith. Pictures of your premiere reached us late but brought much joy to see you happy.*
>   *In prayer—A. Trombello*
> (Translation from Italian)

CHAPTER 13

June 23, 1950
Grauman's Chinese Theater
Hollywood, California

I stumble into the waiting limo, nearly blind from flashing bulbs and my ears ringing with loud voices shouting my name.

"Vivian Snow!" "Vivian!" "Miss Snow!" The photographers and the fans try every version of my name—at least the name they know—to grab my attention. I'm still not used to seeing my face on the screen or seeing my picture in the newspapers. However, I've gotten used to taking orders, smiling in the right direction, and looking happy and gracious, always.

Archie's already inside the limo, half-drunk and smoking a cigar.

"That was one damn fine show. I heard Zanuck chattering about nominations. You're new but not too new, know what I mean?"

He holds the stub of his cigar between two fingers as he dreamily recalls his conversation with the studio executive, Darryl Zanuck. I wave it off, knowing Archie can exaggerate. But even with his blurred eyes and smoky breath, I'm glad he's here.

Soon after my first film with Glenn was declared a blockbuster, Archie moved his whole family out to Los Angeles. Since then, we've had a year of wins. Another film with Glenn at Twentieth Century-Fox,

Flash Point with John Ford, and another signed with Elia Kazan. I can barely keep up between learning my lines, blocking, costume fittings, screen tests, publicity opportunities, parties, and premieres. And on top of it all is the role I've neglected for far too long: motherhood. I wish it wasn't such a puzzle, how to do it all. Right now I manage by sleeping less, eating less, and occasionally using Dr. Youngrin's prescriptions when I'm desperate to stay on top of everything.

"Where to, Miss Vivian?" Tito asks, watching me from the rearview mirror. Glenn offered him a full-time job as my driver once I returned to LA. I think he's already used to the glitz and glamour—almost. I'm not sure anyone is ever fully acclimated to it; I know I'm not, which is likely for the best. But as soon as Tito starts to accelerate, leaving the snapping flashbulbs in the distance, the dreamlike experience of floating through a Hollywood premiere for my newest film leaves, and I remember myself.

You are Vivian Santini. Don't forget it.

My corset cuts into my ribs, and the low-cut bodice of my gown barely contains my breasts as I pant. Sometimes I feel more on the run in Hollywood than I did in France during the war.

"Home for a quick minute. I promised Gracie."

"Yes, miss," he says with an approving smile.

"She'll be up this late?" Archie asks, glancing at his watch.

"I'm sure she is. You know Aria, she's a softy. And I did promise. Besides, I need to change anyway."

"Right. Right," he says as though he understands, though he doesn't. His wife, Clara, puts his four kids to bed at eight and keeps his home running like a tight ship. Aria and I have plenty of love for my Gracie, but with Aria's free spirit and changing moods, and my unpredictable schedule, there's nothing tight about our home. But—we're in the same state, finally, and our Sundays together are the brightest moments of my life.

As we pull up to my Santa Barbara–style home, the white stucco glows in the moonlight. It's past eleven, but only the start of our night.

There's one light on, in the kitchen. It's possible they both went to bed after all. I don't blame them—we're late.

Archie and I have an after-party at Zanuck's that could potentially go until dawn. Not only do I have to go, but I also have to stay as long as possible.

"If you leave early, people will forget what you look like," Archie likes to remind me. If the decision-makers in this town even blink, they forget you exist. So I'll go and do the same thing I learned from my time in the USO—I'll become the girl everyone else wants me to be, which leaves me with plenty of friends but no one outside of my inner circle who truly knows me.

"Want to come in for a drink while I change?" I ask Archie with one foot out the door.

"Nah. I've got enough to keep me busy in here," he says, lifting a full glass of champagne. "Hey, wear something with sparkles, okay?" he says, giving me fashion advice like he always does. I rarely listen, but tonight I already have a dress picked out. It was delivered this morning—a good-luck gift.

"I have just the one," I say and rush inside. The front door is unlocked, which is not unusual. Aria never remembers to lock it, even though I remind her constantly. I don't hear any voices or any signs of life, but when I pass by Gracie's room, I find Aria curled up in bed with six-year-old Gracie, the novel *Little Women* open on the covers between them. I kiss Gracie, leaving a smudge of red lipstick on her cheek, and then tap Aria's shoulder.

"Oh, you're home," she gasps, waking with a start.

"Only for a moment," I whisper, waving for Aria to follow me out of the room. Her hair is flattened on one side, and the outline of one of the buttons on her sleeve is imprinted into her skin. "I have a party in Beverly Park. I'm going to change."

"Into *the* dress?" she asks, absolutely knowing which dress I'm going to wear.

"Clearly," I say, laughing. When the box arrived this morning with the note from Glenn, it came with a card that said, simply, *Wear this tonight if the answer is yes.* The studio chose my dress for the premiere, so I knew this one must be for the party. And I think I know what the question is too.

"Glenn will love it," she says, getting the dreamy, romantic look she usually gets when looking at a beautiful garden.

"I hope so."

My cheeks flush. Glenn Carver—first my director, then my friend, and most recently my boyfriend. He spends more time in my home than I do, I feel like. I return after a long day of filming, and there's Glenn in the living room with my sister and daughter, waiting as though he were already my husband. And when possible, he snaps me up as his leading lady, if Zanuck is willing.

In the past six months, he's asked me twenty times at least if I'd marry him. The first few times, I laughed, sure he must be joking. He was still married back then, though he maintained it was unhappy. I refused his attention, insisting I couldn't possibly encourage a married man.

He asked me again when the ink was barely dry on his fourth divorce filing, and I said no—divorce frightening the good little Catholic girl inside me. According to the church, Glenn would always be married unless he received an annulment, and so if I married him, would our marriage even be binding in the eyes of God? I didn't know the answers to these questions, so I maintained our friendship, refusing to let him into my heart completely. But he didn't leave, he didn't give up, he just kept showing up despite the gossip in the papers. His attentions toward me, a young starlet, caused even more conflict in his already tumultuous divorce.

He spent so much time in my home that I couldn't help but be myself around him, which was refreshing and delightful. Despite my best-laid plans to shun him, I couldn't deny my growing feelings. How could I help myself? He was handsome and kind and so stunningly generous. But will he stay loyal? It's impossible to know. And I know the next man I marry I want to be married to for the rest of my life.

When I started filming *Flash Point* with John Ford, Glenn nearly lost his mind with jealousy. He insisted on driving me every day to and from set and escorted me to and from meals, a devoted suitor. Every girl in every room envied me. Glenn Carver, Oscar-winning director and producer, wanted me. He wanted me not only as his leading lady but as his companion, his wife, and his partner, not for a mistress or some on-set fling.

Last night he put it all on the line—he'd only ask this one last time. He promised he'd pursue an annulment as soon as humanly possible, but he couldn't wait any longer—I had twenty-four hours to decide if I'd marry him or we'd part ways forever. I still didn't know if I could marry him, but I definitely knew I wasn't ready to be without him. Conflicted, I told him I needed more time.

When the dress arrived this morning, a glittering off-white chiffon Fernanda Gattinoni gown with thin straps and a pleated bodice along with a pair of red Salvatore Ferragamo crystal rhinestone pumps, I didn't know my answer. But as I sat through that premiere without him, as I smiled into camera after camera and spoke the same nonsense to people who were also only showing me the parts of themselves that they thought I wanted to see—I missed him. Even though I've pushed Glenn away and acted impartial, turned down his advances, and dodged his affection, since Papà died, he's been here for me and my family, and that means a lot.

So, I slip into my dress and ask Aria to zip it for me.

We both know what this means. Another white dress for another man who is promising me the world. The last time I put on a dress for a man I married, I got Gracie. This time, I hope for nothing more than stability and companionship.

"You look beautiful, Vivi," Aria says with a hug and the lightest of kisses on my cheek. I embrace her and rush out the front door to the smoke-filled back seat of Tito's limo. When Glenn sees me tonight, he'll know in an instant—I will marry him.

~

"I wish he'd keep his hands off you," Glenn says, steaming. I'm in my dressing room, getting in costume for Glenn's newest film.

"He's doing his job, Glenn. It's not like he knows about us. Not officially at least," I remind my director/secret fiancé. Our stealthy engagement is only a few weeks old. There's no way the cast and crew are completely ignorant—we've been attempting to act professional and detached, but the efforts are growing exhausting.

"He's taking advantage of the situation," Glenn rages, his white-blond hair appearing even lighter in contrast to his red face. He paces back and forth, shoving his hands in and out of his pockets, retrieving a dark glass bottle. He shakes the pills inside. There aren't many, which means he's already taken a few today—I just don't know which pills these ones are. There's a delicate balance to Dr. Youngrin's treatments—some pills calm, some energize, some put you under, and others keep you up for days.

"You cast him," I say, trying to sound playful but feeling the tension of the moment, squinting to read the label on the prescription bottle. Glenn opens the cap and shakes one of the small white tablets onto his palm and pops it in his mouth, swallowing. Well, whatever it is—it is. Glenn seems to function just fine on both uppers and downers. I, on the other hand, lose my mind on too much of either and indulge only in the greatest of emergencies or at Glenn's insistence.

"I cast him to be your lover on-screen not in real life."

"You know how it is in this business. Often that line blurs," I say with raised eyebrows. It's not like Glenn is exempt from this form of romancing.

"I'm aware," he says, screwing the lid back on.

I hope the pills are the calming ones.

Glenn's in an impossible position—he needs to make a quality product that'll reflect his talents as a director and display our talents as actors. And if Marlon Brando buzzes around my chair and laughs too readily at my jokes, how can he complain? It creates great chemistry for our slow-burn love story on-screen.

But it's driving him to near furious distraction. My leading man is young, muscled, and completely smitten with me. I'm practically Glenn's wife, but we're the only ones to know it. Keeping our little secret was exciting and fun for the first few days of shooting, but now I just want to be able to kiss him at the end of a long day or discuss what we're having for dinner without acting like superspies.

"He's a child," I say, tugging on Glenn's sleeve, urging him closer.

"He's the same age as you, my dear."

"Shhh," I say, leaning in for a kiss light enough to preserve my lipstick.

His mustache is cut in a short line over his top lip, and his teeth are unnaturally straight in a way that I know comes from porcelain crowns. At forty-nine, he's lived almost two lifetimes to my one. He has four grown children, two nearly grown, and two little grandbabies. With no kids at home, he treats my Gracie like one of his own.

I wrap my arms around his firm, trim torso and press my head against his chest, listening to his racing heartbeat. He kisses the top of my head and encircles me in his arms.

"You're better than medicine," he says, letting out a long breath. "When will you let me marry you?"

"Me? You know I'd marry you tomorrow if only . . ."

Glenn's divorce has stalled in an extended court process. His fourth wife is trying to take him for all he's worth and turn his youngest children against him. It's tearing him apart, and I hate to bring it up and upset him again.

The good Catholic girl in me struggles with the fact that divorce is such a large part of Glenn's past, but he assures me I needn't worry about divorce ever being a part of our love story. He's explained repeatedly that he was never the one to initiate his previous splits. He's convinced that his ex-wives married him for money, for fame, for social status. Once they didn't need him for their egos or pocketbooks anymore, they discarded him for the next shiny object. I know I'm nothing like those women. I love Glenn for the way he twirls Gracie in the air whenever he comes over for dinner and the way he brings Aria seeds for her garden and how he laughs at my ridiculous jokes. I love that he's willing to take care of us, but I'd take care of him if he needed it—in sickness and in health.

"Tomorrow, you say? That can be arranged," he says mischievously. I lean back and raise an eyebrow.

"Wait. It's finished?"

He nods. "She settled this morning. It's done."

"Thank God!" I say, tightening my embrace around his middle until he makes a sound of discomfort.

"Oof. You're oddly strong for such a tiny woman." He chuckles and wiggles against my grip.

"What do you think I do with that trainer every day? Sleep?" I double down on my hold, clenching my teeth.

"My Lord, I hope I don't need to explain why my wife shouldn't sleep with her trainer," Glenn jokes, easily breaking away. I'm embarrassed at my accidental double entendre at first but then pick up on his choice of words.

"Your wife," I echo, dreamily.

"Shall we get married, darling?"

"Of course," I say and reach up for a kiss, but Glenn stops short, studying my face.

"Better not smudge you," he says, not as a fiancé but as a director.

"Kiss me, fool," I say, breathlessly, pressing my mouth to his. He returns my embrace, needing very little encouragement. The heat between us spreads to all parts of my body as his tongue finds mine, neither of us worried about the red lipstick he'll have to wash from his face.

Just as he starts to fumble with the buttons on the top of my costume, there's a knock at the door. We both freeze and then quickly move to return ourselves to the look of normalcy. I rebutton my blouse, he adjusts his trousers and reaches for tissues to clean his face, passing me a few.

"Who is it?" I call.

"Laura, miss. There's a call for you in the booth." Ever since the call from Aria when Papà was dying, it's scary when I receive calls on set. Aria will only reach out in an emergency, but Gracie has recently learned how to use the phone, and Glenn lets her call at will. He'll spoil that girl rotten if I'm not careful.

"Tell them to call me back," I say, holding back a laugh, rubbing cold cream on both of our faces to remove the smudged lipstick.

"I did," Laura says, her voice straining through the door. "But it's the international operator."

"International?" I ask, running through the possibilities of who might be calling from far away. It could be a business call of some kind. Or a relative. Or . . . My heart, which has only recently calmed, explodes.

"Tell him I'll be right there!" I shout, filling Glenn's hands with Kleenex.

"Yes, ma'am," Laura says, her clacking heels signaling her departure.

"Wait, what'd I miss?" Glenn asks, inspecting his face. "Who's calling from overseas? The Pope?"

"Ha. You don't even know how close you are." I reapply lip color and pat on a touch of powder, just in case someone notices the cleanup.

"What does that mean?" he asks. And though whatever pills he has coursing through his veins have widened his pupils and slowed his pulse, he still looks concerned about the mystery caller.

"It's my friend Trombello." Or at least I think it is. "I've been waiting for his call," I say, checking myself in the mirror, my lips freshly crimson. I unlock the door.

"The priest who sends the postcards?" Glenn asks, brushing at his mustache in the mirror and following me into the hall as I give him the all clear.

"Yes! I knew I couldn't write him about . . . everything . . . at least not on a postcard. So I asked him to call," I whisper, though I know he understands my meaning.

"Because you're close."

"Because we're very close."

"I see," he says with a flash of something dark. I don't question it, mostly because I don't want to. Glenn will have no reason to feel insecure in a few days because we'll be married and the world will know it.

Brando sees us and heads our way with a loud greeting. To avoid any awkwardness, I wave goodbye to both men and head to the office.

There, the phone waits, and when I pick up the receiver I know that it's my dear friend on the other end before he says a word, just the sound of his breath is enough.

"Good evening!" he proclaims, and a pure warmth shines down on me like God himself is smiling. Where Glenn's attention burns in a blissful, sinful heat, Trombello's comfort feels like when Papà would light the fireplace on a cold midwestern night.

"Buon pomeriggio, Padre! Sapevo che eri tu." *Good afternoon, Father! I knew it was you.*

"It is a delight to hear you speak, *mia cara amica*. I've not yet forgotten your voice."

"Me either! How are you? How is Nola?"

"It is full of more beauty than should be allowed on this mortal plane."

I sigh, wishing I knew what that meant. "I have to visit. Especially now—in Papà's memory. May he rest in peace."

"Yes, Viviana. Your padre would be proud to know you visited his home. And we will make you welcome."

After a year of mourning, I can finally mention Papà without choking up. Trombello has been a part of that process. We still write to one another, but with my renegotiated contract and increased salary, I've indulged in the occasional long-distance call, as expensive and arduous as that process is. I find it a worthwhile fee for the help he provides me.

When I speak to Trombello, I barely need any of Dr. Youngrin's pills, which Glenn and the studio hand out as freely as candy. The uppers help me stay peppy during twelve-hour days, and the downers drag my hyped-up body into sleep when we wrap for the night. But though they work, I don't like how they make me feel. It reminds me of Mamma, the highs and lows and the drugged-out stupor that filled all the times in between. I can't end up like Mamma, but I don't know how I'd keep up with my rising star without them.

"I've no doubt."

"Besides, you're a bella primadonna here. You'll be carried around the town on shoulders."

"Oh, heavens no. Please." I laugh at the thought of being carried anywhere by a mob of Italian fans. Glenn walks in, and I return to reality. He leans against the door, listening to my side of the conversation, which doesn't bother me. I'm used to having Aria present during my calls. Sometimes she joins in, though she's still unsure if she wants to let a priest too far into her life. It's as if she fears he can read her mind like a magician.

"You have news for me, *mia cara amica*?"

"I do. Do you remember my friend Glenn? The one Ari and I have told you about?"

"The director?"

"Yes. Yes. That's him."

"I read an article on him last week," he says, and I have to control my expression. I know what article he's speaking about—a nasty piece in *Confidential*, the gossip magazine, detailing all of Glenn's marriages, divorces, and settlements and their supposed causes. I removed the pages from our copy before Aria could stumble upon them. It's dirty, nasty gossip and nothing more.

"Yes, well, Glenn and I are going to be married."

Silence.

"Trombello? Did I lose our connection?" I tap the receiver and then put it back to my ear, listening for a dial tone.

"No. No. I'm still here," he says, all humor gone from his voice. This must be the tone he uses for his homily. Glenn takes out a cigarette, lights it, and then settles back against the wall, watching. My nerves start to rise.

"Glenn and I are to be married—soon. Very soon. I didn't want you to find out through some gossip column or a newsreel."

A longer gap ensues, but I know he's on the line still because I can hear him breathing.

"Are you sure of this man?" he asks, finally. I dart a glance at Glenn, who seems to have sensed the shift in the air of the conversation.

"I am. He's wonderful and so good to me and Gracie. Aria adores him. She'll talk your ear off about him if you let her."

"Is he kind?" he asks, which is not a question I expected but is easy enough to answer.

"Yes! Oh yes. So kind. I've never seen anyone kinder other than . . ." I almost say "other than you," but I think better of it, knowing Glenn would be hurt by the comment.

"How do you know?" he asks, pressing the issue. I consider all the little services he's done for me, the thoughtful gestures like when he sent me Tito and Dr. Youngrin for Papà's funeral.

"There's too many ways to list."

"Is he kind when he gets nothing in return?" he asks. *When he gets nothing in return.* The sentence is an uncomfortable one to explore. How often are people kind for kindness's sake? Saints and priests, maybe, but real humans? Not as often.

"I love him," I say instead of answering the question.

"I'm sure you think you do," he says.

"What's that supposed to mean?" I ask, resentment crawling up my shoulders.

"Will you marry in the church?" Trombello asks the one question I'm dreading. I would love to marry Glenn in the church tomorrow, but I cannot. Even if he were a Catholic, he's been divorced . . . more than once. It would take an annulment. Maybe more than one. He says he's willing, but it's a long process and he doesn't want to wait. I don't want to wait either. So we'll be legally married now, make things right with the church soon, and have a Catholic ceremony then.

"Not yet," I say without expounding. I'll tell him more later when I don't feel so self-conscious.

Usually, I can find comfort and refuge in Trombello, but he's never found a way to support me when it comes to choosing a husband. And though I understand his protective nature after what he witnessed with Tom, I thought he'd be happy for me this time around—especially after watching me lose Larry. He tells me all the time I deserve happiness—why can't he ever be happy *for* me?

"Tantissimi auguri." He gives a brief congratulation and blessing and says he'll pray for us both. I thank him, without much emotion, unable to act my way through the disappointment of his response.

"I should go. I'll send you some clippings . . . if . . . if you want them."

"No, *mia cara amica*, of course I want them. God be with you," he says and hangs up. The flat dial tone hurts my ears.

"That man is in love with you," Glenn says from behind me. It's not the first time someone has made that accusation, but I still don't believe it. They don't understand how a man and a woman, a priest and a woman nonetheless, can have a nonromantic, nonsexual love. But it's possible. I've given up on my youthful fantasies of what my life would be like with a man like Trombello as my husband. Glenn is real. Glenn loves me. Glenn wants to take care of me. Glenn is *here*.

"Stop it, Glenn," I say forcefully, not up for a fight. Usually, I'd list all the reasons why Trombello can't have the kind of carnal feelings everyone else assumes a young man would have for a young woman, but I can't muster the energy.

Glenn snuffs out his cigarette in the ashtray and lets out a gush of smoke. I brace myself for his justified comeback, but instead, he rolls his eyes and laughs.

"Eh, you know what, you're right. Why the hell do I care about some priest?" He brushes a loose hair off my cheek and smooths my less-than-camera-ready hair, staring deep into my eyes. His normally green irises look three shades darker in the dim light of the office. He touches my nose and then traces my jawline to my bottom lip, which he presses flat with the flesh of his thumb. "You're mine now."

VIVIAN SNOW

Auction

Lot #14

Hand-painted postcard labeled: Amalfi Coast
 Watercolor on cardstock. Landscape of a small city overlooking the
sea with several boats in the water nearby.

NOLA. ITALIA. 05 OCT 1950

 Dear Mrs. Carver,
  Congratulations on your marriage.
  —A. Trombello
 (Translation from Italian)

CHAPTER 14

October 16, 1950
Carver Mansion
Beverly Hills, California

Glenn's "people" leaked the pictures to the press a month after we eloped at city hall. I'd worn a mint-green chiffon flare-cut dress with a wide waistband and a full skirt, paired with a velvet hat with floral trim. Glenn wore a beige Hallebrook fleck suit and a gray tie. Tito was our witness, on the payroll and easy to bribe into silence.

We spent the night at the Beverly Hills Hotel, making love moments after Glenn carried me over the threshold into our room, and then dining on steak and lobster through room service. I called Gracie and Aria from the hotel as Glenn tipped the bellboy delivering our dinner. I promised them both we'd have a real wedding, soon. Gracie asked if she could have a new dress, and Aria asked if I was happy. I said yes to both. We drank a whole bottle of Dom Pérignon and fell asleep in each other's arms before midnight.

Then, we went back to work the next day as though nothing had happened. Glenn said it was better this way. We'd control the announcement, and time it to line up with some press for the new film. Gracie and Aria were waiting in front of our small ranch house when Glenn and I finally returned home after the long day at the studio. With my left ring finger still bare, Glenn carried me over one more threshold and kissed me in the kitchen as Aria set the table for dinner.

I'm Glenn Carver's wife. For so long I was Anthony Santini's daughter and then the widow of a war hero. Now, I'm the wife of the great, award-winning American icon with a house up Woodhill Canyon Road, six cars in a warehouse-sized garage, a staff of six, and a television in every room, including our bedroom.

Our bedroom. It's strange to call the massive room with a king-size bed, vaulted ceiling, and see-through double-sided fireplace our bedroom. The sheets are an exotic silk Glenn special orders from China once a year. There are three closets—one for Glenn's suits, one for my dresses, and another for our shoes and furs. To think, only a handful of years ago, I shared a small bed with my little sister, made gnocchi from scratch, and hid Papà's liquor from him. Sometimes I feel like little Dorothy Gale from *The Wizard of Oz*.

"Still in bed, are we?" Glenn steps out of the bathroom with only a towel around his waist and a gust of steam trailing off his wet hair and shoulders. I groan and look at the clock. I've been lingering in the afterglow of my real-life dreamworld too long. We're supposed to be on set in an hour.

"Oh, gracious. I've lost track of time," I say, leaping out of bed and reaching for my robe.

"Why do you cover up so much? I buy you pretty nightgowns so I can see you in them," Glenn says as I tie the belt at my waist.

"This wall is made entirely of windows, Glenn. And all the other walls surrounding the pool are glass as well. If we had curtains . . ."

"Ah, you're a modest one, are you? You didn't seem modest last night or the night before or the night before or the night before . . ." He rolls his eyes up in his head as though remembering the hours of lovemaking we've indulged in since our union became official. I would normally blush, but when it's only the two of us, his enjoyment of our intimate moments makes me want to tackle him to make another one.

It'd been too many years since I let a man into my heart and bed. Glenn agreed to wait until we were wed to consummate our physical connection. I wanted to wait even though I was afraid—what if it wasn't good? What if our desire died once the true test came? But I shouldn't have worried. Glenn is a gentle, engaged, and adventurous lover, and I've started to find our sexual connection as electrifying as our emotional one.

I turn and open my robe to flash him quickly, giggling as he rushes across the room.

"That's not fair. Get over here." He lifts me by my hips, and I wrap my legs around his midsection.

"Whatever are you doing to me, Mr. Carver? My director will have my head," I say, mimicking the exaggerated drawl of a Southern belle.

"I'm sure he'll understand this one time," he growls, diving into the skin of my neck, nibbling softly like he wishes he could devour me. He tosses me on the bed, a lustful fire in his eyes.

"I'm sure he will," I say, dropping the robe from my shoulders and letting the spaghetti straps of my nightgown fall down my arms as he seductively pushes the creamy white silk up my pale thighs, forgetting entirely about windows or who might be watching.

An hour later we lie in bed, passing a cigarette back and forth, my naked legs draped over Glenn's. The sheets drip off the edges of the mattress.

"We're late," I say as he takes another puff. I don't normally smoke, but lately it's been fun to add the buzz of the smoke to the hum of my body after my time with Glenn.

"I know. I know," he says, forcing a long stream of smoke out of his gathered lips. He offers me the cigarette, but I decline, so he puts it out in the glass ashtray on his nightstand. "Time to visit the real world, I guess."

"Only visit," I say, rolling to my stomach so I can watch him stroll across the room to his walk-in closet.

"Only visit," he agrees, amused at my demand. I rush to the bathroom with the silk top sheet covering my breasts to wash my face.

"This is better than Oz," I call to Glenn, continuing my thoughts from earlier out loud.

"Huh?" he asks, and I realize he doesn't know what I'm talking about.

"This fantasy world we're living in together. It's better than Oz, don't you think?" I shout as I comb my hair.

"I don't think anyone in Oz was doing what we just did." He laughs, and I join him. I love how beautifully our happiness harmonizes.

"I guess not. But those munchkins had to come from somewhere."

"You just made me imagine the Lollipop Guild in the most demeaning way," Glenn says, exiting the closet fully dressed. I'm back in my robe but naked underneath.

"Still thinking of the Lollipop Guild?" I ask, revealing my shoulder.

"The Lollipop who?" Glenn stares, his shirt buttons only half-fastened.

"Nothing. Nothing. We're late!" I remind myself as much as I do him. If I'm not careful, we'll get distracted again and never make it to work. I leap past his playful, wiggling hands and duck into the lines of clothes in my closet.

All of them are mine, or so he says, but I'd never seen them before I moved in. All of my clothes still hang in a closet in my house on Laurel Street. I told him to send this new wardrobe back, but he refused. I'm still getting used to Glenn's generosity. I don't know where all my clothes will fit once we get them moved over. Aria and I can share a closet, or Gracie's room will have two closets so I could fill one with my things until I figure out how to sneak some of these items back to wherever they came from.

For now, I put on a simple pink cotton dress and a pair of fresh stockings and then tie a scarf around my wild hair, leaving it for my hairdresser to tame. Oversized sunglasses will cover my makeup-less face and add the essential layer of mystery and glamour the world expects from a movie star.

By the time we get to set, we're late but not so late that the day has been wasted. Glenn holds the door for me, and we enter Stage Four from the side.

"Do you think anyone will notice?" I ask him, hoping the preliminary tasks of the day will distract the cast and crew from our tardiness. I lift my sunglasses, but before my eyes can adjust to the dim lighting in the studio, loud applause echoes through the soundstage, and every member of the cast and crew pops out from behind set pieces, behind chairs, and under tables.

"Surprise!" they shout in unison. Music starts playing, and a cake is wheeled out with a little bride and groom drawn in frosting with *Congratulations* written underneath.

"Did you know about this?" I ask, mouth hanging open.

"I had a hunch," Glenn says through happily clenched teeth, smiling as the cheers end. Cameras flash in the background.

"And you let me leave the house like this?" I ask. I put my sunglasses back on just in case there are newspaper photographers out there snapping pictures of me without my "nose powdered."

"You look lovely, my dear," he says, dipping me in a kiss suited for the silver screen, and the room erupts again. The cake is wheeled away, and we accept congratulations from the crew and a few cast members, some halfway through hair and makeup. Brando sits sullenly on a stack of boxes in the back corner of the room, like a child whose sister got the biggest cookie.

The last person to approach us is Darryl Zanuck, head of Twentieth Century-Fox. I've only met him a few times: when I auditioned, when I was called back, and when I signed my contract. We've often been in the same vicinity, at red carpets and parties, but Archie takes care of all our business negotiations. Zanuck and Glenn have a long-standing friendship/rivalry. There's a rumor the two once fought over the same woman. She tragically died while miscarrying a child that belonged to one of the men, but Glenn assured me that the story was nonsense. He claims Zanuck, despite being a powerful producer and executive, always dreamed of being a famous director but couldn't cut it.

"Well, congratulations, you two," he says, shaking Glenn's hand ferociously. Glenn gives back a hearty shake in return.

"Thank you, sir. Did you arrange this?" I ask, watching the line form around the cake table, remembering when I sang at the USO and we'd wait in line for sugarless punch and stale cookies.

"Just a little wedding present. I'd have done more if I'd known sooner," Mr. Zanuck says, folding his arms, a silent message underneath the comment.

"We thought it'd be better to keep things hush-hush, you know, until I had things settled on my side," Glenn tells him.

"Sure. Sure," Mr. Zanuck says, his mustache twisting as he assesses my outfit. I lift my sunglasses, thinking it might be better to see a plain-faced me rather than a woman unwilling to make eye contact.

"Thank you again, Mr. Zanuck. This was lovely," I say with a smile, not sure if the unpolished version of Vivian Snow will work as well at softening a man's heart as the more carefully crafted one.

He shakes his head and tsks.

"How old are you again, dear?" he asks.

"Twenty-six, sir," I say, polite and honest. Most girls would bluff about their age or say something flirty about a lady never telling, especially since twenty-six is nearly ancient in this business. But I've spent too much of my life lying about things. Now that I'm settled with the right man and with a signed contract and plenty of awards buzz, I want to be honest.

"Older than the last one at least. And can act," Zanuck says off-handedly. I don't flinch.

"Yes, well. We have a busy schedule today, so I'll need to ask you to kindly shove off," Glenn says. "That is, unless you have any other questions you'd like to ask my wife." I try not to smile at Glenn's response. It's just aggressive enough to make his point without starting a fight.

"Indeed," Zanuck says, glancing around the room. He gestures at the half-devoured cake. "I'll make sure this gets cleaned up right after you both get a piece. And I'll send a bit home to your daughter. You do have a daughter, is that right, Miss Snow?"

"Yes. I do. And she'd love that." I continue to play nice in hopes the conversation is almost over. Glenn warned me Zanuck would be put off by our relationship—it was another reason we eloped. Zanuck turns a blind eye to extramarital relationships at Twentieth Century-Fox, even if they fester and burst. But marriage? Not unless he's approved it, and the couple has kowtowed and kissed his ring. But Glenn believes everyone is too afraid of Zanuck. He insisted that if we just moved forward, Zanuck couldn't do anything to hurt us.

"And for your kids, Glenn? How many pieces should I send on?"

Zanuck is pushing Glenn past long-suffering. He glares.

"None, thank you."

"Right, indeed." Mr. Zanuck takes a stride away and then another, his hands in his pockets and his head dipped like he's watching his footsteps. "Oh, I'm sorry. I almost forgot. I have one last gift." He snaps, and a young woman in a tan suit rushes over, holding a legal-size manila envelope. "Here you go, dear. Open it when I'm gone. And to both of you, again, congratulations."

He leaves the mysterious envelope in my hands. It's thick. I'm not sure what could be inside, but I can tell from the color of Glenn's face that whatever it is it can't be good.

"I'll take it." He snatches it, leaving me stunned. He unties the red string keeping the flap closed and pulls out a stack of papers. His lips move as he reads the first page in silence and then without warning takes the whole packet and hurls it across the room, papers scattering.

"Damn him!" Glenn yells at full volume, bringing all activity in the soundstage to a screeching halt. It becomes so instantaneously silent that I can hear each piece of paper as it flutters to the cement floor. "Damn him to hell," Glenn curses again, kicking at the pages and rushing out without explanation.

Lulu, my hairdresser, stares at me wide eyed, and I can see Brando skulking across the room as though he sees an opportunity to swoop in during a crisis. The production assistant is frantically picking up pages, and Lulu helps smooth them into a pile. One sheet lands by the pointy toe of my shoe.

I untie my headscarf and drop it on the floor so it obscures the page. I lift it off the concrete discreetly, the first line catching my eye.

"Will be loaned to Metro-Goldwyn-Mayer for no less than six months or the equivalent of three films including promotion and . . ." It's a studio loan contract to MGM. I search the typed page, already knowing whose name I'll find there.

"Ah, that's the last one. Thanks." The PA snaps the paper out of my grip and adds it to his stack.

I don't need to see the name to know it's true. A Twentieth Century-Fox contract player is being traded on loan to MGM. This actress likely won't get a say whether she stays or goes, and she definitely won't get a say in what films she'll do. She can break her contract, but that would mean losing her stability and potentially her career. I've seen it happen. A trade can be great for a career, but it can also be a death knell if there are no restrictions in place on the types of roles an actress will be required to accept or which directors she'll be forced to work with. And what's worse is an actress has very little legal recourse in this situation. Even Bette Davis was placed on the blacklist when she pushed back on a trade and went head-to-head with Jack Warner and the whole studio system. Her massive career still has not recovered. But it's not Bette Davis's name on that loan document.

It's mine.

VIVIAN SNOW

Auction

Lot #15

Hand-painted postcard labeled: Italian House Sparrow
　　Watercolor and black ink on cardstock. Brown-and-white bird with
black eyes and yellow beak.

　NOLA. ITALIA. 10 FEB 1951

　　Vivian—
　　　*To hear your voice has been a great blessing but
　　how shall I practice my drawing if not for our letters?
　　This bird made me think of your father's name for
　　you.*
　　　Always—A. Trombello
　　(Translation from Italian)

CHAPTER 15

April 5, 1951
Carver Mansion
Beverly Hills, California

The phone rings in the hall, and I count the trills.

One.

I hold my breath, the moment between rings feeling like an eternity. Glenn doesn't move, dead to the world like he is most nights, thanks to sleeping pills and a few nightcaps. I used to feel lonely when he'd slip away from reality, and for a short time, I tried to numb that pain by joining him. But then the calls started, and I had a reason to stay awake.

Two.

I strain to hear. It could be Aria calling. She may be having another one of her anxiety spells where she's up all night pacing, or perhaps Gracie has another ear infection. If it's my sister on the line, I'll grab my shoes instead of my slippers, I'll find my dress instead of my robe, and I'll walk the half mile to the small house my sister and my daughter moved into together.

It's hard to blame Aria for the sad spells—we'd lived together for one lovely, bittersweet year after Papà's passing. When I married Glenn I'd assumed we'd live together in his palatial estate as one big happy family. But the room I'd dreamed of painting pink for Gracie is still a pasty yellow with two generic twin beds and Glenn's adult son Peter's oak dresser. And the secluded blue bedroom I'd hoped would be Aria's, with its fireplace and en suite bathroom, is still filled with stuffed poodles and dripping with floor-to-ceiling gauzy white curtains. It looks out on the backyard and has access to the gravel trail through the mossy grass and into a greenhouse of exotic flowers.

But everything changed after that horrible surprise party. That night, Glenn was waiting in our bedroom with a demand—I must reject Zanuck's trade. He vowed to protect me and my career with his power and prestige, insisting every film he made would have a part for me in it no matter what the studios said. I considered it, surrendering not only my future but my family's to him, but the thought of it terrified me. I'd worked too hard to get here and I'd sacrificed too much along the way. So I gently refused to break my contract with Twentieth Century-Fox, pleading for his understanding.

Glenn flipped his lid, tearing through the house, knocking over thousand-dollar vases and tossing my best furs in the pool. He said I clearly didn't trust him, that I was like his other wives who chased money and fame. And when I started on my first MGM film, he stopped coming to family dinner. He threw away Gracie's little drawings and Aria's hand-picked bouquets. And at night, he slept so far away in our giant bed that the silk sheets grew cold between us.

At first, I was sure he'd leave me, but neither of us mentioned the word "separation" or even worse—"divorce." I'm sure he'll warm again as soon as my trade expires with MGM, and he'll love my family like he promised he would. Until then, Aria and Gracie live nearby in a three-bedroom bungalow that feels more like home than this giant palace of a place. Gracie cries herself to sleep, and so does Aria, and if I were honest with them both—so do I.

The phone continues to ring, and Glenn hasn't moved. I've waited and listened longer than necessary. I slide out of bed and wrap myself in a pink silk robe. It's a warm night, so I leave my slippers behind and stealthily move into the hallway without so much as a click of the door handle.

Since marrying Glenn, I've kept Trombello's postcards in a box at the bungalow. No trace of my priestly friend is allowed inside the walls of Glenn's home. I usually don't write back.

Ari has been deeply concerned about my depressive state and how many pills I take to cope with it. She stole Trombello's address off one of the postcards and wrote to ask him to try to cheer me up. She confessed her involvement when I received the letter from Trombello asking for a call. At first I agreed to the call in order to placate Aria and wrote him back with the house number and told him he must call at night. It's the only time I don't feel watched. I know he feels the same.

During our first midnight conversation I remembered the miracle of Trombello's companionship, and he seemed to sense that I needed him more than ever. Plus, I can't take any sleeping pills if I want to be aware enough to hear his calls, and my craving for his friendship is even stronger than for any drug. Every time I hear the phone ring in the darkness, I remember what hope feels like. It's fresh and buoyant, and I haven't felt it in so long. We're both breaking rules, but they feel like they're only meant for everyone else. And it's worth it.

I slip into Glenn's wood-paneled office. The tightly woven carpet does little to muffle my footsteps, but I'm less worried about waking my husband than I used to be. Trombello has called once a fortnight for nearly two months now, and Glenn hasn't missed me in bed beside him even once. I've built a friendship with one of the international operators. She's given us her direct line and knows the drill—she rings the line five times and holds for me to pick up. I affirm the call and the reversed charges, and then she connects us through a tinny, echoey line. She's probably on the line listening, but I don't mind. I need this. My talks with Trombello are my medicine.

"Buongiorno, mia cara amica. You've come at last."

We speak mostly in English so our conversations can remain private on his end. He calls me from the only phone in the rectory, and often that means others are nearby.

"Did it seem longer than usual for me to pick up?" I curl my legs underneath my body and nestle into Glenn's oversized leather desk chair.

"Maybe a bit, but it could be all in my mind," he says. His concern touches me.

"It's a big house. Sometimes it's a wonder I don't get lost."

"Ha," he chuckles, but I detect bitterness at my mention of the home I live in with Glenn. "I'm glad you found your way."

"Me too," I say, ignoring what he implies but leaves unspoken.

"So," he says in a leading way, "are you going to tell me what happened?"

I know what he's talking about—I was nominated for Best Supporting Actress this year for the Golden Globes, Cannes Film Festival, and the Academy Awards. Glenn was nominated for Best Director and the coveted award—Best Motion Picture.

I stare at the shelf of golden statues.

"I won," I whisper into the phone, barely believing it's true. When my name was announced at the Academy Awards last month in front of the audience brimming with talent and beauty, I thought I was hallucinating. Glenn had to nudge me to stand and take my place onstage. I thanked all the right people, sent Gracie and Aria a kiss, and showed my gratitude for the other nominees. Though I'm sure none of us actually like each other, we do a damn fine job of making it seem like we do. It's part of the job, the fake camaraderie, but the truth is every pretty face and nice figure is a threat, especially when that face and figure has been labeled an "up-and-coming star" and is married to one of the most prolific directors in Hollywood. Glenn won neither of the awards he was nominated for and finished the night cold and jealous. We went home in silence, skipping the Governors Ball and after-parties. I haven't let myself celebrate, dodging praise in order to protect Glenn's ego. But I allow Trombello's compliments, and I bask in them.

"*Che meraviglia!* I knew it! I knew you would win. I'm so proud," he gushes, and I blush.

"I still can hardly believe it. There were so many famous people there. I was starstruck."

"*You* are a star, *mia cara amica*. And famous. Your face is on the screen here. The words are covered over in an odd way with a voice that isn't yours, but the rest is you."

Trombello's English continues to improve, but sometimes he has such a delightful way of saying something simple.

"It's called dubbing, and I agree—it can look ridiculous. I guess this means you watch my films, then?"

"I give myself away?"

"A little. But I'm glad. Gracie is begging to see my next one, but I think she's still a little young to watch her mamma kiss men on a big screen. She'd be horrified, I think."

He laughs and agrees, and our conversation transitions to more relatable topics, which is always a relief for me. Everyone wants to talk about my work and wants a picture or a quote, but I cherish talking with those who sincerely care about me and my family.

"Gracie is well, I presume?"

"She's growing and won't stop," I joke, as I normally do. "She can read now. The other day she read me a whole picture book after dinner. Not even one of the easy ones—one with more words than drawings. She's very smart."

"Like her mother, I think?"

"Like her zia, more like it." I deflect the compliment.

"And how is Aria?" Trombello asks, and I hesitate before answering.

"She's in one of her low times. Now that Gracie's in school full time and she doesn't have to take care of Papà or Mamma or me, I thought she'd be happy, but ever since I moved in here she's been unwell."

"This I know to be true. She wrote last week and said she's thinking poor thoughts. She thinks you do not care."

She writes to Trombello? I didn't know she'd be daring enough to continue to reach out to a man she barely knows, even if he is a priest. She must be desperate.

"Of course I care."

"She's lost much in her life. Perhaps with more stillness she can see what she's missing?"

He sounds like a philosopher sometimes. I'm sure it comes from writing homilies and giving advice at confession, but whatever it is, it's like he's lived ten times longer than I have, though we're only a few years apart in age.

"Perhaps, but I don't know how to help her," I say, feeling desperate. I'm trying to understand my sister and not fear her roller-coaster emotions. "But I also worry we're like our mother," I confess.

"You? Like your mamma? No, *mia cara amica*. Don't go looking for troubles that are not yours."

"I know. I know," I say. This is not the first time we've had this conversation. I've often worried I might develop Mother's illness, that Tom's violent end might be a sign of a dangerous personality developing in the darkest part of my mind.

And now Aria's peaks and valleys bring me back to the same concern—that my mother has passed on a ticking time bomb that will at some point explode and spiral us into our own prisons.

"She needs some noise, perhaps?" Trombello offers, but I'm not sure what he's trying to say. "Not noise, but—what is the word? Occupation?"

"She was supposed to go to a gardening class every Tuesday and Thursday, but Tito told me she never came out, not when he knocked or beeped or anything. She told me she didn't want to meet new people, she wanted to be at home, alone. I've tried to have her work here when"—I dodge a near mention of Glenn—"when there's no one home to disturb her, but she says she's unhappy here. She wants to return to Indiana and be near our mother."

Mamma hasn't made the long trip to California yet. She's healthy and stable at Norways, and Margot is there to care for her. Plus, Glenn thinks it's risky to have her close by. He's concerned the tabloids will catch wind of the story and tarnish my reputation. I'll move her here, soon. Just, not yet.

"And so, why not?" Trombello asks like it's the solution we've been reaching for. I sigh and rub my temples.

"I told her she can go, but she wants to take Gracie with her and—I've spent too many years away from my daughter. I can't let them leave again. Besides, Gracie loves California. The snow would bite through her warm spirit, I know it would."

I've convinced myself I'm not being selfish. Gracie needs me. Even though we don't live in the same house anymore, I can still stop by the bungalow and kiss her goodnight or stay for dinner or catch dessert. Some mornings when Glenn and I have different schedules, I can even ride with her to school.

"Perhaps in some time, she will change her mind."

"Something has to change or . . . I don't know, Padre, she might lose her mind. I'm not overreacting, I promise it to you."

"If this is your sincere concern, perhaps she can see a doctor?" Trombello suggests. It's a reasonable idea, one I've played with before. One I've tried, in a way.

"She sees Dr. Youngrin once a week." I'm not proud of this measure. I've learned a lot about Dr. Youngrin in the past few years. He's not only Glenn's doctor, but a doctor to the stars used by most of the major studios. The whole film industry might come to a sudden halt if the pep pills, vitamin shots, and sleeping aids suddenly ran out. Youngrin isn't the only doctor with an open prescription pad and a willing pen. They're everywhere in this town. But Youngrin has *some* humanity, some true care for his patients, and keeps strict confidentiality, so he's my best option for Aria.

Trombello tsks. "That man? The one with the pills? I thought you were wary of him."

"I am, but Ari won't go to another doctor, and Glenn is worried news will get out to the press if we force her somewhere. Dr. Youngrin is very loyal to the family . . ."

"To your husband, you mean."

"Yes, my husband. But even with his faults, Glenn does care about my family. He's taken over payments for my mother's care at Norways, and he pays for Gracie's private school and dance lessons and . . ."

"Money. It's all only money. Is money love?" he asks in a way that sounds identical to how my father used to speak to me when he disagreed with my decisions. I don't like how it makes me feel. I scoff. This is why I avoid speaking of Glenn to him. If money is the root of all evil, then Glenn must be a close second in Trombello's eyes.

"Of course not. I mean, I can afford all those things. I just think it's kind that he wanted to provide them . . ."

"Kind," he says with heavy irony but then clears his throat, likely noticing my silence. I know he's right—Glenn isn't the knight in shining armor I thought he'd be. He's angry with me much of the time, and when he's not using my body in bed, he seems to find my mind useless and annoying.

"He is my husband, Trombello," I say, sounding resigned. "He's not perfect," I admit, "I know that. But he's not a man of God who prays all day as you do." My throat tightens, and I'm sure he can hear it.

"You deserve better than he gives you."

"He's what I have. I cannot divorce without breaking away from God. Our religion makes it clear, and after what happened with Tom . . ."

"I know, *mia cara amica*. But you've not been reading your scripture, have you?" he scolds warmly. He sent me a quote not too long ago, from the book of James, telling me I should read it every day.

"Mercy triumphs over judgment." I recite the simple line as though I'm in Sunday school. "I do memorize things for a living, you know."

"For someone who remembers so well, you seem to forget even more proficiently," he points out.

"I forget proficiently?" I laugh, and it feels so good that I do it again.

"It wasn't *so* funny," Trombello says, also laughing now.

"I know. It really wasn't." I grasp my belly and lean over, the curled cord from the phone wrapping around me as I slowly turn in circles in the chair.

"Wait. Are you making joke at my money?"

"Your money?" I'm sure at this point he said it wrong on purpose to make me laugh again. "You mean at your expense?"

"Yes! At my expen—" He doesn't finish the word as the line goes dead.

"Damn it," I curse and look at the receiver as though it will have some answers. International calls aren't always reliable. The operator should call back in a moment when she reestablishes the line. I spin around in the chair to unwind the cord so I can hang up the phone to wait.

Glenn stands on the other side of the desk with his finger on the switch hook. His eyes are red, and his hair is disheveled. He looks drunk more than drugged. He had enough of a clear head to put on the robe and slippers Gracie gave him for Christmas. How much did he hear?

"Glenn. I'm sorry. Did I wake you? Gracie had a nightmare," I lie. Primal fear kicks in, and my first layer of defense against a man who scares me is to fib, or that's what I learned from dealing with Papà and Tom. Glenn doesn't always scare me but—tonight he does. There's fire in his blurry, intoxicated eyes. And it's pointed right at me.

"You must think I'm stupid," he says, shaking his head, his graying hair scattered across his forehead.

"No, no. Of course not."

He snatches the phone from my hand and doesn't bother to unwind the cord that ties me to the chair. The last bit of the plastic coil is taut against my neck. He yanks on it, causing the chair to sway from side to side.

"You know I see the phone bill, don't you?" he says, tightening the cable across my throat. I shriek, remembering when Tom had his hands around my neck in that locker room and how the world went gray and then black. My heart races. I can't regulate my breathing.

"Your bullshit tears aren't going to work on me, Miss Snow. I know what acting looks like," he says, slamming the handset on the table, the cord slapping against my throat, making my head whip back reflexively.

"I'm not acting," I whimper.

"I believe you. I've never seen you do anything this good with cameras rolling, that's for sure." I ignore his insult. I just want to make it out alive.

Make it out alive? I'm clearly confused. This is Glenn, not Tom.

"Please, Glenn. Let me go. I can explain. I swear."

"I don't want to hear it!" he shrieks. "You're all the same. Actresses. You take and take and take and then leave."

"I'm not leaving, Glenn. I'm your wife. I won't leave you."

"You already have," he says, coming around the desk and blocking any chance of escape with his body.

"I haven't. It was only Trombello. He helps me grow closer to God. You can't be worried about *that*." But I know it's not only Trombello he's speaking of. In his mind I left him for MGM. I was unwilling to sacrifice my career for my husband.

"You'll never speak to that man again, do you understand me?" he says in a low, firm voice. I recoil from his touch. He grazes my skin with every rotation of the chair untangling me from the cord. He places the phone back on the cradle and stares at me, waiting for a response.

"But he's a—" I'm about to say "priest" when the phone rings. It must be Trombello.

One.

Two.

Three.

Glenn picks it up.

"Put him through," he snarls at the operator. After a brief pause, a deep voice murmurs on the other side of the line.

"Stop calling my wife," Glenn orders plain and simple and smashes the phone down. "You know I could divorce you for this," he says, cold and sardonic. "I could tell Hedda about your little priest and let the newspapers eat you alive."

"You wouldn't." I try to stand but he shoves me down again. Hedda Hopper, gossip columnist and life ruiner. I could lose everything. Everything I've worked for, everything that's just at my fingertips if I can only keep moving forward. Glenn Carver giveth and Glenn Carver taketh away.

"Just try me," he says, inches from my face. The skin on my neck burns from where the cord rubbed against it, and his hot breath makes it feel on fire.

The phone rings again. Damn it, Trombello.

This time Glenn snatches it after the first trill and offers it to me.

"Hello? Hello? Viviana? Are you there?" Trombello shouts through the phone. I remind myself of reality just like I did when Trombello protested my engagement last year. Glenn is real. My daughter is real. My career, though fragile, is real. Trombello is no more than a voice on a crackly phone line or a few scribbles on a postcard.

I take the phone, my eyes connected to Glenn's, my breath shaking along with the rest of my body.

"Never call me again," I say as though I'm speaking to my worst enemy. Glenn nods, takes the phone back, places it on the cradle, and then disconnects it.

"Should we go to bed?" Glenn asks, casually backing away, offering to help me up.

I let him assist me to my feet, shivering, suddenly overwhelmingly cold.

"Here, darling." Glenn drapes his bathrobe over my shoulders. The belt to the gown drags on the floor, and he ties it considerately around my waist. "There you go. Wouldn't want you to trip." He puts his arm around me as he guides me back to the bedroom.

I try to look grateful for his sudden change, a tenderness I haven't felt since the early days of our marriage. I crawl under the covers, where Glenn waits for me with eager hands that have forgotten how close they were to harming me. I allow him to take me, fighting back tears, as somewhere in the house a phone rings over and over and over again.

VIVIAN SNOW

Auction

Lot #16

Hand-painted postcard labeled: Tuscan Sunflower Fields
    Watercolor on cardstock. Rows of blooming sunflowers on a rolling hill.

NOLA. ITALIA. 06 AUG 1951

> *Vivian—*
>   *I can see a field of sunflowers from the rectory window as I write. I watch them chase the sun across the sky with great faith. I pray you follow your own light.*
>   *—A. Trombello*
>   (Translation from Italian)

CHAPTER 16

September 9, 1951
Carver Mansion
Beverly Hills, California

"What do you think?" Glenn asks. He's staring at me from the love seat as I read the script for his newest film: *Marry Me Friday*. It's a playful romantic comedy with a strong but loveable leading lady, and he's promised me the part. It's my first film back at Twentieth Century-Fox after being traded to MGM, and Glenn made it clear he had first dibs.

"I love it!" I answer honestly as I read the last line, wishing life had happy endings like the movies. "But, Mick Mitcham? He's not my favorite screenwriter, you know that."

Mick's kept his distance the past several years. Same with just about every suitor from my first year under contract at Twentieth Century-Fox. Glenn's the kind of guy you don't cross. He has a habit of getting rid of anyone who stands in his way.

"Eh, you don't have to worry about that guy. He'll be on his best behavior. I guarantee."

"Well, if you're sure." I look down at the screenplay. I want this part. I haven't felt this way about anything in a long time. I *need* this part. It's light, it's funny, I get to sing and potentially even dance a little.

"I'm more than sure. Hey! We're in business, baby!" Glenn picks me up and swings me around the living room, my feet nearly hitting the edge of the coffee table and the arm of the couch. I playfully slap at his shoulder and back until he sets me down like a ballet dancer releasing his dance partner after a lift. I straighten my dress and smile so big it hurts my face. Before I can get away, he yanks me down into his lap, arms around my waist, entrapping me. I laugh and wiggle against his light grip.

"Hey!"

"You were too far away. This is better." He nuzzles my face and kisses down my neck as a hot thrill shoots through my nervous system.

"I'm not complaining."

Glenn pulls the strap of my dress off my shoulder, leaving his line of light kisses unobstructed. I keep speaking, my train of thought barely coherent.

"I'll get the papers ready. We'll start shooting in two weeks, three tops."

"We can tell Archie tomorrow. Make it official."

"Mm-hmm," he says, working a hand up my skirt, caressing the skin at my thigh and then hip. He nibbles at my neck, and I toss my head back to give him better access, a bit breathless.

"And you don't think you need to tell Zanuck about—you know . . . ," I trail off. His kisses stop cold, his hands go still.

"We shouldn't tell anyone just yet. Not till we've started shooting and there's no turning back," he orders, all desire gone from his touch.

This is how it happens—he loves me, passionately, unwaveringly, until he doesn't. Usually the "doesn't" part happens when I don't do exactly what he wants me to do, my director on and off camera. And right now he doesn't want me to tell anyone about the secret we've been keeping for the past month.

I sit up, resting on his knee, and tread lightly.

"Not even the girls?" I wanted to tell Aria and Gracie tonight at family dinner, then the cat will be out of the bag about the little bun in my oven. A baby. This time, a baby with a father who is alive and able to participate in his or her upbringing. Until now it's seemed a more impossible dream than any of the films I've starred in or awards I've been given.

"No one," he says with finality. I should be used to disappointment. I guess I *am* used to it, but I'm not immune to it, and I feel this setback acutely.

"We can't keep it a secret forever," I mumble, working to hide my frustration and keep the peace. Gracie was a secret for so long, I don't want to do it again. Plus, babies have a way of making themselves known.

"Not forever, dear. I never said forever," he says condescendingly as though I'm a child who still thinks babies come from the stork. "I *have* done this before."

He says that every time he brings up his previous experience as an expectant father. It doesn't bother me, his other kids. I have a child from another father, and he has six kids, most of them grown. The younger two live with their mother in Georgia, who only lets Glenn see them once, maybe twice a year. He misses them and I know it's a constant pain—this loss. I'm sure another baby looks like another potential goodbye. Not to mention the complications this creates for my career—our careers.

"I know, Glenn. I know," I say, twisting his fine hair in my fingers, feeling deflated. I have no choice but to accept his decree. It takes longer for Glenn to explode than Papà, but it's just as frightening when it happens. At least after an explosion, the tension is released nearly immediately. His coldness, on the other hand, is long lasting and brings with it a feeling of desperation I can't seem to evade. Through my marriage to Glenn, I've learned frost can burn as mercilessly as a flame.

I button my lip, kiss his cheek, and saunter into the kitchen. I change the subject and speak to him through the serving hatch as though I didn't notice the change in his behavior, placing items in a netted grocery bag.

"We're still having dinner at the bungalow at six. I'm heading over to teach Gracie how to make ravioli and focaccia."

"You're leaving already?" He folds up the newspaper and peers through the hatch, letting out a heated huff showing he's annoyed.

"It's Sunday. We always have family dinner on Sundays," I remind him. Sunday is the only day we all have off during any busy shooting schedule. Glenn used to beg for an invitation to our Sunday meals, claiming it's better than any Italian restaurant in town. We'd eat, laugh, and drink into the late hours of the night. "We're using Aria's garlic. It's finally ready, and she's been begging me to try it out. She's doing so well. Dr. Youngrin started her on a new medication and it's doing wonders. I was skeptical at first but—"

"Garlic upsets my stomach," Glenn interrupts while I have my back turned.

"It does? But I used it in the lasagna just last week, and you seemed fine." My rebuttal trails off when I turn around to an empty room. He's gone, and the door to his study is closed.

My heart sinks, and I have to brace myself against the counter to keep my knees from buckling. It reminds me of when I used to pluck the petals off the daisies each spring, chanting in a singsong voice, *He loves me, he loves me not, he loves me, he loves me not, he loves me . . .* until I ran out of the delicate white adornment. I never know which it is—he loves me, or he loves me not. It can change from one minute to the next, leaving my head spinning and my cheeks damp.

I use a dish towel to soak up my tears before they ruin my mascara. No one can know I've been crying. Glenn would find my tears irritating and push me further away, Aria would see them as another reason for me to leave Glenn, and Gracie wouldn't hesitate to tell anyone and everyone about her sad mamma.

For now I'll keep it all to myself. The baby will change things, I'm sure of it. Even with the temporary complications, babies have a softening quality to hard hearts. Just look at Papà with Gracie or how he was with my baby brother, Tony.

"We're all counting on you, darling," I say to my unborn child, knowing I'm asking a lot but also knowing he or she might be the only way to unite my fractured family.

I've seen it, his gentleness. When I first told him I suspected I was pregnant, he took me in his arms and kissed me tenderly, promised to name a boy after my Papà and a girl after his long-deceased mother. And when my first bout of nausea hit, he made me ginger tea, rubbed my feet, and called Dr. Youngrin for some natural remedies and vitamins. I don't know what I'll do if he stops wanting this baby like he stopped wanting Gracie, like he stopped wanting Aria, like he often stops wanting me.

VIVIAN SNOW

Auction

Lot #17

Hand-drawn postcard labeled: Festa dei Gigli (Lily Festival)
  Black ink on cardstock. Crowd of men carrying large wooden obelisks through a town square.

NOLA. ITALIA. 02 SEPT 1951

> *Vivian—*
>   *I pick up my pen to write you nearly every day, sometimes I cannot resist the temptation.*
>   *—A. Trombello*
>   (Translation from Italian)

CHAPTER 17

December 16, 1951
Aria's Home
Hollywood, California

I lecture myself internally as Tito drives me to the bungalow. Another argument with Glenn about Sunday dinner. When I say argument I mean I had the audacity to ask him if he was having dinner with us, and he grew icy and made up another excuse. I struggle to hold my emotions nowadays.

I'm far into my fourth month of pregnancy, and though the doctor predicts my nausea will pass soon, I still struggle to keep food down. My hands shake uncontrollably most days, and I have a thirst I can't quench. I've been tested for blood incompatibility, diabetes, hypertension, and all sorts of other ailments. But to no avail.

"Some babies give their mom a harder time than others," my obstetrician explained blithely, as though I'm overreacting to barely being able to function. Dr. Youngrin recommended I take time off from shooting, but Glenn had a fit at that suggestion. The doctor and I haven't been in the house at the same time since.

The shooting schedule for *Marry Me Friday* is intense, and I'm sure my swelling midsection is a major reason why. The tailor had to let out my skirt three times already. Glenn refuses to make the baby announcement official, though the whole crew seems to have a silent understanding based on rumors that I'm expecting, but thankfully the gossip hasn't spread outside of Stage Six.

Mick is around more than I'd like but keeps his distance. Really, everyone is keeping their distance. Crew members I used to joke with or grab a drink with now treat me like I'm a stranger. It's because things are different—I've received important awards, my career has exploded nearly overnight, and I'm married to the director. I wish they could see I'm still me despite marrying Glenn, though I have a feeling many people believe my name is now in lights *because* of who I married. The gossip pages never tire of writing about me, and I find myself dodging cameras and reporters nearly everywhere I go.

The car hits a bump, and the little bit of food I've been able to keep down today threatens to erupt.

"Sorry, miss," Tito apologizes. He knows I'm unwell, probably knows about the baby since he drives me to the obstetrician's office for appointments. His anxious glances through the rearview mirror only make me more self-conscious. I wish Glenn were here to rub my back or bring me tea. He has moments of thoughtfulness that make me think I've gotten him back to who he was in the early days of our relationship, but then he follows up with some cruel comment or he disappears for days without explanation.

It's safer for my heart to assume I won't see him tonight for family dinner. He'll likely stay out with whoever he's using as an excuse to play hooky, and when he gets home, he'll sleep in one of the spare rooms, saying he didn't want to disturb me. And I'll just let it happen so he doesn't use my "bad mood" as a reason to leave again. Damn it, I hate that about myself.

What other choice do I have, though? I don't want to leave Glenn. I want him to open his eyes and see what a wonderful thing he has in his life. I want him to be grateful for his family and to want to be home with us. I know I acquiesce more often than I should, more than Aria thinks I should. But "blessed are the peacemakers," and I care more about peace than getting my way.

I gave up on "my way" the night Glenn caught me on the phone with Trombello. Besides his threats to my career, he followed up with threats to pull strings and get Trombello reprimanded for his "unpriestly behavior." I won't get Trombello in trouble, and I can't let anyone look too far into our past or someone might figure out our real secret, which is far more dangerous than whatever Glenn is worried about.

A familiar car is parked out in front of the bungalow—Dr. Youngrin. My opinion of the doctor has changed over the years. Despite his willingness to be my husband's personal pharmacy, he's always shown me great compassion, especially when it comes to Aria. If I didn't know better, I'd think the handsome and mysterious middle-aged never-married doctor has a crush on my little sister. He's too old for her, and she's too shy to ever allow anything to happen between them, but it's softened my heart toward the physician, especially since lately he seems like less of a spy for Glenn and more of an ally for me and "the girls."

Tito offers to carry my bag into the house, but I see Dr. Youngrin walking down the front path, and I'd like a word with him alone.

"Thanks, Tito, I can manage. See you at ten?"

"Ten it is," he says, never complaining about the hours I keep.

By the time I make it up the sidewalk, Dr. Youngrin notices me. He waves.

"Miss Snow, good to see you," he says with a tip of his hat and a grin that only confirms my suspicions about his feelings for my sister. "I hope you're well."

Dr. Youngrin was the first to know of my condition—in fact, he knew before I did and definitely before Glenn. Youngrin referred me to a well-known obstetrician whom he called "a colleague and a friend."

"This one's not making it easy on me," I say, resisting the urge to touch my belly again in case any cameras or reporters are watching.

"You should rest more." He looks me over. I'm sure he can see the darkness under my eyes and my sunken cheeks. Every ounce I lose elsewhere only makes my midsection more distinct. I know I look unwell. Watching the dailies I think it's blatantly obvious, but Glenn says I'm being too sensitive.

"No rest for the weary."

"Nothing is worth your health," he says, and I detect more of a meaning behind it. He's referring to fame, perhaps, or money, or could he possibly be insinuating something about my marriage? I bat it away with banter.

"If everyone was healthy, what would you do to make a living, Doctor?"

"Become an actor," he quips, his wit quicker than I expected.

"Ah, yes. From doctor to actor—I can see the headlines now." I wipe a hand across the sky like the words are written in the clouds.

Our playful small talk runs out, and he looks ready to make some excuse and leave. He and Aria converse like they speak the same language and everyone else is from an unknown land, but he and I have always been a bit awkward with one another.

"How is Aria doing, you know, overall? Are the treatments working?" That's what I want to know more than anything—is the medicine he claims is a miracle working?

He peeks at the front windows and then back at me. I know doctors aren't supposed to talk about patients, but I have to ask.

"I was seeing positive results. Her mania seems to be under control," he responds, and my heart flutters. Finally, something makes a difference. Dr. Youngrin said this is the latest treatment for the malady Mother and Aria share. He continues with one finger raised.

"But lately, she's shown signs of depression, which I'm treating with great caution. I've ordered a blood test to be sure she's getting the right amount of medication for her condition."

"Should I be concerned?"

"No. No. Not just yet. She's a good girl, smart too. I'm glad to help as much as I can, but"—he squints at me, the early afternoon sun high above the row of palm trees lining our street—"this is strong medicine. Lithium. She needs her levels checked constantly, not only when a concern arises. I know she doesn't like the needles, but you cannot allow her to miss a screening. At some point she may need a specialist. This drug is a miracle in some ways, but there is risk."

"Like?" I ask, eyes wide, unnerved by this sort of warning from a doctor who gives out pills like candies at a party.

"Tremors. Stomach disruptions. Kidney troubles. And especially if she ever finds a nice boy and wants to have a family . . . she can't take this medication when she's in the family way."

I search the doctor's features to see if this last warning is a hint at his deeper feelings for my sister, but all I see is an appropriate level of concern from a physician.

For now, I think. Perhaps there's a happy ending to this story. I thank him for his help.

"I'm sure a busy bachelor like you probably has plans for the night, but if you come back at six, we're having a feast. We'd love to have you."

Dr. Youngrin looks at the windows again and then back at me, and I know I have him right where I want him.

"Six?" he asks.

"Six on the dot," I say, adjusting the bag looped over my shoulder.

"I'll see what I can do," he says and then tips his hat like a gentleman, and we part ways. I feel like a regular ole matchmaker.

As I walk up the front path, I scold myself. Look at all the good in my life: A baby on the way, my sister is healthy and growing stronger, I see my daughter every day, I have a new film and a happy-as-can-be-expected husband. People pay good money to see my movies, hang my picture on their wall, or read an article about my life. If everything is so great, why can't I stop feeling so sad?

The house already smells of garlic and tomatoes when I walk through the front door. The scent turns my stomach. I pop a pepper-mint and hope it'll do the trick.

Within seconds of closing the door, Gracie is wrapped around my legs, and Aria is relieving my shoulder of the bag of supplies.

"Did you two get started without me?" I ask, teasing Gracie with a tickle under her rib cage.

"Only a little, I promise," Gracie vows, her blue eyes deeply serious.

"We peeled the garlic and got the tomatoes stewing, that's all. Don't worry—you still get to do all the hard parts." Aria's lightness surprises me. I want to hug her, but I also don't want to make her feel self-conscious.

"Oh, joy," I kid, tying an apron around my waist and finding the strings shorter than at our last family dinner. The reminder of the life growing inside of me makes the moment of domestic bliss even more dreamlike. The only missing piece is the guiding hands of my mother taking us through each step. I can barely remember when showed me the proper way to feed the dough into the pasta roller and how the flour coating her fingers made the tough calluses feel soft on the back of my hands. She measured ingredients by handfuls or finger lengths. Papà would come through the kitchen and steal small bites of the mushroom filling we made for the ravioli.

Aria was too young to remember, so I'll step in now and give her what our mother grew too ill to share. I only wish the medicine that's helping my sister could help Mamma, but we've been told the brain procedure took away parts of our mother we can never restore.

I take it back—I have another wish: I wish I could talk to my sister about the painful things from our past, from my marriage with Tom, from my life now, without fearing it would drag her back into her darkness. But I'm sure that's a selfish wish.

Gracie bores of the hard, hot work in the kitchen after an hour. She learns the important parts, and I swear I'll call her back in when it's time to put the focaccia in the oven. There's a lull as we wait for the bread to rise. Aria and I crumble vanilla wafers to make the crust for a banana cream pie, Glenn's favorite. No one else likes it, so we've also made a small chocolate cake, but I make the banana cream pie every week, hoping one day he'll show up to eat it.

"Oh, I forgot to tell you. I invited Dr. Youngrin for dinner. I think he might come." I break another cookie in half as Aria looks at me, wide eyed.

"What'd you do that for? He was just here this morning."

"I know. I saw him as he was leaving. I swear he has a thing for you, Ari."

"Viviana Santini, you are a meddling old woman, I swear to God," she says in Italian. We never, and I mean never, speak Italian around Glenn. He gets furious at being left out that way. But I love to hear my old name in my old language, and so I respond in the same way.

"You know he fancies you."

"He brings me medication because I'm going bonkers. He doesn't fancy me." Aria crumbles another cookie, wipes the crumbs into the bowl, and stirs the butter melting in the saucepan on the stove.

"Don't speak that way. You're brave, not sick. I don't know what I'd do if I were . . ."

"What?" She laughs ruefully. "Crazy? I'm sure you're so happy you aren't me."

"No. No, little one. No. I didn't mean it that way." I wipe my hands on my apron and stand beside her at the stove and turn off the burner, the butter melted and starting to brown.

Ari rolls her eyes at herself and shrugs.

"I know you didn't. I'm sorry, Vivi." She lays her head on my shoulder, and I kiss her forehead. I think about the day we buried Papà, when I pledged to myself I'd stop putting Aria in the shadows. I'm failing at that. She's still a little seedling struggling to grab the sunlight, and it's my fault. Maybe that's why I hope Youngrin has an interest in Aria, because she deserves some nourishment, and I'm doing a god-awful job at it.

"You really think he'll come tonight?" she asks after a moment.

"I do," I say, noting the touch of excitement in Aria's voice. "Why? Is that a good thing?"

She pours the warm melted butter into our bowl of crumbles and then stirs.

"As long as you don't make a big deal of it *and* you don't embarrass me"—she uses the wooden spoon to threaten me—"I think it's fine."

"Hooray!" I clap. "A gentleman caller."

"Hey! I said you can't embarrass me." She waggles the coated spoon in my direction, and I dodge a feeble swipe as I grab the pie tin from the freezer.

"Fine. I'll behave."

"You'd better," she says, brandishing her wooden weapon one last time. We press the mixture into the chilled tin, listening to Gracie play with her dolls in the living room.

"So, he called again," Aria says, timidly, still in Italian as though she's sure someone is listening. I know who she's talking about, and nothing good will come from this conversation.

"He shouldn't call. I told him not to. Glenn will see the number and . . ."

"I know, but he's worried. You haven't written him back in months."

She lays a stack of postcards in front of me, tied with a blue ribbon. I recognize the signature at the bottom of the pencil sketch of Fontana Dei Pesci Del Vanvitelli with a brick road leading away from it in four directions. I ache to read them, but if I do, I'll want to write back. I can't. I'm trying to make things work with Glenn. I'm pregnant with his child. I can't be unfaithful, even if that's not how most people would label my relationship with Trombello.

"We only talked for a few minutes, and it was on his dime, so you're safe."

"It'll still show up—"

"He asked me if Glenn hits you."

My longing for Trombello's words evaporates.

"You've got to be joking. What did you say?" I ask, offended that anyone would think my husband might strike me. How dare he? How *dare* he?

"I didn't know what to say, Viv. You don't tell me things."

"What do you mean, I don't tell you things? You mean that you think Glenn is a wife beater?"

"No, but—I've seen him mad. It's scary. I just—does he? Does he hit you?"

My mood turns sour, and I dump the banana mixture into the crust and jiggle it until it lays flat. I'd just been longing to talk to my sister about the hardest things in my life, but now that the opportunity presents itself—it turns out I'm the one not mentally prepared for the moment.

"What the hell kind of a question is that?"

"That's not an answer," Aria says steadily.

"Of course he doesn't," I say, and it's technically true. He's never hit me. He's yelled in my face, he's chased me into rooms where I had to lock the door to keep him out, and I'll never forget the way my neck stung from the cord across it the night he caught me on the phone with Trombello, but he's never gone far enough to hurt me—not physically at least.

Aria lets out her breath and starts to slice bananas for the top of the pie.

"Thank God," she says, and I can tell she means it.

"I know Trombello is trying to help, but you need to tell him to stop. Glenn is a powerful man. He'll make life unbearable for everyone if he wants to."

Aria shakes her head. "I never wish to be married."

"Don't say that, darling. It's not so terrible."

"I've yet to see a marriage that doesn't look like a prison for at least one person inside of it."

"Oh hush, love. That's not true. Glenn isn't so terrible all the time. He'll calm down when the baby comes . . ."

I realize I've just said what I swore to Glenn I wouldn't reveal.

"A baby?" She glances at my midsection and then back at me, stunned. "With Glenn?"

"Yes," I mumble. Aria's expression morphs as though she's in pain.

"Will he let this one sleep inside, or will you buy a third house?"

The remark cuts me.

"You don't understand . . ."

"I do. You've chosen him. You have a new family now with that man, and we don't exist." She throws the spoon into the sink and rips off her apron.

"No, no, that's not how it will go. When the baby is born, I'll make sure you and Gracie can move in. I know Gracie will want to be close to her brother or sister, and we'll need help with the baby and—"

"And you'll have me raise another one of your children while you go live your fancy life. Don't you see how selfish that is? You're delusional, Vivian." Aria picks up the pie and tosses it across the room, where it splats against the wall in an almost comedic fashion. "I know you think I'm sick because of Mamma, but have you ever stopped to think that maybe I'm sick because of you?"

"Ari, no. I'm sorry," I call as she runs out and locks herself in her bedroom. I don't chase her or beg her to forgive me, because what Aria said is one of the most hurtful but also one of the most truthful statements I've heard in my entire life. I envy her honesty. And though I know she's right, I don't know how to change things.

So, I do what I do best—I push down the pain of her words, my husband's neglect, and the loss of my dear friend Trombello. I clean up pie from the wall, ceiling, and carpet, and when that's done I let Gracie help me put the bread in to bake and the pasta in to boil. Most importantly, I hide the beautiful postcards in the silverware drawer. Those cards are a dangerous temptation I must resist, especially when I'm in dire need of the guidance they'd provide.

VIVIAN SNOW

Auction

Lot #18

Hand-drawn postcard labeled: Mount Vesuvius
  Black ink on cardstock. Mountain range surrounded by a city.

NAPOLI. ITALIA. 03 DEC 1951

> *Vivian—*
>   *I've heard from your sister that my concerns are not unfounded. God doesn't desire you to stay in misery.*
>   *Prayerfully yours—A. Trombello*
> (Translation from Italian)

CHAPTER 18

December 16, 1951
Aria's Home
Hollywood, California

When Dr. Youngrin shows up for dinner, I seat him next to two empty place settings, explaining that Aria was overtired from our day of cooking. And when Glenn shows up twenty minutes late and half-drunk, I don't complain, and I pretend not to notice his intoxication, overjoyed he showed up at all.

Without Aria there to engage Dr. Youngrin, and with me fighting nausea through all of dinner, Gracie steps in and charms the guests at the table until her eyelids droop.

"Let's get you off to bed," I say. I stand but then wobble, my knees refusing to lock. Youngrin's hand darts out to stabilize me.

"You should sit," the doctor orders.

"I'm really all right," I say, leaning into his support. "Come on, Gracie."

"I want Daddy to put me to bed." Gracie pouts and clutches Glenn's arm. He starts at her touch but doesn't extract his arm.

Daddy? My head is spinning. I sink into one of the dining room chairs and assess Glenn, worried he might be offended or think I'm behind Gracie's request, trying to manipulate him. But he looks genuinely touched by her request.

"Me?" he asks Gracie, who is wrapped around his forearm now.

"Uh-huh," she says. "Please."

If she's pretending to like Glenn, it doesn't show, or she's a better actress than her mother. I hold my breath as his features soften.

"All right, then. Can't say no to that. Kiss your mom," he says, tossing his napkin on his empty plate. Amazed and slightly stunned, I kiss the top of Gracie's head as she says her goodnights and they go off down the hall. I wish Aria were here to see it and possibly feel some hope about the new baby.

"That's progress," I say as Dr. Youngrin hovers over me, checking the pulse at my wrist and looking into my eyes.

"Vivian. You're not well. I think we should take you to the hospital."

"What? Hospital? No." I remove myself from his inspection and start collecting the plates from the table, putting them in a stack. I can't go to the hospital. Someone will leak news of my pregnancy to the papers before we can tell Zanuck, before I can tell Gracie. "I'm fine. It's been a long day."

"You need help, Vivian," he insists.

"If you want to help me, you'll tell Glenn how well Aria's doing. Or tell him I need some support around the house and Aria is strong enough."

I stand—this time successfully—and take the plates to the kitchen. Dr. Youngrin follows with the glassware. He hovers around me as I clean, like he's waiting for me to break down.

Glenn returns from Gracie's room, and I convince the two men to have a drink in the living room, promising I won't work too hard. As I leave them I hear Dr. Youngrin giving Glenn a rundown on Aria's improvements and the reasons I should have her and Gracie at home. By the end of their conversation, it sounds like Glenn has agreed to finally allow my family to be under one roof. I wish I could give Youngrin a giant hug.

As I fill the sink with warm water and slip on a pair of yellow dish gloves, Dr. Youngrin departs. Once we're alone, drunken Glenn presses his body against my back while I have my arms submerged in lemony scented suds.

"You don't have to do these." He kisses the nape of my neck, his cold side thawed for now.

"I don't want to leave a mess." Aria takes care of so much in my life—I can do this one thing.

"I'll have Carol come down here first thing." He nibbles at the exposed bit of my shoulder, and I tremble.

"I'm sure Carol will love that." I chuckle, closing my eyes, relishing his touch. Glenn's had his housekeeper longer than any of his wives, and she's definitely not a member of my fan club.

"Eh, she's a sweetheart under all that prickliness. Anyway, she'll do it if I ask her."

The last thing I want to do tonight is a sink full of dishes. If Glenn wants to care for me, I should let him. I peel off the gloves but leave the water in the sink, placing every pot and pan inside to soak.

"That should make her job easier."

"You're a sweetheart," he says, turning me around for a kiss. His approval is the nourishment I've been craving, and I consume it greedily. "Let's get you home," Glenn says, tucking a stray clump of hair behind my ear. "Tito's waiting outside."

I nod, and then hesitate, remembering the pie on the wall and the look of betrayal on Aria's face.

"Let me tell Aria we're leaving." She likely won't open the door, but my bladder is aching, and I can take the opportunity to sneak in a quick trip to the bathroom.

"Of course. Take your time."

I fill Aria's empty dish with pasta, salad, and bread, pour a tall glass of milk, and walk down the hall. I have so much to tell her and apologize for, but tonight isn't the night.

I leave a plate outside Aria's room, choosing not to knock.

I hurry to the bathroom, the urge to relieve myself impossible to ignore. As I pull up my skirt and down my undergarments, a warm trickle rushes down my leg. I've never wet myself before. Pregnancy is so inelegant. I sit on the toilet, ashamed but also glad it happened in the bathroom instead of the kitchen when a flash of red catches my eye.

I inspect the trail on my inner thigh and then the cotton crotch of my underwear. I cover my mouth to keep from screaming. It's blood. Lots of it.

"Glenn," I whisper as I limp into the kitchen, a wad of toilet tissue wedged between my legs. "I think the doctor is right. We need to go to the hospital."

The yellow light over the stove and the lamp in the dining room are on, and the light seems eerily bright.

"Glenn?" I call again, a little louder this time. No response. I peek through the back curtains to see if he's stepped out to smoke on the porch, but it's just dark and empty back there. I stumble to the front door. It's possible he decided to wait in the car with Tito. But not only is Glenn nowhere to be found—Tito's car is gone too.

My ears start to ring, and the room spins. How could he have misunderstood? Why would he leave me behind?

I use the furniture as a support line until I reach the kitchen counter, sweaty and out of breath. I dial our home number and let it ring. It rings five, six, ten times with no response. *Maybe he's not home yet,* I think, wondering if I should wake Aria.

Would she even want to help me? I wonder. *Of course she would.* I calm myself. *She's my sister.* We get frustrated with each other, but I know she'd step in front of a bus for me, and I'd do the same for her.

I'll try Glenn one more time. He's probably still in transit, and next time I call he'll pick up and rush back and take me to the hospital, and everything will be all right. I dial the number to the house again and stretch the cord into the dining room, grasping for a chair when I notice the table is covered in scattered pieces of paper that I recognize immediately—Trombello's postcards.

He found them. A cold sweat covers my forehead and the skin at my wrists and ankles, a shiver running through my entire being like an earthquake. I shove the stiff paper rectangles onto the floor with a swipe of my arm. These are why he left, why he's not answering.

"Come on, Glenn," I say through clenched teeth into the phone, almost like a prayer of desperation. But no one answers. As the phone continues to ring, the trill on the line grows hypnotizing. The room goes fuzzy around the edges until the lights dim and then go black.

"Mamma? Mamma?" Little hands shake me, and I slowly come to. Gracie stands over me where I'm slumped in the chair with the phone lying on the floor. I've failed to reach help. My mouth is horribly dry, and each parched taste bud stands sharp and erect on my tongue, making it painful to speak.

"Gracie! My good girl." I want to touch her face, but my hands are heavy. "Mamma is ill. Won't you please wake Zia and tell her I need her?"

"I can't," Gracie says, her bottom lip quivering as she twists her doll's hair around her finger over and over till her nail turns blue. I've scared her, I'm sure.

"It's all right, darling. All will be fine. Will you please go and get your zia Aria? Tell her Mamma needs her. She won't mind."

"I can't," she repeats, her cheeks already wet like she's been crying.

"Why not?" My sharp query makes her blink in fright, and I try again, calmly. "Why not, darling?"

"I already tried. She won't wake up."

She won't wake up.

Terror floods my body with enough energy to stand. The moment I'm on my feet, there's an uncomfortable gush between my legs I'm forced to ignore. I replace the phone on the hook, and Gracie holds my hand and leads me down the hall to Aria's room.

"Be a big girl and get mommy's purse from the kitchen. There's a little book in there with numbers. Bring it back, but don't come in unless I tell you, all right? You promise?"

"I promise." Gracie nods somberly and runs off on her errand.

I sidestep the untouched tray of food, and I find my sister in her bed, vomit on the pillow. God no.

I put my cheek close to hers, listening for any sign that it's not too late, that I still have a chance to say I'm sorry, to change my ways, to relieve her burden. Aria's raspy breath in and out sends another quake through my body so strong that I can do nothing but sit and wait for it to pass.

"Mamma? I'm here," Gracie yells from the hall.

"Good girl. Now, leave it there and go back to your room. I'll read you a story in a minute."

We both know my last offer is a lie. Aria is not taking a long nap, and I'm not sick with the flu. We both need help, and I can think of only one man who I can rely on. I dial his number on Aria's bedside phone, and it rings once.

"Hello?" a deep voice answers, and it's like seeing a rescue ship after being stranded on a deserted island.

"Please come . . ." My energy wanes.

"Who is this? Are you all right?"

I try to wet my tongue to speak again but find it difficult to form words. Gracie's voice comes on the line, likely from the extension in the kitchen.

"Mamma is sick and Zia is asleep."

There's what seems like an eternal pause.

"Gracie? Is that you?" the voice asks.

"Uh-huh," she says and then seems to get nervous about breaking the rules. "I'm not supposed to talk on the phone so I gotta go now. Bye."

"Vivian? Are you still there?"

"Yes," I manage to utter.

"I'll be right over."

"Thank you," I say, hanging up the phone and curling up on the bed next to Aria like we used to sleep when we were little girls on cold winter nights. I kiss her hair, count her breaths, and whisper every apology I can conjure as I feel the life of my own little one inside of me slip away.

VIVIAN SNOW

Auction

Lot #19

Hand-drawn postcard labeled: Struffoli
   Pencil on cardstock. Deep-fried morsels of dough arranged in a wreath shape.

   NAPOLI. ITALIA. 22 JAN 1955

   Vivian—
        God bless you and your family.
        —Father Trombello
        (Translation from Italian)

CHAPTER 19

June 17, 1957
Rome, Italy

"I can't get you out of my head," he says, hair mussed, eyes flaming with passion. He takes my shoulders roughly, and my head bobbles back like I'm a rag doll at his whim.

"That's not my fault. That's your fault. I can't fix your brain any more than I can fix mine." I gasp, thinking of Aria lying beside me the night we almost lost her. Tears spring to my eyes immediately.

"Let me give it a try," he says, smashing his mouth against my lips, my lipstick powdered so it won't smudge during our big moment. I push him away.

"No. No." I run across the room and stand behind a chair in the corner. "Get out." I point at the door, the tears falling down my face. I feel the real emotions of my character as though she's a part of me.

He looks torn between arguing and accepting the rejection. I already know what he's going to do—this is our sixth take. But I still find his reaction as believable as I did at our first rehearsal. Johnny has grown as an actor, and he challenges me at every turn. When he walks out the door and I collapse on the bed sobbing, I know it was our best take yet.

Vittorio De Sica, our director, calls cut and shouts, "That's a wrap!"

The crew breaks out in applause. I tear up again, this time without using any trigger other than the joy of acting again. Johnny runs around the front of the set and picks me up in a giant hug. It's been two months away from home, two months in the sticky, hot city center of Rome. Two months of rehearsing, working on my craft, and putting myself in front of the camera again, and eventually the world. It's been too long. I've missed this *so, so* much.

"Damn good work, Miss Snow," Johnny says, his arm slung casually around my shoulder like my best friend. I blush. It's been five years since *Marry Me Friday* was a box office hit and I was nominated for nearly every Best Actress award. I didn't win the more notable ones, but the nominations looked to be a pivotal moment in my career that would shoot me into the stratosphere of fame and success.

But that's not what happened, not even close.

"Pretty damn good job yourself, Mr. Scott."

"What are you doing tonight? Wanna have dinner at Al Pompiere? I'm dying for some good wine and a pile of pasta."

"Gosh, I'd love to, Johnny, but I'm leaving tomorrow for Salerno. I'll be gone two weeks and I gotta pack," I say. As we walk toward the makeshift dressing room, I hear congratulations and thank-yous in more than one language. This is a lower-budget film, the first independent film I've done in my career. Glenn made sure my opportunities were limited after I moved out of the house and into the bungalow with Aria and Gracie.

"I could get the food to go. Grab a bottle of wine. I could help you pack. You never kick back and relax." Johnny's at it again, but I'm not interested in romance of any kind. I've been alone for five years now, married, yes, but alone. Ever since I woke up in the hospital the morning after that dreadful dinner, I've had an emptiness in me that goes beyond the loss of my unborn son and the loss of the capability to grow life inside of me. I've lost my ability to trust anyone outside of those in my closest circle.

"I need sleep more than I need pasta." I keep the rejection delicate. There will be reshoots and press and red carpets with him, and if I'm lucky, other films, so I tread lightly around his ego like most women in the industry must. "I'll be back to tie up any loose ends if you'd like to have lunch then."

We've reached my dressing room and the end of his cigarette. He crushes it on the ground, looking disappointed.

"Yeah. Sure. Lunch."

I wait by the dressing-room door, my name taped on it two months ago when we started filming in this soundstage. I feel like a girl trying to slip inside the house after a date without getting kissed, because Johnny definitely has kissing eyes right now.

"It's been an honor working with you," he says, leaning against the doorframe. He could seduce any of the scantily dressed screaming fans that follow him around, or any other actress in this film, but he continues to pursue me. Why? Is it the challenge? Or a feather for his cap?

"You too," I say, offering my hand for a shake. He takes it reluctantly and kisses it as his eyes hold mine. I ditch into my dressing room, wipe the back of my hand on my dress, and get to packing. My train leaves at five thirty tomorrow morning. I'm visiting family in a small town outside of Salerno. I sent a letter ahead a few weeks ago, and a great-aunt on my father's side replied, assuring me she'd show off the place my parents fell in love. It's bittersweet.

I feel compelled to connect with my roots, my heritage, but I've kept my grief for my father's passing and my mother's illness locked behind strong doors. It's only by seeing my parents as flawed figures that I can stop looking to them or their memory for comfort. But to see where they were children, where they grew up and had hopes and dreams of their own—I'm frightened to unlock that door.

But there's another door I'm even more scared of. My train goes straight through Nola, the small village where Trombello serves.

I took my first call from Trombello after I lost the baby. I was settled in with Gracie at the bungalow, and Aria was nearing her release from the psychiatric hospital. He and I made small talk and caught up the best we could without walking down paths paved with remorse. I told him how Glenn didn't come to see me once at the hospital and that when I came home from my convalescence I'd found he'd petitioned to have Aria committed. I told Trombello how I left that day and moved into the bungalow, how I used every cent I could access to fight the petition and get Aria released. I told him I wished I could divorce Glenn and cut him out of my life like a cancer but that I knew it would cost me my career, my family's financial stability, and God's approval.

Trombello claimed God would understand if I divorced Glenn. I told Trombello I've tried God's patience too much already—this marriage is something I can give him as a show of sacrifice. He disagreed. I didn't care. We hung up with bitterness traveling the phone line between us.

I called him one last time a few weeks later and told him I could no longer afford the expensive calls. I'd been cut off from Glenn's accounts, accounts that held all of my income and savings. Trombello acted like he understood, though I wonder if he knew I was also avoiding my holy friend's difficult counsel. I couldn't say I'd divorce Glenn, but I could promise that if Glenn chose to divorce me, I wouldn't fight back. Trombello said he supported my decision and he'd pray for me. We've exchanged cards and letters occasionally in the years since.

And in that time I've lived apart from my husband, and Glenn has done everything within his power to keep me as his wife. At first, he tried to make me jealous, dating his new leading ladies and holding all-night parties that were so large the parking overflow clogged the street in front of the bungalow. And after my awards nominations for *Marry Me Friday*, he begged Archie to get me to work with him again. When I refused, he said I'd never work with anyone else in Hollywood if I wouldn't work with him.

And he was right.

It didn't take long for the offers to dry up. Soon I was labeled a "flash in the pan" like so many girls who try to make it big in the industry.

Over the next several years, I took small modeling jobs and performed in eleven different live teleplays with *The Philco Television Playhouse*, *The Elgin Hour*, *Ford Television Theatre*, and *Robert Montgomery Presents*. Between my acting jobs and Aria's position with Westwood Village Memorial Park's landscaping crew, we got by.

With Glenn's influence gone, we moved Mamma to San Diego and hired Nurse Margot to be her caregiver at Bayside Assisted Living Facility. Aria continues to blossom with Margot only a train ride away, and I take great joy in seeing her bask in the sun for once in her life.

I grew used to it, the ache where my little boy once grew, the absent husband who won't let me go, the coolness of an extinguished spotlight that used to burn so brightly I worried I'd be burned. But the bills were relentless, the stress too.

Then this opportunity fell in Archie's lap. He could've pitched one of his younger clients—he has quite a few now—but instead Archie had me get a full makeover and paid for a new wardrobe. I did more screen tests than I could count, and just when I'd decided it was a lost cause, the offer came through. I'd forgotten how good it felt to not give up.

"Buona sera, Carlo!" I call out to one of the gaffers, busy packing away lighting equipment.

"Buona sera, Signorina Snow," he calls back with a wave. A few more farewells and I escape into the darkened streets of Rome. I've been told I shouldn't walk alone, but my rented apartment is only a few blocks away, and I enjoy the independence this new city provides. In America, people still recognize me. I don't mind the requests for an autograph or a quick moment of my time, but when the questions get personal or even aggressive, I wish I'd never left the house.

Here, I fade into the background. The streets are full of life and passion, and the smells of the city remind me of my days at Camp Atterbury. Laundry hangs on lines across the streets and alleys like celebratory banners, and carts of fresh fruit and flowers shift from corner to corner. I've never seen so much living crammed into one place.

Men are flirtatious, yes, but the women are self-assured and strong. I hold my head high here and imagine a life where I'm not pretending to be strong but have true strength. Being immersed in the Italian culture, *my* culture, is a balm for some of my childhood wounds. I've found a fire in the women here that's barely flickering inside of me. Just try to kiss an Italian woman when she doesn't want it and see what happens. A slap across the face and a few choice words, I'm sure. My mother wasn't passive, but I saw where that got her. Papà was loud and sure of himself, but I learned to be the opposite. Aria too, until the night we almost lost her. From the moment she threw that pie, she's been different—bold. It was like that night showed her that her life and sanity were on the line, and she chose to never surrender again.

Some people may call me strong because I moved out of Glenn's house and finished the film without letting my miscarriage and failing marriage and Aria's suicide attempt stop me. But it wasn't bravery as much as desperation. I saw Dr. Youngrin only one more time after he showed up at the bungalow that night, red and white lights following close behind. I was heavily medicated in the hospital after surgery, but he spoke with such force that I'll never forget it: *He did this to you. If you stay in that house, you will die.*

I discard the memory of that eerie moment where I knew he was right but didn't know why by stomping up the stairs to the top floor of the small apartment building where I've been staying. I have a simple room with a double bed, a kitchenette, a table, a few overstuffed chairs, and one understuffed couch. A few years ago I would have considered these sorts of accommodations an insult, but after living in a 1,200 square foot home with a preteen and my sister, this seems like a mansion now that I'm living on my own.

I'd always thought that the little three-bedroom bungalow would be Aria's home one day, where she could have a family of her own. Dr. Youngrin seemed interested in her; he visited her in the hospital a few times, but he soon cut his connection with Glenn, and Aria held fast to her belief that she'd never fall in love and get married. A year or two after his warning to me, I saw an announcement in the newspaper with a picture of Dr. Youngrin and his new bride.

I don't know what exactly led to the breakdown of Glenn's relationship with Dr. Youngrin or what fueled his ominous warning, but a new doctor replaced him within a week, and Dr. Youngrin moved into private practice, last I heard.

I pour myself a glass of wine. I've always found the smell and flavor distasteful, but in Italy it's different. It's part of the experience of this place, my parents' origin. Plus, there's little else to calm my nerves at the end of the day now that I've given up pills like the ones Youngrin prescribed and Glenn constantly pushed on me. I'm learning to celebrate even when I'm alone, and the warm, earthy comfort of my indulgence gives me enough thrill to finish my packing quickly. I'll be back in two weeks, and I'll return home to the room I share with Gracie soon after that.

And tomorrow I'll see my dear friend for the first time in thirteen years and tell him that I've finally decided he was right—it's time to move on with my life and leave Glenn for good.

VIVIAN SNOW

Auction

Lot #20

Hand-drawn postcard labeled: The Voice of One Crying Out in the Desert
  Pencil on cardstock. Portrait of a lion.

NOLA. ITALIA. 25 APR 1956

Vivian—
  The feast of St. Mark is upon us once again. As
every year, it makes me think of the time we met long
ago. It's been many years since I've heard your voice
or read your words.
  May God's blessings be upon you.
  —Trombello
(Translation from Italian)

CHAPTER 20

June 18, 1957
Nola, Italy

My eyelids feel gritty as I wake from a long nap. The conductor is tapping me on my shoulder to remind me of my stop just outside of Naples, a small town called Nola. It's one of those times that having a familiar face has been a help rather than a hindrance in public. I thank him and place a tip in his palm.

"Thank you, signorina. Thank you," he says, helping me with my bags.

My hat is a bit ridiculous for the one-room train station. An older Italian woman sits fanning herself on a wooden bench as two small children sit at her feet, playing marbles. She's dabbing at tears with a handkerchief as a man and a woman stand a few feet away locked in an emotional discussion.

I avert my gaze, but the grandmother notices me watching and watches right back as though I'm an exotic bird that's landed in the middle of Piazza Campo de' Fiori. I consider removing the wide-brimmed hat and stowing my sunglasses in my satchel, but then the woman smiles at me as though the unusual sight brings her joy.

I smile back, and the little girl follows her grandmother's gaze and whispers something. Just as I'm considering asking her where the cathedral is, last call is made, and the man tearfully kisses each of the children and the grandmother as they chirp farewells.

I don't want to disturb their private moment, so I walk through to the other side of the building before the train leaves the station. Outside, a single taxi idles, the front grill broken in two places and plumes of exhaust gathered around it in a toxic cloud. I can remember wishing I had enough pocket change to take a taxi when I was alone and pregnant with Gracie.

The driver, Enzo, is friendly but seems distracted by my appearance. I give him the name of Trombello's church but keep my replies to his questions simple. He tells me he's sure he's seen me before. Do I know Rocco Bianchi?

"I'm not from around here," I explain in Italian.

"That's easy to see." He looks me over in that way I hate. I clutch my bag across my body. "But a good girl going straight to church."

"I guess."

"Or a very bad one, eh?" He laughs and flicks his cigarette out the window as we pull up in front of a small cathedral, though small is a relative term. The modest cross on the apex of the pointed roof towers above the neighboring village homes, many of which look as though they haven't been repaired since before the war. The countryside behind the church is green and lush and spotted with what must be sheep. Farther in the distance are thickly wooded hills.

Enzo hands over my bag, and I pay him in a large-enough bill to cover the trip and leave him with a tip. He thanks me profusely and asks my name.

"Santini. Vivian Santini," I say, and decline his offer for help up the steps.

"Signorina Santini. Should I wait?"

I consider the offer. I haven't seen Trombello in years, and we have so much to catch up on. My train to Salerno isn't until five. I'm hoping Trombello will find a moment to have lunch and walk me to the station.

Then again, another thought hits me. He might not be here. I didn't give him any notice of my intent to visit.

"Wait for five minutes, and if I'm not out by then you can go."

"Sounds good, Signorina Santini."

He's watching my ass as I walk up the steps, I can sense it, so I hurry my pace. I think I'd rather walk back to the station than get in Enzo's cab again, no matter what awaits me inside the cathedral.

When I crack open the solid oak doors I'm surprised at their hefty weight, and when I walk through it's like entering a different land. The ceilings are nearly as tall as the tower and are covered in wood paneling. The walls are lined with stained glass windows, and the marble altar is elevated and covered in velvet. I love churches in Italy. I can imagine the hands that built them, the workmanship it took to carve each statue and to paint each mural. Even the most grandiose structure in Italy reminds me of the humble Chapel in the Meadow at Camp Atterbury, built by POWs determined to bring God with them to their prison and worship him there.

A group of parishioners waits in line outside an ancient-looking oak confessional. There's no guarantee Trombello is inside, but I haven't gone to confession since I've been in Rome, so even if it's another priest it won't be a waste.

I stash my bags under a pew and join the line. Two of the parishioners are women in simple dark dresses, each with her hair pinned in a bun at the nape of her neck. The third is a young man twisting a cap as though he's wringing it out after being stuck in a rainstorm. When a young woman exits the confessional with her eyes cast downward, cheeks flushed, the hat goes still, and he looks like he wants to say something. Instead of acknowledging the young man, she lights a candle and kneels to pray. He plunges the hat into his coat pocket and takes his turn in the tiny confession box. It's ungodly to have impure thoughts in church, but I can't help guessing at the backstory to their visit.

The two village women are too busy whispering to notice the big-ticket gossip item right in front of their eyes.

The young man leaves the confessional, wiping at his face. He kneels next to the girl and looks to be praying, but in my imagination he's whispering words of love or apology, whatever will make it right. The couple leaves one at a time, though I'm not fooled by the staggered departure. Perhaps it will work for them—love, that is, simple and pure without all the strings and baggage that came with my marriage.

The other two women pop in and out of the confessional box, likely devout. Thankfully, I'm the last in line, which means if it's some strange old priest on the other side of the screen, I can confess a handful of sins and escape without embarrassment. And if Trombello is on the other side, I won't feel pressured to rush.

As I pull aside the curtain that separates the beautiful imagery of religion from the true work of religion, of sculpting and perfecting the soul, I know immediately I've found him. I've missed his friendship and guidance. I know I pushed him away, but back then I didn't know how to be the woman he encouraged me to be. I'm stronger now. Surer of what I want. Will he be proud of me now? Will he know my voice? Will he feel the same longing that's coming close to suffocating me inside this little box?

I'm unexpectedly nervous as I kneel at the screen.

I keep my head bowed and whisper, "Bless me, Father, for I have sinned. It has been two months since my last confession."

A part of me expects him to recognize me as instantly as I recognized him, but I realize that's unfair. He hasn't even glanced toward me. It might be easier this way, with a wall between us. I bow my head, so my hat obscures his eyeline.

He welcomes me and gives the sign of the cross and says a brief prayer. "May the Lord be in your heart that you may know your sins and be truly sorry . . ."

As he prays with his eyes closed, I try to make out his profile through the ornate screen and absorb his voice as he speaks. It's the same as the first day I saw him in the office of the internment camp at Camp Atterbury.

He finishes his prayer, and it's my turn. Normally, I'd list my sins, but today, with my dear Antonio Trombello sitting so close, I have only one confession on my heart and mind.

"I'm so sorry I didn't listen to you," I say. Trombello's head tilts, but he still doesn't look through the screen long enough to see me clearly.

"We all have our weaknesses. You are here, and that is good. It is not me you need to listen to—it is God. It takes time to change, become new. First is to name your sin. Next, to renounce it in Jesus's name." He's so priestly he feels like a new person in many ways. We'd become casual in our conversations, jovial, friendly, and to see him like this, so spiritually humble and empathetic, it's almost like when I see myself on film playing a character.

I clear my throat and try again. "I've committed the sin of pride. I've rejected and hurt people who cared about me because I was too ashamed of my weaknesses."

"Have you apologized and made restitution for these sins?" he asks. He's shifting in his chair now, and I wonder if he's catching on. My accent is different from his parishioners', and by now he must have noticed my appearance. I wonder if he can smell my Diorissimo perfume through the thin divider.

"I'm sorry, my friend," I say, lifting my head, hoping he'll look at me. "I'm sorry I took you for granted and didn't listen to your kind words of counsel. It seemed impossible at the time. I felt trapped, you know? I'm not sure you know. It's hard to explain."

As I stumble through my confession, the fear and confusion of our years apart rush in all at once, and my breathing becomes shallow. The walls seem to be closing in on me, inches at a time, threatening to crush me. I feel trapped in this little box the same way I've felt trapped in my marriage. Trombello speaks, but his voice is so quiet it can't even be called a whisper. I lean closer to the screen to hear him only to realize—he's gone.

"Vivian?" The curtain to my left swooshes open, and fresh air floods inside. There, standing in front of me, is Antonio Trombello dressed head to toe in priestly attire. I've never seen him this way. I've seen him in a prison uniform and an army uniform but never in the uniform of his true job, his real calling. Despite the black robes and the white collar, his face is the same. He's still the young man who saved my life, who buried the man I killed, who guarded me after Larry died, who paid for a headstone that made my career possible, and who kept all my secrets.

"Trombello," I say with a tentative smile, enjoying the taste of his name on my tongue. He helps me up from where I'm kneeling, his warm touch steadying me as the blood returns to my feet.

As soon as I'm stable, he pulls his hand back, glances around the sanctuary, and puts several feet between us. I recognize the reason for his caution when I notice the two older women who were in front of me in line sitting in a pew with their heads bowed.

"I'm sorry to surprise you, but I've been shooting a new film in Rome. We just wrapped, and I'm on my way to visit my family in Ogliara. My train leaves at five. I remembered you'd settled here in Nola for a bit, so I took a chance and thought I'd make a few calls to hunt you down and make some amends, you know, face-to-face. Well, almost face-to-face," I say, gesturing to the confessional. He doesn't smile at my explanation—in fact, he seems very serious.

"Shall we sit?" he asks, this time in English. I remember from our phone conversations that he preferred English in case someone was listening. I'm sure the same goes for now, but why is he ashamed to speak with me? We're not breaking any rules that I know of. I'm confused, but I go along with it and sit in a pew, where he joins me.

"How are you?" I ask, holding in a torrent of apologies and regret.

"I'm well, thank you," he replies formally, as though I'm little more than a stranger. I check on the women in the front pew again. They seem to be preparing to leave. If I bide my time a few more minutes, I'll be able to say everything I've been holding in my heart for too many years now.

"Well, that's good. It's beautiful here. I understand why you missed it so much when you were in America."

"Every place has its beauty." His eyes are distant, and he's speaking in generalities like an oracle from an ancient Greek play.

"Rome is dazzling. Everything is just so old. I can't wrap my brain around how long people have lived there. Everything in Los Angeles is brand new. I don't like it. It seems so"—I search for the word—"disposable."

He nods, staring ahead at the crucifix. The women have left, and the heavy doors shutting into place send an eerie echo through the cavernous space. I have no reason to hold back now. No busybody parishioners or secretaries or nuns or clergy. Just me and Trombello, alone.

All the thoughts I've stored up come pouring out.

"I haven't treated you fairly. And, I don't know, I think I'm ready to change, really change. I came here, didn't I?" I gesture to my surroundings, but I mean far more than the church itself. "To Italia. And now I have a second chance with this film. I'm nervous about seeing my parents' hometown. My zia Nina wanted me to stay with them, but I got a hotel room instead, which caused a few ripples, but you know how I can get around strangers."

He still says nothing in response to my rambling, though I know he's listening. I change the subject to something I know he's interested in.

"Gracie is so grown up now. Archie and his wife have taken a liking to her and have her in acting classes, and she hangs out with their kids. It's like she has cousins nearby. And Aria is so much better. The medicine is working, and she sees a special doctor. Oh, we moved Mother closer, and Aria's friend Margot is her nurse . . ."

I can't bring myself to continue. He's hardly paying attention.

"You seem bothered that I'm here," I say, consumed with disappointment. I know I've hurt him through the years, and I know it's unfair to expect him to be perfect, despite his religious devotion, but I didn't expect him to hold a grudge. "I guess I should've written."

He sighs, the cloth of his robes gathered in his clenched fingers.

"Yes, that would've been best," he says simply.

"That's it? That's all you have to say?" I feel the ember glowing inside me, the one I've seen in other women of my heritage, the fire I've been jealous of. Maybe I don't need to douse it immediately. Maybe I deserve a better explanation.

"That's all I *can* say, *mia cara amica*." He looks in my eyes, and I see a glimpse of him, the real him. A quiver of relief ripples over my skin, leaving goose bumps in its wake.

"What do you mean?" I ask, touching his arm. He opens his mouth as though he's ready to explain, when the church doors open and close, making us jump. A mother and her children slip inside, a reluctant husband following close behind.

Trombello stands, hands clasped behind his back.

"Do you need a ride to the station?"

I almost offer to wait so we can try this whole conversation over again when he's finished taking confession. But I'm certain he'd encourage me to leave, and I'd rather walk away with my head held high than beg for his attention. It seems I've neglected this friendship for too long and it's blown away like the dried-out seeds on a dandelion puff.

"No, I'm fine. Thank you," I say, gathering my bags. As he holds the door for me, I think of my departed taxi. But I wouldn't mind a good long walk right now to clear my head and relieve my embarrassment.

As I walk past him, feeling like a child who's been cast out of her Sunday school class for misbehaving, I stop short of the steps to the street. Glancing back, I squint against the afternoon sun, courageous enough to ask one last question.

"Why do you keep sending me postcards?" If he's this offended by me, why send me picture after picture, year after year?

He shrugs. "Habit, I suppose?"

"I see," I say, sliding on my sunglasses and hefting the big suitcase off the ground. "I guess I have a few bad habits myself. Goodbye, Padre."

"Arrivederci, signora," he says, closing the door behind him.

"Goodbye, dear friend," I whisper to myself, tears running down my cheeks as I head to the dusty road. "I will miss you."

VIVIAN SNOW

Auction

Lot #21

Hand-painted postcard labeled: Ceppo
    Watercolor on cardstock. Pyramid-shaped wooden frame with shelves, a small Nativity scene, candy, fruit, small gifts, and a star on top.

ROMA. ITALIA. 25 DEC 1956

   Vivian—
     Christmas wishes.
     —Trombello
     (Translation from Italian)

CHAPTER 21

July 1, 1957
Ogliara, Italy

A rooster cackles outside, and my eyes fly open at the sound. The tiny twin-size bed is thin in the middle and bulging at the edges, but I've grown accustomed to it in the past two weeks. I spent my first night in the hotel I'd reserved ahead of time, but Zia Nina, my great-aunt on my father's side, made it clear once I got to her house that it was unacceptable for her great-niece to stay anywhere but with the family.

Since then, I've stayed here and taken a tour of my parents' lives. I met my mother's family, who found a way to rejoice in her new experiences in California and sidestep any mention of her lifelong illness. I brought pictures and gifts from America, and I spent the first two nights at Zia Nina's eating too much and drinking too much and going to bed far too late.

It's helped me forget about that uncomfortable meeting with Trombello. It was more than uncomfortable, it was heartbreaking. In all our years apart, I never considered that my distance hurt him so profoundly. He always seemed like an island in a still ocean, while I was a ship blown about in a storm. I can't let myself believe he's gone forever. I've lost people I love to death, but I'm not prepared to lose a friend I hold so dear without the barrier of mortality between us. But any thought of returning to that church where he basically cast me out leaves me cold and anxious. So for now I'll allow him the same space I took for myself when I chose my marriage over my friend.

Morning is filled with purpose here. All good things made in my zia's kitchen are thanks to the work of the women. But it's a happy work, and Zia Claudia, Nina's sister, is generous with her praise when it comes to my cooking. My attempts at scrubbing a floor or hanging laundry on the line in front of the house, on the other hand, incite peals of laughter. I don't mind, though. I enjoy the energy of the people here, and even the laughter feels like love.

After one day of living with Zia Nina, I came to realize that none of my clothes were appropriate.

"It is the woman in the dress that makes it beautiful," Zia Nina declared when she finally convinced me to switch into one of my cousin Maria's dresses. Maria is married to a baker and lives down the street with her six children, her hips now too wide for her former wardrobe.

"Don't worry, we'll fill you out before you leave," Zia Claudia said, the dress loose around my hips and bosom. For Hollywood standards, I'm the exact measurements I should be. I should know—I work hard to keep trim with a restricted diet and plenty of swimming and biking to stay slender but not too muscular. Three years ago I had a few nips and a tuck or two on the advice of Archie, who was just as frustrated as I was at the lack of offers coming my way. He helped fund the surgery, but even a "perfect" 36-24-36 didn't get my name off that blacklist.

It feels liberating to eat until I'm full and drink until I'm laughing. I'll never fully enjoy the flavor of wine, I think, but I see the joy in it and why Papà thought it might be the magic elixir to fix mother's illness.

Ah, Papà.

My zio Mario, Zia Nina's husband, is much like my father, or like I always imagined my father would be as an old, old man. They mourn the loss of my papà as though he were still a child, which I'm certain in their minds he always will be. I went to church with Zia Nina and Zia

Claudia, and we lit a candle for Papà and I wished they'd been there the day he was buried.

"We cried all day and night when he left here with your mother," Zia Claudia told me.

"He used to beg us to come join him in America. Said there was plenty of land and jobs. But then there was war, and it was impossible to get out to—anywhere. Once our sons were forced into the army, we didn't want to leave. We wanted to be here when they came home," Zia Nina added as we turned down the lane leading to a line of little cottages, each with a sizable slice of land reaching out behind it. I see why Papà felt at home in the cornfields of Indiana—he came from a world of agriculture. I can't wait to bring Aria here.

"Now we understand why he went to America. Look at the good fortune it brought to his family, eh?" Zia Claudia says, caressing my cheek. Her touch fills some of the emptiness I've felt without my mother in my life and gives me a profound sense of not being alone in the world.

"Viviana!" Zia Nina calls from the bottom of the stairs, reminding me to hurry my morning routine. Her knee is bad, and she makes the arduous trek up or down only twice a day—once at dawn and once at night. Today she beat me to the kitchen.

I throw on a brassiere and a white dress with pink flowers from Maria's collection. I'll change back into my "movie star clothes," as Zia Nina calls them, before I leave for the train tonight. I've convinced Zia Nina to let me help with the laundry and make dinner before I leave as a thank-you for her hospitality.

I run a brush through my wild hair.

"Breakfast is ready," Zia Nina says as I rush down the stairs, the smells of a hearty meal hitting me as my feet settle on the landing.

"Thank you, Zia," I say, kissing her cheek. I eat quickly, but not too quickly that she scolds me. The only way to get Zia Nina to let me do a single chore without her by my side is to get her out of the house.

Zio Mario is taking her into town for a shopping trip and to pick up a part for their old truck.

"You look lovely, Zia," I say as she pins her straw hat into her hair.

"I look like a tomato left on the vine too long, wrinkly and ready to fall to the ground and rot," she says, waving off my compliment.

"Zia!" I laugh, the image too grotesque to imagine.

"My wife, the beautiful tomato," Zio says, kissing Nina on the cheek as he walks past. "The car is running. We should go."

"Fine. Fine." Zia Nina retrieves her bag from the closet, a straw color that matches her hat. "Viviana, don't work too much. You have a long day."

"Yes, Zia. I know." I intend to do as many chores as possible and prepare a meal of tortellini. She knows I'll do "too much work," but we have to perform this dance in order to make it acceptable in her eyes.

I kiss her goodbye and thank Zio Mario.

As I set to work cleaning the kitchen, I get lost in the steady hum of housework. It's a satisfying monotony. The tasks seem far more achievable than reestablishing a film career or keeping my sister from falling into another depression or mania or raising a daughter without the help of a husband.

The work goes fast, and I head outside to wash the bedsheets and undershirts in warm, sudsy water.

When the linens and other white articles of clothing are rinsed and wrung, I make a line of clothespins on the collar of my dress and drape each damp item over the line in the yard. As the sun reaches its pinnacle in the cobalt sky, dotted sparsely with fine, fluffy clouds, my stomach grumbles. It's well past lunchtime, but I can't waste the sun and wind of the afternoon by leaving even one wet undershirt in the basket. I imagine Zia Nina's relief as she comes up the drive to see the spotless white flags waving in the wind and forget about my hunger.

Almost finished, I wrestle with one particularly troublesome sheet. I climb under the cloth to smooth it on the line, the cool touch of the moist textile refreshing. I could stay here in the shady tent, the sun a minuscule yellow spot on the opaque fabric above me. It's dreamlike here, but it also feels more real than most of the important moments in my life. But then the wrinkles flatten and the wind stops as though it's been inhaled. The pocket of protection collapses, and I wiggle out of the sheet, the magical moment passed. I reach for Zio Mario's nice dress shirt he wore to Mass on Sunday, his first time in a year, Nina said.

"Vivian?"

I freeze with the shirt halfway on the line. It's like hearing the voice of a dead man, the one I've spent the last weeks mourning. I toss the last sleeve up over the line and pin it in place before ducking under the pure white fabric fluttering in the breeze. There, on the other side, stands Trombello in his priestly vestments, holding his wide-brimmed *saturno* in front of him. A leather satchel hangs at his side, its strap cutting across his cassock. I raise my hand to my forehead to block the sun and squint at him.

"Trombello?" I ask. Is he real or a specter? Am I being haunted by a man who isn't dead?

"Sì," he says, walking up the drive to where I stand under the broad, towering plume of the Italian stone pine.

"How did you find me?" I ask at the same time he says, "Forgive me."

We both laugh a little, though I'm guarded, unable to forget his coldness at our last meeting. I'm so exhausted by changeable men. Why are women called the weaker of the two sexes when we carry so much?

"You told me you were visiting your family in Ogliara, and I'm a priest, so the rest was easy." He gestures to his vestments. He's right. Everyone here trusts a man of God. All it takes is asking a friendly face on the street and he'd have Zia's address and a loaf of bread for his supper. "My only worry was that you'd be gone."

"That thing's not fair," I say, pointing to his collar. "Everyone has to be nice to you when you wear one of those."

"Eh, there are always a few atheists out there who give me dirty looks, but perhaps you're right. It's hard to truly know someone when they think you're holy."

"It's impossible to know someone based on outward appearances alone," I agree. I can count the number of people on one hand who truly know me. This man used to be one of them.

He nods and then stares at the house and then back at me. The wind plays with my thin cotton dress and the unruly strands that have escaped from my bun. The threadbare fabric flits around my calves, and hair tickles the side of my face.

"Can you forgive me?" he asks again. He nervously spins his hat in a circle, waiting for my verdict.

I study him, taking my time before answering. I see a few signs of age I didn't notice in the dimly lit church. Some wrinkles at his eyes, some on his forehead. Some silver strands in his dark hair, curled at the tips. But his eyes are soft and welcoming today, and even with these minuscule changes, this Trombello, the one asking for forgiveness, is the Trombello I used to know.

"Can you forgive *me*?" I ask, snapping a small twig off the branch hanging between us and fiddling with it so I don't have to look at him when he answers. This is the more important question, in my mind.

"I already had," he says.

My head pops up, and I survey him with suspicious eyes. "You could've fooled me."

"I know. I know." He shifts his weight from one foot to the other. I see shame there, shame and regret. Two emotions I'm far too familiar with.

"It's all right," I say, cracking the twig in half and tossing it on the ground. "I wasn't fair to you, cutting you off like that. All I do is take, Trombello. It's wrong."

He shakes his head. "It's your life, Vivian. God is the only one who can touch it. I tried to steal God's role, I tried to be God for you."

He's wrong. He hasn't tried to be God for me. I've made him god-like all on my own.

"No. I deified you, made *you* my saint." It's a painful admission, and I pick at the bark on the trunk of the pine. "So when I knew I'd displeased you, I hid, like Adam and Eve in the garden."

"I'm no saint," Trombello says without meeting my eye, shame showing again. He places his hat on his head, looking more holy than ever before. But as much as his previous coldness hurt me, I'm grateful to get a glimpse of the flesh-and-blood man under his pious persona.

"You shouldn't have to be." I stare into his eyes, trying to let him feel how deeply I mean it. He doesn't have to be perfect with me.

He shakes his head and looks at the house.

"And . . . how is your family?" he asks, urging a change in the subject.

"Better than I could've hoped." A healing warmth spreads through me as I tell him how Zia Nina sent Zio Mario to the small hotel in town to retrieve my bag the morning after I arrived. I tell him of Zia Claudia's gentle nature and generosity, assuring him I have six other dresses just like this one hanging in the closet upstairs that used to belong to my cousin.

The stories pour out of me, and he says, "You've always been so nervous to come here." He smiles tenderly as though he's proud of me.

"I had so many excuses. They were all stupid." I laugh and roll my eyes at my foolishness.

"But you did it. You look like you belong here," he says, acknowledging my outfit, bare feet, and low-profile hairstyle. I wrap windblown strands behind my ear and straighten my dress, which I fill out a little better than when I first put it on.

"I could move here and fit right in. No one would know I'm a runaway actress. Look, I even do chores now." I sweep my arm in the direction of the laundry. Another laugh, and then a moment of awkwardness passes between us. He's blushing, and I don't know why.

"Could I . . . ," he starts and then tries again. "Would it be too presumptuous of me to meet your family?" he asks. I'm sure my family would be honored to have a man of God in their home, but I don't know if it'd be considered rude to invite a guest without asking ahead of time.

"Gosh, it wouldn't, but they're not home," I sigh, frustrated. I'd love to have some time to catch up, to make sure this forgiveness isn't momentary or fleeting. "I'm trying to finish a few chores for them before I leave tonight."

"Leave?" he asks, catching on the one word.

"I leave for Rome tonight," I explain. "I have a few meetings later this week and reshoots starting next week, and then I'm heading back to California." I long to hold my Gracie in my arms and measure how much she's grown and find out how much I've missed in my time away. But even so, I'm sad to leave because Italy has changed me. This ancient land shushed and comforted the unsettled part of me that felt unmoored, not American enough or Italian enough at the same time.

"Ah," he says, looking disappointed.

"I'll be back," I rush to reassure him. I'm not going away forever. "Aria needs to see the sunflower fields, and I know my zias will gobble up Gracie, even if she thinks she's too old for hugs."

He watches me with a grin. "I hope one day to meet them both."

"I'd love that. And one day you could visit us in California, see the Walk of Fame and the big white letters of the Hollywood sign. Wouldn't the papers love it if I brought a priest to my next opening?" I laugh at the idea, knowing how easily they find ways to make terrible accusations about anyone, including a member of the clergy. "Are there tuxedo cassocks?"

"I do not think so." He chuckles, his cheeks going red again. My God, I've missed him.

"Thank you for coming here," I say, but what I mean is "Thank you for forgiving me."

"Thank you for coming to confession," he says, and I'm sure his gratitude also has a double meaning. He starts to back away. "I shouldn't steal any more of your time, seeing it's so short. I'll leave you be."

I grumble. Time is running out just when we're finding our comfortable rhythm again. I stop him, filled with a rash, sudden idea.

"We could ride the train together—later tonight. We go right past Nola. We'll finally have a chance to catch up," I suggest, remembering we're headed in the same direction. We could sit face-to-face, tell our stories and pick through all the carcasses.

He squints against the sun. His feet shuffle in the dust as though he's planning out a detailed choreography, and then he exhales as though he's completed some internal debate I'll never be privy to.

"What time do you leave?"

VIVIAN SNOW

Auction

Lot #22

Hand-drawn postcard labeled: Colomba
    Pencil on cardstock. Sweet bread baked into the shape of a dove, decorated with nuts and sugar.

    NOLA. ITALIA. 22 APR 1957
        Happy Easter.
        (Translation from Italian)

CHAPTER 22

July 4, 1957
Bari, Italy

The sea breeze feels different here, thicker, like I'm breathing in the sea with each inhale. I remember a similar feeling in the South Pacific, but there we also inhaled fear and danger, and I breathed out grief and loss. Walking down the rocky beach with Trombello—no, with Antonio, as I'm now working to call him—those mournful, salty memories seem a lifetime ago, and though he hasn't said it, I know he's as reluctant to leave tonight as I am.

He's wearing the off-the-rack suit I purchased for him the morning after our escape from reality. I'd said farewell to my family, and we boarded the five o'clock train, thinking we'd spend an hour together reminiscing and healing, but when we reached the station near Nola, it felt like only a moment had passed since we sat down together.

The idea started as a lark. I offered it knowing he'd refuse. He laughed as though I were joking, and I pretended he was right. He took me into an unexpected embrace as the train shuddered to a stop in Nola, and we both swore we'd write. I kissed his hand, and he grasped my fingers fiercely. I covered my face with a handkerchief as he slung his satchel over his shoulder and disembarked. I couldn't watch him walk away, so I tilted my hat to cover my face.

As the last calls were made and the other passengers settled into their seats, a man slid into the empty spot beside me, and I curled into myself further, bitter at the intrusion.

"Let's go on an adventure," Trombello whispered in my ear. I squealed, making the other passengers whip around, but with my tears and a few comforting gestures from Trombello, it looked as though he was caring for a grief-stricken passenger. What they couldn't see was the smile hidden behind the handkerchief.

"Yes!" I whispered back, and we planned our wildly spontaneous escapade. I didn't need to return to work until Thursday, and he'd been given a week's holiday. In Naples, we purchased tickets on the new electric train, and after a short wait and a quick call to Aria explaining my change in plans so she wouldn't worry when I didn't answer her call at my Rome apartment later that night, we were on our way to the seaside.

I didn't tell Aria about Trombello. I hadn't even told her that I'd seen him in Nola or that he'd broken my heart there. That should've been my first clue that what we were doing was wrong. But it was only when my eyes drooped and our conversation faltered because of fatigue that the oddity of our impromptu trip truly sunk in. A priest and a young woman traveling together alone, overnight, is an uncommon sight. It's one that grew more awkward as the miles flew by, the landscape made invisible by the thick blackness of the night outside our train window.

It was simpler in Indiana, when he wore a POW uniform and didn't look like a priest, though still fully devout. As we exited the train at the eastern seaport of Bari, we kept space between us, using our fellow passengers as cover. I wore a scarf high on my neck, my too-large hat tipped low, aware that I might be recognized, especially in a town flooded with American tourists.

It felt like a secret mission, like we were behind enemy lines together, dodging Soviet spies and taking on cover personas. Trombello became just Antonio, and I became Ana. We were once again cousins, a role we'd played before, this time visiting the seaside together in memory of our lost grandmother. Or at least that's the story I wove at the small shop on the corner of Via Napoli and Via Trevisani where I chose a suit for my cousin Antonio and a plain brown dress with no accents or frills for myself because the shop had nothing in black.

I walked out of the boutique, wearing the dowdy dress, a simple cap hat, and low heels, and handed him the box with his disguise. He assessed my getup.

"You still look like Vivian Snow," he said, mocking my attempts to blend in.

"The costume is only one part of the façade. Are you doubting my acting skills?"

"No. No," he assured me. "You're a fine actress, but no matter the part, even on the screen, you look like Vivian Snow."

I rolled my eyes and pointed to his new uniform.

"Change." We agreed to meet at the Veronero Caffè down the street. I sat at a small, circular table made of heavily lacquered wood and traced a work-worn nail over the bubbles stuck just underneath the surface. I'd ordered espresso and biscotti for both of us, but when I reached the bottom of my first cup and he hadn't returned, I started to wonder if he'd changed his mind and caught the first train back to Nola. Strangely, I wasn't hurt by the thought. Selfishly disappointed, yes, but how could I blame him? This was a rash and impulsive trip, and if he'd chosen to protect himself by leaving, I'd understand. To comfort myself I thought through what the next two days alone would look like. I'd sleep, eat, and prepare myself to finish this film and then go home and face Glenn. I couldn't ignore that situation any longer.

It'd been half an hour, and I was suddenly certain Trombello wasn't coming back. I ordered a second espresso to fight my exhaustion after our all-night adventure and gave in to the temptation of the biscotti.

"Is this seat taken?" a young man in a suit asked right as I bit into the sweet, crunchy pastry I'd been dipping into the rich, steaming beverage. I was about to mumble a polite reply, not in the mood for company, when I saw the interloper.

There stood Trombello in the suit and matching felt hat that I'd picked out. Though the suit sagged around his waistline, and the coat and pants were made for a shorter man, he looked the part of a dashing, young Italian on holiday with family.

"Well, look at you," I exclaimed in English, far louder than I meant to. The whole room quieted a bit like they thought I was about to make an announcement.

I did the only thing I could think of and stood and wrapped my arms around him, declaring loudly how good it was to see my dear cousin, whom I hadn't seen since he was a small child. We were convincing enough that the room quickly lost interest after our awkward embrace, but I couldn't forget how his touch made me feel. Before this trip, I hadn't been in his arms since we danced together at Blinstrub's, but after the train and our playacting, it was becoming a familiar and exciting sensation.

I ordered him a fresh drink, and we sat and whispered to each other in English until lunch. I never knew I had so much to say.

We checked into our separate rooms as soon as they were available but only stayed apart for a brief nap. Over the next two days, we spent every moment possible together, walking, exploring, talking. But it's not only the chatty moments where we talk of our childhoods or we laugh at stories of Gracie or he tells me what it's really like working as a parish priest or what it was like to return to his battered country after the war. It's also how little I'm required to say when I'm around him.

And now as we take one last walk down the shore, sweating in our suit and dress while children flit about in swim bottoms and not much else, their mothers shouting words of caution from the shore, we've grown mute. It's an intimate silence, one that welcomes a reprieve but also doesn't require it. My arm is looped through his when he speaks first.

"You'll have a ride to your apartment from Roma Termini?" he asks for the third time today.

"Yes, I'll take a taxi. Don't worry. I'm used to traveling alone." I've never minded it before, but now it seems a touch lonely after having a constant travel companion.

"I know."

We walk in silence again, until we're well away from the over-crowded public beach. Here, it's rockier and the waves are choppy. As we reach a dock only a few blocks away from the hotel, sweat drips down my back and my shins are damp with perspiration under my thick nylons.

"That's it!" I say, stopping at a large boulder to sit down. "It's too hot to walk like this. I haven't come all this way to not even put one toe in the water." I take off my shoes. Trombello watches me, but when I lift my skirt to unbuckle my stockings, he averts his gaze.

"I thought we were trying to keep a low profile," he says, amused but also confused at my outburst.

"Low profile, my foot." I roll down my sweaty stockings, pull them off, and stuff them into my empty shoes. "We look ridiculous walking around like this on the beach. You're gonna die of heatstroke with that thing on. Come on, join me." I unpin my hair and let it roll down my back as I wade out into the water, carefully navigating the smooth rocks that line the shore. The surf is warm and rushes up my calves and halfway up my thighs as a big wave hits. I inhale, laughing in the sea mist and wishing I had my swimsuit so I could dive in and really experience the ocean.

Trombello watches from the shore for a moment and then says, "All right, then," and peels off his shoes, socks, and coat, rolling up his slacks and the sleeves of his shirt.

"Take off the tie," I holler.

"What?"

"Your tie!" Another wave smashes against my legs, nearly sending me tumbling. He removes it along with his hat.

"There you go," I yell, as he gingerly walks out to where I'm standing.

"This is insanity," he says after tripping and nearly falling into the waist-deep water. Usually, any reference to psychosis would upset me, but not today. Today, I'm glad for being a little mad.

"Isn't it glorious?" I ask, jumping over a wave and landing with a wobble. He steadies me, touching my waist as another, smaller surge hits. He's watching me like he's memorizing this moment, like he's memorizing my face and this place, like he wishes he could stop time. My breath catches in my throat. I wish it too, but nothing can stop time.

Another wave slams into our legs, and we grasp for each other's hands so we don't fall, though my skirt is already soaked, and his pants are on their way there.

"Ready?" I ask, taking his hand and smiling mischievously.

"For what?" His eyes are wide and brown, and I can't imagine ever forgetting them and this moment.

"This!" I shout. "Jump!" I tug on his arm and leap into the air, as I do with Gracie at Venice Beach when the tide is high. We jump together, she and I, flinging our legs over the sea-foam crests until they grow too large to conquer, and then we give in and let the tide sweep us into shore.

But Trombello doesn't know the game and doesn't know the right moment to leap. As the next wave peaks in front of us, I jump, but he hesitates, and instead of flying over the swell, I fall backward into him, and we both tumble into the ocean. The water is shallow, and we pop up, saltwater streaming from my eyes and mouth, stinging my nose and the back of my throat.

"Are you cool now?" he asks, coughing as another wave hits us. We both laugh and help each other up.

"That wasn't planned, I swear," I say, trying to sound innocent.

"I know. I know." He staggers, and I steady him this time, taking his hand. The moment our palms touch, I feel a shock of energy, similar to when we embraced in the café but stronger, as though the water carries the current at a greater intensity. I lace my fingers through his as we tiptoe cautiously to our clothing on the shore. When we reach the large rock, we don't let go. Instead, Trombello takes my other hand and stares deeply into my eyes.

I've had many moments of romance in my life where I thought a man loved me. But Antonio Trombello is the only man I've known who loves me without doubt or reservation, a love that is beyond lust or fame or greed.

I step closer to him, and he shuffles closer to me until I can feel the heat of our skin in the space between us. His chest rises and falls rapidly, and I tilt my chin up. I know what I want more than anything. But he doesn't kiss me. Instead he leans down and places his forehead against mine, his eyes closed.

"I had a dream last night you were my wife." I close my eyes, too, and let his breath wash over me as he speaks. "We had a house and children and a little cat you snuck bits of anchovies to when you made dinner." He laughs as though the dream were real. "We lived a whole life, in that dream. And when I awoke I cried to lose it."

I touch his cheek, and he burrows into my caress.

"Come home with me," I whisper. I can see it, I can feel how perfect it would be. "No one's stopping you."

"God is stopping me," he says, but doesn't pull away.

"God will understand."

"No, no, he won't." He shakes his head very slightly. I open my eyes and watch him.

"You told me God understands hard things. You told me he wouldn't blame me for Tom"—it's difficult to say his name after all these years, but I get it out—"and Glenn."

"That's the other thing stopping me," he says, leaning back, physically repelled by the mention of my husband. He unrolls his pant legs and sleeves, mumbling to himself.

"Were you lying to me about God?" I ask, feeling betrayed. How is God's forgiveness enough for me but not Trombello? I touch his shoulder and he stops fidgeting. "When you said I could be forgiven for Tom, when you said I could leave Glenn, were those lies?"

He yanks me in again, pressing me against his chest, holding me tight like he's going to kiss me as I've never been kissed before.

"I don't know what's real anymore when it comes to you," he says roughly, and then releases me and steps away, far enough that I don't think he'll make the same mistake again.

"I was going to leave him when I got home," I call to Trombello as he walks up the berm, dragging his suit coat. "Are you saying I shouldn't?"

"Don't ask me that."

"But will God understand?" I ask, pleading for an answer.

"Viviana!" he shouts, turning to look at me, tossing his hands into the air. "I am not God!"

Damn it. I'm doing it again. I grab my shoes and stockings and run after him.

"I'm sorry. You're right." I stop him, touching his elbow. "Please, I don't want to go back to the way things were."

"We won't. I just need some time to consider these things carefully, to think, to pray." He wrestles the word out of his mouth as though he feels unworthy to say it.

"Really? You might . . . you might come with me?"

He nods but doesn't look at me.

"But I must do this part alone," he says forcefully, keeping a wide berth between us. "As should you."

"How long?" I ask, unsure if his praying and pondering will take a day, a week, or a year.

"Next week. I'll come to you in Rome before you return home and tell you which way I must go."

"Next week," I say, a tickle of excitement starting in my core and running through to my fingertips.

Trombello and I walk back to our hotel in silence, pack in our rooms, and then take a taxi to the station without a word exchanged other than for logistical reasons. He's back in his black shirt and pants with his clerical collar displayed. The moment has passed, this trip, these days together, were nothing more than a dream. He's Trombello the priest again, and I'm the actress he knew during the war.

When I asked him to return to California with me, I was living in a dreamworld that existed for the briefest moment in time. Truthfully, I'd expected a flat refusal. It was an offer fueled by loneliness and unmet desires, but knowing that Trombello is seriously considering the monumental life change makes it seem like anything is possible.

I follow him onto the train, parting ways to separate cars where he will start his private pondering, and I wave goodbye to the dearest friend I've ever known. I never thought I'd love again or let someone in again, but perhaps that's why this might work—because I already love this man. And the only thing that stands in the way of our happiness is God.

Well, God and my husband.

VIVIAN SNOW

Auction

Lot #23

Hand-painted postcard. No label.
Watercolor on cardstock. Cherry tomatoes ripening on the vine.

FIRENZE. ITALIA. 12 NOV 1957
-BLANK-

CHAPTER 23

March 26, 1958
Carver Mansion
Beverly Hills, California

I stare at myself in the mirror. Looking back is Vivian Snow, Best Actress nominee, Golden Globe and Laurel Award winner, hair up in an elegant twist with a strand of diamonds around her neck, a Dior dress on the bed waiting to be photographed on the red carpet. Vivian Snow with a wedding band on her left hand, thick with gold and precious stones, and her husband half-drunk, shouting in the background. Vivian Snow, her eyes glassy and lost, dreading the most important night of her career, trying instead to remember what the sea air in Bari felt like in her lungs.

I should've known we'd end up here again, I think to myself, wishing I could go back in time to when I returned to my tiny Rome apartment after a day of reshoots and found the door unlocked. I should've run away. I think I was hoping I'd push open the door and find Trombello waiting inside, his bags packed and our future limitless. I was leaving the next day, and my nerves were frayed waiting for his final decision. Mine was already made—if he was willing to risk everything to be with me, I was willing to do the same.

But it wasn't my dear Antonio I found on the other side of that door, it was my long estranged husband, Glenn. He was sitting at the small circular table with his feet propped up. It looked uncomfortable, and I'm sure he'd been planning the moment in his head, like any good director. I screamed even though I recognized him immediately.

"Hush, you'll get the police called on me," he said, dropping his feet with a heavy thunk. He wore a dark suit, one I'd never seen before, expensive looking, and a gold Rolex probably worth more than my house.

"What are you doing here, Glenn?" I asked, shaking. He hadn't spoken a word to me in years, literally years. After my miscarriage and the critical success of *Marry Me Friday*, he tried to convince me to work with him again. When I refused, he had me fired for breach of contract. But he didn't stop there.

He pulled a surprise visit to my dressing room after the live television performance of *A Doll's House*. And when that didn't convince me, he showed up at Gracie's school and drove her home in his Rolls-Royce, chatting with her the whole way about how wonderful it would be to have us move into the big house. He promised her candy and toys in return for putting a good word in.

When she didn't get off the bus, I called her school in a panic, and they told me her father had picked her up. I called the police and ran down the street to the house we used to share. Gracie was sitting at the table with a glass of milk and a plate full of cookies.

He begged me to move home, but as soon as I asked if I'd be guaranteed freedom to choose what and where and with whom I work and if he'd be loyal and treat me as an equal—that's when he turned fierce. And when I dared to question where he was the night of Aria's suicide attempt, the same night we lost our baby, he started to rant and rave about the postcards he'd found and Trombello's influence on our marriage.

The police arrived a few minutes later. Glenn calmed and packed up Gracie's cookies in a paper bag with a heart drawn on it. I told him to never speak to my daughter again, and the policemen looked at me like I was insane.

Aria begged me to divorce Glenn, Archie told me it couldn't hurt my career at this point, and I didn't ask Trombello's opinion because I already knew what his biased advice would be. So I spoke to Father Peter from my home parish and told him the story of my terrible marriage. He told me that even if we hadn't married in the church, matrimony is a holy sacrament and that I should never leave it.

"Divorce is a grave offense against the natural order." He said that any question of dissolution must come before a church court for an annulment, but it could take years to be granted. His advice was to live in whatever way would preserve the marriage, even if that meant living apart. So I didn't divorce him, and he didn't divorce me. Instead, Glenn just did everything within his power to ruin my life and career. As soon as I rebuilt some of what he ruined, as soon as I was prepared to leave him forever, he was back, sitting in my apartment in Rome as though he belonged there.

"What, I'm not allowed to visit my wife?"

"I'd hardly call me your wife," I said, tossing my netted bag filled with a wedge of parmesan, a loaf of bread, and fresh produce onto the counter. I removed the scarf from my head and sat on the bed to slip off my shoes, dusty from the streets. I glanced around the room for anything that might help me defend myself.

There was no phone in the tiny flat, only in the hall. I made my collect long-distance calls each night to Aria and Gracie and sometimes Archie with my face pressed into the corner to keep our conversations private. I didn't know who to call in an emergency. I didn't know the number for the police. I knew I could walk out the door and scream, but who'd hear me? Would they get here in time if Glenn did something truly nefarious? Would I even get one sound out before he silenced me for good?

"You're my wife whether you like it or not," he said, his tone softer than I expected, mournful maybe.

"What do you want, Glenn?" I said, tying on an apron to make dinner. It was the easiest way to get a knife in my hand without setting him off.

"I told you, to see my wife. That's all."

"You want something," I insisted, refusing to be a sucker.

"I want you to come home."

"Home?" I laughed ruefully. "I have a home, and I'll return there tomorrow."

"I want to work things out. I want to go back to the way things were."

"The way things were?" I gripped the knife tightly. I was no fool. He wanted me for the same reason he always had—money. His last hit was *Marry Me Friday*, and if I was going to start getting jobs again, he clearly wanted in on the action. But I couldn't say that without fear of his reaction, so instead I said, very politely, "No thank you."

It was a relief to hold the blade in my hand as I set out the tomatoes, garlic, and onion in a line on the cutting board. Abruptly he was behind me, his body trapping me against the counter. His scent was familiar and the heat a reminder of times past when I welcomed his touch instead of fearing it. I kept working without recoiling.

"You have every right to hate me, but please, please give me one more chance." He kissed the nape of my neck, and I fought off a wince. I didn't crave his touch anymore, I craved Trombello's.

Seeds and pulp gushed out of the tomato at my first slice. I cut and chopped on autopilot as he begged, pleaded, bargained.

"I know I've gone about this all wrong. I'll make it up to you. Move in Gracie, your sister, anyone you want. I know MGM wants to sign you. Nunnally Johnson wants you. And I won't interfere this time. I promise—I promise!"

I finished the tomato and moved on to the onion, unmoved by his offers. It was everything I'd ever wanted to hear him say. It was everything I'd ever hoped for in my career. It'd keep me from returning to the tiny soundstages filming the macabre teleplays, or even worse, giving up on acting entirely to get a steady job to keep our family afloat.

But I didn't want what he had to offer.

"I already told you, no thank you." I filled a pot with water and lit the burner as he followed my every move like a shadow.

"That's all you have to say? No thank you?" I began chopping the garlic, my eyes still stinging. I hoped the smell would make him recoil like it always used to, but it didn't. He put his hand over mine, halting the movement of the blade and taking away my greatest chance for escape if it came to it.

"I'll tell everyone about the priest," he said, his passionate, generous pleading turned dark. The knife fell with a clink as my extremities went numb.

"You said that last time," I said, bracing myself on the counter, calling his bluff. I knew how to take care of myself and my family without Glenn, protect them. But Trombello? "There's nothing to tell."

"I didn't think so at first, but a good private eye can uncover some scandalous things."

"You don't know what you're talking about," I said, my voice shaking, the tears in my eyes no longer a reaction to the onions. He turned me around, my empty hands frozen like a freeze-frame as my body trembled.

"I know enough. Antonio Trombello, that's his name, right? At least that's the name he used when he ordered that headstone, the one he bought you for your dead husband." I held back an exclamation. That was one of the many secrets known only by Trombello and me. "Sloppy of him to use his real name at that dinky cemetery. But I guess priests aren't known for being smart—"

I lunged against his towering form, trying to get past. "Leave Trombello out of this. He's a good man," I commanded. He grabbed my wrists and squeezed so tightly my fingers turned blue.

"Listen!" he shouted and then said it again calmer as I stopped trying to free myself. "Listen, I don't give a shit what happens to that creep. I'm worried about *you*. If Hedda Hopper were to hear about your scandalous fling with a priest and write about it right as this hack film you're working on comes out . . . Damn. That'd be messy. Don't you think?"

I stared up at him, horrified. He was acting as though he wasn't the one wielding my past as a weapon. "Come home," he pleaded again, his mouth nearly on top of mine, his breath smelling of cigarettes and strong coffee.

I didn't say yes, not right away. I didn't collapse on the bed in a fit of passion and let him kiss me and take my body in ways that used to thrill me. I told him I'd think about it, I fed him dinner, and I sent him back to his hotel. I was stalling. I had a plan. When Trombello came the next day, we'd face Glenn together. He'd know what to do. He'd know.

But Trombello never came. In fact, it's been over a year since I talked to the man I was sure I loved.

When it became clear Trombello had made his God-centered choice, I knew I had to make mine. At first I played along with Glenn's truce as a hostage, to keep Trombello safe and my career safe, to keep my marriage sacrament intact. But then Glenn followed through on all of his assurances, including giving back every cent of my income he'd held hostage in his bank account during our separation. He also gave me complete autonomy financially and creatively.

Three months after I returned to LA, I agreed to move back in with Glenn. Gracie joined me, overjoyed with the pretty canopy bed he'd purchased for her and the record player in her bedroom stocked with vinyl records. Aria chose to stay behind in the bungalow, living alone for the first time in her life, with Margot and our mother visiting often.

In the big house, Glenn threw parties, and I was reacquainted with famous friends and artists. Gracie went to school with a few of Mickey Rooney's kids, and once again my kitchen counter held stacks of scripts and my social calendar brimmed with parties, appointments, and red carpet appearances.

It seemed like God was rewarding me for staying in my marriage. He may have taken my baby and my ability to have any more children, but he gave some of my dreams back. I missed my Trombello, but I did my best to not think of him.

During nearly the entire premiere of *The Love of a Woman*, I sat in the ladies' room, feigning illness. The sights of Rome and the footage of the countryside brought back my time there and when I last saw Trombello as we walked away from one another in the Roma Termini train station. I thought I'd see him again. Truly, I thought I might never be without him, and that hopeful moment hurts more than some of my most painful memories. And as the nominations rolled in for all the biggest awards in the film industry, I almost wished I'd be overlooked so I could forget my time in Italy altogether.

But, like any dream, even the best ones, this fairy-tale life with Glenn didn't last forever.

At first it was Glenn's drinking, then it was the pills. He needed them to sleep. He needed the other ones to wake up; he swore they were all medicinal. He swore it. He started to lose track of time, he started to get angry again, he started to treat Gracie strangely.

Last week he insisted I star in his next film. He took my new script for MGM and burned it in the kitchen sink. He hasn't started making threats, not yet, but I can feel it building.

Tonight he seems more on edge than usual.

"You have to tell him you won't do it, no matter what." Glenn is fully dressed, tuxedo jacket and pants pressed to perfection, with a simple bow tie, which he's now retied seven times. A cigarette hangs from his lips as he dumps several pills into his palm, drinking them down with a mouthful of whiskey. This is not a good start to what will likely be a long night.

"Tonight?" I ask, snapping out of my daydream. "I'm not sure that's possible, Glenn," I say, trying to keep my husband calm.

"Yes, damn it. Tonight. He's been champing at the bit for another opportunity to steal you away from me, and I'm not letting it happen,

Vivian. You promised you'd play Cora in *Twelve Flowers*. I don't care what kind of offers they make—you have to say no."

I try not to let my frustration show as I add one last puff of powder, checking all angles of my updo. Tonight is a big night for me—a nomination for Best Actress is nothing to scoff at, and I might have a real chance.

Glenn wasn't nominated this year, not for a single one of the films he worked on. He wants me to believe that my comeback is because of him, but he had nothing to do with *The Love of a Woman*, and he'll do anything to make this night miserable for me.

"I already signed the contract, Glenn. I can't back out or he'll sue." Studio contracts are a thing of the past, but Archie and I already agreed to my next film, the ink barely dry. I can't back out now.

I slip into my Dior couture gown, asking Glenn to zip it, which he does in such a rush it pinches my skin. I glance in the mirror and feel fully beautiful. The stiff pink satin skirt of the gown engulfs my legs and hips, displaying my corset-enhanced waist and pushing up my breasts into a tasteful display of cleavage.

The Academy Awards will be televised live, and that means from the moment we arrive, the eyes of the world will be focused on us with no breaks for lighting changes or touch-ups or directors calling "cut." We'll be performing from the moment we step onto the red carpet, and I, for one, want to make a good impression—on the audience at home but also on the Academy and my peers and secretly even dear Trombello all the way in Italy. So the pills and the booze Glenn's helped himself to are a bad sign.

"Don't forget Gracie's contract. I can't steal away her first speaking part," I remind Glenn. It's my first film with her.

While I was in Italy, Archie signed Gracie up for acting classes, and she took to it like a pro. Everyone says it must be in her genes, but I think it's from being on set since she was six. Aria says it's because she learned how to act normal when everyone in her family was losing their minds, which I take slight offense to but pretend to laugh at.

Now Gracie's going to be in an actual film, and I won't take that away from her.

"Eh, I'll put her in *Twelve Flowers*. She can be young Cora. Works perfectly because you look so much alike."

We look nothing alike, I think as I smooth my hair and touch up my lipstick, tossing it in my clutch when I'm finished. My husband barely knows me, barely cares about me. If only Trombello had come to me. If only things were different . . .

But he didn't come and they're not different. I exhale and work on my most difficult job by far—keeping Glenn happy. I turn and kiss him ever so lightly on the lips, making sure I've left not one bit of color.

"Let's just try to get through tonight. We can talk about it all in the morning."

"Fine," he says, sighing and downing the last bit of his drink.

As I get into the limo with the fairly intoxicated Glenn, Gracie watches from the front steps.

"Good luck!" she yells, holding Poncho, her miniature poodle, in one arm and waving with the other. My bright pixie girl, more fairy than human. I blow her a kiss and settle in for a silent ride with my ice-block husband. I can't help but hope I win tonight, but I fear his response if I do. In the back seat of an expensive limousine, smelling of fancy perfume and surrounded by yards of stiff pink satin, I wonder if I'll ever feel as happy as I did wearing an old brown dress, soaked to the bone in seawater, standing face-to-face with a man I thought might kiss me on a rocky beach in Bari.

VIVIAN SNOW

Auction

Lot #24

Hand-drawn postcard labeled: Fireworks in Florence
   Black ink on cardstock. Fireworks around Ponte Vecchio on river Arno.

FIRENZE. ITALIA. 01 JAN 1958
   Happy New Year.
   (Translation from Italian)

CHAPTER 24

March 26, 1958
RKO Pantages Theater
Los Angeles, California

A life-size version of the Oscar statue looms upstage center at the podium, where John Wayne holds an envelope and our rapt attention. It's the second to last award of the night and the reason I'm here.

"And the winner is . . ." He glances around the room coyly, making the most of his moment onstage. They always wait for an obnoxious amount of time after that sentence. It's annoying. It's manipulative. It's—glorious to hear your name.

"Vivian Snow, for *The Love of a Woman*."

The applause swells and the room sways. I squeeze Glenn's hand before I stand to take the stage. He tugs it away, and my stomach tightens. I don't dare look at him, knowing the blank expression I'd likely find. My face must show joy for the cameras, it must show gratitude.

The statue I receive looks the same as the first one sitting on a shelf in Glenn's office that I accepted in 1951. But back then I didn't go to any of the parties before or after the awards. Glenn was bitter at his loss that year, and I was a fool who still cared about protecting my husband's fragile feelings. That was before I knew how deeply cruel he could be.

"Keep it short," Bob Hope, host for the night, whispers as he shakes my hand, smiling for the cameras. Last year Dorothy Malone took a full two minutes for her Supporting Actress acceptance, thanking her producer and dedicating the award to her dead brother. My thoughts go dark, and I momentarily consider dedicating the award to my dead husband whom I stabbed, or my stillborn child, or my friend the Italian priest whom I thought I'd fallen in love with during the filming of this movie. By the time I have the heavy statue in my hands and get to the microphone, I say only, "Thank you to Vittorio De Sica for his faith in me. And to the Academy for this honor."

The crowd applauds, and John escorts me to the press pavilion, where I'm handed a glass of champagne. He has the same dry personality and slow drawl offstage as he does on camera. I make small talk as we sip the bubbly and wait for our turn to face the horde of journalists. I haven't eaten all day, and the buzz from the alcohol comes quickly, making the whole experience even more dreamlike.

I pose holding my heavy golden statue and smiling so hard my teeth ache and cheeks crease.

"Come on, dear. This way." A man in a short coat with a golden braid at his shoulder urges me forward as though I'm a kid in the lunch line at elementary school. I take another glass of champagne, and I'm rushed off to another station where more flashbulbs pop and lenses click, and then to another room where members of the press shout questions at me. They want to know how it feels to win three separate awards for my performance in *The Love of a Woman*.

"Surreal," I reply.

They ask if the other actresses seem jealous.

"They've been so sweet. I adore them," I lie. Yes, they definitely hate me.

They ask if Glenn is jealous. My words evaporate, and I focus on keeping my features neutral.

"Of course not. He's my biggest fan," I say after the briefest pause. Curse the press. Curse their nosy little questions that hit too close to home.

I smile, I thank, I make small jokes that elicit bursts of laughter from the men in dark suits and glasses. At long last, I hand over my award, which I'm assured will be returned to me with all the correct details engraved in its base. I kiss the statue on the head, which makes the crowd laugh, and then give one last wave to the room.

When I'm released on the other side, I'm exhausted. I scan the room, hoping to see Glenn. The night isn't over—in fact, the awards ceremony is only a small sliver of activity on this day. But it's not Glenn I see—it's Tito.

"The car is around back," he says.

"Where's Glenn?" I ask, my head starting to spin as I glance around the receiving room. The show has been over for twenty minutes. Perhaps he's waiting in the car, having another drink before we head over to the Governors Ball at the Beverly Hilton Hotel.

Tito's expression softens as we slip out the back door of the theater. He's about to tell me bad news. I should've expected this.

"Mr. Carver went home early, I'm afraid."

"Is he all right? Was he feeling sick?" My shoulders slump with disappointment. I try to conjure a reason that will make this all okay, that will save me from the embarrassment of showing up alone and sitting next to an empty seat meant for Glenn.

"I'm not sure, miss. He took another car, asked me to stay and wait for you. Said he'd see you at home." He points to the limo idling in a line of cars. I sniff. Home. He wants me to go home on a night like this? No way.

"We're not going home, Tito." I open my own car door and collapse into the familiar back seat, no longer worried about creasing the creamy pink satin. Once he's behind the wheel I call out in my best fancy British accent as though I'm the queen, "Take me to the Beverly Hilton."

"Yes, miss," he says, looking at me through the rearview mirror, pity and, if I'm not mistaken, a touch of respect showing in his wrinkled features. He puts the car in drive but doesn't take his foot off the brake when he speaks again. "Congratulations on your win, miss," he says with a tip of his hat before driving away from the RKO Theater.

"Why thank you, Tito," I say, wishing it were my husband and not his driver saying those words. "Thank you."

Traffic is thick and heavy but flowing at a steady pace as I sit in the back seat of Glenn's Rolls-Royce, blinking away tears.

VIVIAN SNOW

Auction

Lot #25

Hand-drawn postcard labeled: Grace Highward
Pencil on cardstock. Profile of a young teen girl.

FIRENZE. ITALIA. 12 MAR 1958
Birthday salutations to little Grace.
(Translation from Italian)

CHAPTER 25

March 27, 1958
Los Angeles, California

At the Governors Ball, the seat beside me is rarely empty as actors, directors, and producers I haven't seen in far too long come by to congratulate me. It seems the invisible veil that separated us for so many years is now gone.

Johnny Scott saunters over to my table toward the end of the ball. On my third drink, fifth if I count the champagne from earlier, I don't mind that he's moved into the chair beside me as though we're there together. His date, a young actress who goes by the name Lila Lockwood, sits alone at his table, pouting.

Johnny escorts me to the next few parties, leaving Lila in the dust. Mick Mitcham is at the second party at Sam Spiegel's house. He tells me how I haven't aged a day, and that he's written another movie with me in mind. As he traces the strap of my gown with his eyes, I tell him I've heard his wife is pregnant again, this time with their seventh or eighth. Apparently, Mrs. Mitcham is a devout Catholic, obviously more devout than I am, I tell him, too intoxicated to hold my tongue.

Johnny urges me into the back of the Rolls-Royce, giving Tito an address in Beverly Hills, barely keeping his hands to himself as my loyal driver glares at the handsome young actor from the front seat.

The last party is more intimate, a small house with a pool in the back and a U-shaped drive out front. After following us across town, Mitcham wandered home to his wife and glut of children around two a.m.

By three a.m., Scott sits beside me on a sofa with scratchy brown fabric. My third martini has taken me from loopy to sloppy, but I don't stop. And when the fourth is in my hand and Johnny is rubbing my shoulders and my arm and whispering things in my ear that'd make me blush if I heard them sober, a tall man in a dark suit asks if he can have a moment of my time.

"Do I know you?" Johnny asks, glaring at this man interrupting his chance at a drunk Vivian Snow.

"I'm her doctor," the familiar voice, deep and calm, replies. My head snaps up.

"Dr. Youngrin," I slur and then cover my mouth, embarrassed at my sloppy state.

He holds a small sandwich, a glass of water, and two little pills I recognize as aspirin.

"I'm fine, Johnny. Have Tito take you home. Tell him to pick me up when he's done." I give my order in a trancelike voice as I stare at the man who'd all but disappeared seven years ago. Johnny argues for half a second, but Dr. Youngrin cuts him off, and the actor takes the hint.

"My God, men can be relentless," Youngrin says, taking the now empty spot at my side.

"You're telling me."

"Bet you haven't eaten all night. Here." He passes me the triangle of white bread with cheese and pressed ham and puts the water on the table. "This should help."

The first bite turns my stomach, but he insists, so I power through. After a few minutes, the spinning in my head slows, and though I'm still very intoxicated, I can focus.

"My God, that's the best sandwich I've ever had," I rave, wishing I had another.

"I doubt that's true," Youngrin says. "Don't forget the water."

I drink it, maybe a little too fast, my bloated stomach pressing uncomfortably against the tight bodice of my gown.

"That was a mistake," I say, clutching my midsection.

"Here, this should help." He puts a pillow against the armrest and gently guides me into a reclining position, places a wet rag on my forehead, and kneels on the floor in front of me. "Keep that sandwich down and we'll try a little coffee."

I shake my head with my lips pressed closed. He laughs. I stare up at him, remembering the last time he took care of me, after Gracie let him in and led him to the bed where I lay, blood between my legs and my dying sister in my arms. He called an ambulance, he cleared Aria's airway, he breathed for her. He saved her life.

As the first ambulance drove away with Aria, he tried to convince me to let an ambulance come for me as well. I knew I needed to go to the hospital, but I wanted Glenn to take me. Dr. Youngrin tried him several times, but he didn't pick up the phone.

"Let me drive you," he said, worry etched on his face. "You're losing a lot of blood."

So we went, Gracie lying in the back to sleep and me in the front. I laid a towel and thick blanket on the seat so I wouldn't ruin the upholstery even after he told me not to worry about it. By then, I could barely walk, and the dull cramps in my stomach had begun to cut and burn. The lenses of his glasses were dirty like they are tonight, I remember that, the headlights of the passing cars catching them as they sped by. Tonight, the flames from the fireplace make me remember that night and how I wished I could wipe them down, help the man who was helping me.

"I never got to apologize," I say. He didn't save my baby, but he did save my life.

"Apologize? For what?" He flips the wet rag on my forehead to the cool side.

"For that night." I settle into the couch cushions, my nausea starting to pass. "For getting you involved. For getting you fired."

"Fired? What do you mean?" Dr. Youngrin takes a deep breath, looking unnerved.

"Glenn. When I didn't see you again, I assumed he let you go."

Dr. Youngrin chuckles but without humor, his jaw tensing and releasing.

"I wasn't fired. I quit." He clears the plate and goes to refill the water glass. There's a couple kissing on the couch across the room, and the record reaches its last groove and starts to skip. A heavy layer of smoke hangs low in the air like clouds haloing the mountain summit before a storm.

My head spins when I try to sit up, so I surrender to gravity and return to the safety of the couch. Youngrin is back. He lifts the tone-arm of the turntable to the beginning of the record. As the sound of the Everly Brothers fills the room, he kneels by me again, the scent of strong coffee following him.

"I couldn't find their sugar, so I hope you don't mind taking it black."

"I don't mind. I got used to it during the war." He helps me sit up, and this time I'm able to stay upright. I sip the bitter liquid, remembering my days on the Foxhole Circuit.

"Yeah, I guess we all did. I never told you, but I saw you perform once, way back then. I was a medic stationed in Guam."

"I had no idea," I say, shaking my head, remembering the stifling heat clearly but the faces of the men blurring.

It's been years since I've thought of those days of darkness after Larry's death. I was on autopilot, working because I had to and because I knew it was what Larry would've wanted.

"I don't think any of us had seen a woman in a month and then here's this vibrant star, singing and dancing in front of us. I don't think you know how much that meant. After the show, you came to the hospital and talked to the men for hours. I could see the goodness in you. It's far rarer than beauty, that's for sure." He pushes his glasses up his nose, and I wish he had come back to see Aria instead of marrying that woman I read about in the newspaper. He's a genuine man, despite his faults. But I'm the last one who should be tallying faults.

"I'm certain your perspective on me has shifted quite a bit since then." I pick at the napkin in my lap, ashamed of the side-by-side comparison in my mind.

"No. Not at all. I only wish—" He stops himself. "Never mind."

"You only wish what?" I ask, hanging on the ragged edge of his unfinished sentence.

He places the coffee on the table, stirring it to help it cool. The tink of the spoon against the white ceramic is soothing. He offers it to me, but I decline, wanting my question answered first.

"I only wish . . . ," he starts again, glancing over his shoulder at the entwined lovers, and then lowers his voice so no one can hear it above "All I Have to Do Is Dream." "I only wish you'd listened to me."

"About Glenn?" I ask, remembering the warning clearly: *If you stay in that house, you will die.* It was the most shocking diagnosis I'd ever heard from a doctor. I readjust in my seat, either the coffee or the confessions starting to sober me up.

"Yes. I'd heard years ago that you'd left him, but then I saw you together at Musso's a few months back and could've been pushed over with a feather. I was in such a shock my wife left in a huff, sure that you and I had been lovers." He snickers dejectedly.

"Did you tell her the truth?"

"I told her what I could, but it wasn't . . . everything."

I hold my breath, waiting for him to fill in the details he couldn't tell his wife. It was my body, my baby, my marriage, my life—I have a right to know.

"I think it's time you tell me it all."

"Are you sure?" he asks, as though he's assessing whether I can handle the secret he's been keeping.

What's been hidden from me, an affair or a violent past or whatever it may be, only serves to hold me prisoner. Truth is the only way to be free.

"I'm positive."

VIVIAN SNOW

Auction

Lot #26

Hand-drawn postcard labeled: Tuscan Cypress
    Black ink on cardstock. Long gravel path lined with tall, narrow cypress trees.

LUCCA. ITALIA. 18 MAR 1958

> *V—*
>   *Best wishes for your nomination.*
>   *—A*
>   (Translation from Italian)

CHAPTER 26

March 27, 1958
Carver Mansion
Beverly Hills, California

I'm still in my gown, though I lost my shoes somewhere between the party and my front door. I'll pack what I can, get Gracie up and we'll leave—for good. Then, I'm getting an attorney and filing for divorce. I don't care what God thinks or the church thinks, I don't care if Glenn tries to come after me or even Trombello. I don't care. Dr. Youngrin is right—if I stay, I'm going to die.

All the lights are off in the house, and I slink through the back hall to our bedroom. I'd leave everything behind and run down the street to the bungalow, but I'm no fool—Glenn will lose it when he wakes and finds me gone. Anything I want from this house I must take tonight, and that includes pictures of Gracie from when she was little, letters from Papà and Aria and Larry when I was on tour, Gracie's baby blanket, and the collection of Trombello's drawings and postcards. Most of those things are in the spare room, safely stored away in an old suitcase I never unpacked after our move. But in my bedroom I also have $10,000 in cash hidden under my mattress, an escape fund in case things went south again, and a large jewelry box filled with expensive pieces that can keep us afloat once the mattress money runs out.

I don't care if I'm blacklisted again or never appear in another film. I can't stay with the man who killed my baby.

Dr. Youngrin told me the story, and immediately I knew it was true. After he left me in the hospital, near death, my baby already gone, and after he left Aria in the psych ward, also battling to stay alive, he returned to the big house with Gracie to wake Glenn. He said Glenn was callous and removed, barely concerned at the news of the pregnancy loss or the other traumas from that night. Glenn left Gracie with the housekeeper and then went about his day, more irritated that I'd be missing work than anything.

His heartlessness set off alarm bells for Dr. Youngrin, who was still very shaken up from the harrowing events of the evening. As he returned to his daily rounds, he thought through everything, every step of my pregnancy, every adjustment to Aria's treatment. He recalled my endless nausea, weakness, fatigue, fuzzy head, extreme thirst, Aria's sudden depression after so much success with her lithium treatments, and that's when he realized it.

Glenn had swapped my vitamins with Aria's medication. Dr. Youngrin had warned us over and over again to keep the bottles separate. I remember his warnings to Aria about the risks of continuing the lithium treatments if she were to marry and want children one day. It's too dangerous to take lithium while pregnant. He warned and warned and warned, and Glenn must have been listening.

When the doctor confronted Glenn, he did what he always does, he threatened Youngrin. He said he'd get the physician's license taken away, blaming him for his addiction to pills. Youngrin was scared into silence. He quit and changed his entire career path but carried a load of shame for what happened to me and Aria. But when he saw that Glenn and I had reconciled, his conscience begged him to speak up. So when he saw me alone at the party tonight, he knew it was time to be the brave man he once was in the field hospitals of the South Pacific when he looked the horrors of war in the face and kept going.

When his words sunk in, I knew I had to be brave too. I needed to gather my courage and run and never look back.

So I am.

"Gracie, Gracie honey, wake up." I shake her slender shoulder in her queen-size canopy bed. It took me seven years to move her into this house, this fancy room, this family, and now after a year, I'm yanking her out of it again.

I shake her a little harder, and she lets out a small yelp that I muffle with the light touch of my hand. She blinks and rubs her eyes like she's sure I'm a dream.

"Oh, Mamma! You won!" she gasps, engulfing me in a hug. I remove her heavy, sleepy arms.

"Fill the bag with what you can. We have to leave—now."

"Leave?" she asks, hefting herself up till she's propped against the wall of pillows behind her. "Are we going on a trip?"

"I'll explain later, but we have to go to Zia's house."

"Zia's house?" she says, her eyebrows tipping inward.

"Yes. You can have your old room like before." I rummage through her drawers, gathering the items I know she'll need. "Put on a dress so we have less to carry and then bring one other." I point to the closet. "I have your underclothes and nightgown. We'll buy more when we can. And be as quiet as a mouse, okay?"

Gracie doesn't budge. She flops back into the pillows and crosses her arms over her satin comforter.

"No. I like it here. It's pretty and there are fun parties and Glenn treats me like I'm grown up and . . . if you want to go to Zia's house, go. I'm staying."

"You can't stay here," I say, still packing, my anxiety building. When people tell women to leave, to walk away from bad husbands or situations, they don't tell them that once they find the courage to get out, it's not an immediate happily ever after. They don't tell them leaving is dangerous and that sometimes even their child might not understand.

"Glenn says I can be in his next film. He says I'll be a star. You can't do this to me." She kneels in the middle of the bed. I flick on a light. No reason to keep the room dark with Glenn asleep down the hall.

"We can't stay. It's not worth it. I promise." I toss her a dark dress from the closet and a pair of socks and saddle shoes that are practical for walking. "Put these on."

She starts to dress but continues her rant. "Why do you always get to decide these things? It's not fair!"

I finish packing everything I can think of off the top of my head and turn and stomp my foot lightly on the floor.

"Basta!" I say in Italian, what my father used to say that would stop me in my tracks. Gracie's eyes go wide. "You want to be treated like an adult? Then act like one. Finish packing *now*, Grace."

I don't speak to my daughter this way, I try not to speak to anyone this way, but I won't let Glenn take another one of my children away from me.

She listens, and I leave her to dress. I tell her I'll be right back and then slink through the hall to the room I share with my husband.

Glenn is sound asleep in our bed wearing only his silk boxers. The underwater pool lights outside the window give the room an eerie, bluish tint like I'm walking underwater without holding my breath. Hitching up the wrinkled skirt of my gown, I tiptoe over to my makeup table, where my jewelry box and a row of perfumes sit. I load several gold chains, diamond bracelets, and strings of pearls into an overnight bag I retrieved from the hall closet.

I slide in earrings and combs and rings. In the bottom drawer I find my engagement ring, the one I wore when I married Tom, when I killed Tom, when I mourned Tom. I hesitate. The stone is worthless, but the band is white gold. But I wouldn't sell it anyway. It's become a symbol of Gracie's origins and a symbol of how much we've suffered to get to where our little family is now, how much struggle it's taken to be the woman I am now. I toss it in and then remove the large gold and diamond band Glenn gave me when I moved back in and place it in the middle of the now empty tabletop.

Trombello's postcards are still hidden in the suitcase in the corner of my side of the closet. I dump them on top of the jewelry. The most recent card came a week ago, a simple wish of luck sent to the bungalow and passed to me by Aria. For a short while I kept it taped to a random page in my latest script to keep me company, remind me of the maybes I had to give up on when Glenn showed up in Rome instead of Trombello. But then it fell out one day and Glenn walked right past it, nearly giving me a heart attack, so I put it in the box, which was probably for the best. If it'd stayed in my script even a day longer, I'm not sure I'd have been able to avoid the temptation to call him.

The bag is growing heavy. The only thing left to retrieve is the cash sandwiched between our mattress and the box spring. When I first started my secret savings, I'd considered hiding it in the spare room, but whenever Glenn has insomnia, or if he's taken too many uppers and can't make his brain quiet down, he hides out in there, crying, talking to himself and sometimes talking to invisible vestiges of his children who no longer take his calls. I didn't want him to find it during one of his episodes. Plus, I felt safe sleeping on my money. Now, I'm cursing the idea.

The crinoline petticoat under my dress is infernally loud as I kneel to reach under the mattress. I'm cautious at first, creeping my fingers between the fabric by centimeters. But when Glenn changes his position in bed with his face turned in my direction, my pace quickens. I had arranged the stacks neatly in a row, and they're easy to locate and retrieve. I wiggle them out one at a time. One thousand. Two thousand. Three thousand. Four . . .

The overnight bag is nearly full, though I haven't packed one item of clothing, but financial security is more important than any designer label. The last stack is just out of reach so I shove as much of my shoulder under the mattress as I can, using my painted nails to maneuver it out and then toss it into the bag with the rest.

"What the hell do you think you're doing?" Glenn bellows, watching me from his prone position on the bed. His eyes are glassy, like dark marbles in his swimming-pool-blue-tinted face.

"I'm leaving you," I force out.

"Where have I heard that before?" he asks, rolling onto his back and slapping his leg as though I'm Jerry Lewis doing stand-up. I glance at the light coming through a crack in the door. Can I get to Gracie before Glenn realizes I'm serious? Can I grab her bags and convince her to run?

"Wait. What's in your hand?" He bolts upright, squinting at me in the ghostly darkness. I swing the bag behind my back, hoping he's too intoxicated to have noticed what's inside. He leaps off the bed, and instinct sends me diving for the hall door. He's fast though clumsy. His feet get twisted in the sheet, the silk holding him back just enough that he misses my body and ends up with the hem of my dress crumpled in his palms. As I run, he tries to hold me back, and a loud rip bounces off the walls and ceiling.

I stumble. The bag drops. Trombello's drawings spill out, and my safety net of cash scatters over the floor.

"You little bitch," Glenn barks, finally understanding I'm definitely not bluffing.

I shovel postcards and money from the floor into the bag, both valuable in their own way. Before I know what's happening, Glenn is on top of me, grabbing for the case. I writhe beneath him as he tears at my arm, scratching deep gashes into my skin and ripping the shoulder strap of my dress.

"Mamma? Did you want to take this?" Gracie stands framed in the doorway, a slender silhouette against the white of the hall light. She's holding my first Oscar, the one I got for Best Supporting Actress. Seeing Glenn sprawled out on top of me, the money on the floor, my ripped dress, and the bloody lines on my arm, she screams.

"Gracie!" I cry. "Go to Zia. Go now."

She doesn't move, she just keeps screaming. Glenn releases me and addresses Gracie calmly as though he's directing a young actress on set.

"Shhh. Everything's all right. Your mom had a little bit too much fun tonight. I was trying to help her change. Why don't you just give me that and head on back to bed." Glenn takes the statue from Gracie. She's silent now but hasn't taken her eyes off me, blood soaking into the side of my pink satin gown and spilling onto the bills scattered around me.

"Mom?" she asks, droplets on the edge of her bottom eyelashes, reflecting the blue that illuminates the whole bedroom through the sliding glass door.

"Go," I mouth so Glenn can't see. She's old enough to find her way to Aria's house and get help. This is her opportunity to escape.

She blinks, and a tear falls down her cheek and onto her collarbone. She backs away, and I can see the suitcase I told her to pack standing behind her.

Glenn slowly closes the door as she leaves.

She's safe. Thank God, she's safe.

It takes a moment to understand what that means.

Gracie is safe . . . and I'm not.

I have to get out too.

As I gather the last of the bills and cards from the floor, Glenn slaps the statuette against his palm and saunters in my direction. He thinks he has me. I'm petrified of his determination, but he's inhibited by a cocktail of liquor and drugs, and for once I'm grateful he's an addict. I need my own escape plan.

I scan the room. The wall on the far side of the room is made entirely of glass with a sliding door latching on the far right side. It opens to the pool and the garden. If I can get out that way, I can run around to the front of the house, and join Gracie at the bungalow. All I have to do is get past Glenn.

"I didn't think your head would get this big this fast," Glenn says, standing over me as I zip the bag closed.

"Please let me go, Glenn. You're not any happier than I am." I try to reason with him, though I know it's likely futile.

"Don't pretend to know what I feel or do not feel." He slurs his words, and I scoot farther away from him before standing.

"Well, either way, I'm not staying." I make a false move toward the hallway door, and he mirrors my action. *Perfect.*

"The hell you aren't," he says, spreading his arms wide like he's a wall I'll have to run through to get out of the room, clearly forgetting about the glass exit behind me.

"Glenn, I'm not changing my mind this time. I'm leaving. You can fight me in court, but I'm done." I speak evenly with self-assurance, though it's all pretend. My whole body is trembling with terror.

"Go ahead. Leave. You know what I'll do, what I'll tell people." This is it—the threat—the one that's always worked to bring me home or keep me quiet. He'll tell people about Trombello. He'll tell the press I'm a cheater, with a priest, nonetheless. He'll tell them about the headstone, he'll dig and dig and dig until he finds out why my priest paid for Tom's final resting place. He'll expose me. He'll continue to ruin me.

I toss my shoulders back, my broken strap hanging down my right breast, my skirt holding on by only a few threads in the front.

"I could not care less what you tell them," I say with a sniff.

"You'll care when you can't book a job again and your priest's face is in every newspaper. All I have to do is make a call." Hedda Hopper has a story written and on hold, I know that. He puts out his empty hand, gesturing for the bag.

This is how he forced me home, how he kept me, and how he's been planning to take over control of my career. But this time his threats won't stop me, because I can finally see that staying would ruin me and my daughter worse than leaving ever could. Besides, I'm not the only one with deadly secrets.

"I saw Dr. Youngrin tonight."

His eyes darken. He doesn't respond, so I do instead.

"He told me everything."

"I doubt that."

"He told me what lithium toxicity can do to a forming baby and to a pregnant mother," I say with narrow eyes, the meaning clear.

He staggers again like the implied accusation knocked him off balance.

"No one will believe you," he says, his back now against the door to the hall.

"I don't think I'll need to tell them," I say, backing up toward the bed, putting more space between us. I'm hurt, frightened but also stronger than he expects me to be. Normally, I give in when he threatens me, I placate and cajole, I twist my brain into believing his fairy tales and lies. But not tonight. I won't let him control me ever again.

He glares with a look of pure hatred.

"You're blackmailing me?" Though I already believed Dr. Youngrin, Glenn's response is painful proof of the story's authenticity, and irrefutable evidence that my husband has no remorse for causing the death of our child.

I speak in an unruffled tone.

"Let me go, Glenn. I'll keep my money, you keep yours. No fighting. Let me go quietly and quickly and we'll call it even." *Even.* As though poisoning me and killing our baby is equivalent to a few letters and phone calls from an old friend. Not to mention the fact that my sister nearly succumbed to her depression because he swapped her lithium with tablets of vitamin C. I hold my breath as I wait for his response, eyeing the sliding door to ascertain if it's unlocked.

"Fine," he finally agrees, slithering down to the floor like his bones suddenly turned to spaghetti. He places my Oscar statue between his legs. "Go. I don't give a shit. Get out of here. Go! Go!"

It's my chance. He thinks he's challenging me to another altercation by blocking the exit, so I make a sharp turn on my heels and run in the opposite direction toward the glass door. He curses. I don't look back, but I know he's scrambling after me. I reach the door and fumble for the handle and tug, nearly free. It doesn't budge. I yank again but it holds firm with a clank.

It's locked. Oh God, no.

He can't be far now.

I grapple with the twisting latch, forgetting which way it turns, when an object hits the glass wall beside me, and the loud thunk elicits a network of lines, emitting delicate crackling sounds as they spread. On the ground next to my foot lies the large golden statue I received for Best Supporting Actress years ago.

I whip around to find Glenn standing in the middle of our king-sized bed, wearing just his boxers, panting heavily. My heart is racing, mind spinning, adrenaline coursing through my veins.

"You could've killed me!" I shriek, sure Glenn has lost his mind. Why do I keep ending up in this situation? How is this love? Would it have been different with Larry, or would he have found his trigger point and blown up just like Glenn, just like Tom? How about Trombello?

I don't have time to ponder the frightening question. Glenn's face is red, his lips turned white, clear murderous rage in his glowing blue eyes.

I fumble at the latch behind my back, but it won't dislodge. I'm trapped. Just when I finally found the strength to leave, there's no way to escape.

The statue on the floor catches my eye. I pick it up and hold it in front of me like a weapon.

Glenn leaps off the bed, his arms extended, malice and rage in every movement.

"Stop right there," I shout, my hands shaking.

I consider raising the statue over my head, all eight and a half pounds of it, and slamming it against his skull like he just tried to do to me. It'd be fast, maybe not lethal, but I'd be free.

He charges, and I'm sucked back in time to that stale locker room in Edinburgh, Indiana, where Tom pressed me against a line of metal doors and tightened his fingers around my throat until I was sure I was about to die. I'd clasped the knife I still had in my hand after taking it off Tom during his fight with Trombello. With one last bit of energy, I sliced outward as I lost consciousness. When I awoke, Tom sat in a puddle of blood, Trombello explained he was dead, and I was whisked away never to see my husband again other than as a ghost in a crowd or in the features of my daughter's face. I've lived with the guilt of that day ever since. It's haunted me and limited me. Now, I'm in a position to make that same decision once again.

With Glenn's outstretched hands only inches away, I drop the statue and duck.

Glenn misses me and crashes against the fractured glass. His thick body hits with a thunk, and the wall of glass shatters into a shower of crystalline shards. He falls straight through and skids across the concrete pavement, coming to a stop on the edge of the pool.

"Glenn!" I lunge forward, afraid I've killed him after all. I almost run to him through the glittering landscape of razor-sharp fragments. Then he turns over, muttering angrily. No. I can't stop to make sure he's all right, I can't call for help. I have to leave, and this time I can't look back.

I run.

I run out of the bedroom and down the hall. The front door is open, and Gracie's bag is gone. I pray she's found safety. I run down the long winding driveway and up the side streets that lead to the little house. I arrive on my sister's doorstep, struggling to breathe. Her door flings open, and I fall into her arms.

"You're here. Thank God," she says, petting my hair and gently kissing my forehead. Margot is here, sitting in an armchair in her robe. She bolts up and helps me onto the sofa while Aria locks the door behind me. I didn't know the nurse was visiting, but I'm grateful for her soft hands and well-trained eye as she checks my cuts and bruises. Once she's sure I don't need to go to the hospital, I lean my head on Aria's shoulder. Gracie leans into my side and I pet her arm, as we three become one in our comfort.

In the background, the sound of sirens interrupts the silence of the cool spring air, and instead of being consumed by fear of Glenn's anger or retribution, I feel free. It's over. I'm done with Glenn and anyone who dares to control me. Even if he spreads nasty rumors and no one believes my story, I'll survive. I have my secretarial degree, I was a trusted interpreter at a prisoner-of-war camp, I can speak two languages, I can memorize and recall pages and pages of information at a glance, I'm good with people, I've traveled the world. I have value outside of my face and my body and the things men want to do to me. This is my life now—and it's time to actually live it.

VIVIAN SNOW

Auction

Lot #27

Hand-drawn postcard labeled: Cinema Teatro Odeon
    Black ink on cardstock. Illumined lettering reading "Cinema Teatro Odeon" above arched doorways.

    FIRENZE. ITALIA. 05 MAR 1961

    Vivian—
       You and Gracie were a lovely pair in your last film. I'll never be ready to call her Gracelyn, though. She is growing up too quickly.
       —Trombello
      (Translation from Italian)

CHAPTER 27

March 31, 1961
Blessed Sacrament Cathedral
Hollywood, California

The bells chime and echo through the cathedral, arches framed with Roman columns lining each side of the rows of pews. Blessed Sacrament Cathedral isn't as imposing as the grand cathedrals of Europe, but I don't go to church to see grandeur, I go to look for God.

I only wish Gracie could find some peace here. I've been waiting for two hours, sitting in this pew, thinking and praying and waiting. Gracie promised she'd be finished on set by four today, and I changed my dinner plans with Joanne Woodward and her husband to meet her for confession. It's six now, and she's still not here. Mass is about to start. I walk out as the organ begins to play, more furious than I should be when leaving church.

Standing on the top of the front steps, I narrow my eyes against the afternoon sun. The thirty-foot-tall palm trees cast long, slender shadows down Sunset Boulevard. Tito's car is nowhere to be seen. He left to pick up Gracie immediately after he dropped me off, and even if he'd been stuck in traffic, there's no reason the seven-mile drive should take two hours. I'm sure she's stood him up.

At seventeen, she's more rebellious than I'd ever have dared to be at her age. It's just the two of us living in our home on Laurel Street now. Aria moved into a small apartment down the street soon after I showed up on her doorstep in my demolished gown the night I left Glenn. I think it all became too much, the real-life drama of my love story. Margot suggested Aria could maintain a better equilibrium in her own place, preserve her health and peace of mind. I can't blame her—the divorce wasn't easy on anyone.

That night Aria and Margot bandaged my wounds and held my hand when the police showed up. Glenn refused to press any charges, and I followed suit. I filed for divorce the next week and began the process of starting over. Severing the marital ties left me feeling like Pinocchio discovering he could walk without strings.

Though Glenn didn't pursue legal action or try to stop the divorce proceedings, the media still had a heyday, speculating who each of us might be having an affair with. We were stalked by papàrazzi day and night, and I'm glad Aria doesn't have to walk through the hornets' hotbed that sets up its nasty, papery nest wherever I go.

Thankfully, Archie, with the help of some of his associates, found a way to shift the narrative. Soon every news brief about our family focused on my daughter's film debut. Gracelyn Branson is the name she and Archie chose for her first film, where we were cast as a mother and daughter pair. We both received award nominations for the roles, and Gracie won a Golden Globe.

She deserved it. I always knew Gracie had star potential, but I didn't want to acknowledge it. Stardom has an alluring glow that ends up burning most who pursue it. But after our first day on set together, when action was called, I knew she had talent, and it was too late to stop her.

My girl, my little girl, is a natural. Not only a natural but a hard-working natural who's willing to learn and constantly evolving.

But she's also still a child. She dodges her tutors and insists school isn't important, but I know exactly how fickle fame can truly be. I'm trying to keep her grounded, keep her innocence intact, but I can't shield her from the gaze of grown men. The longing looks that used to make me blush now fill me with fury when I see them directed at my child. I know there are good men in the world, men who don't want to possess or use up the women they love, but I don't know how many of them live in this town.

Finally, a shiny black Corvette with the top down pulls up in front of the church. A man in a dark suit is in the driver's seat, and a glamorous woman sits beside him wearing sunglasses and a headscarf. It takes half a second, but as he puts the car in park, I recognize the man: Mick Mitcham. He's not the kind of person I can ignore anymore.

He's moved up in the world, going from staff writer to screenwriter to studio executive, and now he produces films. Some he writes, but most he adapts from books or classic movies. I never would've thought when I first met him as a small, greasy, handsy writer that he'd end up a big name in the industry. And I never would've guessed he'd be the kind of man who'd go to church on a Friday afternoon. I'm about to wave when the woman beside him beats me to it. I immediately recognize her despite the headscarf and oversized sunglasses. It's definitely not his wife.

It's Gracie.

"What the hell," I whisper, as I fake a smile and rush down the rest of the steps, eager for an explanation. What is Mick Mitcham doing with my child?

"Mom!" she calls, waving as she climbs out of the car. She's wearing snug blue capri pants and a button-up white blouse, her blonde hair cut just under her chin with the ends curled outward away from her face.

"You're late," I say, slapping my clutch against my knee-length pencil skirt, and then I gesture to her outfit. "And you're wearing pants."

What I want to say is, Why are you in a car alone with a married man who is old enough to be your father? But I'll save that question for when we're alone.

"I'm so sorry. I just changed and ran out the door. It was chaos on set today. Frank had an allergic reaction to some new powder the makeup lady was using, and I swear it looks like his face is a bloated tomato on top of his super skinny neck. It's a huge bummer. So we had to change the schedule and move up a few things. I got out as fast as I could . . ."

"Where's Tito?" I ask, inspecting the street in case I missed him.

"Oh shit. You sent Tito? I must've ditched him." She bites her lip, feigning innocence.

"Grace! Language." I glance meaningfully at the spire of the church and the cross atop it.

"Ugh, Mom. You're so uptight." She waves me off. "Everyone at work talks like this. It's not a big deal."

"It's a big deal to me," I say and then beckon her in my direction, trying not to lose my cool in front of Mick, who I wish would just leave.

"Well, I can tell the priest all about it in confession if that'll make you feel better."

"Confession is over. I waited two hours."

"I know. I know, but I told you what happened. The tomato-face thing. Remember?"

"Yes. Yes," I say, on edge. "I'll see if I can call the studio and get word to Tito." I can't help but add under my breath, "I wish you'd be a little more considerate."

I head up the steps, feeling exposed standing outside of the church. It's impossible to know when someone might recognize one of us, ask for an autograph, or start taking pictures. Even worse is if those rogue cameramen roaming the streets of Hollywood, looking for an easy payday, come by and snap a shot of the three of us together. Surely the press would find something stupid and salacious to put in print.

Gracie calls out, "Hey, Mick said he'd drive us home. It'll definitely be quicker."

Mick is behind the wheel and looking smug. He's been flirting with me since before the ink on my first contract was dry. I've made it clear that I don't date married men, but what I haven't said is I also wouldn't date him even if he were single. He's a well-known womanizer, and as much as he pretends to be enamored with me, I know he has six more women he treats the same, and none of them are his wife. It's his money and power that get him women, I'm sure of it. He's not an ugly man, and over the years he's had all the procedures most Hollywood men get: hair plugs, teeth caps, lifts for his shoes. But using my daughter to get to me is a new low, and I wonder if I can hold back my true feelings. Archie will kill me if I don't play nice, but the older I get, the worse I am at this kind of acting.

"All right, then," I say, knowing that agreeing to a ride is the fastest way to get home and likely the fastest way to get word to Tito since I'm not sure if anyone is manning the church office.

"Great!" Gracie says, climbing into the back seat so I can take her spot up front.

"Hey, Vivian." Mick greets me as though we're friends who see each other every day.

"Hi, Mick. Thanks for the ride." I give him the address, and he pulls onto Sunset and heads north.

"How's the family?" I always ask this question first when I see Mick, so he knows I haven't forgotten about his wife and eight kids.

"Good. Good. Just left Barb at Brown. And Bobby is directing his school's one-act."

"That's nice," I say, noting that none of his family stories reference his wife. We make small talk about travel and second homes, and he congratulates me for the Hollywood star I received last year in front of the Chinese Theater.

"Gracelyn is very talented," Mick says, glancing back at Gracie. "I've been telling her about a new screenplay I'm writing with her in mind. I think she's got some amazing potential."

"Well, that's kind of you. I'm sure Archie would love to hear all about it." Archie always tells me to let him do any negotiating. I know he's told Gracie the same thing, but I'm not sure she's listened.

"That's another thing I was talking to Gracelyn about. Archie's a good agent for a gal like you, but your girl here needs someone more in tune with her generation. I was thinking Norman Brokaw from William Morris. Archie's connections are old as dust, and she needs someone who knows what it means to be fresh."

Frustration rolls through me.

"Archie is doing a fine job, thank you," I say coldly.

"But Mom," Gracie says, taking her sunglasses off so I see her eyes, her father's eyes, staring at me. "Mick says Archie's gonna retire soon, anyway. He *is* getting pretty old, and I don't think he tells me about all the offers I get."

"No, because he tells *me*," I explain, wishing we weren't having this conversation in front of Mick. I put on my best impression of a patient mother and describe it to her in the simplest terms. "I'm your legal guardian and know you better than anyone, and I've been doing this long enough to know what makes a script work or if the timing is reasonable. We're both just looking out for you."

"Oh, come on, Vivian. You're treating her like a child," Mick says with a huff as he pulls into the driveway of our modest home.

"Because she *is* a child," I snap. Her seventeenth birthday was just two weeks ago, and it feels like she was in knee socks the week before that, even if it's been years.

"You can't force her to stay a child forever. And either way—Archie isn't the right guy for her, you gotta know it deep down."

"Archie is good at his job and he's a dear friend. He won't let Gracie get swept up in sex and drugs like that oversexed Monroe girl. I won't sit here and listen to this any longer. Come on, Gracie." I shove open the door and hold it for Gracie to climb out from the back seat. She's beet red, clearly embarrassed, but compliant.

"Sorry," she says to Mick, but it gets lost in the slamming of the car door.

"Gracie, please go inside," I say. She doesn't budge at first, but I give her a look with raised eyebrows that says, "Don't cross me, you're already in trouble," and she shuffles up the drive and through the side door without further protest.

I stay for one extra moment. I need to establish clear guidelines with this man—again. As soon as Gracie is inside, he starts up. This time in a soft, creamy voice and a sultry glance I'm sure works on plenty of girls.

"I'm just trying to help, Vivian." He reaches out like he's asking for my hand, but I keep my arms crossed. "You know I've always wanted what's best for you."

"You've always wanted . . . period," I say, tired of holding back. I think of the women I met in Rome, and the women in Ogliara, the sure-footedness of their thought and expression, and I point a gloved finger at Mick and continue. "Gracie is my child, my responsibility. And Archie has been there for us since the beginning, so he'll be representing me and *my* daughter until he's no longer willing or able. And you, sir, will leave us alone. I don't want to see another offer come across his desk from you, do you hear? I'd rather starve."

I've let him get to me, and I've broken the cardinal rule for an actress by showing that I have free will, but damn the consequences. I expect him to rage, like Glenn, or to drive away incensed, but instead he laughs as though I'm putting on a comedy show.

"I'm sure it won't come to that," he says, still chuckling at me like I'm an adorable child having a temper tantrum over ice cream. "I'll talk to Archie, and I promise to be nice."

I stare at him, confused.

Talk to Archie? But I just said . . .

"Goodbye, Miss Snow," he says, putting his car into reverse and tipping his hat as I watch him in stunned silence.

He'll go away for a little bit, I'm sure, but he'll be back. It's one thing to mess with me, but another to mess with my daughter, and Mick will not be laughing the next time he tries.

VIVIAN SNOW

Auction

Lot #28

Hand-drawn postcard labeled: Settimana Santa
   Pencil on cardstock. Large crowd facing the front of grand cathedral St. Peter's Basilica.

   ROMA. ITALIA. 02 APR 1961

   V—
      Holy Week brought many wonders. I pray you continue to delight in His light.
      Best wishes—Fr. Trombello
      (Translation from Italian)

CHAPTER 28

March 31, 1961
Laurel Street Bungalow
Los Angeles, California

"What was that about?" Aria asks when I walk in the door a few minutes after Gracie's stormy entrance.

I tear off my gloves and hat and toss them on the counter next to the large wooden bowl filled with leafy greens and colorful tomatoes and peppers from the garden and hold up a finger. I call the switchboard at MGM and find someone willing to locate Tito before returning to Aria's question.

"She skipped confession again," I say, popping a cherry tomato in my mouth, wishing it had magical calming properties.

"If I remember right, you were skipping confession to go to voice lessons when you were her age. I mean, correct me if I'm wrong." Aria turns the issue back on me, not at all angry at the child we've been raising together.

"It's different."

"Why? 'Cause she's yours? She has to start making her own decisions one of these days."

"I know. I know," I say, taking the admonition from my sister better than I did from Mick, who barely knows her. "But this guy is bad news."

"Guy?" Aria stops slicing and looks at me with concern.

"Oh yeah. Creepy Mick Mitcham. He drove us home. It was so uncomfortable."

"He's the married writer with a bunch of kids, right?"

"Yeah." I reach for another tomato, but she intercepts me and knocks it out of my grip.

"Yuck," she says, shoving the salad tongs into the bowl and placing it on the table. "Hey, do you need to change or anything? Margot will be here soon."

"Margot? Oh, shoot. I forgot. Dinner with Margot tonight. I'm so sorry. I have plans tonight at the Brown Derby with Joanne and Paul." I have to get changed and out the door in twenty minutes to make our dinner reservation. I met Joanne when we were both stuck doing teleplays. She was new to Hollywood; I was an unwelcome longtime guest. We've both moved on to bigger and better things, but I seize every opportunity I have to connect with Joanne and her handsome actor husband. The way they love each other is mesmerizing. It makes me wonder if real love might be possible after all. But I guess I'll never know because I'm not interested in trying again—at least not anytime soon.

Without commenting, Aria counts out three plates and three sets of silverware, though I can tell she's frustrated with me.

"I'm sorry, sweetie. You know I love the girls' nights with you and Margot and Gracie, but this is important. I have to make connections, be seen out and about, or I'll lose work."

"I know, but we scheduled this weeks ago," she pushes back, which is unusual for her now that she's stabilized.

"I'm sorry, Ari. You must feel like I take advantage of you." I often think of that night we nearly lost her, how she told me I am one of the reasons she's sick. I've made sure she has a good doctor now, and Margot helped her find the right kind of analyst to meet with weekly.

When Gracie and I moved back into the bungalow and the divorce didn't destroy my career, I started paying Aria a salary for all she does around the house, and I paid the rent on her apartment. I thought it was enough, but the look on Aria's face tells me that whatever she's been feeling, she's been enduring it for quite some time.

"It's not that. I wanted to tell you and Gracie together, that's all."

"Tell us? Tell us what?" I ask eagerly. Aria is never mysterious, and this seems like a happy mystery, one that's forcing her to pretend she isn't smiling.

"I'm moving," she says, blushing and fiddling with the place settings.

"What? Where?" I'd always imagined Aria and me living in this house and growing old together. She's continued to insist she never wants to get married, but maybe the time has come. Maybe she wants a family of her own.

"To San Diego. By Mamma. Margot thought it might be good for me."

"You'll be living with Mamma? That seems like a lot for you."

"No, no. I'll be living with Margot," she says, placing folded cloth napkins in the middle of each plate.

I tear up, and Aria notices.

"I'm sorry, Vivi. I'll miss you both desperately . . ."

My baby sister will be gone, the spot next to me on the porch when I'm an old woman that I'd always thought would belong to her will sit empty. But I'm not angry, I don't feel rejected. My heart warms. Aria is leaving the nest.

Plus, there's no denying the medicinal value of Margot's friendship. Aria and I have always been close, but our relationship has shifted back and forth with each of us taking turns parenting the other. And though I love her more dearly than any creature aside from my own child, if I'm honest, we'd die of boredom if we were each other's only companions.

"No, no. I'm happy for you!" I toss my arms around her neck, and she leans into our embrace, her head nestled just below my chin. I'd never begrudge her happiness. "You've given so much to me and Gracie. You deserve some of your own dreams."

I lean back to look at her, and we both have wet eyes and glowing cheeks. She's unstuck, the inherited trauma she's carried hasn't kept her chained in one place for good.

"I'm so relieved," Aria says, the tip of her nose red from crying.

"You thought I'd be mad?" I ask, curious about how she views me.

"Not mad but . . . I felt guilty leaving you."

"That's 'cause you're a thoughtful girl. I bet you'd never leave if it wasn't for Margot," I say, drying Aria's cheeks with a napkin.

"I doubt it," she admits.

"She's been such a good friend to you."

Aria nods and smiles wistfully as she steps away to dry her face properly.

"She says I'm her *anamchara*. It's an old Gaelic saying, I guess. Means 'soul friend.'"

"Soul friend," I repeat. Soul friend. *Anamchara.* "That's lovely. I wish I had one of those, an *anamchara.*"

"I always thought you did. He sends you postcards and lives in Italy," she says with a wry smile.

My dear Trombello. She has no idea how close my friend and I came to entwining our lives. Since then, our correspondence has been limited to once or twice a year. After I wrote and told him I'd left Glenn, I thought he might call me, check in, tell me why he changed his mind about coming to the States with me. But he didn't call, his only messages coming on four-by-six cards with his drawings on the other side. In the past three years he hasn't mentioned my divorce once. I'm not sure whether he's proud of me or disappointed.

When I went back to Ogliara with Gracie and Aria, I made sure to take the express train that didn't stop at Nola. But I still read his postcards over and over, old and new. When a new drawing arrives, I place it on my mirror, and the old one goes in my memory book that I keep in my bedside table. I flip through it often to remind me in my loneliest moments that I'm not alone. If Margot is Aria's *anamchara*, then she's right—Trombello is mine, or at least he used to be.

I change the subject.

"I'll call the restaurant and let them know I'll be late. I won't eat, but I want to see Gracie's face when you tell her."

"All right. Margot should be here any minute." Aria unties her apron and hangs it on the hook, revealing pea-green slacks and a white blouse with tiny matching green polka dots. She looks fresh and as happy as new buds in the springtime.

"I'll get Gracie," I offer, heading into my bedroom to change. Gracie will be sad to see her zia move, but she has been trying to set Aria up with all the available men on set for eons. She'll no doubt come up with a list of eligible men in San Diego, and Aria will roll her eyes and we will all laugh.

Then I remember the two hours I waited at church, and then the ride with Mick. Officially, I'm mad at my daughter, but I'll put it on hold for now. I call the Brown Derby and ask the hostess to give Joanne the message that I'll be late. Gracie will need a consequence for her behavior. Perhaps she can go to work but has to be home on time every day. If Aria or I can't be there with her on set, I'll make sure one of Archie's assistants stays with her, and no nights out with friends for a week. No—for two weeks. Not until she's gone to confession *and* Mass for two weeks straight and hasn't missed any school assignments.

Yes. There we go.

I hear Margot arrive and I change quickly into my cocktail dress, a deep-purple Ports knee-length silk dress with a crisscross back, teardrop earrings, and dark heels. I touch up my makeup and glue a strip of lashes to each eyelid. With a swipe of pale pink lip color and a quick fluff of my already styled hair, all I need is a quick spray of Diorissimo and a touch at my pulse points.

One last look in the mirror confirms I'm ready. Seventeen-year-old Vivian Santini wouldn't recognize the thirty-seven-year-old woman I am today. Styles have changed, yes. Hemlines and necklines have risen and fallen at an unprecedented rate, as all the traditionalists moan constantly. I have wrinkles around my eyes and mouth that I try to treat with creams and masks, and gray hairs I've started to color. I've had dark moments, ones of my own making and ones brought upon me by fate. But overall, I'm proud to be where I am.

I put my clutch under my arm and head to Gracie's room. I can hear Elvis singing loudly on the other side of her door. I knock softly to show I'm not angry, a bit of a peace offering.

"Gracie. Sweetie? It's time for dinner. Margot is here and there's cannoli for dessert."

No answer. Either she can't hear me or she's giving me the silent treatment. Usually, I'd leave her alone, unwilling to drag her out of her bedroom, but tonight I want it to be perfect for Aria and Margot.

"Sweetie. Come on out, honey." I knock louder, getting aggravated.

There's still no response. Damn it, I've raised such a belligerent child. I love that I've taught her to be outspoken and self-reliant, but this is ridiculous.

I test the doorknob. It's unlocked. I swing the door open and brace myself for her to yell at me for invading her privacy. The record player blares a jaunty rhythm with maracas that back up Elvis's smooth voice singing about now or never. The window facing the front yard is open, the curtains blowing inward, the screen on the floor, the room empty.

Gracie is gone.

VIVIAN SNOW

Auction

Lot #29

Hand-painted postcard labeled: Fiat 600
   Watercolor on cardstock. Two-door light-blue compact car parked by a dock with tall ships in the distance.

SALERNO. ITALIA. 02 MAY 1963

Vivian—
   I know you must be lonely with Grace and Aria away. Please know my thoughts are your constant friend.
      —A
      (Translation from Italian)

CHAPTER 29

May 23, 1963
Waldorf-Astoria Hotel
New York, New York

"She looks so beautiful," I whisper to Johnny Scott, my date for the party. Though technically a Democratic Party fundraiser, the invitation read *New York's Birthday Salute to the President.* I've done some work with the Kennedy campaign after representatives from his reelection committee reached out to me as "a fellow Catholic." I know it's an honor to be in a lineup with the likes of Jimmy Durante, Louis Armstrong, and Mitch Miller, but I heard through the grapevine Gracie was also invited.

Thankfully, Johnny was willing to tag along so I didn't have to go alone. He and I are working together again on another film. We still have plenty of on-screen chemistry, but it seems he's given up his attempts at seduction, with me at least. And with both of us single, it's been a lovely and convenient friendship with no messy strings attached that the gossip pages find exciting to write about.

"You should go talk to her," Johnny urges, taking a sip of his drink and touching the curled ends of my bobbed hairdo. He's a pro at making it look like we're flirting. Usually, I join him in the game, leaning into his caress. But whenever Gracie is around, I can't be anyone but her mother.

"It's too painful. Plus, Mick is there."

"I never liked that guy much," Johnny says, lighting a cigarette and blowing a thick cloud into the air.

"Me either," I say, allowing myself one last glance at my daughter before returning to acting like we're strangers.

Gracie, wearing a silver metallic brocade gown with cap sleeves and a belted waist, her blonde hair piled high on her head, looks every bit the movie star she is. When I see her on a magazine cover or in one of her films, or when I watched her accept the Oscar for Best Supporting Actress at the age of eighteen, I can't believe she came from my body. I miss her, I miss hearing her laughing in the hall while talking on the phone, and I miss holding her when she goes out for an audition and doesn't get the part. I miss going on adventures together around the world or simply popping popcorn on the stove and watching *The Ed Sullivan Show*.

But those days are gone and will never return. For a while after I found her room empty and read the note she'd left on her dresser, I thought I could coax her home. I thought if I appealed to Mick, if I got the police involved, if I told the press how a man twice my daughter's age swept her away without my permission to Mexico where he kept her hidden until they were married, that someone would bring my girl back to me. But all it did was estrange her further.

"You don't understand, Mom. I love him," she told me on the long-distance phone call facilitated by the police after I reported her missing. "I want to be here."

And that was it. She married Mick, of all people. His divorce had been quiet and swift, and his marriage to my daughter just as clandestine. When she returned from Mexico to finish her contractual obligations on our film, she was furious that I'd tried to get Mick fired. No one cared that this man had seduced my child and taken her out of the country to marry her, that he'd hitched his wagon to her rapidly rising star.

Now I have to sneak glances across a smoky room to capture a glimpse of the child I risked my life to create. The band starts to play a slow song, and the dance floor turns into a swaying sea of bodies, each one paired with another. Circles of light bounce off the mirror ball hanging above the floor, spinning about the room like an Indiana January snowstorm. Johnny puts out his Lucky Strike and offers his hand.

"Shall we?" How can I say no to this man? Now that he's not trying to make me one of his harem, I can appreciate his good looks without anxiety. His straight, bright smile is warm, and his bronze skin and dark black hair reminiscent of my other dear friend who I danced with only once, long ago, the night I found out Larry had died.

"Naturally," I say, accepting his offer and letting him escort me to the floor. He's a brilliant dancer, though nothing like Danny Kaye, but this kind of dancing isn't for a stage or a camera, it's for us. I enjoy the way he guides me with his strong arms and a firm hand on my lower back.

As he spins me in a moment of playfulness, I catch a glimpse of Gracie still sitting at her table. She's watching me and Johnny. She doesn't look angry or judgmental, she looks sad. Perhaps she misses me as much as I do her.

My turn falters and I trip. Johnny catches me, and we pick up where we left off.

"Whoa there. Too much champagne?" he asks, bringing me closer and slowing our pace to a light swaying motion as we turn in a leisurely circle.

"No, no. I'm fine," I say, putting my head on his chest.

"Sure you are," he whispers, and like the good actor he is, he pulls me in as though we're lovers. I stay that way until the end of the song, cherishing the moment our turn reaches its full rotation and I get to see her again, watching.

"Would you be a doll and grab my wrap?" I pass Johnny my coat-check ticket. He's chatting up a lovely blonde bombshell nearly half my age. I like to give him some space when we attend these events together. "I need to powder my nose real quick."

"Of course, darling," he says with a debonair flair I'm sure the starlet appreciates.

The bathroom is covered in mirrors and marble, like a castle bath hall. I know I have silly thoughts like this when I've been drinking, which I'm ashamed to say I do more lately than I ever have. Loneliness is a painful affliction, one that alcohol numbs, at least for a time.

I wrestle through layers of my dress and hosiery and garter belts once I'm in the stall. It hurts to see Gracie, but I truly believe there was something different about her this time.

I rearrange my gown and unlatch the lock, my purse under my arm. A primly dressed bathroom attendant sits on a stool in the corner of the room, and I fumble for a tip after I wash my hands. She says thank you as someone opens one of the stall doors behind me.

"Mom."

Emotion fills my throat and tears swell in my eyes at the sound of her voice calling me the one name that's more important to me than any other. She says it like not one day has gone by. I blink and turn to face my daughter.

"Gracie," I say, trying not to appear too eager. "You look beautiful tonight."

"Thanks. It's Givenchy. Saw it in Paris and had to have it," she says hotly, like I'm one of her Hollywood friends who only cares about labels and status. She steps past me to wash her hands and adjust her hair and then reaches into her purse for a tip but comes back empty. I toss another dollar in the jar.

"Oh, thank you." She looks embarrassed, but I'm happy to help in any way she allows.

"Congratulations," I say when she's pulled on her gloves and it looks like she's about to walk out the door. "On your win. You deserved it."

"I got your flowers." I sent two dozen daisies just like the ones on the comforter in her room, even though Aria told me not to. I thought it would be an olive branch, a gesture of kindness.

"Sorry, I couldn't help myself. You'll always be my little girl," I say. She shakes her head as though I'm speaking in another language.

"I'm not a little girl anymore."

"I know." I rush to fix the mistake, walking on eggshells, not wanting to ruin my one moment. "I only meant I'm proud of you, and I wish I could call you sometimes. Hear about your day."

"After all you did to Mick, to his career and mine? Don't you remember how hard it was with Glenn when he spread lies about you? And you did the same thing to me like it was nothing." She snaps her fingers, her gloves muting the sound.

My chest tightens like it's in a tourniquet. I don't want to fight, but the unfairness of the past two years is crushing, and with the drinks mixing with that stored outrage, I can't pretend she's not hurting me.

"They weren't lies, though. It was all true. That man stole you from our home, from your family."

"I told you—I chose to leave. You have to let this go. I'm an adult now. I can make my own choices. And Mick is my husband, and since you can't accept that, I can't accept you."

"If you want me to think of you as a grown-up, stop behaving like a child," I spit out and immediately regret it.

"What's that supposed to mean?" We both know what I mean. An adult wouldn't run off with a notorious playboy, a cheater. An adult wouldn't have believed his lies about true love and being married forever. What everyone knows, including the gossip pages, is that Mick is already cheating on her with Natalie Wood—but I won't say it.

"Nothing. I'm sorry. I'm so sorry." She pushes past me as I apologize. I latch on to her arm. "You don't have to stay with him. I can help you . . ."

She tears her elbow from my grip, glaring.

"Help me? You couldn't even help yourself, Mother." Then she adds with an air of cruelty, "And stop sending me flowers."

She's gone. The bathroom attendant is staring at me. Our eyes meet through the reflection in the glass, and I wonder if she pities me or thinks me a fool. When I don't look away, she does and pretends to clean a spot on the counter. I take a moment to collect myself and to give Gracie time to find Mick and go back to their house full of kids that belong to another woman whom he left. I hate that man, and yet somehow, scandal after scandal, no one else seems to hate him longer than the length of a news cycle.

When I told Trombello I was pregnant with Gracie, he told me my penance for taking her father's life was to raise her well. For a brief moment after I left Glenn and before Gracie left me, I thought I'd fulfilled my duty. But now, my daughter, Tom's daughter, hates me. She hates me for trying to protect her, for trying to save her, and I hate myself for giving up. Then again, I should know better than anyone that it's impossible to save someone who doesn't know they're in a trap or—worse yet—doesn't want out.

VIVIAN SNOW

Auction

Lot #30

Hand-drawn postcard labeled: Rocca Maggiore, Assisi
    Pencil on cardstock. Stone castle on hillside.

LUCCA. ITALIA. 23 SEPT 1970

> *V—*
>   *Your letters are much appreciated. I'm sorry I don't have time to write more than a few lines, but know I treasure every message.*
>   *In gratitude—A*
> (Translation from Italian)

CHAPTER 30

October 16, 1970
ABC TV-15, The Elysee Theater
New York, New York

"*Mama's Girls* opens next week, October 23, at the Shubert Theater, and you, Miss Vivian Snow, play Mama to five girls in this modern retelling of *Little Women*." Dick Cavett, with his sharp features and sharper wit, starts speaking as soon as we settle into our seats. I lean forward and speak into the silver microphone, keeping my good side in full view of camera three.

"Yes, it's been a delight working with Bobby Van and Jack Gilford and to be onstage singing again." I keep my voice demure, blinking against the glare of the studio lights. I can see only the front two rows of the audience, but my raucous welcome let me know there are plenty more fans out there in the darkness.

"Yes, yes. That's how you started your career, am I right? You were on tour with Danny Kaye and later Bob Hope?"

"Yes, overseas for the Camp Shows. Delightful group." My nerves are higher than usual, the tension in my neck giving me a headache. Interviews are frightening to me, with no filter or editing, no rehearsal or previews. I've been on a few shows—Jack Paar, Steve Allen, Merv Griffin—but mostly to wear something pretty and laugh at the host's jokes. But Dick is different. He likes to dig a little deeper with his guests, and there are too many topics I'd rather not talk about.

"I'm sure. I'm sure. And we'll get to hear your lovely voice later when you share one of the songs from the show."

"Uh-huh. I'll be singing 'How Fast They Grow.' It's a delightful ballad."

"That's grand. I'm sure it's different for you this time around. Last time you were on Broadway it was for, what was it"—he looks at his cards—"Shakespeare, correct? *Macbeth*?"

"We prefer to call it 'the Scottish play,'" I tease, referencing an old belief that saying "Macbeth" in a theater is bad luck.

"You theater types are very superstitious. Does the curse count on a soundstage?"

"I'm not sure, but I'm not going to be the one to test it out." I laugh, and the audience joins me.

After the laughter diminishes, Dick grows serious, leaning in as far as his microphone stand allows.

"Tell me—how has it been playing the role of a mother to all these girls? It must feel odd to go from being cast in those youthful roles only a few short years back, to now being cast as the matron. It must be quite the adjustment."

His question stuns me, though it's not the first time I've heard it. My hips have widened, and my stomach isn't quite as flat. I've had a few lifts and tucks to help stay camera ready, and I use every cream and ointment suggested for a woman of my age. But nothing can halt the sands of time, and though everyone ages, there are versions of me on film that will never age, and I'm constantly judged against those earlier iterations of my face and body. But I can't say that here. As the battle rages on for equal rights, no one wants to hear a middle-aged movie star complain—even if good ole Danny Kaye is thirteen years my senior and no one blinks an eye when he plays lover to girls half his age in his shows.

"When I start getting cast as a grandmother, then I'll worry" is my good-natured reply. Dick chuckles, and the audience claps.

"Ah, but you already have that role in real life, do you not? Your daughter, the glamorous Miss Gracelyn Branson, just welcomed her second son, correct?"

I keep a stiff grin and nod, my headache only growing.

So, she had a boy. Another grandson. My beautiful grandsons born only two years apart. After her divorce from Mick, Gracie was distant but not cruel. I worked to forgive her for what I'd decided was a childhood folly. She continued to succeed, and all the parts that once would've gone to me now go to her. Which, I guess, is how life should go.

She did alert me to her second marriage before it was leaked to the press. And though I wasn't invited to her baby shower a year later, she mailed a thank-you note for the pram I sent, though it wasn't in her handwriting. When Jimmy was born, she allowed me to come see her and the baby in her home. But her shaman said I left too much bad energy that stopped her milk production, so from that point forward I saw Jimmy only when she was on set or location. When I was in LA, the nanny brought little Jimmy to my home for afternoons of fruit-juice ice-pops and playing in the sprinklers. Once, we went down to San Diego to visit Aria and show Mother her great-grandson.

When Gracie found out she was expecting a second baby so soon after Jimmy, she came to me and cried and cried and cried. She told me her second husband, Mark, was addicted to heroin, and when I suggested she leave him, she exploded and left in a huff. Jimmy and his nanny didn't show up for his next visit, and my heart still aches at the loss of those special moments. Previews for *Mama's Girls* started a week later, and I haven't spoken to Gracie or seen Jimmy in far too long. And this is how I find out about the birth of my second grandson—from Dick Cavett, live on his show.

"Can I tell you a secret?" I say and lean into Dick like I'm really going to whisper in his ear. He plays along.

"Ooo, I love secrets." He leans in as well.

"Grandma is my favorite role," I whisper.

"Oh yes? Do you like being called Granny? A beautiful woman like you?" He slaps his desk, indignant.

"Well, I won't be retiring to a rocking chair anytime soon, if that's what you're asking."

"I should hope not!" Dick says, his eyes twinkling. He looks into the camera and invites everyone to hold on tight because, after a momentary break, we'll be back with Vivian Snow singing "How Fast They Grow."

"You're a gem. Sorry if I threw you off with that last question," Dick whispers as he shakes my hand and thanks me for my time.

"No, no. You were fine," I reassure him, because what else can I say in the ten seconds before I'm whisked off for a sound check. After the "On Air" sign illuminates and Dick reads a brief blurb detailing my awards and films and promoting the opening night of *Mama's Girls*, the band plays my intro and I dive right into the song, gazing into the camera as if I'm singing to my own daughter. I relish the momentary inhale from the audience and perhaps from Dick as well when my voice comes through the speakers in a smooth, vibrant mezzo-soprano, and I imagine a husband and wife sitting on their couch, watching at home, wondering to one another how they never knew Vivian Snow could sing.

~

"Miss Snow! Miss Snow!" Every night after a show, a crowd waits at the stage door, waving pens and pictures or programs. All the faces blend together as I sign the name Vivian Snow with a heart beside it, over and over again.

Every performance has been sold out for the past three weeks, and the reviews are strong enough to keep us going. One of the girls got laryngitis in the first week, but her understudy stepped in seamlessly.

And when my onstage husband broke his leg after having too much to drink one night after a show, he missed only one matinee and has done the rest of the performances in a cast. The show must go on—and go on it has.

I've continued, though every bit of me wants to jump on a plane and show up on Gracie's doorstep and beg for forgiveness for whatever failings she holds against me. There are many, so many that when I try to list them in my letters to Trombello, I have to stop short because my guilt overwhelms me.

At least I have Trombello again. He won't speak on the phone, but I write to him often and he returns the favor when he finds the time. I've gone as far as having my personal assistant look up his number, but I've never been desperate enough to call, though I know he'd know exactly what to tell me, how to comfort me. Perhaps he could point out exactly what I need to change to heal my relationship with Gracie so she'd speak to me and let me welcome my grandsons into my life.

Until I figure it out, with or without his help, I throw myself into work. Some nights I'm restless and I go for late walks on the dark streets around my building. Lonzo, the night doorman, tries to dissuade me every time.

"It's not safe," he insists. But it's either a walk or it's a drink.

Since I left Glenn, I've refused to take any of the sleeping pills or nerve pills prescribed by my doctor. But I've found some relief in the wine I used to despise because of my father's dependence.

I don't drink during the day, I tell myself, *so it's not a big deal.* But it is a big deal when I can't sleep without a glass or two before bed or, even worse, on a night like tonight when cold champagne was waiting for me in my dressing room after curtain, a gift from one of my fans.

I've lived behind my Vivian Snow mask for so long that it's become second nature, but lately I've found myself wishing I could take it off, at least occasionally. I used to be myself at home with Gracie and Aria, which gave me a break from the façade, but "home" now is just another word for "alone with my ficus plant."

"My ride is here," I tell the stage manager as I see my car pull up to the curb.

"One more for Miss Snow!" Buck calls out to the crowd, and a sea of waving hands surges in front of me. I scan the multitude for someone who looks like they've come a long way to be here. I see a figure in the distance. A tall man about my age, wearing a dark suit and a short-brimmed gray fedora that casts a shadow on his face. I squint. I think I know him.

"Do you see that man?" I ask Buck, pointing with my pen, not sure if I should believe my eyes. I'm tired, it was a long show, I'm not sleeping well, I've had a few drinks.

"You, right there." Buck bids a clean-cut teen in the back row to move closer, and the rest of the crowd groans.

"No," I whisper, "not him. Him." I point again, beyond the crowd, but the man in the fedora is no longer there.

"The guy with the sideburns?" Buck asks, pointing at the hippie in the back row wearing hip-huggers and a loose pastel shirt.

"Yeah, uh, sure. That one," I agree, confused, unsure of what I've just seen. I finish signing and hand the pen back to Buck, blowing my fans a kiss as I leap into the back seat of my waiting car.

"Good show, Miss Snow?" Mike asks like he does every night.

"Great show. Thanks for asking," I say, my pulse pounding behind my eyes, breath leaving a fog against the chilled windows that I wipe off as we pull away. I study every person we drive past, trying to get another glimpse of the man I saw standing in the alley by the stage door. The man who I'm pretty sure was Tom Highward.

VIVIAN SNOW

Auction

Lot #31

Hand-drawn postcard labeled: At Flight
   Pencil on cardstock. The agrarian landscape of a field with birds midflight in a cloudless sky.

LUCCA. ITALIA. 30 NOV 1970

My Dear Friend,
   I'm concerned for your safety. Do you have a doctor to visit? Have you told your sister of your worries? Please do not wait too long. I shall call you later this week.

   —A
   (Translation from Italian)

CHAPTER 31

December 7, 1970
Midtown East Apartment
New York, New York

"I saw him again," I write to Trombello. I've been using my letters to help me keep track of all the times I've spotted the man. He's the only one who knows why this specter is so frightening. Trombello wrote back only once and didn't mention my ghostly visitor on his postcard. I'm sure he thinks I'm losing my mind.

Or he knows something I don't.

I take a sip of my wine to ease the growing sense of suspicion swelling inside me. Trombello never told me where Tom is buried. What if this man I keep glimpsing isn't a ghost? What if all these years he's been hiding? Would Trombello have lied to me all this time? Is that why he got so upset when I told him about my engagement to Larry and to Glenn, because in his eyes and in the eyes of God I was still married?

No. No. I can't let the paranoia get to me. Tom is dead. My mind is playing tricks on me. My guilt and the isolation of this city is getting to me. Trombello would tell me if Tom were alive, wouldn't he?

I continue writing.

I saw him in Central Park. He thought he was being sneaky, but he wasn't. I was on a jog with Jane so I couldn't say anything, but it was him. I know it was. That's twelve times in six weeks. I can barely bring myself to leave the house anymore. My nightly walks are a thing of the past, which is a relief to sweet Lonzo, but it's left my head in a whirl. Most nights I struggle to sleep. My entire life exists now in the moments between leaving my apartment for the theater, performing, and returning home.

What does one do to rid themselves of a ghost? I'm sure a man of God like you would say I need an exorcism. I'm sure a psychiatrist would tell me I need an antipsychotic or Valium or something like that. I believe I need a full night's sleep and a week or two at one of those health resorts where they feed you nothing but bean sprouts and beet juice.

Do you think I'm mad? Do you think I'm ill like my mother and my conscience is playing tricks on me? I know you don't like me to ask for your guidance, to look to you instead of God, but I've been praying to God for a long time now and he's yet to answer me. Please, please call me, or at least write me something more than those little cards you send.

I need you.

Always yours,

V

I shove the letter into an envelope and scrawl out the address on the front as my phone rings. It's Lonzo, letting me know my ride is here. I grab my bag, cover my sunken eyes with a pair of sunglasses, pull a poncho over my brown jumpsuit, and take the elevator to the lobby.

"Would you send this out for me, please?" I pass Lonzo a twenty-dollar bill to cover the international postal rate with enough for a tip.

"Yes, miss. Break a leg," he says as he always does, holding the door as I jump into my hired car, sliding down into the seat while watching for a man with square shoulders, graying blond hair, and a haunting gaze that knows my secrets.

"Are the lights brighter tonight?" I whisper to Buck as I exit from the opening number. He's focused on an illuminated script, whispering cues into a microphone. I strip off my flowy peasant dress and allow the costume assistant to help me into the fitted evening gown for my next scene. The whole process is made even more complicated by the way my eyeballs pound in their sockets.

"Not that I know of," he says. I'm sure I'm being irritating. Buck's got a tough job, and he's the only reason we don't fall into complete chaos. He smiles and says with a slightly patronizing tone, "I'll ask Woody."

Woody is our lighting designer and I'm sure he'll say the same thing Buck did—there's been no change. But my head feels a change, and the room is starting to spin a little. With my dress zipped and hair touched up, Buck calls standby for the next lighting cue and says "Go."

The lights lift and I saunter onstage with a winning line that always brings a laugh from the audience. Tonight is no exception. I try not to squint at the glare from the overhead floodlights, and when the music starts to play, making me jump, I ad-lib a line about my nerves that gets another solid chuckle from the audience. The house is full, from what I can tell. I usually avoid looking into the audience, allowing the light barrier to be like the invisible fourth wall.

This is my favorite part of stage acting, this melding of self with character. I love these girls with the same love I have for Gracie, and I cry the same tears I shed for her when their characters are hurt or disappointed. We break out into a big dance number with bouncing choreography that makes me feel like I'm flying.

A few scenes later, I have another costume change. The timing for this one isn't as tight. The assistant stage manager, Betty, is waiting with a glass of water and two white pills.

"For your head," she says.

"Aspirin?" I double-check, holding the pills in the palm of my hand. She nods and says they're from Buck, who gestures silently for me to take the tablets.

I pop in the analgesics, a tangy, bitter taste left at the back of my throat.

"Drink it all," Betty urges. I know she's right, my big solo is coming up.

I have a moment to relax before the big first act finale. I do the yogic breathing I learned during my fitness class when I still went, when I still left the house unescorted. Each breath washes over me in a calming wave. When my cue comes, I'm ready.

I enter for my solo, the song I sang on *The Dick Cavett Show*. The lights dim, and I walk to downstage center. I stand in a single spotlight as the intro swells. This is one time during the show I allow myself to really look at the audience. Even the balcony is full.

I sing the song, a melancholy ballad expressing the desire to see children grow but the grief at having them leave, and stare into the spotlight as my eyes fill with authentic tears. On the last note, a high C, I make one last connection with the audience and see women grabbing for their handkerchiefs and dabbing their eyes.

And just as I'm letting my vibrato enrich the extended note, something catches my eye. Him. The note falters and my voice cracks, but I don't care. The man who's been chasing me, the one so ghostlike that I'd convinced myself he is just a figment of my imagination, is sitting in the second row, watching me.

"It's you!" I say, pointing at him, unable to stop myself.

The music continues to its natural conclusion, and the spotlight starts to fade. I'm supposed to stand in place and wait for applause in the silent dark, but instead, I shout it again.

"I see you! You're not a ghost. You're real." I call up to the kid manning the spotlight. "Bobby! Bobby! Put a spotlight there. Put it there!"

My breathing is rapid, my heartbeat pulsing in every extremity. I stand on the edge of the stage, my right knee goes weak unexpectedly, and the crowd gasps. Mary, the young woman who plays my eldest daughter, holds me up with an arm around my waist.

"Come on, Ma. Time for bed," she says, still in character, which makes me want to scream. All this fakeness, this playing pretend, when I'm being stalked by a real-life apparition. The stage is bathed in black now and I can't see anything, much less old man Tom glaring at me from the audience. I start to protest but the entr'acte starts to play, drowning out my voice. Instead of leaving the stage in an onslaught of applause, I'm dragged behind the curtain to the sound of concerned murmurs from the audience.

"You have to go back out there. I saw him. It was Tom. I saw him!"

Buck is here and I grasp at his shirt, pleading. He keeps looking at someone past my shoulder and mouthing words I can't make out because my head is pounding like it's trapped in a thousand vices. I try to look at who he's talking to, but my head is too heavy and it's painful to move.

"Is it him? Do you see him? Is he there?" I cry as I'm heaved backward, away from Buck. I continue to beg and plead as hands pin me to the floor and pry my fingers off his sleeve.

"Please!" I beg. "Please let me go." I reach for anyone I can get hold of, but my hands remain empty. Skirts swish past, shoes in desperate need of a polish stomp by, panicked voices rush over and around me, and finally a cool breeze from the stage door touches my cheeks. A paramedic bends over, flashing a light in my eyes, asking questions I'm unable to answer. All I can do is whisper desperately.

"Please help me . . . please . . . please . . . help . . ."

VIVIAN SNOW

Auction

Lot #32

Hand-drawn postcard. No label.

Black ink on cardstock. Black Bible with ornate cross drawn on the cover.

ROMA. ITALIA. 18 FEB 1971

> *My Dear Friend,*
> *It sounds like you are working very hard, and I feel much pride at your progress. I know God looks on you with kindness. Never forget: James 2:12–13.*
> *—A*
>
> (Translation from Italian)

CHAPTER 32

February 21, 1971
Silver Hills Hospital
New Canaan, Connecticut

"Vivian, did you hear what I said?" Dr. Fiedler, my analyst, sits in his overstuffed armchair as I continue looking out the window, tapping on the glass at the little birds, wishing they'd hop closer.

"Hmm?"

"You can go home anytime you want. We'll continue treatment in an outpatient program."

"Anytime you want," what a misleading phrase. At first I was compelled into the hospital against my will, the whole padded-room thing in movies, just like I'd seen with my mother. I was told I'd lost my connection to reality from sleep deprivation, drinking too much, eating too little, and whatever was in those little white pills Betty gave me. I heard she was let go. I feel terrible about that.

I also heard my understudy took over after intermission, and she did her best for the next three weeks until it became clear I wasn't coming back and the show folded. Another thing I'm sorry for. I know Broadway is a risky business, especially for new musicals. Many shows don't even make it past previews much less through an eighty-six show run, but the show's demise is my fault.

When Aria and Archie got the call about my "incident," they worked together to find a place more suitable for my recovery. I like to imagine they asked Gracie's opinion too, but if they did, no one mentioned it to me.

This place, Silver Hills, is half mental institution, half rehab and only a step away from what I'm pretty sure is a front for a cult. Dr. Fiedler says joking is my way of resisting treatment and hiding from the real work I need to do, but if I have one more glass of what tastes like ground-up grass clippings, I might scream. But then why don't I want to go home?

"Maybe next week," I say, curling my legs up underneath my body on the stool he leaves by the window for my sessions.

"What will change next week?"

"I don't know. Maybe I'll be ready then."

"Vivian, you can stay as long as you wish, but it's a waste of time if you won't talk to us. It's just another way of avoiding your healing work."

"You think I'm doing this on purpose?" I ask, irritated. My overly polite, always gracious persona is difficult to keep on here. It's uncomfortable not being allowed to hide behind my name.

"I think part of you is doing it on purpose, yes. It's excruciating work to process trauma, and you've had a lot of it. You've been brave, very brave. But I know how carefully we protect those secret pains because it seems easier than rehashing them."

"Why pick at a healed wound?" I ask, questioning his logic.

"Because it's *not* healed. It's like covering a mortal wound with a bandage. And if you'll indulge my analogy, if one part of your body becomes septic, do you know what happens?"

I know from my time in the field hospitals what sepsis does to a person, how it can kill an otherwise strong and vibrant young man, how one cut can turn into the loss of a limb.

I nod.

"Emotional wounds are very similar. But how can we help you if you continue to pretend you're not even injured? Perhaps it's time to talk about Tom."

I wince at the mention of my first husband. If I tell him about Tom—how will he view me? How will I view myself?

"I'd rather not." Even hearing Tom's name makes his face flash through my mind. I have to pretend I didn't see him, that it was illness and exhaustion that brought my dead husband back to life, but I'm still not convinced. And Silver Hills is as good a place as any to hide from a ghost.

"I was overtired and overworked," I repeat for the hundredth time. "I don't need to be psychoanalyzed. I need more rest and recovery, and then I'll be ready to go home."

Dr. Fiedler takes off his glasses and runs a hand over his face. He's a kind-looking middle-aged man who spent much of my first weeks here listening. I liked him then, the thoughtful man who nodded along to the crescendos and decrescendos of my life story. Then he started to ask questions, challenging me, asking me to do "the work," and since then I dread my sessions.

"You've been through so much, so much. If you'd like to stay at Silver Hills a little longer, I'm sure no one here will stop you. But this isn't a spa, Vivian. You're stable, and I think you'd benefit greatly from outpatient treatment. You can't hide here forever."

I sit silent and glance at the door. I want the session to end. He notices my change in focus and sighs, closing the folder on the desk in front of him.

"We can do this every day, Vivian. Every day I can ask you, and every day you can walk away. What if this time you don't run from it? Face it," he urges.

I hold my breath and think of everything I'd need to tell him to make him understand. If I explain about the locker room, the blood on the floor, Trombello's assurance that he'd "take care of everything," the military police, the Highwards, the lies Larry wrote, the headstone

Trombello purchased, too many secrets to list, will he understand that I might not be totally delusional when I question if Tom is truly dead? *If I say the words, will I be free?* But then the panic comes, the paralyzing clutch of anxiety that makes my head spin.

I let out my breath and unfold my legs. I'll stay in Silver Hills a little longer.

"Maybe next week," I say again, standing and gathering my journal.

Dr. Fiedler tsks and puts down his pen, replacing his glasses. A younger version of me would find it unbearable to leave someone this frustrated, especially a man. But what good would explaining do?

"You know, Vivian," Dr. Fiedler says as I reach for the doorknob. "I find it fascinating that despite being so afraid you'll end up like your mother, you're choosing to stay in this place."

I turn on my heels, my ears ringing. *How dare he?* I hold my spiral notebook across my chest like a shield.

He's watching me with his elbows on his desk, lips puckered like he's tasting something sour. I want to swear at him, tell him that he has no idea what he's talking about. He didn't live with her, the woman who stole my childhood and killed my brother. The woman who left scars on my arms where she tried to rip my infant daughter out of my grip and now walks around in a world of half reality.

"I'm nothing like my mother," I say defensively.

"No, you're not." He makes a note in my file before placing it on the stack. "*She* didn't have a choice."

The statement guts me. He's right. My mother grew up in a time when mental illness was considered supernatural possession or a defect in genes or parenting. After losing her youngest child to her illness, she was locked away in an asylum only to have a part of her brain scrambled because no one knew a better way to help her. If only she could've had access to the kind of help I have at my fingertips—maybe she'd have had a life outside the walls of an institution.

"I'm not ready yet," I say honestly, staring at the floor. My voice is trembling, and the admission is different from my blasé, avoidant response earlier. Then I add, meeting my doctor's empathetic gaze, "But maybe next week."

The pinched look of disappointment on Dr. Fiedler's face is gone. I think he can tell I'm sincere. I'm not ready yet but I *will* try again, soon. He smiles kindly and says, "Yes, maybe next week." And we both mean it.

"Your ride is here," Tammy, the day nurse, says when she pops her head into my private room. The bed is stripped, a small green suitcase sits at my feet. It was hastily packed three months ago when Aria flew out to New York and ransacked my apartment for pajamas, slippers, a robe, and a bag of beauty supplies.

Three weeks have passed since I told Dr. Fiedler that I'd try again, and I'm finally ready to go home. Or at least ready to go back and tie up the loose ends I left dangling in New York before my breakdown. I'll attend a few weeks of outpatient treatment at Dr. Fiedler's Manhattan offices. Then, I can head back to my real home: California.

I pick up my hardback suitcase and follow Tammy down the carpeted hall. The walls are a light blue that looks soft enough to use as a swaddle blanket. Edie Sedgwick sits in the TV room wearing baggy sweatpants and an oversized T-shirt. She's been here three weeks now, and her face has finally started to lose the hollow look she came in with. She told me last night that she asked Dr. Fiedler to take all the mirrors from her room because they reminded her of how "fat" she's getting. I'm sure we'll see each other at some banquet or red carpet and nod in a silent pact, knowing we saw each other at our sickest.

Aria wanted to fly out again, but she and Margot were out of the country on a trip they'd planned for months. She said she'd send a car to take me back to Manhattan with an assistant to help me transition back to my apartment, where I'll finish my treatment. It's better this way, I think. Dr. Fiedler says it's good for family to support one another, but he says in the second half of my life I've asked Aria to carry me. It used to feel like an exchange, I'd shelter her from Papà or pay the bills and care for my mother, but over time I've taken more than I've given. It's unfair and unhealthy and has left me infirm when I should be perfectly able to carry myself. Dr. Fiedler assures me it'll take some time, but he's certain I'm growing closer to independence every day.

Dr. Fiedler shakes my hand after I sign some papers. I hug Tammy, and she walks me to the large double doors that mark the exit and the entrance.

"I'm such a huge fan," she says in my ear so no one else hears. The staff isn't supposed to acknowledge the celebrity status of any of the patients, but I guess it's all right now that I'm no longer a resident.

"You too," I whisper and then catch myself. We both giggle at my error as I correct it. "I mean, thank you. Though, I am a fan."

A black Cadillac with darkened windows sits at the curb outside. A man wearing a dark suit meets me halfway up the stairs to retrieve my luggage. A temperate spring wind whips at my loose ankle-length skirt and sends a ripple through my silk blouse. My hair has grown during my stay here, and nearly touches my shoulders. I relish its weight. When I was younger the black locks cascaded down my back, and Papà called it my "natural beauty." It's been lightened and shaped so often since then I hardly remembered the original state of it until now.

The chauffeur offers to get the car door for me, but I decline. I take one last look at Silver Hills, grateful for my time here, relieved to be leaving, and determined to never return. With a wistful sigh, I slip into the back seat. Waiting inside with his hands clasped in his lap over his dark slacks, is the last person on earth I expected to see.

"Oh my heavens," I squeak, laughing at the shock of seeing Antonio Trombello, his dark hair graying at the temples, the lines around his eyes and mouth reminding me that time hasn't stood still since our last good-bye. My cheeks flush like I'm a schoolgirl sitting next to her first crush. When he finally speaks, his voice brings tears of gratitude to my eyes.

"Hello, Vivian."

"Oh, Santo Cielo! Antonio Trombello. You almost gave me a heart attack." I pinch him, blinking away the moisture in my eyes.

"Ouch. What was that for?" he asks in Italian.

"To make sure you're real," I say, staring at him in the same way I would if the president were sitting inside my hired car. "I don't know if you've heard but—my sanity has been up for debate as of late."

"I may have heard a bit of the story," he confirms.

"Aria?" Clearly, it's Aria. Dr. Fiedler wouldn't break confidentiality, and Gracie knows nothing of my priestly friend.

"Yes. Somehow she found me in Calcata and told the story. I remembered your last letters and understood. She said she felt guilty she couldn't be here for a few weeks, and so I told her I'd come to help you."

"Just like that," I snap. "You've never visited me before, but now . . ."

He shrugs. "Now is the right time."

I look over his uniform of black pants and shirt and a simple collar. It's a step away from the street clothes we wore during our trip to Bari.

"And your responsibilities in Calcata?" I ask, grateful he's here but confused by his sudden appearance. I've prayed for him to visit, longed to sit by his side and listen to his baritone voice, but now that he's here—it feels unreal.

"They will keep," he says simply and firmly, and I push no further. During the rest of the drive, we speak as though we've never been apart. The creases around his lips give him an air of authority, and the lines beside his eyes, a promise of kindness. The stubble on his chin is fine, and flecks of silvery gray mix in with the rest. I wish I could reach out and touch it, see if it's rough like Papà's unshaven face or soft like Larry's.

As we get close to the George Washington Bridge, traffic slows. Trombello, sensing my weariness, suggests I give in to my droopy eyelids.

"We will have much time to speak later," he says, removing his coat and offering it to me as a blanket.

I cover myself with the wool jacket, burrowing into Trombello's scent, his warmth still lingering there. He's definitely real. I feel solid with him here, less afraid of running into the ghost that chased me out of my sanity.

As I give into sleep, I listen to his breathing beside me and pretend we're an old couple sleeping side by side, even though I know it's a silly dream. I've forgotten what a puzzle Antonio Trombello can be. He might be my closest friend in this world, but he's also hidden behind barriers of propriety and rules. Usually, those walls become thin if I'm patient. I'm almost grateful they've never toppled completely. I'm not sure what either of us would do if we tore through them or what we'd find on the other side.

VIVIAN SNOW

Auction

Lot #33

Hand-drawn postcard labeled: The Torch
    Black ink on cardstock. Woman's hand holding a metal torch, likely from the Statue of Liberty.

NEW YORK, NY. AUG 23 1971

My Dearest Friend—
    Thank you for every minute.
    —A
(Translation from Italian)

CHAPTER 33

August 22, 1971
Midtown East Apartment
New York, New York

"I'll be back in an hour," I say, pulling my hair into a short ponytail and slipping on a pair of oversized Coach sunglasses. I have on a lightweight green tracksuit and my favorite pair of walking shoes. It's a little over an hour before sunset. Usually, Trombello and I take an evening stroll together, but he's so wrapped up in whatever he's studying that I know we won't fit it in if I wait. Exercise is an important part of my treatment plan, so I stick to my routine with or without a companion. I should probably get used to walking alone, anyway. I can't expect Trombello to stay in New York forever, though I can't imagine my life without him now.

"All right. I'll start dinner once I finish here," he says. A slew of old-looking books with leather binding and gold embossed lettering on the spines are scattered across the kitchen table, where he's taken to studying.

Antonio Trombello is a quiet, scholarly man. During the day, he's at the table reading or off to the library in search of a book. He attends Mass daily, but never in the same location and never with me by his side. I know he's right, it's best to be discreet. I invited him to stay with me in the guest room of my apartment, but he insisted on lodging at the Vanderbilt YMCA nearby. But during the day, he's here and has been since March.

After his surprise appearance at Silver Hills, we returned to my apartment and found it much like I'd left it. Aria had at least done me the kindness of tidying the place, putting empty wine bottles in the garbage and rinsed dishes in the sink. Later, she told me that she'd intended to hire a cleaning service, but Dr. Fiedler suggested it might be best if I saw how bad things had gotten before I went into treatment.

Trombello and I spent hours of that first day cleaning the apartment, emptying half-full bottles of wine and visiting the local market to fill the refrigerator with fresh food. That night, I ordered pizza from Sofia's, too tired to cook. Antonio snickered at the New York version of one of his favorite foods, but ate it willingly.

We laughed through dinner and listened to a record on the couch, sipping herbal tea instead of wine as we reminisced. Through the next week or so, we cleared out the most obvious evidence of my breakdown, including a stack of programs for *Mama's Girls* that I'd signed six months ago for my publicist to send out.

I see Dr. Fiedler once a week, now at his Manhattan office. He's clearly still waiting for my breakthrough moment, the one where I'll discover the true reason behind my "psychotic break."

I have told him about my fears of ending up like my mother and the horror of that tragic day she killed baby Tony and how I couldn't stand to wear blue after seeing him cold in my mother's arms. I told him about life without a mother, my father's anger. I told him about losing Larry and my baby and feeling as though I've lost Gracie. I told him about Glenn's torture and coercion, and I saw his eyes grow misty when I recalled the night I finally left him. I told him about my dear friend Antonio Trombello whom I'd once thought I might be in love with and how he's an example of the kind of pure love I've always hoped a man can have for a woman. I told him of how I'd failed as a daughter, mother, wife, sister, and friend.

I told him everything—except for the one thing he keeps asking about. Tom. But we haven't gotten there yet. I sort of hope we never do. I haven't seen the man with his face since the night I screamed into the audience of *Mama's Girls*, and I'm halfway convinced everyone else is right—he was a figment of my imagination. Besides, the only other possible explanation, other than something supernatural, comes at the expense of my trust in Trombello. If Tom Highward is alive, that'd mean my oldest friend has been lying to me for the past twenty-eight years, and that's the most terrifying possibility of them all.

Lonzo holds the door.

"No preacher man today?" he asks. Lonzo hates when I walk alone near nightfall. Though I'm sure he's glad I'm no longer a drunk recluse, he still would prefer I take a cab any time past six p.m.

"Not tonight," I say, waving and tying a thin scarf under my chin. "Busy reading about Babylonians or something."

"Of course he is," Lonzo says. "Have a good walk, Miss Snow."

"Thank you, Lonzo," I say, waving as I pick up my pace.

Trombello has made friends with plenty of people during his stay in New York City. I'm always surprised to hear his name as we walk down the street. It's a comforting change in dynamics. I still see photographers snapping a picture of me here and there, and there was a particularly painful headline that hit the gossip pages, touting my return to New York from "rehab." But all in all, this city is too large to keep the spotlight on one person for too long. I'm enjoying the taste of anonymity.

The sun is nearing the strange twilight hour where it shares the sky with the moon. The temperature drops and the scents of cooking food and shrub roses rise above the lingering smells from garbage and the heavy odor of exhaust. Most people who can afford it leave the city in the summer months. Work weeks are shortened, and on particularly scorching days, fire hydrants are unleashed into the streets, to the delight of all neighborhood children.

The sight of children always makes me think of Gracie's kids. When I'm ready, I'll return to my house on Laurel Street and try to see my littlest grandson for the first time.

"You'll get there," Dr. Fiedler promises, "but you've got to be strong enough to stay there."

A line of sweat trickles down my spine when I reach Central Park. Usually, I'd follow the outer loop before heading home, but I've started out too late, and even I know it'd be reckless to be in the park past dark.

Instead of crossing at Fifth Avenue, I make a quick last-minute turn and increase my speed in the opposite direction. *I'll stop at Sofia's and pick up some garlic bread to have with dinner,* I think. For a moment I wish I could bring home a fancy wine for Trombello, something he'd never buy himself, but then throw away the idea, knowing it'd be one step down a road I'm trying to get far away from.

That's when I see him.

He tries to cover his face as though he's wiping away perspiration, but our eyes connect for just long enough for it to register.

It's Tom.

My throat clamps down on a building scream. This can't be happening again. Can my mind have made something so convincing? He looks so real, so, so real.

"Tom" steps toward me, his mouth open like he wants to talk. He is real. I'm certain.

But how?

The same suffocating anxiety from the night I screamed at Tom from the stage floods my senses. It's like I've been given a vitamin shot or one of Glenn's pep pills. But this time I won't confront this man here on the street and get tossed in a padded room again. Instead, I turn on the balls of my feet and sprint in the opposite direction, confused and desperate to escape.

I dash up Fifty-Ninth Street and down Park Avenue, knocking into a couple, my sunglasses skittering across the sidewalk. The man curses at me, but I don't stop. After a series of unpredictable turns, I end up half a mile north of my building, drenched in sweat and out of breath. Tom is nowhere to be seen.

I don't know where to go now. I could go to the airport and back to Hollywood. But I have no money or ID. Usually I'd turn to my dear Trombello, trusting he'd know what to do. But if that man was Tom and not some hyperrealistic hallucination, it means Trombello has been lying to me for decades. I'm confused, frightened, and sure of one thing—I must leave this city before Tom, dead or alive, finds me again.

Tearing the scarf off my head, I hail a cab and crouch in the back seat after giving the driver my address. The cabbie pulls up in front of my building, and I slip inside the lobby as he shouts at me through his window. Lonzo stands stunned at his post as I rush past. I'm beyond logic and reasoning, the panic-fueled hysteria affecting my every move. My hands are shaking and lungs aching as I explode through the apartment door. I lock every bolt and chain and dash to my bedroom, where I drag out my green suitcase and toss it on the bed.

"Viviana?" Trombello calls from the hall, knocking and then pushing the door open without waiting. He watches as I toss clothes and toiletries into the open suitcase. "Are we going on a trip?"

"I'm going somewhere, anywhere but here."

"Lonzo called just now. Asked if you were hurt."

I take an envelope of bills from my underwear drawer, pull out a hundred-dollar bill, and then toss the rest on top of the clothing.

"Here. I forgot to pay for the cab. Can you make sure Lonzo gets this?" I hold out the bill, and it quivers in the space between us. Trombello doesn't take the money, but does cover my hand with his, speaking calmly.

"Yes, but first, answer. Are you hurt?" he asks, looking me over from head to toe and then stepping closer to check my head and my eyes. I duck away, remembering the last thing I need to take with me—the scrapbook with all of Trombello's postcards lies on the nightstand. I place it in my luggage and then snap the lid closed.

"I'm fine. I just need a ride."

"To?"

"The airport. I . . . have to go home. I can't be here anymore."

"You can go anywhere you want, *mia cara amica*, but I thought you wanted to finish the program with Dr. Fiedler. Perhaps we should call him . . ."

"No," I say, dragging the heavy suitcase to the front door while Trombello follows behind. "I'm not crazy. He'll put me away again. But I know what I saw."

"What you saw? You mean . . ."

"Yes! Him. Alive and well and following me. Ghosts don't get spooked when you suddenly change the direction you're walking, do they?"

"Good heavens, Viviana! This again?" Trombello proclaims, slapping the wall with frustration.

"Yes. This. We never talk about this." My hands move wildly as I speak like Papà used to do when he was making a point. I'm exhausted by it all, the secret we never speak about, the reason we're bonded closer than I've ever been with another person.

"You mean, Tom Highward?" It's a relief to hear him say the name. We have to talk about it. Dr. Fiedler is right, it's festering inside me, rotting a hole in my soul.

"Yes." I stomp my foot, resolved. "Tom Highward. My husband."

He sighs deeply like he's been holding in a breath for thirty years.

"What do we have to say? Huh? We've said it all." He clutches my shoulders in a firm but tender grip, and my trembling calms.

"I saw him, Antonio," I say, weakly.

"Oh, *mia cara amica*," he says and leans his forehead against mine like he did in Bari. His eyes are closed, mine are open. The warmth of his touch comforts me, and I indulge it.

"He was real. I . . . I'm sure . . ." With the adrenaline rush gone, I run out of words, and we stand together. I breathe his air as he breathes mine. I glide my hands up his neck and frame his face. He traces his thumb down the outline of my jaw to my chin. I lean in, wanting to close the space and he does the same.

My lips brush his and he takes in a shuddering inhalation that reverberates through his frame and sends a thrill through my core. He wants me as urgently as I want him. He wants to take me. He doesn't have to say it, every inch of his skin touching mine screams it. I wait, sure it's finally time to cross these holy lines. But instead of kissing me deeply and allowing passion and desire to do their unrighteous but delicious work, Trombello shuffles back, disconnecting all carnal connection.

He shoves his hands in his pockets and asks curtly, "What more do you want to know?"

It's a rejection as harsh as the day I visited him in the confessional, or when he never met me in Rome. We've lived in this space of want and withholding for too long to play with it casually. And to think it's possibly all balanced on a lie.

I wet my unkissed lips and speak the one question I've never had the courage to ask.

"Is Tom still alive?"

Trombello, who's been staring at the top of his scuffed leather shoes since pushing me away, lifts his eyes to meet mine, a deep hurt residing inside them.

"Che cosa?" *What?*

"Is he alive?" I ask again more forcefully this time.

Trombello takes another step backward, tripping over the suitcase, catching himself against the wall.

"This is what you think?" he asks, tossing his hands in the air, flustered. He walks away to his spot in the kitchen, closing and stacking books and placing piles of notes into his satchel. I don't let his agitated state stop me. I press forward with my investigation.

"I know you're trying to protect me, but don't you see? If Tom is alive—I'm sane. If Tom is dead—I'm seeing ghosts. Tell me. Which is true?"

"I'll call Dr. Fiedler, but once he gets here, I have to leave." He continues to pack, ignoring my questions. All I can think is *He's abandoning me again.* He almost kissed me in the doorway, and now he's going to disappear.

"You're always running away." I stamp my foot, putting my body between Trombello and the phone. I take the receiver and hug it against my chest. "You can call him, but first—the truth."

"What is this truth you speak of?" he asks, clearly frustrated. He slaps the table with both hands, knocking over a stack of books and staring at me like I'm a stranger. His outburst doesn't frighten me.

"It's the only thing that makes sense," I insist. "You've always maintained his death wasn't my fault, and you helped me falsify his headstone and death certificate." All of the pieces start coming together as I speak them aloud. I should've seen it before. "He didn't die, did he? You helped him run away."

I point at him with the phone receiver. Trombello shakes his head deliberately and curses under his breath.

"You want to know where he is, do you, Viviana?"

"Yes." I stand tall, resolved. "Where is he?"

"I hate to speak of it, but I will tell you." Trombello tsks, sighs, and collapses into the wooden chair, a fully deflated man. He speaks again, cautious with each word he uses.

"Tom is buried under the Chapel in the Meadow. Dead. There was a hole in the fence. Everyone knew it. Soldiers snuck in and out through it, a few desperate prisoners too. That night we slipped in with your husband's body. I administered his last rites and buried him under the foundation, knowing concrete would be poured the next day. He rests there, still." He takes the phone from my hand and places it back on the hook. "I swear it to you, and I swear it to God."

I shudder. Trombello would not lie, not about God.

"Then who did I see?" I ask feebly. Has my mind gotten so practiced at creating false realities that now I imagine people who aren't there?

"I do not know, Viviana. I don't know how to help you. Only the doctor knows."

Trombello restacks his tower of books and retrieves a paper bag from the cabinet beside the fridge. It's a simple act of intimacy that makes it feel like he lives here, but the fact that he's packing up his belongings reminds me that Trombello cannot stay forever.

"Must you leave?" I say, ashamed I suspected him, accused him.

"I will speak to the doctor to be sure you are safe, but then, I will leave." He shakes his head and continues to clear his belongings from the table.

"But why? I believe you're telling the truth. You're a good man, Antonio. I don't doubt it for one minute."

"But you did doubt me. And you should," he says, taking one of the bags of books in his arms and placing it by the front door.

"What? What do you mean?" I ask, inhaling quickly, afraid of the sudden reversal. He returns to the kitchen empty handed.

"All these years I helped you, advised you, and protected you for one reason and one reason alone." He lifts one shoulder and shakes his head like he's scolding himself. "I'm in love with you."

When he didn't come back for me in Rome, I assumed I'd imagined that he returned my deeper affections. But I was wrong. My stomach flutters. He loves me.

"I love you too," I say, reaching out to take his hand, but he tugs it away. He finishes collecting his belongings and places the last bag by the door.

"You shouldn't," he says over his shoulder, his warning echoing through the hall.

"I know," I say, following him.

"And I shouldn't," he says, standing in front of me, the same stubble on his chin as the day he picked me up from Silver Hills. I know what it feels like now—soft, like cashmere. I want to lay my cheek against it.

"I know."

"You are so beautiful," he whispers quickly, as though the words were escaping. He tucks a lock that's fallen from my short ponytail behind my ear, and exhales.

I've been called beautiful by many men, by reporters, directors, and fans, but this is the first time the phrase has made me feel beautiful. He puts distance between us. He's clearly struggling with the same urges I'm fighting.

"Would God really mind so much if you stayed?" I ask, caressing the button on his shirtsleeve as he watches.

"This is a question I've asked of him countless times. He has not answered." He chuckles, cynically. "It's the only reason I've managed to stay on the other side of the ocean. Every day I sin in my love for you. I don't know if God will forgive me for it. He surely hasn't spared me from my longing for you."

I think of his lips, the near kiss, the life we would have had if he had been the one to get on that plane with me, instead of Glenn. Perhaps this is my atonement, to live a life without him.

Just as my touch drifts off his cuff fabric onto flesh, a loud knock at the door makes us separate with a start.

"It's probably Lonzo," he says. "I can explain to him . . ."

"No, it's all right. He might want to see that I'm safe. I can get it."

"Do you feel up to it?" he asks as another series of knocks rolls through the apartment and bounces off the walls. I blush.

"There's no such thing as ghosts, right?" Neither of us laugh. "Can you get the cash?" I ask, hand on the doorknob.

"Of course," Trombello agrees and goes to retrieve the cab fare and tip from the bedroom while I get the door.

I straighten my hair, run a finger under my eyes to clear away any running mascara, and put on my best Vivian Snow smile.

"I'm sorry, Lonzo. I had a slight emergency situation . . ."

I don't have the chance to finish. With my door wide open, I'm standing face-to-face not with Lonzo or even the angry taxi driver. No, the man at the door wearing a brown suit with a wide maroon tie, his light, slightly thinning straight hair combed to one side, is the ghost of Tom Highward.

This time I don't run.

This time—I scream.

VIVIAN SNOW

Auction

Lot #34

Hand-drawn postcard labeled: Sofia's
    Pencil on cardstock. Slice of New York style pizza with pepperoni.

SALERNO. ITALIA. 13 NOV 1971

    V—
      Move forward with boldness (and then have a slice of Sofia's cheese pizza afterward). You know how to reach me if you need to talk.
      —A

(Translation from Italian)

CHAPTER 34

November 16, 1971
Law Offices of Simon, Barrows & Murphy
New York, New York

"Sign here and here and here." An attorney wearing a Baroni pinstripe suit points to the pages where my signature is required. Across the table sits a team of attorneys, a middle-aged woman in Chanel, and an older man in a well-tailored suit. When I first saw him outside my apartment door, my scream brought Trombello running to my side.

"You," Trombello said, in shock. The fact that Trombello could see Tom made all the difference. This was a real man, flesh and blood, not a vision or ghost. And Trombello's shock confirmed that he hadn't been lying—he sincerely believed Tom Highward was dead.

That's because—he is dead.

The man on the other side of the door and the man sitting across from me today isn't T. B. Highward, son of Richard Arnold Highward. This is Tom Howard Highward, younger brother of Richard A. Highward and uncle to my dead husband. He's ten years older than my Tom would've been and his spitting image. He's also an attorney, which he made clear from the first moment he spoke to me on the threshold of my apartment.

"Miss Vivian Snow, I presume?"

"Tom?" I asked, trying to recall his voice from the few months of courtship that led up to our marriage.

"You may call me Mr. Highward," he said with a nod. "I have here important paperwork I need you to review and return. It's of a sensitive nature, and I hope you'll keep it to yourself." He held out folded pages. "There's a letter in there from my niece, whom I'm aware you've met with, and a number you can call with any questions."

At that moment, Lonzo appeared at the end of the hall, out of breath. He shouted at the intruder, who turned and walked away without acknowledging any of our questions or pleadings.

I shuffled through the stiff pages. The top sheet was a cream-colored letter. I passed it all to Trombello, who read through the document as we waited for Dr. Fiedler to arrive. The letter was from Moira, Tom's sister, the gray-haired woman staring at me across the table today. I haven't heard from her in decades. I'd read in the society pages that she married and had a few children of her own, which took care of any inheritance concerns, or so I thought.

Dear Vivian,

I hope all is well with you and your family. I've followed your career closely and I've cheered with each of your successes. Your dear Grace has turned into a lovely and talented woman. I'm sure you're incredibly proud.

Today, I write you with the most somber news. My father, Richard Highward Sr., has passed away. At the reading of his will, we were surprised to find that my father left his entire company, fortune, and inheritance to his eldest son—Tom Highward. My father never believed in Tom's death, and I think some part of him thought if he left this fortune to him that he'd return home.

But as we both know, Tom is dead. We've produced his death certificate, but all that did was change the path of inheritance from Tom to you and Grace.

This is why I come to you now, Vivian. Attached are papers that will legally disclaim this inheritance and refute your claim that Grace is Tom's child. I know this is a painful request, but one I'm sure you'll understand as a mother. My husband took his own life two years ago after some legal issues, leaving us with nothing. You're a strong woman, Vivian. You've built so much out of nothing. I have deep respect for you, so it's with great shame that I come on my knees with this appeal.

It's not only selfishness that brings me to this point, but my uncle Tom has threatened to speak publicly of his and my father's beliefs around Tom's death. I begged for the opportunity to entreat you in a private manner. I pray we can protect one another.

Sincerely Yours,

Moira Highward Lane

Trombello and I discussed the letter and the risks involved with fighting back to claim Tom's inheritance for Gracie. Within five minutes, we both saw what needed to be done. Gracie doesn't need Tom's money, and neither do I. But what we both need is privacy, and that's worth more than any dollar amount.

We didn't tell Dr. Fiedler, and when he left around ten, Trombello departed immediately after. Instinctually, I knew that was the last time I'd see him before he returned to Italy. I couldn't expect him to stay, not after everything we'd said and felt that night. He promised to write, and I promised back. I miss him, terribly, but he's done what he does best—he's taken me through a dark night to a new dawn, and now I'm ready to move through this day on my own.

"No one will know?" I ask after signing the pages in all the spots they highlighted. I have an attorney with me, but beyond that, this has been a secret proceeding, a closure for this chapter.

"No one will know," Mr. Highward echoes. Moira's eyes have been damp since the moment we walked in. She went to hug me, but Mr. Highward held her back by her elbow. Moira knows I was Tom's wife and Gracie is his child, but she's choosing her children's future over that connection, and I can't hold it against her. She's clearly been under the thumb of the men in her life since she was young.

I don't want Richard A. Highward's money. If he'd truly cared about Tom, he'd have attempted to visit Gracie at least once in his long life.

"Thank you," Moira says as she walks out the door behind Mr. Highward, before the ink is dry. It's over—I'm no longer attached to Tom Highward or his family. The only Tom that still exists in my story is the one I've made up for Gracie, and that's the only one who matters.

VIVIAN SNOW

Auction

Lot #35

Hand-drawn postcard labeled: Bardonecchia
   Black ink on cardstock. Snowy mountain with ski tracks visible through the trees and a small village at the base.

TORINO. ITALIA. 31 JAN 1972

> V—
>   I've been sent north to Bardonecchia. The chill here in the mountains reminds me of the shipyard, but my old bones shake easier. I long for home but will go where God needs me.
>   Your frozen friend—A
> (Translation from Italian)

CHAPTER 35

March 2, 1972
Dr. Fiedler's Office
New Canaan, Connecticut

On days like today it's worthwhile making the drive to Connecticut to meet with Dr. Fiedler. Our hypnotherapy sessions are intense, and he likes to do them here, close to Silver Hills, just in case I . . . I don't know . . . I guess just in case I lose my mind again.

I don't mind his overcautious approach. I always welcome getting out of the city, and I like watching the birds from his office window as we talk. The starlings fly like they're members of a Broadway company doing a choreographed dance they've polished to perfection over a long run. The sparrows play on the windowsill, reminding me of Gracie when she was a toddler collecting Easter eggs in the yard of the Norways' cottage. The cardinals turn a bare, brown cluster of branches into a brilliant red blaze.

It's been nearly a year since I left Silver Hills, and Dr. Fiedler has slowly introduced hypnotherapy to our sessions. Under hypnosis I'm able to look at my life experiences from a dispassionate distance, which helps me analyze and process with some clarity. Sometimes my realizations come after a session, like a picture appearing on photo paper drenched in developing fluid.

Last week as I was running through a scene from *Imitation of Life* in a class at the Actors Studio, a sudden understanding parted the chaos in my mind.

"All these years I've been bashing my brains in trying to figure out why Gracie hates me," I say to Dr. Fiedler. I curl up in a ball, leaning against the window. "I think I've figured it out."

"I'd love to hear your thoughts on it," the doctor says cautiously, as though any sudden movements might distract my train of thought. He leans back in his chair and listens with a finger over his lips like he's muting himself. I find the words again, and force them to stay in my mind, fogging the glass with each rapid exhale.

"I killed her father." It sounds like a line from a film or a play, something by Tennessee Williams, no doubt.

There. I said it. I told someone other than Trombello, who insists on forgiving me for everything I've ever done wrong.

Dr. Fiedler leans forward, elbows on his desk, head cocked to the side.

"What exactly do you mean by killed?"

"Killed. Murdered. Stabbed."

"Tom, your first husband, the one who died in France . . ."

"He died in the locker room of Edinburgh Middle School." Now that I've started I have to get it all out. It's like I'm purging a poison. "Three days after we were married."

"But, but why?" the doctor asks, stuttering. I know he intended to be calm, indifferent, but how could he have prepared for this? I knew I'd shock and horrify anyone who heard the truth.

"I worked at the POW camp. There was a dance for the Italian prisoners. I was in charge. Tom and a few other soldiers interrupted the dance, and he was angry, so angry."

I'm experiencing it again. The way he dragged me back into the locker room, leaving bruises on my wrist that took a week to fade, and how he called me a whore for singing and dancing with the Italian POWs, men he'd been trained to fight overseas.

"And then?" Dr. Fiedler asks. His momentary horror has passed, and he looks professional, focused again.

"Then . . . Trombello . . ." Antonio Trombello's voice comes into my mind.

Non è sicuro. It's not safe. *Per favore vieni con me.* Please come with me.

"Your priest friend who I met at your apartment last year? The Italian?"

I nod.

Do I tell him the rest? Do I risk letting the truth out? I glance at his pen standing at the ready.

Noticing my hesitation, he lays his writing utensil down and adds, "Just to remind you, Vivian, all you tell me here is confidential. I take my ethical obligations seriously. If it makes you feel an increased sense of safety, I can stop taking notes."

At least in confession I don't have to look the priest or God in the eye and see my darkest sins written down. I whisper a thank-you and stare back out the window at the birds so I don't have to watch the doctor as I continue.

"Tom had a knife." I run my fingers over the delicate scar on the side of my neck. "Trombello had a bat. Told me to run, but Tom was in a rage. He was killing Trombello, slamming his head on the floor." I can hear the sound of my friend's head hitting the brown tiled floor over and over again. I didn't know if it was the tiles cracking or his skull. "I grabbed the knife and . . ."

"Yes?"

"I didn't stab him."

"You didn't?"

I look down at my empty hand. "I didn't even think of stabbing him. I didn't want to use the knife. I wanted to hide it so he couldn't use it. I used the bat instead. Hit Tom hard enough to distract him, get him off Trombello."

"Did it work?"

I nod, trancelike.

"It worked. But then . . ." I remember Tom's rageful frenzy, the murderous wrath in his eyes as he barreled toward me, tossing the bat aside as though it were a stick in a child's hands. The feeling of the knife's blade cutting into his skin as I defensively sliced at him. My overpowering guilt when he saw what I'd done to him.

"I warned him to stay back. He reached for me but I . . . cut his hand."

You're crazy, he screamed, blood dripping down his fingers and soaking into his sleeve. I still hear that voice inside my head nearly every day.

I wipe the condensation from my breath off the window and focus on a large bird of prey making leisurely loops up and around the meadow that surrounds Silver Hills. It's a hawk or eagle, I can't be sure from so far.

"He said I'd end up crazy, you know." I laugh sardonically. "He was right, I guess."

Dr. Fiedler says something in an attempt to comfort me, but I'm too far away from the book-lined room, from his wispy goatee and tobacco-stained teeth. I'm still back there, with Tom's hands around my throat.

"He pinned me against the lockers and . . . his hands were so large. They fit all the way around my neck." I inhale rapidly like he's choking me again, squeezing life out of me one second at a time.

"Vivian? Are you all right?" Dr. Fiedler asks. My breathing is raspy now, my head starting to spin. He stands, shoving his chair into the wall. My vision grows blurry as he touches my arm, the one that propelled the knife forward only a few inches into the soft flesh of Tom's thigh.

My breathing recovers, eyes focusing once again on Dr. Fiedler, who is now standing over me.

"Then I killed him," I say, matter-of-factly, staring up into his normally stoic face, which is now twisted with concern and curiosity.

"With the knife?"

"Yes," I say, opening and closing the hand that held the handle covered in his blood.

He settles into the chair next to me.

"Vivian, you do understand that this is not murder, correct? This sounds like a clear-cut case of self-defense. Why didn't you just report it as such?"

"How could I prove it?" I say. What would've changed if I'd gone to an officer, one of the superiors in charge or Lieutenant Colonel Gammell? "And the prisoners involved—who would've believed them? I needed to work to take care of my family, and those men were just trying to help me. I couldn't betray them."

"That makes sense, but it doesn't change the fact that you were defending yourself. What happened next?"

I flash back to the moment I woke up and saw Tom on the floor, lying in a pool of blood. Trombello helped me to my feet, sent me off with another Italian prisoner, Gravano, who took me to the car where my parish priest, Father Patrick, waited to drive me home. I never told Father Patrick the truth of why I was bruised and beaten, why my new husband never returned after that night, why I had blood on my hands. I never knew how much the Father knew, and I thought he'd bring it up to me if he felt it needed to be addressed. He never did.

"Trombello took care of it all."

"It sounds like you trust him."

"I do. More than anyone."

"I can see that. Does he believe this was homicide?"

"Well, no, not exactly. He said I was justified, but he's biased."

"So you don't trust his assessment?"

"I do, but . . ."

"But not about this."

"I guess not."

"Hmm." The doctor pauses and rubs his chin before speaking again. "Now, let me ask you something different. You said Gracie hates you because you 'murdered' her father. Does she know what occurred between you and Tom?"

"No. I was just thinking that in some cosmic way she does, and that's why she found it so easy to leave and cut me out of her life."

"But, Vivian, no matter what happened to Tom after your altercation with him—an altercation he started—you saved Gracie when you saved yourself. She wouldn't exist otherwise. Do you truly feel that's murder?"

I think of her as a baby, lying in my arms, taking long, hungry gulps from my breast, the sky blue of her eyes the only blue I've ever loved. I imagine the way that night could've gone if I hadn't lashed back, if I had surrendered to the darkness as he choked me. I'd have died that night instead of Tom, and with me our little girl. To take a life in order to save one, that I can understand. I protected myself and my baby in a way my mother was unable to with Tony—that's not a crime.

"I don't know for sure, but I . . . I don't think I do." A weight lifts from my body like bubbles off a glass of Coca-Cola as soon as I say the words out loud, and I laugh at the sensation.

"That's a really good start, Vivian. Very good," Dr. Fiedler says. He inhales deeply like he's taking a hit off a joint and holding in a cloud of smoke to increase his high. He lets out the breath and speaks at a measured tempo.

"Our time is up, but before we go, I'm going to leave you with a thought that might make you uncomfortable," Dr. Fiedler says with an empathetic sternness. I try to look back at the birds, but he retains my focus with a heavy look. "Your relationship with Gracie is complicated and layered. It cannot be boiled down to one act and should be the subject of future psychotherapy and family therapy. It's a lot of work. Often, we tell ourselves we're unworthy of love because of the past as a way to avoid the emotional labor of relational healing."

I think of the last thirty years and how I've worn Tom's death as a layer of armor. I ran away to the USO, I ran away to Hollywood, I ran away to live with Glenn, I ran away to Italy—and when I stopped running away, it was too late. Gracie has built her own armor. I did the same thing to Trombello, always pushing him away, hiding from his care, until he didn't have the desire to keep coming back.

I told myself I needed it, the shell that kept me close but unreachable. I wore it to protect my family from my past, and to protect me from making any more horrendous mistakes. But really all it did was keep me from feeling the touch of another human heart or the deep intimacy that would allow me to be seen spiritually naked.

"I'm willing to work."

"Good. Good. So, does that mean I'll see you next week?"

I ponder his question. I've stood up to frightening men and I've sung with bombs echoing in the background. I've seen death with my own eyes, and I've endured abandonment from those I hold most dear. But by far the most frightening thing I've ever done is sit in this office and face my past with new eyes, my present with forgiveness, and my future with a hope that it's all been worth it.

"See you next week." I nod and gather my things and exit his office where I'll return next week and next week and next week—as long as it takes.

VIVIAN SNOW

Auction

Lot #36

Hand-painted postcard labeled: Saint Agnes
   Watercolor on cardstock. Young girl in white robes with angelic halo, holding a lamb.

SALERNO. ITALIA. 24 JUN 1984

    V—

    A granddaughter! Many congratulations at your continued blessings. Give my best wishes to Aria and your mamma and wholehearted congratulations to Grace. I'll continue to pray her heart is softened.
    —A

    (Translation from Italian)

CHAPTER 36

July 3, 1984
Bayside Assisted Living Facility
San Diego, California

"Here you go, Mamma." I run a brush through Mamma's silver hair. It's smooth and thick and smells of argon oil and lavender. Her private suite looks out on the ocean, and a warm, salty breeze rushes in through the screen door. Whenever I get a good lungful of sea air I think of Italy, Trombello's arms, and more than one regret.

"Thank you," she says with a slight slur like her tongue is too wide for her mouth. She doesn't fight back when I call her Mamma anymore. It's like she's accepted it as a name rather than a title or role. I place a comb on each side of her head to keep the strands from tickling her face.

"You look very pretty today, Mamma," Aria says loudly from the kitchen, where she's cutting vegetables. Mamma's hearing has gone downhill in the past few years, and since she finds hearing aids irritating, we've all taken to shouting.

"Thank you," she slurs again, her head bobbing as she reaches for a tube of lipstick on the table. She applies it with a shaky hand, using the tabletop mirror, and I tidy the edges with a tissue.

"Lovely," I say, encouraging her efforts. Margot likes Mamma to do as much of her own self-care as possible, but I've taken to playing beauty parlor with her during my visits.

Her doll, Miriam, is tucked to her side and she caresses it tenderly. "Now Miriam?"

"Yes, take her bows out. She needs a new hairdo," I say gently. Her wrinkled, knobby fingers with manicured red nails work methodically to remove the braids and bows from the doll's hair. These are the hands that raised me and the hands that held my brother as he took his last breath. She's been through more torture and terror than I can possibly imagine. I used to think I'd never be able to look at her hands again without feeling the dread or the anger from that horrible day. But Dr. Fiedler helped me understand that Aria and I could've easily ended up in the same place as our mother if we'd been born in a different era. I still mourn the loss of the healthy mother I never had and the brother who never had the chance to live. I also mourn for my mother herself, how we all failed her in our own ways.

But we're not failing her anymore.

"Here, let me help," I say, watching Mamma struggle with the latch on one of her doll's bows. We're working together to get her hair braided just right, when the doorbell rings.

My stomach drops.

I'm leaving in the morning for Greece, where we're filming on location, so Aria planned one last dinner together, all us girls. Mamma, Aria, me, and—Gracie.

"I've got it!" Aria runs to the door, and as soon as it's opened, a burst of energy floods through.

"Grandma!" Seven-year-old Lawrence runs and jumps onto my lap. Mamma starts and glares at us both, protecting her doll like we're obnoxious kids on the bus. I scoop up my little grandson and apologize, collapsing into a chair by the window.

"I didn't know you were coming!" It was supposed to be just the four of us, even Margot stepped out so we could have some uninterrupted time as a family. When Gracie agreed to the luncheon, I was shocked. Gracie has kept her walls pretty high over the years, though I've been given open access to my grandchildren. Her newest husband, actor Clark McFadden, invited me to Christmas on his Montana ranch, but Gracie remains cold.

Years ago, Dr. Fiedler, who I still see as often as my schedule allows, reminded me to be patient, that it might take some time to reconnect with my daughter. His constant reassurances have kept me from showing up at her house with a pan of lasagna and a tray of cannoli and pleading for her to let me in.

I missed the first few months of Chris's life, but I've been around for each birthday and holiday since. Today, it seems we have the younger two of the crew.

"The big boys with their father?"

"Yup," Gracie says, holding six-month-old Elise on her hip. My first granddaughter.

"Where's the baby?" I ask, in a playful voice, reaching out for the chubby infant.

"Here. Take her. She's fussy. You'll need this." Gracie passes me a damp spit rag, and I toss it over my shoulder. She's dressed in an ankle-length skirt and platform sandals with her long hair parted down the middle. I can see stress in the corners of her eyes, and she barely looks at me.

I try not to focus on the tension and snuggle into the wiggly infant in my arms. I missed this phase with Gracie. I was in Europe when she was a tiny little lump like Elise. Did her head smell this fantastic? Was her hair as sweet and fine?

I don't get far into my wonderings, when Gracie, beautiful, polished, self-assured Gracie, collapses into a puddle, sobbing.

"Oh heavens," Aria cries from the kitchen, running into the small dining area, where I'm holding Elise and Lawrence is playing with a truck on the floor. Aria's still holding a sauce-covered wooden spoon, and I've adjusted Elise onto a hip so I can kneel beside my daughter who is crying unconsolably.

"Sweetheart, whatever is the matter?" I ask, petting her silky hair like I used to do when she couldn't sleep at night.

"Are you hurt?" Aria asks, searching Gracie's crumpled form for an injury.

"Ari? Ari?" Mamma calls out from the sitting room, clearly upset by the commotion.

"I've got her and the kids. I'll call Margot over, and you take Gracie into the bedroom," Aria suggests, peeling the baby off my side and calling out words of comfort to Mamma.

"Come now, Gracie. I've got you." I half carry, half guide her into Mamma's bedroom. There's a hospital bed against the side wall, and I help her onto the mattress, the rubber sheet underneath crinkling as she returns to her fetal position. I rub her back and run my fingers through her hair, remembering Dr. Fiedler's suggestion of patience.

After a few minutes, Gracie rolls onto her back, her face wet and eyes swollen. Her freckles have faded, but there's still a handful that dot the bridge of her nose. Her cheeks are flushed, and I stop myself from drying her tears.

"I feel so alone," she says, looking at the ceiling with a dead-eyed stare.

I blink slowly, thinking I might understand the reason behind her collapse. Clark has finally had enough of her affairs and moved on. I knew there was gossip in the papers, but I hoped they were lies. Gracie's tears tell the truth. My girl is adrift once again, this time with four children in her boat.

"You're not alone," I say. I push a damp clump of hair away from her eye and then stop, hoping she'll continue talking. I'm disappointed in Gracie's choices. I have been from the moment she crawled out the window of her bedroom twenty-three years ago, but she's not the only person riding the tide of her unpredictable love life—her children are too. I made the mistake with Gracie of thinking the dysfunction in my home only affected me. Clearly, I'd been wrong.

"Clark left me." Another rush of emotion bubbles up, but she forces it down before it erupts. "He's jealous of Phillip," she says, referring to her costar in her latest film. She slaps at the wrinkled comforter. "He said after the baby was born that he tried to love me again, for the kids' sake. Tried to love me *again*, Mom. He'd already stopped loving me after six years."

"Oh, sweetheart. I'm so sorry," I say, genuinely sorrowful for her loss but also holding back the comments I may have made in the past about her habitual infidelity and how this Phillip person left his second wife for her and how that's a sign he's not a trustworthy man. I leave out all mention of religion and judgment when it comes to divorce. She needs me to listen, to caress and cajole, not judge her. That's one thing I've come to understand as I've evolved—very rarely is judgment the correct response to a cry for help.

"We made plans for our lives, for our careers," she continues. "We made a child together. Can you believe it? Just like that—he's gone," she snaps. "He promised to help with Elise, pay for things and take her places, but it still stinks. They all loved him. Jimmy's already started asking for him 'cause their dad is so shitty, so, so shitty."

"He'll be there for them. Clark's a good man."

Gracie punches at the mattress and sobs again.

"He is. I took him for granted. I know I did. But he won't take me back and . . . the papers . . . the papers are going to say the worst things."

They already are, I think. I often wonder if fame is a gag gift that looks beautiful on the outside but has little inside other than a few fear-inducing tricks. If I had to go back and do it over again knowing what I know now, would I trade the money and the notoriety for a peaceful life with a loyal husband and happy children? Does fame have to lead to infamy?

"Mamma? How did you do it?" she asks after a peaceful moment, her voice small and childlike.

"Hmm?" I ask, worried I've missed something, so lost in my thoughts.

"How did you do it on your own?" She dries her face with the long sleeve of her floral dress and props herself up on her elbows.

I think back to when I found out I was pregnant after Tom's death. I remember my father's joy at having a grandchild, my sister's concern that my love for her would wane with the addition of another hand to hold. I remember feeling Gracie squirm inside of me. I remember how right it felt to hold her in my arms even though I believed I'd stolen something from her when she was no more than an imagining.

Dr. Fiedler was right—I love my baby girl, but she and I have spent a lifetime holding each other at arm's length.

"I didn't do it alone," I say, tucking a strand of golden hair behind her ear. "I did it with Nonno and Zia, and I did it with you. I wasn't a good mom to you, Gracie. I know it. You have every right to be hurt by the way I raised you."

She collapses into my shoulder.

"You thought you were doing the right thing. I just didn't understand how hard it was to know what the right thing is most of the time."

I caress her cheek and run a finger under her chin. She's a woman now, a mother, but she's still my daughter, and if she'll let me help her, I will. "I'm not perfect." I correct myself, "*We're* not perfect. But, you don't have to do this alone."

"I love you, Mamma," she says quietly. Her makeup has washed off with her tears, and I know in this moment she's sincere. There's no guarantee she'll feel this way when the press has moved on to a new scandal and she has a new award in her hands, but for now, it brings more healing to a wound that I've been trying to close since the day I defended my life not knowing I was also protecting hers.

Her nose crumples, creasing the dusting of freckles like cinnamon dissolving into the foam of a cappuccino. I gather her in my arms and hold her the best I can, rocking her back and forth. I'll never be the perfect mother, neither will Mamma, or Gracie, and if she chooses motherhood one day, neither will Elise. But perhaps we don't have to be perfect—perhaps we only have to be better than what was given to us.

VIVIAN SNOW

Auction

Lot #37

Hand-drawn postcard. No label.
    Pencil on cardstock. Masculine hands held together in prayer.

SALERNO. ITALIA. 25 JUL 1998

> *Dear Viviana—*
>   *Thank you for your ongoing support. I know you are worried, but I have faith all will be as it should. I need no money—only prayers. When I'm well again, we will visit.*
>   *Till we meet again—A*
> (Translation from Italian)

CHAPTER 37

December 20, 1998
Acton Cottage
London, England

The phone rings for the third time. I check the clock—it's three a.m. I bolt up in bed and grab the receiver, interrupting the fourth trill, doing the math in my head. At home, I'd assume an early morning call was bad news, but London is eight hours ahead of LA, so this could be anyone from the States. I include in that Gracie, who is supposed to join me and Elise here for Christmas.

Dear God, please don't let her cancel on Elise again, I plead mentally.

"Hello?" I whisper into the receiver. My fourteen-year-old grand-daughter, Elise, is in the next room, sleeping off her jet lag. We've been in this quaint cottage two days already, and though I know Gracie is going to find it stifling, Elise and I have enjoyed playing pretend in the little house. My first great-grandchild is due in two months, so Jimmy and his wife won't be visiting this year, but both Chris and Lawrence are planning to meet us in London in the New Year.

"Buongiorno." It's a woman's voice. I don't recognize her immediately, though I probably should. Anyone who has this number must be someone important in my life. Zia Claudia and Zia Nina passed years ago, but I've stayed close with my cousin Maria and her crew of kids. But this isn't Maria. I respond in my native tongue.

"Good morning. May I ask who is calling?"

"Yes, this is Nurse Christine Lombardi. I'm calling from Giovanni da Procida Hospital. Dr. Franco gave me your number."

I know who this call is about.

"How is he?" I ask, without saying Trombello's name. He told me last fall of his diagnosis. I tried to visit then, but he asked me to wait until he'd grown stronger. I've had three letters from him in that time—two saying he was getting better and one written in a shaky hand, telling me not to worry. I've written and asked for his number, location, his doctor's name—but he's kept me in the dark. I think I've known, just like I knew with Aria's cancer, that the end was coming. I can only hope that it's not too late.

"Weak. His time is near."

"How long?" I ask, understanding that it's impossible to predict, but asking anyway.

"A day. Maybe two."

"All right. Thank you," I say, collecting information for what I know must come next.

As I call my travel agent and wake my long-suffering assistant and ring through to Gracie, who is in New York with one of her boyfriends, my heart aches with sorrow.

The older I get, the more I should expect these calls, but they never get easier. Mamma passed in her sleep unexpectedly of a heart attack at Bayside when Elise was a toddler. And Archie passed from a stroke a few years after that.

The most painful loss was ten years ago when my Aria passed. It took me years to be able to look at a blooming garden and not break into tears. Gracie, Margot, the kids, and I planted chrysanthemums around her grave one year after her passing. I still visit her every time I return to California. She's buried in the same cemetery she tended for so many years, and Margot has a spot reserved right next to hers. They may never have shared a name, but they shared a life, and that might mean even more than any of the marriage certificates I've signed.

Now, my dear Trombello. I'm in my seventies, but there's always been a part of me that thought I'd find my way to my friend's side or him to mine. His book of postcards is my most priceless possession, and I share it with Elise, telling her stories of the places in his drawings. She has no idea who they're from, and I dream of a day where I might tell her all about the artist who created those cards. But knowing Antonio Trombello is ready to cross over to his eternal reward, I find myself filled with intense regret for all the could've beens and maybes, and I know I must see him one last time.

~

Trombello was sent home to spend the last of his hours in his one-bedroom house on the edge of Salerno. I've been traveling for half a day, leaving Elise with my assistant, knowing Gracie is on her way to the cottage. I told her an elderly relative is ill, and she was more compassionate than I expected.

"Go be with her, Mom. I've got Christmas covered."

Our relationship has never been sturdy, but we go through cycles. The ups and downs are heavily affected by her relationship status, but there are plenty of good times to equalize the rough ones. And even when things are rocky with my daughter, I've found a deep connection with my grandchildren that brings a profound richness to my life.

"Come in. Come in." A young woman in a white uniform meets me at the door. It's been drizzling today, and I know I must look a fright. I've found freedom in aging. As my wrinkles have set in and my hair turned white and men's eyes grown numb to my appearance, I've spent less time worrying about how I look and more time worrying about what meaning I'll leave behind. Besides, there's always a role for a grandmother in Hollywood, and though I only accept an offer or two a year, I still know how to find my light.

Christine takes me to a room in the back of the small apartment, where a hospital bed has been squeezed into the bedroom. The shades are drawn and the lights are off, making it feel like night. Trombello lies propped up with pillows, his eyes closed. His hair is white, like mine, and his wrinkles soft looking and deep like they've been carved in wet sand. He's thin, sickly thin, and a monitor beeps in the corner, letting me know I'm not too late.

"*Mia cara amica.* You silly girl. You came." His eyes crack open, and he squints at me as though I've brought light into the dark room by entering it.

"Silly, perhaps. But girl? I think not." I blink back tears and swallow the sob that's creeping up my throat. His voice is the same as the first time I heard it in the Camp Atterbury POW office. How will I get by without him?

"You look like an angel to me," he says in Italian, not caring that Christine is in the room.

"I'll be in the kitchen," she says, closing the door behind her, seeming to recognize our need for privacy.

"You finally let me visit," I say, leaving my bag by the bedroom door and settling into the chair next to his bed. I take his hand and he doesn't stop me. There can be no sin in our love now.

"I hate for you to see me this way."

"I'd have cursed you forever if you'd stopped me."

"That's a poor way to start eternity," he says, laughing and then flinching and closing his eyes. I kiss the back of his hand.

"You should rest," I say, moving to stand, but his weak grip tenses.

"I'll have plenty of time to rest later. Please don't go."

I return to my previous position and reassure him with a squeeze.

"I'm here for as long as you want me."

"Thank you, *mia cara amica.* You bring me comfort."

We sit in silence until the darkness isn't only in the room but also outside the windows. His breathing is slow and ragged, and there are spaces between breaths that make me wonder if he has already gone.

His nurse comes in and does a check, her face subdued, telling me all I need to know about his prognosis.

"Would you like some music?" she asks, and Trombello mutters the title of a collection of classical songs. Christine inserts the CD, dims the lights, and leaves once more.

"Where are you?" Trombello asks. I'm holding his hand, but it seems he can't feel it.

"Right here, Antonio. I haven't left."

"Come closer," he bids. I measure the space remaining on the bed, and instead of thinking of propriety or sin, I think of human kindness and lay my body next to his and place my head on his shoulder. His skin is chilled, so I pull up a thin afghan and tuck it around him, kissing his cheek with a love that's lasted longer than any in my lifetime.

"I hope there's a God," Trombello says. It's the first time I've heard him come close to hinting at doubt of a supreme being.

"Me too," I agree honestly rather than spouting comforting placations.

"What if we were wrong?" he whispers, and I curl against him, trying to give him some of my existence to keep his going a little longer.

"Do you truly question your faith?" I ask, unsure where his thoughts are leading him and fearful where his lack of faith would leave mine.

"No. Not truly," he says, lifting his arm with great effort and cupping my cheek with his cold touch. "But with you beside me now, I only worry it wasn't worth it."

I press my lips against the palm of his hand, my hot tears bathing his skin in much-needed heat. We had chances to change our trajectory, to have a family and future together, and every time, God got in the way.

"You were worth it," I say, wishing we had more time but knowing if Trombello were healed and lifted from his deathbed today, his doubts would clear once again, and he'd choose God. Tom chose anger, Larry fame, Glenn greed, and my dear Trombello chose God Almighty. It might be asking too much, it might make me a selfish and heretical woman, but I wish someone had chosen me—at least once. He drifts off to sleep again and I close my eyes, listening to his breathing, clinging to his side as though I could force him to stay.

A light from the hall wakes me after some time, and a light touch on my elbow shocks me to full consciousness. It's Christine. I want to wave her away and get her to close the door quickly to keep from disturbing Trombello, when I see the sympathy on her face.

"Miss. They are here to take him."

"Take him?" I ask, disoriented at first and then noticing the strange silence in the room—no music, no beeping, and no ragged breaths outside of my own. I turn around and see what I already know, just as every other time he's shown his love for me, he's left me alone. My Trombello is gone.

I return home in time for New Year's Day, though the celebration seems brash and out of place after sharing Trombello's deathbed. I try to imagine he's in heaven with Aria somewhere, acting as my guardian angel, but it all seems so futile.

I'd hoped Trombello had left me a letter or note of some kind telling me his true emotions, but Christine said he'd been too weak to write for a long time, and so I hold on to our last night together as proof of his care for me. I move on with life, I spend time with my grandchildren and great-grandchildren. I watch Gracie fall in and out of love and make all the mistakes I wish I could spare her but that she has to experience for herself.

~

One year later, on a cool January morning in my Laurel Street bungalow, I receive a letter with a familiar postmark—Salerno. My heart leaps as though it's been sent straight from heaven. The handwriting is feminine, and I calm my outrageous imagination as I open the envelope.

A small sheet of stationery slips out folded around one of Trombello's postcards.

This is one I've never seen before. It has my name in the address section on the back but no street number or city and no postage, and the message looks to be in English rather than Italian. The card itself is tattered along the edges of a pencil drawing of a woman sitting beside a man at a café, staring out at the ocean.

The stationery has a short note from Christine.

> *Dear Miss Snow,*
> *I found this card with your name on it. Though I cannot read it, I know you'd hoped for some parting words from Father Trombello. I thought this might bring you comfort.*
> *Sincerely,*
> *Christine*

My hands shake as I turn the card over and see a simple message written on the back in English. I let out a little whimper as I run my eyes over his handwriting over and over and over again.

"Nonna, are you all right?" Teenage Elise, who is staying with me while her mom films on location in Thailand, puts a comforting hand on my back, concern spelled out on her face.

"Yes dear," I say, sniffling. I wipe my nose and cheeks with the tissue I keep stashed in my sleeve, and then I ask Elise for a favor. "You know that book of pictures we used to look at when you were a little girl?"

"The ones of all your trips and stuff that's next to your bed?" Elise asks, her eyes bright with curiosity.

"Yes. That one," I say, turning the card over so the words are hidden. "Could you go grab that for Nonna?"

"For sure," she says, dashing through the kitchen and down the hall to snag the scrapbook. I put the nurse's letter in my pocket and then read Trombello's message one last time, kissing the cardstock where he signed his name. When Elise returns, we flip through the pages to one of the few empty ones and carefully slip it into the slot. The spine crackles when I close it.

"Was that one a picture of you, Nonna?" Elise asks, running her finger along the metal corners of the book.

"I think perhaps it was, darling."

"And the man?"

I shrug.

"Only a dream."

EPILOGUE

Fifty years later

The auctioneer, wearing a pair of cotton gloves, takes out a stack of postcards from a specialized clear envelope and spreads them on the glass countertop.

"I'm glad to see these all go together," he says with a stiff smile. Kara counts each of them and checks them against their lot number before signing the auction papers that make them legally her property.

"Yeah. My mom was devastated when they went up for auction. We're all pitching in to surprise her for her sixty-fifth birthday."

"Is she a big Vivian Snow fan, then?" the man in the suit asks. The twentysomething young woman shakes her head and laughs.

"Not exactly. Vivian Snow is my great-grandmother. My mom tells stories of seeing these cards in a book a long time ago. When my grandma passed away, they got lost, so you can imagine what an awesome present this is gonna be."

The auctioneer's eyebrows shoot up as he replaces the cards in the clear envelope.

"Your grandmother was *the* Gracelyn Branson?"

"Yes, she was, and she was a hoot right till the end."

Emily Bleeker

"So I've heard. Did your great-grandmother ever mention this priest guy? I watched a documentary that said he and Vivian had some sort of love affair."

"That was just gossip. As far as I know, they were only friends. Grandma never met him and neither did my mom."

Kara passes a credit card across the table.

"Interesting," the auctioneer says as he excuses himself to run the payment. He returns with the receipt in one hand and a weathered postcard in the other.

"Payment is official. Here you go." He passes the receipt, which has more zeros on it than are in his paycheck. And then he holds up the other item, tucked in a plastic sleeve. "We couldn't authenticate this one so we couldn't include it in the auction, but it only feels right that you should have it."

He slides one additional postcard across the table. It's a pencil-drawn picture of a young man and woman sitting at a restaurant, with the out-line of the ocean in the distance.

"Whoa, this is amazing," Kara says, examining the picture. "It matches the others."

"Yes, but there's no postmark or address or even date on it," he says, flipping the card over and revealing three lines of handwriting.

Kara's mouth hangs open as she reads the lines.

"Could this be real?" she asks, turning the card over, squinting at the details.

"We couldn't be sure, but it looks real. The only thing we know for certain is—it was never sent."

"So, they really were lovers?" Kara asks, mostly to herself.

"I guess we'll never know." The auctioneer shrugs and replaces his magnifying spectacles on the top of his head.

"Huh," Kara, Vivian Snow's great-granddaughter, says with a blithe wave, "I guess not."

"Congrats again," the auctioneer says, with a firm handshake. "And happy birthday to your mom."

"Thanks, I'll pass it on."

She places the collection of cards in a padded case, keeping the bonus postcard in her hand as she walks out the door. All of the other cards were friendly, but this one, this one is different.

> *Dearest Viviana,*
>
> *I have wrestled against my own heart for too long. Love will not let me rest. I will meet you at Parco Savello at noon on Wednesday and start living the dreams that have haunted me since we first met.*
>
> *Till then—all my love is with you.*
>
> *Antonio*

Kara ponders the note as she returns to her hotel to prepare for the evening's festivities. It's impossible to know what the mysterious message means or if it changes the narrative of Vivian Snow's life. The only thing that is clear to Kara is that Vivian and her friend Trombello had a private love story. She reads the note one more time before placing it in the case with the rest. Now, the world will never know—which, for a woman who lived so much of her life in the spotlight, only seems right.

ACKNOWLEDGMENTS

First, thank you profoundly to my readers, who make all this worthwhile. If you read *When We Were Enemies* and came here looking for the rest of Vivian and Trombello's story, I hope you enjoyed it! If you are new to the Santini family, I thank you for taking a blind chance on a story that was inspired by a novel I loved writing and felt compelled to continue.

Thank you also to the hardworking team at Lake Union. Thank you to Melissa Valentine, who trusted me to write this book. Thank you for supporting this project every step of the way. I'm grateful for your vision and fortitude and feel lucky to work with you. And to Jodi Warshaw, thank you for the phone calls, emails, and deeply insightful thoughts that helped me write a story that spans more decades than I've been alive. It wasn't an easy task, but it was made clearer with your guidance. Thank you as well to a wonderful editorial team who fact-checked and fine-tuned a nightmarish timeline and made me feel secure sending this book out into the world.

Thanks to my agent, Marlene Stringer, for your ongoing inspiration and support. I'm grateful for each and every project we work on together—past, present, and future. And of course, a hearty dose of gratitude to my friends and fellow improvisers at Improv Playhouse for keeping my brain active and being my second family. And for my actual family, I love and thank my parents and siblings, who cheer me on and keep me believing in myself.

To my children—from the time I wrote my first novel to now, you've gone from toddlers to teenagers and some of you to adults, but you'll always be my babies. I hope you all find your own light as you venture out into the world. I adore you.

And to my husband, Sam. Honestly, you make this all possible. You make it a joy to wake up every day and create. I'm glad we found our way to one another. I love you.

ABOUT THE AUTHOR

Photo © Organic Headshots

Emily Bleeker is a *Wall Street Journal* and Amazon Charts bestselling author of seven novels. Combined, her books have reached over two million readers and counting. When she's not writing or mom-ing, Emily performs on the house team of a local improv group in suburban Chicago, where she lives with her husband, kids, and kitten muse, Hazel. Connect with Emily or request a Zoom visit with your book club at emilybleeker.com.